where the grass grows blue

HOPE GIBBS

---

1.   http://StreetlightGraphics.com

For my husband, Patrick, for always believing in me, and my children, for your love and support through this journey.

Spring 2008
Atlanta, Georgia

Chapter 1

Breakup at Tiffany's

"Good as new," the young woman behind the Tiffany & Co. customer service counter says, handing Penny a three-carat emerald-cut solitaire diamond ring. Still warm from the steam, this classic yet understated stone—as much as a diamond that size can be—still takes her breath away. Other than her school ring, it was the first one she ever owned.

Over the years, her husband, Teddy, made several attempts to trade it in for a much larger, more ostentatious one. Several of the Crenshaws' friends around Atlanta had swapped their original engagement rings—small oval or marquise-cut diamonds adequate for a starry-eyed twenty-year-old to swoon over—for monstrous rocks adorned with halos of diamonds, enlarging the gem size by several carats in a perfect compromise for the jaded over-thirty crowd. It quelled their appetites for keeping up with the Joneses while putting a little spark... or rather, sparkle back into their stagnant unions. But Penny still loves the ring given to her in New Orleans all those years ago.

"Thank you," Penny replies, slipping it back on her finger. "I'm sorry it was so dirty. My son and I got a little carried away yesterday." She spent the afternoon basking in the beauty of her backyard, making dozens of mud pies with Sammy, her youngest and most precocious child. Enjoying the invigorating spring air, they used Dutch clover and its ivory blooms as decorative touches for their mucky masterpieces. She forgot to take off her symbol of love, since it never left her finger, and it became caked with dirt. Her attempts to clean it with dish soap, water, and even Windex only made it worse. After her husband's passing comment at dinner about how her diamond's luster was gone, she decided to drop by Phipps Plaza to have it cleaned and its prongs tightened.

"It's no problem. We're always happy to assist our customers," the girl replies in a professional tone. "A ring like that doesn't come my way every day. It's gorgeous."

"Thank you," Penny says, turning to leave the posh store. The Crenshaws' three sons' afternoon activities await.

"Oh! Mrs. Crenshaw, I almost forgot." The girl slaps her shiny forehead. "Your bracelet is ready. Our jeweler was able to repair the clasp quicker than he expected."

Penny turns around. "My bracelet?"

"Yes. I was about to call your husband to tell him it was ready, but since you're here, I'll give it to you instead. And. Oh. My. God. It's stunning. I thought your ring was something, but wow, this bracelet is beyond," she gushes, disappearing beneath the mahogany-and-glass case before springing back up like a jack-in-the-box. With the aplomb of a game-show model, the girl reveals a black velvet box containing a breathtaking twenty-carat-diamond tennis bracelet. All that's missing is a delicate flick of the wrist. "You're such a lucky lady to have a man like this."

The blood drains from Penny's face, and she must have a deer-in-headlights expression, because the Tiffany's employee's blinding smile fades.

"Oh no," the girl says. "Did I ruin the surprise?" Her youthful cheeks are now fire-engine red. "I'm so sorry, Mrs. Crenshaw. I assumed you knew about the bracelet, since the clasp was broken, and it needed to be—" The girl purses her lips in a bid to keep her mouth from speaking.

"Fixed," Penny finishes. New jewelry doesn't require repair.

The girl snaps the top of the box back in place, and the pop startles both of them, breaking the awkward moment. After shoving the velvet box into a larger blue one, she tosses it into a Tiffany bag without bothering with the customary white bow. "Have a nice day," she says, throwing the package across the counter and into Penny's chest like a live hand grenade.

"Y-You too," Penny stammers, taken aback by the forceful throw. As she places the bag in her navy Tory Burch tote in an attempt to hide the evidence of her husband's possible transgression, Penny's throat tightens, and her eyes begin to burn. Before she can collapse into a puddle of tears, she musters her last bit of strength and forces her body through the heavy brass doors while ignoring her woman's intuition screaming, *This bracelet isn't yours!*

Though Penny's of average height, around five feet four, she possesses a bone structure that any ballerina would kill for. Her wrists and fingers are particularly slender. Because of her inability to procure jewelry that accommodates her dainty frame, she wears only one bracelet, a custom-made Cartier Love bangle given to her by Teddy when their oldest son, Trey, was born. If this extravagant bracelet is a gift for Penny, he would've remembered his beloved's unique sizing requirements.

After navigating her way through a labyrinth of opulent stores and high-end dining establishments, Penny finds the exit to the parking deck, praying she can remember where she's left her SUV. After several fruitless trips up and down the long, narrow rows of minivans and overpriced coupes, she resorts to using her key fob. With unsteady hands, she presses the emergency button in hopes she's close enough to set off the alarm. If ever there was an emergency, this is it. Her car horn screeches only two rows away.

Once she unlocks the door, she jumps into the driver's seat. Clutching her purse, which contains the little blue box without the white bow, she begins shaking with fear, as if a poisonous snake is slithering around, trying to escape its leather confines so it can strike, injecting her with its venom. But in this case, it will sink its sharp fangs of truth into her crumbling heart, which will be more destructive than what any neurotoxin can foment. It's no use trying to avoid the inevitable, so Penny rips off the bandage and faces the ugly truth.

"Wow." She gasps, looking down at the bracelet, which is stunning—a real showstopper. One could not wear a piece of jewelry like this without the whole world taking notice, marveling at its beauty and insane cost. Penny would never wear such a garish display of diamonds. Simplicity is her style trademark, as she opts to wear only her engagement ring with a thin plain band resting below, one set of diamond studs her in-laws bequeathed her on the eve of her wedding, and one bracelet, the one her husband *did* give her.

Lifting the bracelet from its box, she allows the precious stones to encircle her wrist. The coolness upon her skin causes it to prickle, and the fine blond hairs on her arm stand at attention. She admires its beauty while noting how heavy twenty carats of diamonds feel. Right now, it's hard to fathom that something so simple as compressed carbon could also be the demise of her marriage, her life, or worse, the lives of her children.

Once she clicks the double clasp into place, she lifts her hand parallel to her face, inspecting the bracelet. The bracelet dangles, creating a gap so large that she can fit most of her left hand through it. Her mouth begins to water, and she swallows hard, trying to suppress the warning sign that her stomach is about to betray her. Knowing her lunch from Henri's is ready to reappear at any moment, she lowers her wrist to end the excruciating suspense once and for all. As she fears, the twenty carats of diamonds slip effortlessly from her wrist, falling into her lap. Nothing stops their short journey down. Obviously, this piece of jewelry isn't hers.

"Dammit," she whispers, resting her head on the steering wheel while the grandiose display of affection remains untouched in her lap. The dreaded waterworks she's kept at bay release. However, these tears are not just from grief but anger as well. Once again, Penny's been let down by yet another man, an all-too-common occurrence for her. Though she's never believed in fairy tales—growing up with an alcoholic father will steal any childhood fantasies of happily ever after—the prospect that her husband has cheated still stings.

After twenty minutes of sobbing alone in her car in the parking garage of Phipps Plaza, Penny pulls out her cell phone. It's time to call for emergency backup.

"What?" a woman answers curtly.

"Dakota?" Penny asks timidly.

"Of course it's Dakota. Who else could it be? You called me," Dakota teases. She's Penny's closest confidant in the Peach State. Their husbands, who graduated together from Westminster, introduced them when Penny moved to Atlanta from Nashville. They vacation together each summer as couples, going to the Crenshaws' Sea Island cottage every Fourth of July. Since their children are close in age, they're more like siblings than friends.

"Hey," Penny says, trying to sound casual to her best friend. "Could you do me a favor? I've lost all track of time today, and I'm stuck in traffic. There's no way I can pick up Sammy by two. Maybe grab him for me?"

A long pause follows. "Jesus Christ, Penny, what's wrong?" Dakota asks.

"Nothing."

"Nothing? You've never been late for anything in your life, let alone for pickup. What's going on?"

"Please grab Sammy for me," Penny asks and clears her throat. "And if you don't mind, could you pick up Trey and Drew too? Maybe keep them until dinner?"

"Dinner? You're scaring me now."

"Dakota, I need you to get the boys," Penny repeats slowly. "Please take them to your house, and I'll call you later."

Penny Crenshaw never passes her duties of being a mother off to someone else. In their eleven years of friendship, Penny is the one in the front of the school pickup line, filling her SUV with other children if another mother finds herself in a jam. Every afternoon, like clockwork, she's painfully punctual. Dakota, on the other hand, has used her as her personal carpool chauffeur, never once batting an eyelash when a Brazilian wax or blowout appointment is running late.

"I'm on my way. Tell me where you are," Dakota demands.

"No. The boys. Please get the boys," Penny says, her voice cracking.

Another long pause follows. "One Mississippi," Dakota says in a robotic voice. "Two Mississippi."

Dakota's counting in a bid to suppress the slew of F-bombs ready to come pouring out of her mouth. The tactic was recommended by Dakota's husband in hopes that it would curtail the use of his wife's favorite word after their three-year-old daughter, Kadyn, blurted, "Fuck me," in front of a class full of impressionable toddlers last month when she spilled paint down the front of her Hannah Kate jumper. Naturally, the entire class began parroting what she said, to the horror of her preschool teacher, who had never witnessed anything like it in thirty years of teaching.

"Three Mississippi."

The family had made phone calls and sent multiple emails and letters of apology to the teacher, the director of Northside Methodist Preschool, and its senior minister, trying to clean up the mess.

"Four Mississippi."

Instead of the customary three Mississippis most people use in an attempt to calm down, Dakota's husband recommended that his wife count to at least ten, since she needed more time than the average person to contain her emotions—or her tongue.

"Five Mississippi." Dakota's voice trembles.

Penny senses she's becoming more agitated with each reference to a state she has nothing in common with, since she's a "damn Yankee and proud of it!" She's about to break.

"Oh, fuck it. I've got the boys," Dakota blurts. It's surprising that she's lasted this long, as she rarely gets past three. "Just text me when you get wherever you're going so that I know you're safe." This time, Dakota's voice is the one that's quivering, and it has nothing to do with the three additional children being dumped on her with no warning.

With her boys safely in her best friend's hands, Penny begins her journey toward home in Atlanta's bumper-to-bumper traffic, readying herself to face Teddy. Though Phipps Plaza is only a few miles as the crow flies from her house, at this time of day, it can take twenty minutes by car.

Navigating her oversize SUV down Lenox Road, through a sea of BMWs, she tries piecing together what her husband has done, thinking of all the places he could have taken this other woman, the one with the much larger wrist than hers. Because Teddy controls his work schedule and is constantly traveling, it isn't a huge shock that he could carry out an affair. Maybe there's a standing date for them at the St. Regis in Buckhead on Thursday mornings, when Penny runs her usual ten miles before meeting up with her nonrunning friends after their Atlanta Lawn Tennis Association, or ALTA, matches for a quick lunch. The Caroline Astor suite is just the spot for sipping champagne and nibbling on ripe strawberries in bed. Perhaps they had a secret rendezvous in Napa, sampling the finest wines at the French Laundry before taking respite in a cozy cabin at Meadowood. In January, he traveled to California without her to meet with some car developer who had the idea of battery-powered cars. Or worse, she fears, Teddy whisked this woman away to their family cottage on Sea Island, where she decorated and shared so many memories with him and their boys. Now she remembers his sudden impromptu visit to their second home in late February, the worst month of the year to visit the island. The thought that this other woman joined him on his golf sabbatical causes her stomach to churn.

But the details of Teddy's potential affair aren't what's ripping Penny up inside. This isn't the first time she's suspected unfaithfulness on her husband's part. Whispers have swirled about it for years, but she's ignored the talk because there's never been any hard evidence supporting it. No, this is about her children and what will happen to them as a result of Teddy's reckless actions. Because divorce has never been an option for her, Penny turned a blind eye to the sad state of her marriage. A stable home with two loving parents, something she'd been denied as a child, was what she wanted to give her children. So hell-bent on keeping her family together, she's adopted the strategy of "not poking the bear" as it pertains to her husband. She learned that punishing lesson from her childhood. But Teddy isn't a monster. On the contrary, he's mild-mannered, even if he has a wandering eye. But now that eye has done more than just wandered. It's bought some woman a very large piece of jewelry.

When Penny finally arrives home, ready to face the bear, her husband is packing up his car. Judging by the scene, she realizes the management at Tiffany & Co. has probably called their "special" client, warning him he should seek cover for the colossal screwup they've created. Steering her SUV down the long, winding pea gravel driveway, she knows that their brick traditional, with its blue-gray slate roof, will never look the same again. Though the house itself was never to her taste, she happily went along with her husband's whims as he painstakingly oversaw every detail. He gave her custody of its sprawling grounds, and that was all she wanted. The flower beds, trees, and hedges are hers alone. Every free moment she can spare away from her boys has been spent here, sometimes with them next to her in a Moses basket, sleeping while she worked.

As she pulls in next to the garage, the row of large scarlet azaleas she planted eight years ago—for no self-respecting Georgian would have a yard without the Southern staple—causes her throat to tighten. Mid-April, and they're in their blooming glory. The groundskeepers at Augusta have nothing on her. She fears that all her blood, sweat, and a couple of tears spent creating this outdoor masterpiece is now for naught.

"Going somewhere?" she asks, rolling down her window and trying to steady her trembling hands.

Without so much as a passing glance, Teddy throws his satchel into the trunk of his car before slamming down the lid. "I don't want to talk right now."

The curtness in his voice causes Penny's pulse to quicken. Resisting the uncontrollable urge to hurl his love trinket into the back of his thoughtless head, she closes her eyes and says, "I went to Tiffany's today. They gave me a bracelet."

"I told you I'm not doing this right now," Teddy says, opening his car door and still refusing to make eye contact.

Exiting her car, Penny reaches for his arm. "I think we need to talk. Maybe this is all a big misunderstanding."

"Stop it, Penny." Teddy lowers his voice, still averting his eyes.

"Just tell me what's going on," she pleads.

"I'm in love with Jessica. Okay?"

"Jessica?" she repeats. "Jessica who?"

He finally turns around to face her. "Knox."

"Jessica Knox?" she asks in disbelief. Her eyes widen. "My Pilates instructor?"

"Your former instructor," he corrects her.

She gasps in horror. "My God, Teddy, she's only twenty-one." Penny has fifteen years on her new adolescent love rival, and Jessica has several bra sizes—though not by nature's design—on her. It never occurred to Penny on her drive home that the other woman was barely a woman at all.

Teddy lets out a nervous chuckle. "That's what you're concerned about right now? Her age?"

Shaking off the temporary shock and dismay in regard to what decade of life Miss Knox checks on her medical forms, Penny asks, "How did you even meet her?" But as soon as those words pass her lips, a wave of nausea envelops her body. "The club."

"Yes."

"I got her that job." Indeed, Penny made the introductions for Jessica Lyn Knox—one *N*, not the customary two—to obtain a position in the pro shop of their country club after Jessica had mentioned how poorly the owner of Peartree Pilates treated her. Being a trusting Gen Xer trying to help a struggling millennial find her way in the world with new career opportunities, Penny was happy to step up. Though she's heard rumblings around the club regarding Jessica's snug, ill-fitting golf skirt along with her penchant for provocatively leaning over tables of Peter Millar clothing while wearing said skirt, it never crossed Penny's mind that Teddy was one of the members enjoying the view. Now, she realizes she's become a suburban cliché—or worse, a perimenopausal cautionary tale.

After taking in a long, deep breath, Teddy says, "I love her. It's that simple. I hate that you found out like this. Really. That wasn't the plan. Jessica and I were going to come clean, but we wanted to wait for Sammy to get older."

The Crenshaws' youngest is a month shy of his second birthday. It's not lost on Penny that it would look worse for Teddy to leave his wife and three sons when one child's age is still being counted in months rather than years.

"I guess the cat's out of the bag now," she says, handing him the diamond bracelet. Though it has left her grip, she can feel the round indentations it made in her palm with her fingers.

Teddy takes the bracelet from her and sighs. "Look, we were never good together. Deep down, you know that too." His eyes soften. "Something's been missing from the very beginning. It's like you never gave yourself to me completely. I've always felt you were holding something back."

Penny's chin trembles because she knows there's truth to what he's saying. She hasn't given herself to him fully, but she hoped he hadn't noticed. Some parts of her—her past, her traumas—she refused to share with him. Only one other person on the planet knew the real Penny Ray Crenshaw, and Teddy wasn't him. That man, the one who understands her to her core, lives in Kentucky, and she hasn't spoken a word to him in almost two decades.

"I'll call the boys in a couple of days," he tells her, getting into his sedan.

"Okay," she whispers. *No reason to fight for him now when his heart is with another.*

Before Teddy makes his hasty exit from his old life with his wife and three children, he leaves her with a parting shot. "I may have been the cheater here, Penny, but at least I gave you my heart for a few years. I'm not sure you can say the same thing."

Penny's back stiffens, while the tips of her fingers begin transforming into a sickly yellowish color, her natural reaction to fear, anger, and heartbreak. Instead of replying to her husband's callous words, she becomes cold and robotic, unable to show her true emotions. *Don't go poking the bear.*

The next morning, still in a daze and with a mug of steaming black coffee in hand, she walks to the end of her driveway to retrieve her *Atlanta Journal Constitution*. Sleep was elusive the first night without her husband, the boys without their father.

As Penny reaches for her paper, a baritone voice rings out. "Nadine Penelope Ray Crenshaw?"

Startled, Penny jerks backward, spilling coffee down her robe, perplexed that anyone's awake at this hour, let alone calling her by her first name.

"Nadine Penelope Ray Crenshaw?" the man repeats. Not only is he using her first name, but he's using her maiden one as well.

"Who's there?" she asks, looking around her lawn, unable to see who's calling to her. Only a handful of people in the world know her full name, like her doctor and her husband.

"Are you Nadine Penelope Ray Crenshaw?" the stocky figure huffs, hobbling toward her.

"Yes," she replies, squinting to get a better look at who's approaching.

"You've been served," the man says, handing her a large manila envelope, then shuffles back to his seedy sedan parked next to her mailbox. Though it's pitch black, Penny knows exactly what she's holding in her shaking hands: divorce papers, compliments of Teddy, before the sun even has the chance to shine.

A week later, Penny and Dakota sit at a long mahogany table in a conference room at the Law Offices of Higgins, Barrett & Bray. The walls are covered in neoclassical oil paintings of Italian landscapes, while the floor is dripping in an array of deep-red Turkish rugs. Across from them is Ruth Higgins, Penny's newly acquired divorce attorney. Though she's barely five feet tall and has the look of a benevolent grandmother who might pinch your cheeks while offering you warm cookies, she's known around Atlanta as a pit bull in pearls, striking fear into the hearts of even the most cunning opposing attorneys. That's precisely the reason Dakota insisted that Penny hire her.

"Your husband's attorneys have sent over an offer." Ruth slides a bundle of legal papers across the table.

Dakota's thick eyebrows shoot up to her chestnut hairline. "Hold on. I thought we were here for a consultation. Who makes an offer after only seven days of separation?"

"Someone who wants out of their marriage quickly," Ruth says bluntly. "In a nutshell, your husband is willing to give you a monthly alimony allotment plus a decent cash settlement. There's enough that you'll be able to buy a new house."

"Excuse me? A house? What's wrong with the one Penny's living in now?" Dakota asks, looking both confused and furious.

"The marital home isn't in her name but rather in a family trust," Ruth says.

"What does that mean?" Penny asks, pinching the bridge of her nose and hoping she can quell the massive stress migraine forming behind her left eye.

"It means you have no legal rights to it. The same goes for the vacation home on Sea Island. Actually, most of your assets are tied up or worded in such a way that you have no access to them. As far as I can tell, you have no land, no stocks, no bonds, or even a 401K. It's almost like Penny Crenshaw hasn't existed the last fifteen years. At least in the financial sense, which they've kindly pointed out."

Dakota turns to Penny. "Did you know any of this?"

Penny ignores the question. "W-What about the boys?" Her mouth is so dry that she can barely eke out a sound.

"If you agree today, he will give you primary physical custody. He's only asking for two weekends a month and a couple of weeks in the summer."

"Thank God. That's all I want. The boys."

"He's also asking that you not return to full-time employment until your youngest child is of school age," Ruth tells her.

"Whoa!" Dakota's hands fly up. "Let me get this straight. Not only is Teddy kicking Penny out of her home, but he's also going to control if and when she can get a job? You cannot be serious about her entertaining this shitty offer."

"She should absolutely take this offer. Today, in fact," Ruth says. "I don't think we want to get mixed up in a messy court battle with Teddy Crenshaw. Or his family."

Penny turns to Ruth, who's staring a hole through her from behind her burgundy Valentino glasses.

"His connections in Atlanta run deep," Ruth continues. "One call to a friendly judge could muddy this case."

Penny's pit bull is turning into a shih tzu right before her eyes.

Before she can absorb the enormity of Ruth's message, her purse vibrates. Though a phone call is the last thing she wants right now, it could be one of the boys. All three have been complaining about a variety of ailments since their father's departure.

"Hello?" she answers.

"Penny," a man says somberly. "It's Jimmy Neal."

Usually, she would be happy to talk with her favorite cousin from Kentucky, but these are not ordinary circumstances. "Hey, Jimmy Neal. I can't really talk right now. I'm kind of in the middle of something at the moment. Can I call you later tonight?" She closes her eyes. The lights in the conference room are aggravating her impending headache more.

"I'm afraid this can't wait," he says.

"Okay. Go on. What is it?"

"I hate to tell you this over the phone."

"Tell me what?"

"Mama went over to check on your grandmother this morning. And well... I'm so sorry, but Ruby Ray has passed away."

Penny's phone tumbles to the ground as the ornate conference room rocks back and forth, like a small ship caught in a perpetual swell. The motion causes her stomach to lurch, yet she remains frozen, holding it all in.

Dakota leans over and asks, "Are you okay?"

The thick mahogany beams on the ceiling close in around her while the row of arched windows behind Ruth's head blur into the exposed brick wall. Penny can no longer make out where one begins and the other ends. Yet she doesn't move. Nor does she blink to clear her vision.

"Can you hear me?" Dakota touches her shoulder. "What's going on? What's happening?" Alarm fills her voice.

Every cell in Penny's body screams at her to get out, to run away from this place and this unbearable pain. It's what she's always done, yet she can't. Her body and mouth are paralyzed.

"Should I call someone?" Ruth asks, reaching for the intercom.

"Say something. Anything." Dakota spins Penny's leather chair toward her and grabs her face with her hands. "Speak!"

Without meeting her friend's steely gaze, she says robotically, "They're all gone now."

After that, Penny's world goes black.

One year later
Atlanta, Georgia

Chapter 2

Out of Africa

The cool, damp dirt covering Penny's hands on this spring afternoon is better than any salve. Calmness spreads throughout her body as she forgoes her trusty gardening gloves and plunges her fingers deep into the earth, the soil pressing against her skin and nailbeds, rubbing against her cuticles. It's therapeutic, connecting with nature this way. The garden is one of the few places that fill Penny with joy. For her, spending a little time outdoors, among her beloved flowers—or her "girls," as she calls them—is better than any antidepressant she could ever try. They are her friends and have never once disappointed her.

After her divorce was finalized in the fall, Penny packed up her boys, per court order, and moved three miles away into a quaint 1920s Dutch colonial. Dakota encouraged her to buy it, pointing out that the house was bursting at the seams with potential. From its large backyard, which would provide her rambunctious brood plenty of space to throw a football or pitch a tent for an impromptu campout, to the thick swaths of ivy covering the back of the house, giving it a cozy cottage feel, it was the perfect place to start over. Plus, Dakota was one street away. But the real selling point for Penny, what pushed her to buy it, was the almost two acres of soil to transform. The second she signed the closing papers to her new home, she dove headfirst into her new project, spending hours diligently selecting various plants, trees, and flowers for each season that would complement the exterior of her new home.

With spring's arrival, it's evident that her hard work has paid off. Though Dakota chastises her daily for spending more time with shrubbery and mulch than with other human beings besides her children, looking around her lawn, Penny knows it was well worth it. Not only has she created a minimasterpiece, but it's here where she almost feels whole again. *Almost.* Whenever the pressure of her divorce comes up, she grabs her gardening tools and starts digging, hoeing, plucking, and planting.

Today, she's putting all her stress to good use. The recent talk surrounding Teddy's wedding, the one that has all of Buckhead reeling, reached a fever pitch earlier in the week.

"Did you see those pictures from the wedding on Facebook yesterday?" a woman said in the entrance of Sammy's preschool Tuesday as Penny was picking up her toddler.

Penny froze, stopping in her tracks.

"Not only did he marry that woman, but he did it in Cabo San Lucas, of all places," the woman continued. "On Valentine's Day. As if there's anything more cliché than marrying your mistress on that day."

Penny craned her neck around the corner, looking for the person discussing her life. She discovered three "friends," Mary-Alice Warren, Carley Crews, and Lorie Duncan, huddled near a row of cubbies full of *Thomas the Train* backpacks and Elmo lunchboxes. They were all in various hues of Nike tennis outfits, none of which had an ounce of sweat on them, since all three women were low-C-level ALTA players at best. They only "participated" for the social connections and cute outfits.

Carley lowered her head. "At least they had the decency to wait a few weeks before they posted about it on social media."

"Did you see? All three boys were ring bearers *and* groomsmen," Mary-Alice said. "I would absolutely die if those were my children.

All dressed up in little linen suits next to their new stepmother on a beach."

Penny's fingers turned cold and started transforming into their usual sickly yellow when she was stressed.

"I heard Teddy dropped a hundred grand on the wedding alone. Renting out the entire resort," Carley said.

"I'm sure it was quite the affair." Lorie added, "No pun intended, of course."

A thunderous roar of laughter followed. A wave of anger pulsed through Penny's body as she listened to their cruel assessments of her shitty life, as if she weren't already keenly aware of it. Their gossipy play-by-play was only pouring more salt into her already-raw wounds.

After they controlled themselves, Carley said, "I don't know how Penny can even stand upright, let alone find the strength to get out of bed."

Mary-Alice shivered. "I wouldn't be able to show my face in public for years after all she's been through. Not in Atlanta or anywhere within the state of Georgia."

"And what about *the club*?" Lorie asked through the side of her mouth. "From what I hear, she can't even step foot in there anymore, thanks to Teddy."

"And Jessica," Mary-Alice pointed out. "I heard she put her bedazzled foot down on that one."

"Those feet are now covered in Manolo Blahniks." Lorie threw her head back with wicked laughter as the other two joined in on the fun.

Mary-Alice crossed her arms. "I think it's best if Penny steps away from polite society with as much grace as possible. If she has any left at his point."

"You're right. This is Teddy's town. He was born and raised here. The Crenshaw family has deeper roots in Atlanta than Coca-Cola.

He's one of us, and we have to rally around him, even if he's made some missteps." Lorie shrugged. "Penny's a laughingstock now. There's no coming back from that."

As Penny was preparing to run away and bury herself in her beloved gardens next to her Dutch crocus and grape hyacinths, Dakota came up from behind, breezing past Penny and toward the group of heartless Botoxed women.

Never changing her pace, gait, or stone-cold expression, Dakota said, "Lorie, your husband's been inside more hookers than Charlie Sheen. Now *that*'s something you can't come back from."

With those words, the conversation and faux friendships ended right then and there in the entrance of the church's preschool.

Penny smiles, thinking of her best friend's antics and the sheer fearlessness of them.

"When the shit hits the fan," Dakota always reminds Penny, "I bring the Charmin, because your skinny derriere deserves the best."

"This one's for you, Dakota," Penny says, covering the base of a hybrid tea rose bush with the last chunk of dirt in her bare hand and admiring her newest addition. Lorie Duncan's husband does have a taste for a certain type of woman, yet no one will dare speak of it around Buckhead, except for the incomparable Dakota Reisner.

With her little horticultural revenge project complete, she turns her attention toward something sweeter, her daffodils—or buttercups, as she's mistakenly called them since childhood, and she will never deviate in her habit.

"Hello, ladies," she says softly, both delighting in their presence and basking in their beauty. Much like for William Wordsworth, they never tire her. Though they're almost finished blooming for the season, she cuts six stunning jonquils for a simple arrangement that will brighten her kitchen for the week. Before placing the last one in her basket, she lifts it to her nose and closes her eyes.

"There's nothing more determined in the world than a buttercup," Penny's beloved late grandmother used to tell her. "They bloom in spite of their circumstances. Rain or shine, snow or heat, they refuse to wilt before their time. In a world full of impatiens, be a buttercup instead."

A small tear rolls down Penny's cheek. She would give anything to spend one more day with her grandmother, especially on a glorious afternoon like this. Not a cloud is in the sky, and a warm breeze blows, swirling around. Ruby Ray was the strongest, kindest, most God-fearing woman Penny knew. For some reason, everyone in Camden, Kentucky, grandchildren included, called her by her full name, Ruby Ray. As bad as Penny's divorce was, losing her was the harshest blow of all. Her death left a gaping hole in her heart.

Before she can have a much-needed full-on crying spell, Penny spots her former husband's car pulling into her driveway. Music blares from the radio, mixed with squeals of delight. The boys are home from the weekend with Teddy.

Penny discreetly wipes away her tears and waves at them. "Be a buttercup," she whispers. "Be a buttercup."

"Mommy!" Sammy says before bolting from the car.

"Samuel Matthew Crenshaw, what did you get into, young man?" she asks, pretending she doesn't know her three-year-old has been overserved copious amounts of sugar for the past forty-eight hours.

"I had blue cotton candy and a Coke for lunch, and I love it!" he yells, running past her, as high as a kite from the rush, heading straight toward the wooden swing set in the backyard. His tiny feet barely touch the ground, while his curly auburn hair, the same hue and thickness as his mother's, bounces up and down.

"Of course you did," she says through a tight smile.

"Hi, Mom," Drew, her middle and most thoughtful son, says, going in for a big hug around her waist.

"Hey, sweetheart." She kisses the top of his head.

"How was your weekend?" he asks.

"Wonderful," she replies with masked enthusiasm, disguising that it was another boring break from motherhood. A weekend without the boys usually consists of a glass or two of sauvignon blanc with some rosemary Triscuits for dinner—and maybe a cube of cheese if she's feeling adventurous—while reading *To Kill a Mockingbird* for the hundredth time. *Fun times.* "And yours?"

"It was okay. Nothing big," Drew tells her. He never divulges whether or not he had a good time at his father's, probably so she won't worry—or worse, make her feel left out of the fun they were having without her. He's always so considerate of Penny's feelings.

"We went to a basketball game," Sammy boasts, running circles around his swing.

"It wasn't that fun, and it was too loud," Drew says, looking up at Penny with his big blue eyes, which are just like hers. "Plus, the Hawks lost. They always lose to the Celtics."

"Hi, Mom," Trey says, giving his mother a passing nod before heading toward his room. The oldest Crenshaw child is twelve now and the most upset by his parents' whirlwind divorce, not to mention his father's sudden marriage to a preschooler. What he craves is space, which Penny dutifully gives, no questions asked, since preteens rebel at the very existence of adults, especially parents.

"There're some fresh strawberries in the fridge and cookies in the pantry if you're hungry," Penny says quickly before he can disappear into the abyss. Food will always draw him out. He's an eating machine and growing by leaps and bounds. Some mornings, Penny hardly recognizes him.

After easing out of his car, Teddy walks toward her. Sweat is dripping down her chest, her face—everywhere. She's covered in potting soil, leaves, and a little Georgia red mud.

"Drew, why don't you take your brother inside so Mommy and I can talk," Teddy says, motioning toward his son.

Without saying a word, Drew obeys his father's directive.

"Your flowers are coming along nicely. You always did have a green thumb," he says, looking around Penny's lawn. "It's nice."

"Thank you. It still has a long way to go," she says, wiping the beads of sweat rolling from her brow while staring a hole through her ex with her piercing cerulean eyes, which he used to love and admire. They drew him to her in the first place. She wants him to feel uncomfortable since he's on her turf now. He stares down at his shuffling feet, away from her gaze, as he often does when he's uneasy.

After a long, awkward pause, he begins. "I'm planning my summer trip with the boys."

Penny braces herself. Since their divorce, she's known this day was coming, but she would rather not think about it. This will be Teddy's first vacation with them since a judge in Atlanta family court signed off on their parenting agreement, which allows each parent a two-week vacation with the boys every year. Now, she really feels divorced from her old life.

Smiling, she says, "I'm sure the boys will have a nice time with you. Let me know the exact dates and where you plan to go."

"Well, there's more." Teddy pauses. "I'll need the boys longer than two weeks."

"Oh," she says, surprised.

"Since I haven't had the opportunity to use all my weekends from this winter or last summer because of work, I thought I could use some of those days now."

Work was the last thing on Teddy's mind when he whisked Jessica away to Italy and Greece for two months after their affair was exposed. The thought of him gallivanting around the world with his neonate causes Penny's blood pressure to rise, since her passport remains stamp-less.

"I don't think that's how it works, Teddy," she says slowly. "We agreed to two weeks."

"Look, this is simply a courtesy on my part, telling you I'm taking the boys to Africa. I don't need your permission for my visitation time. It's mine. John McGinn assures me I'm well within my rights as a father to spend time with my children. He's prepared to take you to court if you don't agree."

"Hold on." She lowers her voice so as not to alarm the boys, who are peeking through the dining room window, watching them. "Did you just say Africa? What on earth are you going to do there? Sammy is only three."

"It's Jessica's idea. A great one, at that, to take the boys on a familymoon, celebrating our marriage. Our new family. She even asked my parents to come along," he says.

"Teddy, that's a huge trip."

"It's only twenty-five days."

"Twenty-five days!"

"We'll need that much time to do Africa properly."

Penny closes her eyes, shaking her head at the prospect of being away from her children for a month.

"Are you going to deny our boys a once-in-a-lifetime trip? Deny Sammy a chance to go on a safari and spot a real-life Simba or a Mufasa? Deny him the chance to sing every single song from *The Lion King* in Africa?" Teddy asks, implementing a new tactic—a side of guilt, since they both know their toddler's obsession with the movie.

"It's such a long time," Penny replies. "I've never spent five days in a row away from the boys in their lives, let alone a month. Plus, that's a long time away from their friends. I mean, it's a large chunk of their summer vacation."

"That's the great part! They won't be alone. The Walkers are coming along with their kids. Tess and Jessica have become really close.

She's been a tremendous help, so I asked them to tag along as a thank-you for that friendship."

Penny's jaw drops, and her eyes widen at the shocking revelation that her dear friend Tess Walker has become friends with the woman who slept with her husband. Not to mention that she's willing to travel halfway across the world for said friendship.

"Here's the itinerary," Teddy says, handing over a stack of papers. "The boys will need some shots, so you should call their pediatrician. Maybe get the ball rolling with that?" The tone of his voice is more like a boss's while dictating orders to a beleaguered secretary.

Reaching for the handle of his car door, he suddenly stops to face her. "Oh, and by the way, I can't take the boys the weekend of the fifteenth. You'll need to make arrangements."

"And why is that?" Penny asks, pinching the bridge of her nose, hoping to avoid an impending splitting headache.

"Because I'm having surgery that day, and I won't be up for taking them, since I'll be recovering."

"Oh my god, Teddy, are you okay?" Old habits die hard. Though divorced, Penny doesn't wish him ill. He's still the father of her children.

"I'm having my vasectomy reversed next Friday. As I understand it, I'll need some time to rest."

A loud cackle at the absurdity of the situation escapes her lips before she even realizes it.

Teddy, however, isn't amused. "Go ahead and laugh. Jessica wants children of her own. She loves being a mother to the boys, and she wants the opportunity to expand our family."

"Of course she does. Good luck with that," Penny says, shaking her head.

"Forget it. You need to get on board. Africa is happening."

"Wait." A forcefulness she hasn't used with Teddy in many years fuels her voice. "I haven't agreed to anything yet. I'm not saying no, but I certainly haven't said yes. I'll need some time to think about this."

"Don't make this difficult," Teddy says, getting into his car. "If I have to, I'll get John involved."

Once Teddy's car is no longer in view, the pounding headache she's been hoping to avoid unleashes itself, but she has no time to dwell on it at the moment. Sammy's bouncing off the walls, with blue cotton candy stains around his mouth. Tomorrow, she will think about this ludicrous trip.

"Be a buttercup," she says, walking up the stairs of her Dutch colonial. Though right now, Penny needs to be more like a Venus flytrap.

Chapter 3

Gossip Girls

"Tess Walker? I always knew she was a bitch!" Dakota says before taking a long drink of coffee. In her case, it's a cup of cream with a splash of the dark stuff mixed with two packets of Sweet'N Low. "I told you after that trip to Charleston four years ago that she was looking out for herself and herself only."

Last night, Penny texted Dakota an SOS that coffee and calories were needed, since her former spouse had just hurled three little surprises upon her: Africa, Tess Walker, and the cherry on top, a vasectomy reversal. Advice was needed ASAP. The two have been sneaking away for caffeine hits for years after dropping off their older children at Lovett and the babies at Northside Methodist Preschool. The Starbucks off West Paces Road is their usual spot. If they have time, the Corner Café is the perfect place to commiserate and indulge in an order of their white chocolate French toast. But this morning, Penny needs more. A little Southern comfort is required. A bowl of The Flying Biscuit Café's warm grits with a dollop of their famous cranberry apple butter is what she craves. Besides, it's the perfect spot to go incognito. There will be no chance of an awkward encounter with Tess "Benedict Arnold" Walker. So obsessed with improving her social status, she wouldn't dare step foot in a place where she can't network with other Lovett moms.

"Tess is a social climber. She gets all she can from one friend, then she moves on to someone who can give her more," Dakota says. "Like free trips to a beach house or flying around on someone else's expense. She's always trying too hard to get connected to the right crowds, weaseling into conversations. I mean, she joined the Junior League, for Christ's sake."

"I guess I was more important to Tess when I was Mrs. Teddy Crenshaw than I am as Ms. Penny Crenshaw," Penny says, defeat creeping into her voice.

"Tess is a user and a phony about everything. Remember when she had her new 'Mommy makeover' last year, pretending it was *all* the result of her new dedication to yoga and conversion to a gluten-free diet? Claiming it's the reason her body miraculously transformed overnight? As if there are enough downward dogs or vinyasa flows in the world that can make your tits grow three sizes and stand at attention like those monstrosities."

"I know," Penny says, closing her eyes in embarrassment at her former friend's antics. She made quite a spectacle of herself back then. Yet Penny always defended Tess. That's what friends do.

"*Then* when I called her out on her new boobs and that liposuction on her fat ass, she finally came clean and admitted to the surgery," Dakota says. "She only did it because she wanted her old body back. The one she had when she was younger, the one before children." Dakota uses a fake Texas drawl in an attempt to mock Mrs. Walker's, which, sadly, is spot-on. "Who the hell was she in high school? Pamela Anderson? What a phony. She's full of shit *and* silicone."

Dakota came from family money and grew up on Long Island. As an only child, she's the apple of her parents' eyes. After forty-four years, they're still married and madly in love. She had a carefree childhood and never worried about what people thought of her. Frankly, she didn't care. Penny, on the other hand, grew up in rural Kentucky with two parents whose tempestuous relationship ended in a divorce when she was very young. She had three older siblings. None survived past their midtwenties. The Ray coffers never had any money to spare. On a good day, they had maybe a handful of S&H Green Stamp books. And unlike her Yankee friend, Penny very much cared what people thought of her.

"I know. You warned me about Tess," Penny says. "But it still stings that she's suddenly friends with Jessica. I had no clue she even knew her, let alone had befriended her." Sometimes a two-timing friend can hurt just as much as a two-timing man.

Combing through the detailed itinerary, Dakota says, "Obviously, Teddy's footing the bill for Africa. Tess and Reggie can only dream of having that kind of money. Again, users."

The lavish trip begins with the nonstop flight from Atlanta to Johannesburg that American Airlines recently debuted—first class, of course. After the long journey across the Atlantic, the group will spend a few days at the Saxon Hotel, relaxing in their private villas, before embarking for the Singita Boulders Lodge in the Sabi Sand Private Game Reserve for their African safari. After twelve days of admiring the majesty of the continent, they'll set out for the Four Seasons Resort in the Seychelles for a little R and R before heading back to the doldrums of the ATL.

"This trip is crazy, right?" Penny asks. "I thought he might take them to Disney World or a water park for summer visitation, but Africa? That never crossed my mind. I mean, the thought of Teddy being in charge of the boys for twenty-five days on another continent that happens to contain the deadliest creatures on Earth. Lions and cheetahs and hippopotamuses. It's absurd. Did you know that hippos kill more people in Africa than any other animal? Not to mention malaria, yellow fever, and snakes. Guess how many people die of snakebites there every year. At least fifty thousand!"

"Fifty thousand?" Dakota asks, arching an eyebrow.

Penny's numbers might be a tad inflated. Math has never been her strong suit.

"It's preposterous, right?" Penny continues, ignoring Dakota's reaction. "Sammy is only three. He'll never remember this trip, and Trey isn't exactly jumping up and down to spend time with his new stepmother. I'm so tired of Teddy always getting his way."

A long silence stretches between them before Dakota reaches across the table to hold Penny's hand. "We have an opportunity presenting itself."

"I know what you're going to say." Penny shakes her head. "When life gives you lemons, you need to make lemonade."

"No, Penny. When life gives me lemons, I throw them out. I fucking hate lemonade."

Penny chuckles because it's exactly what Dakota Reisner would do.

"You know I think Teddy's an idiot. This is some pathetic attempt to buy your kids' love and forgiveness. I get it, and I'm on your side. Always. But you need a break. You haven't had any time to decompress after the divorce, let alone face Ruby Ray's death." Dakota squeezes Penny's hand extra hard at the mention of her grandmother. "I know how you feel about Kentucky. You only go back there for... funerals."

A tear slips from Penny's eye at the mention of the word. Penny Crenshaw's an expert in those, having buried her entire immediate family over the last twenty years. Seven people, to be exact, though thanks to her best friend, she can't remember the most recent one. Ruby Ray's was the most painful. One part genius and one part diabolical, Dakota spared Penny immense pain by slipping a couple of Valiums into her iced tea the second they reached the Kentucky border last year. Dakota's excuse: "After a triple whammy of an affair, a divorce, and a death in a seven-day period who wouldn't need to be tranquilized?" Unaware of her friend's plan, Penny could barely remember her name, let alone the day, but she was grateful for the respite from grief.

"I get it," Dakota says. "I wouldn't want to go back, either, if I were you. But that house is just sitting there, causing more problems for your family. It'll be good to go home. Maybe while you're there, you can spend some time with your ten thousand cousins." A crooked smile spreads across Dakota's face. "Or better yet, you could look up an *old friend*."

"Dakota." Penny groans at the insinuation, which hurts almost as much as all the funerals combined.

"Okay, we'll get to that later." Dakota winks. "But now's the time. Go to Kentucky while you have the chance. Box up the house, and finally put it on the market. Holding on to your grandmother's house won't make her come back. It's time to say goodbye to it and to Camden. Then..." She sits back. "You and your true friends, excluding that traitor Tess, will go to Rosemary Beach for a week. I've already worked out the details with Leslie, who has generously offered up her house. Annie's on board too. We'll get some sun, sleep late, drink mimosas for breakfast, ride our bikes to George's for lunch, and every night, we'll head over to Red Bar for dancing and beer sponsors. Then we'll find some random hot guy and get you laid. God knows you need it."

Penny rolls her eyes—sex is the last thing on her mind.

Dakota continues, "This isn't about Teddy or Jessica or Tess or even Africa. This is about *you*. It's a blessing in disguise. Maybe a blessing wrapped in a big pile of dog shit but a blessing nonetheless."

Dakota is right. Though Penny doesn't want to give in to her ex's demands, Dakota has her best interests at heart. It's time to go back to Kentucky, but even entertaining the thought causes her anxiety.

"Why don't you go for one of your ungodly runs and forget about everything for a little while," Dakota says. "Don't worry about carpool today. Leslie and I will grab the boys after school, feed them dinner, and take them home in time for bed. Once they're settled, we'll open a bottle of wine, and we'll log on to Facebook and unfriend the now-unmentionable Tess Walker. Then we can talk about the most absurd part of all of this."

"And what exactly is that?" Penny asks.

"Teddy's vasectomy reversal, of course." She snickers. "Think of all those sleepless nights, shitty diapers, and temper tantrums coming his way over the next few years. And that's just from his wife."

Chapter 4

American Woman

Dakota's right. A good run is just what the doctor ordered or, in this case, what a trusted confidant has prescribed.

Running six days a week has been Penny's routine for decades, as essential to her survival as air. Nothing stops her regimented exercise schedule. Rain, stifling heat, hail storms pelting her with ice balls the size of grapes, and daily IT band flare-ups causing shooting pain down her leg and her knee to scream in agony are a part of Penny's life. So are the blisters on her feet, which resemble weathered docks growing barnacles. She's lost count of how many toenails have become ingrown or fallen off for her sport—or rather, her obsession.

When she was a child, she discovered the solitude in running. It allowed her young mind to become as still as a morning pond, clearing it from all the doom and gloom she was always watching and preparing for. The sky was perpetually falling for young Penny, between her pugnacious parents and the health of her brother and sisters.

Before long, Penny found she had a gift, excelling at distance running. When she was offered a scholarship to Belmont in Nashville to run cross-country, it made college possible, no small feat for a poor girl with an inauspicious start to life and whose parents were often the talk of the town.

Taking her friend's advice, Penny grabs her iPod, which is full of her favorite songs by Alanis Morrissette, Blues Traveler, and the Counting Crows, laces up her worn-out Nike running shoes, and jumps into her SUV. Instead of running around the hilly Buckhead neighborhoods like she would normally do, dodging cars and avoiding double strollers along the narrow streets, today, Penny goes OTK, as it's known in Atlanta—outside the perimeter. With Dakota's offer of picking up the boys this afternoon, she's been presented with a rare opportunity—time. Now she can go to her favorite place, the Silver Comet trail right outside the city. It's a sixty-mile path stretching all the way to the Alabama border and is relatively flat and straight. It will be quiet on a Monday, unlike a weekend, with few tourists and cyclists clogging up the space. Just rolling creeks and scenic views will keep Penny company. Though fall is a spectacular season there, spring is when the magic happens because it's covered with trees in all their blooming glory. Redbuds, Japanese cherries, and Penny's favorite, the flowering dogwood, remind her of Ruby Ray's yard in Kentucky.

As she's finishing the last remnants from her water bottle and preparing for the mileage goal she's set, her phone pings. It's a text from Dakota.

Have you made it to Silver Comet yet?

Penny begins typing out her response on her new iPhone, which makes the task remarkably easier than the old flip phone she converted from earlier in the year.

How did you know? Penny replies.

Because when you really want to punish yourself, that's where you go.

"If you only knew," Penny says as she pecks out a response.

About to start.

Did you take your mace? Dakota asks.

She worries about Penny's safety, and since the divorce, it's only grown.

Yes. I have it. Great Christmas gift, by the way. Just what every girl wants for the holidays. Nothing says I love you like pepper spray.

Dakota texts back, *I don't have time to find a new best friend. I've invested too much in you for you to keel over now. Text me when you're heading home.*

After sending, *I will*, Penny places the phone in a special running pouch around her waist. Though she used to leave the phone behind, two years ago, she snapped a tendon in her foot and had to hop then crawl back home, since she had no way to call for help. That changed her mind about the extra weight she now carries—and Dakota's constant nagging.

As she does before every run, Penny inhales a long breath through her nose before slowly blowing it out through her mouth then repeats the process twice more, starts her music, and takes off.

At mile five, she passes a bicycle shop on the trail. Though this was going to be her turn-around spot, her body's in such a sweet rhythm that she keeps going. Despite some pesky pollen floating about, which is typical in Georgia this time of year, her lungs fill easily with air. Her quads no longer burn, while her calves tingle with energy. This is the feeling she craves like a drug. She's found her high. It would be easier to run fifty miles than to stop now.

With Alanis belting the final lines of "You Oughta Know" in her ears, she's so confident in her body's abilities that she makes the Sailors Parkway trailhead her new mental goal post. It's farther than she planned, but she can't waste a day like this. The temperature's in the low seventies, and there's hardly any humidity. Endorphins flood her bloodstream. This is the best run she's had in years. The last time she felt like this was before she got pregnant with Sammy and finished second in her age division in the Peachtree Road Race. That year, her friends set up a tent off Piedmont, cheering her on with signs, balloons, and of course, adult morning beverages. While Dakota, Leslie, and Annie noshed on apple fritters and chocolate croissants from Henri's and sipped Bloody Marys from sterling-silver julep cups, Penny sped past them, recording a personal record for the distance.

Lowering her head, she picks up her pace.

Two covered bridges and five miles later, taken by the beauty filling her eyes at this point in the trail, Penny pulls out her earbuds to listen to the sounds of Mother Nature. It's a wonderful feeling, peaceful and calm.

"Mommy!" a child screams in the distance, causing Penny to stop.

As a mother, she knows that sound. Something is terribly wrong. She looks left then right then back again.

"Mommy!"

"Hello?" Penny yells, still searching for the source. "Where are you?"

"Over here!" someone calls out.

This time, she sees what's wrong. A woman is lying on the ground, next to a bicycle with a trailer, fifty feet ahead, near a row of pine trees.

Penny rushes to her aid. "Are you all right?" she asks, kneeling.

"I don't know," she says. "We hit a rock and flipped."

Another round of wails ensues, and Penny turns toward the trailer. "Is there a child in there?"

"Yes. My daughter. I can't get to her because I can't move my leg." Panic fills her voice.

"Don't worry. I'll grab her."

When Penny unzips the black mesh front, a tiny child lunges into her arms, almost knocking her to the ground.

"Is she hurt?" the woman asks, her voice trembling. "Please tell me she's not hurt."

"She seems to be moving pretty well," Penny says as the girl clings to her neck like she's holding on to a life preserver, wailing.

"Shh," Penny whispers into her ear. "There, there. I'm going to sit you down to get a good look at you." She begins checking for injuries, starting with the girl's legs before moving up her body.

"What happened here?" a cyclist asks, jumping off his bike.

"I hit a rock, and we flipped," the mother repeats.

Without turning her eyes away from the child, Penny says, "Could you tend to her while I keep checking this little one?"

"Sure thing," he says, offering the water bottle from his waist to the injured woman.

"I'll call for help," someone else says.

"I'll grab some paper towels" comes a different voice before the person sprints toward the cement restroom fifty yards away.

A small crowd—a mix of joggers, power walkers, and bird watchers—begins forming around them. Penny's heart rate slows, since she's no longer alone.

"How's Addie?" the mother asks.

"So far, so good. Not a scratch in sight on sweet Addie," Penny tells her.

"I want my mommy," the girl says between hiccups.

"Just a second. I'm almost finished," Penny says.

"She looks good to me," the first cyclist says, motioning toward the child. "Other than a little blood from her nose and a broken crown."

"My cwown's bwoken?" the girl asks.

Slowly, Penny lifts her head and eyes. Up until now, she'd been so focused on Addie's knees and elbows that she hasn't bothered to look at her face or notice she's wearing a yellow chiffon dress.

"She loves Belle," her mother explains to the crowd through clenched teeth. "It was her Halloween costume back in the fall, and she refuses to take it off."

When Addie's face comes into focus, Penny's breath catches. Before her stands a little blue-eyed girl with full cheeks and rosebud

lips. Her auburn ringlets are pressed against a sweaty forehead sprin-
kled with light-brown freckles.

"Excuse me." Penny bolts upright and sprints toward the cin-
derblock restroom, ignoring the crowd's confused gazes and whispers.

After locking herself in the first stall she comes to, Penny leans
down and vomits over and over again until she dry heaves. Up come
the biscuit and grits she had earlier. This is her body's way of ridding
itself of the picture of Addie, who's the spitting image of Penny in the
summer of 1976, down to the bloody nose and broken tiara.

In this cold room, Penny is helpless. Though her stomach needs
to purge itself, her mind is forcing her back there, making her relive
it once again.

Summer of 1976
Camden, Kentucky

Chapter 5

American Girl

Camden, Kentucky, was like most towns in the US the summer of '76. The entire community was making preparations to celebrate the country's bicentennial. The mayor promised fireworks, parades, cotton candy, and even ponies. The town had never had a bigger celebration. All five thousand-plus residents were going to participate in some form or fashion, and the Ray family was eager to do their part. While the men in the family worked on a float for the Spirit of '76 parade, Ruby Ray and her sisters-in-law were busy at the dining room table, sewing together patriotic costumes from Simplicity patterns for the children.

Excitement filled the air, an energy little Penny had never felt before. Though she couldn't put her finger on it, something was different, especially with Daddy. His breath no longer smelled of sweet caramel and butterscotch, which always lingered on him. She even caught a glimpse of him smiling at Mommy. They seemed to like each other. She'd never witnessed what a loving relationship looked like between the two.

But the best part was that Daddy hadn't yelled, slapped, or choked Mommy all summer. Penny didn't know what had gotten into him, nor did she care. All she knew was the summer had been the calmest season she'd ever experienced in her short life. Though she couldn't put it into words, she'd finally found peace.

"You did what?" Ruby Ray gasped, looking up in horror from her sewing machine.

"You heard me," Mommy said smugly before lighting one of her Kool cigarettes. "I've entered all three girls in the Spirit of '76 beauty pageant next week."

"What's a beauty pageant?" Penny asked her older sister Janet, who was standing next to her, peeking through the door from the kitchen along with Janet's twin, Julie.

Janet lowered her head toward Penny's ear, since the girls were supposed to be outside on the porch swing, keeping their brother, Jack, company, instead of inside, looking for lemonade and pecan bars. "Remember Mommy's crown?"

Penny nodded.

"In order to get one of those, you gotta get up on a stage with a bunch of other girls and let people decide who's the prettiest," eight-year-old Janet whispered.

"She was the Dairy Princess the year before Jack was born," Julie added softly.

"It's all right here." Mommy pulled out a flyer and handed it to Ruby Ray. "See? The winner in each age group will get a crown, flowers, and a twenty-dollar gift certificate to Farley's. But the best part is they get to be in the parade, riding in their very own convertible, compliments of Oliphant's Oldsmobile."

"They're already going to be in the parade, Zelda. On the float our family is working on outside for the Lion's Club. I've been sewing day and night, getting ready for it." Ruby Ray held up Jack's Paul Revere costume. On the table were Julie's Martha Washington dress, Janet's Abigail Adams bonnet, and Penny's pint-size Betsy Ross mobcap.

"Don't you see? This is special. They won't be lost on some cheap trailer made from chicken wire and tissue. They have a chance to ride around town in a five-thousand-dollar car," Mommy explained. "All they need is a Sunday dress and a costume representing the bicentennial, which, thanks to you, they already have."

"Are you asking me to come up with three new Sunday dresses by next week?"

"Of course not. Homemade ones won't do for an event like this. I went last week to Castner Knott in Bowling Green for proper dresses."

The three girls began quietly jumping up and down. "New dresses," they mouthed.

"And just where'd you get the money from?" Ruby Ray asked.

"I've been saving all summer."

Ruby Ray's eyes narrowed. "Saving or hiding?"

"Don't go concerning yourself with how I got the money. That's my business," Mommy said, snatching the flyer from Ruby Ray's hands.

The two had a rocky relationship. It all started because Ruby Ray refused to give her blessing to Mommy and Daddy's marriage. She told them the match was doomed because all they did was fight like cats and dogs. Their only real connection was their love of rebellion—going out drinking, smoking, and dancing the night away. In the process, they broke the three cardinal rules of the families' strict Baptist religious teachings at once—no alcohol, no dancing, and no rock 'n' roll. Because Ruby Ray had vocalized her misgivings, Mommy paid her back by eloping with Daddy the day before her eighteenth birthday, denying her the chance of a church wedding.

"Does my son know any of this?"

"For your information, he does. And Charlie's thrilled about it." Mommy took a drag off her cigarette. "It was his idea to enter Penny in the first place. I wasn't going to, because she can't possibly win, thanks to you and all those angel biscuits you keep feeding her. I swear that girl's tummy is swollen tighter than a tick. But with the right dress, that can be hidden. Unlike the rat's nest," she said, referencing Penny's thick, coarse hair with curls galore, which was in stark contrast to the long, dark, flowing locks the twins possessed.

Julie gave Penny an empathetic smile while Janet squeezed her hand. They'd all overheard Mommy speaking about Penny that way before. Beauty was important to her, so much so that after the twins were born, she switched their names. For the first hours of their lives, Janet was named Julie, and Julie was Janet. Mommy used to say the name of a person gave vital insight into their future. It could change their life and alter their destiny. Convinced her own name was a curse, for it meant "dark battle," she put effort into naming her children. Jack was the first-born child, but she wasn't concerned with his name. He was a boy. He already had a leg up in the world. A year later, when the doctor informed Mommy she was carrying twins, in keeping with the "J" tradition, she decided to name them bearing the same first initial if they were girls. Julie would be given to the first twin born because it meant "beautiful and vivacious," while the second would be called Janet, meaning "God's gift." However, when Mommy peered through the glass of the nursery window soon after their delivery, it was undeniable that one twin was head and shoulders above the other. Twin number two was the epitome of beauty. The newborn possessed locks of thick, flowing black hair like her brother's. Many at the hospital fancied it would need to be cut within weeks, since it was "halfway down that child's back." An old wives' tale said that a child's hair should never be touched before their first birthday.

Twin number one was not as fortunate as her enchanting sister. She was yellow and flaccid. Her arms looked as if they could break with a puff of wind, and worse, she was as bald as a bat. Without consulting anyone, Mommy switched the names. After that, their world changed forever.

"I don't want to hear any more talk about Penny," Ruby Ray said. "Do you hear me? She's fine just the way she is." Her tone was sharp, causing the girls' eyes to widen. Ruby Ray never let her temper show, at least not to them. "If you'd pay that child some attention, you might see it."

Ruby Ray had done her best to shower Penny with love and affection, but no matter how hard she tried, she'd never filled the parental void Penny craved or eased the burden that came with being the healthy child, the one who could live a life free of pain and worry and had the ability to survive in the first place—unlike her siblings.

Mommy took another long drag. "You've always had a soft spot for her, and I've never understood why. Penny's the healthy one. Lord knows she doesn't need you doting on her all the time, spoiling her rotten. It's your other three grandchildren who need looking after. The sick ones."

That time, Penny's tiny hands reached over and squeezed her sisters'. The three of them knew the story by heart. An hour after the infamous name change, Janet began struggling. She was jaundiced, her abdomen swelled, and she couldn't keep down a bottle, so she was rushed to a larger hospital than the county one she was born in. There, after dozens of blood tests, X-rays, liver biopsies, and some serious scouring through medical journals, they came to a diagnosis. Janet had Wilson's disease, a rare genetic disorder that caused excessive amounts of copper to build up in the body, especially in the liver and the brain. Two malfunctioning genes, one from Daddy and one from Mommy, caused her sister's plight. They'd both been unwilling, unknowing accomplices.

Six months later, Jack's constant colds, which turned into serious bouts of pneumonia requiring long hospital stays, caught his doctor's attention because he was showing telltale signs of another genetic disorder. Shortly after his third birthday, it was confirmed—he had cystic fibrosis. The insidious monster caused Jack's body to produce a thick mucus, especially affecting the passageways in his lungs. Over time, his breathing became difficult, which caused the passageways to grow and harbor bacteria, which scarred the organs. Yet again, the cause was genetic.

Since two of the three Ray children had been diagnosed with rare and serious diseases unrelated to each other, they checked Julie for her siblings' ailments. A week later, they discovered Julie didn't have Wilson's disease or CF, but she had Von Willebrand disease, type three, to be exact, which was the rarest, most deleterious form. In layman's terms, it was a bleeding disorder. Julie's blood couldn't clot, for it lacked the Willebrand factor in plasma. Once again, it was because of a faulty genetic combination. It seemed as if God Himself was conspiring against the two from successful procreation, at least until Penny's unexpected arrival.

"I don't think you've thought this through, Zelda," Ruby Ray said, pushing away from the table. "Julie and Janet are twins. Maybe not identical, but they still have an uncanny resemblance to each other. Don't you realize putting them in a contest to see who is the prettiest is a recipe for disaster? Haven't those poor children been through enough?"

Mommy whipped her head around. "You're right. I didn't think of that."

"Of course you didn't."

"I'd better cancel that registration today. Maybe if I do, I can get my money back on the pageant fee."

Ruby Ray sighed in relief. "I'm glad you're thinking clearly now. The flyer said LeeAnne Williams is in charge of the pageant. I'll call her and cancel for the girls." Ruby Ray walked toward the wall phone.

"Hmm. Just one," Mommy said, blowing a plume of gray smoke into the air. "I'll only need a refund for Janet."

"I thought we agreed that this is a terrible idea. Why are you only canceling Janet's?"

Mommy threw her cigarette into an open Tab can and blew out her last stream of smoke. "You're right. Janet's starting to look like Julie now. She's not as pretty, of course, but it could confuse the judges. That would hurt Julie's chances."

"What did you just say?"

"Don't look so shocked, Ruby Ray. Everybody in this town has been crowing about Julie's looks since the day she was born. Nobody in this town can beat her. She's a shoo-in for a convertible ride."

"Don't you mean *your* convertible ride?" Ruby Ray asked, seething.

Mommy ignored the comment. "Just watch the kids for a couple of hours, will ya? I need to run over to Castner Knott and return Janet's dress."

Ruby Ray followed her to the door. "I won't be a part of this, Zelda. What you're doing to those children isn't right, and you know it. One day, you will reap what you sow."

After Mommy left, Penny and Julie moved closer to Janet. New clothes from a high-end department store were rare for the Ray girls. So was Mommy's love.

"We can share my dress," Julie offered, stroking her twin's cheek. "I'm sure it'll fit you."

"Thank you," Janet said weakly.

Penny caressed Janet's other side. "And we can share my crown too."

Janet laughed through her tears. "What crown are you talking about, Little Bit?"

Penny looked up at her innocently and said, "The one I'm gonna win for you."

A week later, Penny took the stage of the Miss Spirit of '76 with a plan... or as much of a plan as a five-year-old could concoct. Knowing she wasn't as pretty as the other thirty-nine girls, she was determined to steal the judges' attention. A prim and proper little girl hitting her marks and posing with her red carnation in hand while smiling on command wasn't going to cut it. No, little Penny Ray took a far different approach from the rest of the field. As she entered the stage on that hot July day, Penny threw caution to the wind and her flower over her shoulder with the most devilish grin she could muster. When she hit her mark under the spotlight, she spun around, throwing her hands up in the air, screeching, "Ta-da!"

The crowd went wild for the littlest Ray, and when her name was announced as the winner of the Tiny Tot division, Penny caught a glimpse of Mommy's face. Finally, she'd stolen a bit of sunshine for herself.

As expected, Julie won her division, besting twenty-five other girls in her age group—the one without Janet. The plan came together beyond all expectations, with two Ray children earning their convertible rides in the local parade. The day was perfect for Mommy, and Penny was happy to have been a part of it. Though like most things in Penny's life, the joy was fleeting.

Becoming impatient with Mommy's multiple victory laps around the crowd, Penny headed to the car with Daddy. The two rarely got any one-on-one time, for there'd never been a real connection there. Not every little girl was lucky enough to have a daddy they could love.

"Look at you, Little Miss Sassy. You won the whole goddamn thing!" he roared. "That momma of yours never thought you'd win. But you know what? I did." He picked her up in his arms, the same ones she'd seen used in a very different manner throughout her brief life. "You out-showed your sister today, and your momma never saw it coming."

Lapping up his compliments like a kitten with milk, Penny smiled. She'd never known what it was like to be deemed special by him. "Daddy," she whispered, "I love you."

Those words would never pass her lips again.

As the two made their way along the sidewalk under the sweltering afternoon sun, Penny relaxed a bit, laying her sweaty head upon his shoulder. The crease between his chin and chest allowed her a perfect pillow to rest upon, a place that was foreign to her. Daddy rarely allowed her the pleasure of his fatherly touch, and she usually recoiled around him, for she knew his movements better than most. The moment was sweet, but all that changed when they turned the corner.

"Well, you know why the Ray girls won, don't ya?" someone said. "'Cause all them kids are gonna die soon enough. It's the ultimate sympathy card. I mean, you saw that little one, with the belly poking out. Lord knows she ain't no beauty queen."

"That's right," someone else replied. "Even her knees have rolls of fat on 'em."

"Today was all about giving those sick kids one last day in the sun. And you just know Zelda Ray ate it up, 'cause today was all about her. Like everything else round here. That woman's been playing up that sympathy card for years. It's a shame how she acts like the devoted mother in public while leaving those kids whenever she gets the chance. I guess dying children ain't as important as scratching a certain itch, if you know what I mean. Sneaking off with Terry Sutton in the middle of the afternoon must be exhausting."

"The whole town's been talking about how she's been messin' around with him, leaving those poor kids alone. I guess if her husband wasn't such a drunk, he'd know it too." Laughter ensued.

And just like that, Penny's infinitesimal peace was shattered.

"Hey, ladies. You know I'm standing right here with my fat daughter, right?" Daddy spewed, marching toward the women and tossing Penny from his arms like a bag of flour. Her imaginary pillow, her safety net, was once again lost.

"Charlie? Congratulations on your girls," a blond woman said. Her gossiping tongue had been caught red-handed by the town's drunk, who was currently as sober as a judge.

"You just said my kids are all gonna die and my baby girl is fat. Oh, and I almost forgot, my wife is screwing one of my cousins. Is that right, or am I so goddamned drunk I can't understand?" he asked, venom dripping from his lips.

Mommy rushed toward the scene. "Charlie Ray, what are you doing?"

"They called one of our kids fat and said our other ones are dying. Oh..." He turned toward her. "And they said you're sleeping with Terry Sutton."

"Come on," Penny said, trying to extract him from the situation. She knew the signs that his explosive temper was about to get the best of him.

"Go home. Now!" Mommy demanded. "You're embarrassing yourself."

"Me? I'm the embarrassment? Are you kidding me? You turned our daughters into a couple of show horses today so that you could feel young and beautiful again. Guess what. You ain't young, and you ain't beautiful no more. Have you seen yourself in a mirror lately? You look hard and old. You look like a woman who's been ridden hard and put up wet."

"Go to hell, Charlie!" Mommy yelled before grabbing Penny's arm and dragging her along with Julie to Ruby Ray's house.

Daddy was a ticking time bomb, ready to explode. Mommy needed cover. As hotheaded as he could be, he would never slap her around in other people's presence. Some things were best left in the privacy of a marital home.

After a couple of hours had passed, Penny began to relax. In her short life, she'd mastered the roller coaster ride of two combative parents, and she was in the safe confines of Ruby Ray's home. It had always provided her with a sense of security and normalcy. Her kitchen was always clean and stocked with food. The milk was never soured. The house wasn't filled with thick cigarette smoke. She could always count on running hot water, and the electricity was never cut off by Kentucky Power for insufficient funds.

After the unexpected arrivals, Ruby Ray headed to her bountiful garden for some vegetables. Penny followed, with her crown on top of her head. Because the children were rarely treated to a decent meal at home, Ruby Ray made sure they had something to eat. A couple of big purple tomatoes she picked quickly turned into a pie with the help of some biscuit dough. The English cucumbers and white onions she grabbed were transformed into a salad using white sugar, ice cubes, and vinegar. Since there was no time to defrost any meat from her deep freezer, which was full of beef and pork from animals the family raised and slaughtered the previous winter, she fried up some hog's jowl she and Pops had been feasting on all week.

As Ruby Ray finished doing the dishes, Penny spotted a truck swerving down the street from the kitchen window. "Daddy's coming," she said.

"Homer. Get down here!" Ruby Ray cried out to Pops, who was watching *The Great American Celebration* with Jack, Julie, and Janet. Then she rushed to the back porch, where Mommy was smoking a cigarette. "Charlie's here. Let me handle this. Do you hear me?"

"Don't let him in here, or he'll kill me," Mommy said.

As Ruby Ray and Pops waited for Daddy to walk up the steps, Penny joined them.

"Zelda and the kids here?" Daddy asked as Ruby Ray opened the door slightly. His thick tongue caused his words to blend into each other.

"You've been drinking, son," Ruby Ray said, her tone clipped.

"I just had a couple of beers with some friends to celebrate Zelda's big victory today. You heard, didn't you?" he asked, losing his balance. "How my baby girls won? I know you weren't there, since you didn't approve of my wife's little plan, but let me tell you what—they was the stars of the show."

"Yes, we heard. We also heard what happened afterward. It's best you go home and sleep off all this *celebrating*," Ruby Ray demanded.

"So my dearly beloved is here, then? Did she tell you everything?" Daddy sneered.

"It doesn't matter what she told us other than you made quite a fool of yourself. One of these days, you're gonna learn how to control that tongue and temper of yours. Good night," Ruby Ray said, trying to shut the door, but Daddy's foot stopped it from closing.

"I don't think you understand. I'm here to get my wife and my kids. It's time to go home. My home." He jabbed his finger into his chest. "We got ourselves a big day tomorrow, remember? My girls are going to be riding around in their convertibles, blowing kisses to the crowd, with Zelda right next to them. So like I said, it's time for my wife and my children to go home. With me," he said in a menacing tone. It sent a cold shiver down Penny's spine. She knew exactly what was in store for them if they left Ruby Ray's.

"You'd be better off if you'd go on by yourself and get some sleep," Pops said.

"Not until I see my wife."

"There's nothing you can say to her tonight that can't wait till the morning," Ruby Ray said slowly.

"I ain't going nowhere until I see her. I'm fairly certain she hasn't told you what all transpired today, did she? I'm guessing she left out the whole part about her affair with Terry."

Ruby Ray cleared her throat. "Well, whatever she's done, it can wait till tomorrow. You're drunk, and nothing good will come of it if you see her tonight. Leave."

"So you're going to let that whore sleep here tonight?"

"Don't you use that kind of language with me, Charlie Wayne. I won't tolerate that behavior."

"Won't tolerate what behavior?" He laughed. "My wife can sleep with whoever she likes? My own cousin?"

As Penny stood behind Ruby Ray and Pops, watching the events unfold, Jack tried in vain to pull her away to safety, as he'd done so many times before, to hide along with Janet and Julie, but she refused. They were unaware of the danger Daddy posed at that moment, not just to her mommy but to them as well.

"We can deal with all this tomorrow in the light of day. But know this, son—you're not stepping foot in this house tonight," Ruby Ray said with a fortitude in her voice warning that she meant business.

"I'll leave. For now. But this ain't over. Far from it. You tell Zelda there *will* be a reckoning. She can count on it." Daddy stumbled down the steps before turning around. "Oh. And one more thing. Could you let her know that Terry won't be sniffing around her little honeypot no more? Me and Ricky Lambert done paid him a visit tonight, and he won't be up for any of her company for a *real* long time."

"*What did you do to him?*" Mommy screamed, rushing past Ruby Ray and Pops.

"Zelda, no," Ruby Ray said, reaching for her arm.

"I hate you!" Mommy charged toward Daddy like a crazed bull, slapping him across his cheek.

A sinister smirk spread across his face. "Well. I guess I got your attention now, didn't I?"

"You'd better not have hurt him. He's twice the man you'll ever hope to be," Mommy said.

"I just gave him some friendly advice that messin' around with a married woman around these parts was frowned upon. Especially with family. Then I beat him up. Not 'cause I want you, but now he don't want you either. He's done. He hightailed it out of here. You ain't never gonna see him again."

"No!" Mommy cried.

"And, Zelda? Don't you ever think you can step out on me again," Daddy said, rearing back with a clenched fist. He struck her squarely in the mouth with such force that she fell to the ground like a limp rag doll.

"Mommy!" Penny screamed, rushing to her side as Daddy landed a barrage of punches to her stomach. Blood poured onto the sidewalk, which was still warm from the sweltering summer day.

Though Penny tried her best to pull Daddy off Mommy with all her might, her efforts were fruitless, and she was greeted by a swift backhand to her face, the same one that only hours ago had been deemed the prettiest in the county. Penny and her rhinestone crown tumbled to the ground.

"Stop this!" Ruby Ray commanded, scooping a stunned Penny into her arms. Like Mommy, she had blood pouring from her nose.

Pops tried in vain to stop the rampage, but he, too, was no match for Daddy's strength, which was fueled by the hate coursing through his veins. But the Rays' next-door neighbor's teenage son, Josh, a giant of a boy who played nose tackle for the Liberty County Rebels, saw what was transpiring. Like an angel sent from God, Josh came rushing over and took Daddy to the ground.

Josh's parents, after hearing the commotion from their living room, hurried over to assist after calling the police. Together with Ruby Ray and Pops, they helped move Penny and Mommy into the house to get a better look at the destruction Daddy had caused.

"Is everything all right in here?" Officer Ricky Lambert asked, peering through the front door.

Mommy sat up, grabbing Ruby Ray's arm. "Don't let him in here. He's Charlie's best friend."

"Now, Zelda, that's no way to speak of an officer of the law. Is it?" Ricky said.

Ruby Ray turned toward her. "Hush. Let me handle this. And this time, I mean it," she commanded. "Where's Charlie?"

"Evening, Miss Ray," Ricky said, tipping his hat. "Don't worry, Officer Owens is outside with him, taking his statement."

"His *statement*? What statement could he give?" Mommy yelled. "Don't you see what he did to me? The only statement you need is mine. Get out there and arrest him."

Ricky eyeballed her. "I'm not gonna be told how to run this investigation by a woman."

Ruby Ray stepped between them. "I'm afraid my son has lost his mind tonight," she said. "He's a danger to us all. Even the children aren't safe. I'm sure of it. I think he needs some time to cool off and think real hard about what he's done."

"Just what are you askin' of me here? You want me to arrest him? Your son? Your own blood?"

"Yes, I am. There are consequences for your actions," Ruby Ray said.

"And he needs to answer for what he did to Terry," Mommy added. "You, too, Ricky. I know what you did, and I'm gonna make sure Chief Cooksey knows it."

"Ladies, y'all sure you want me to arrest Charlie? 'Cause the way I hear it, Zelda was the first one to land a punch tonight. She instigated this whole mess when she charged after him. A man's got a right to defend himself. Nobody can blame Charlie. His wife goes into a fit of rage and resorts to violence. Looks to me like if I arrest Charlie, I'd have to arrest Zelda first."

"*What?*" Mommy asked in disbelief.

"Another word out of you, little lady, and I'll haul you in for failure to comply with an officer. You hear me?" Ricky shot back. "It'd be in everybody's best interests to chalk this night up to some poor choices."

"Poor choices?" Mommy repeated mockingly, spitting a mouthful of blood onto one of Ruby Ray's handkerchiefs.

"Here's what I propose. I'll take Charlie with me and clean him up, and he can sleep this off on my couch. I suggest you and Homer get on down to the hospital so they can stitch up that little cut Zelda's got. Then come on home and tuck them kids into bed. In the morning, get yourselves to church then on to the parade. Nobody has to know the difference. You hear me?"

Ruby Ray bent down and whispered, "As much as you want Charlie to pay for his sins, are you willing to spend the night in a jail cell next to him?"

"Fine," Mommy said. "I won't be pressing charges." Her voice cracked.

"Well, I guess I'll be heading on, then," Ricky said as he swaggered toward the door. "And, Zelda..." He turned and faced the women. "You should learn how to leave well enough alone. Don't go poking the bear, if you catch my drift. You might not be so lucky next time. Evening, ladies."

Mommy lost her convertible ride in the town's parade. The horror that had transpired the night before was written all over her battered face. No amount of Maybelline could cover up the truth. Though the girls were traumatized, Penny the most, since she bore the physical scars, she wouldn't let her girls miss out on the opportunity.

"No one will know the difference unless they get real close," Mommy kept repeating between taking drags off her cigarette with one hand while plastering globs of Avon foundation onto Penny's black eye before supergluing rhinestones back onto her broken tiara.

Mommy patched Penny back together again piece by piece—at least, on the outside. The brokenness she carried on the inside was never dealt with. Out of sight, out of mind.

Three things changed for Penny the summer of 1976. First, no one would ever refer to her as fat again. Though she didn't fully comprehend what it meant, it was an ugly word, and she made a vow to herself to never be called it again. Second, she stopped calling her father "Daddy" or any other term of endearment. He was Charlie from that moment on. And third, and the biggest lesson of all: "You don't go poking the bear. You might not be so lucky next time." All those things proved to be pivotal for young Penny Ray, and it shaped the person she would become.

Penny pulls out her phone and dials her ex-husband's number from the bathroom stall. It goes straight to voice mail.

"Teddy. It's Penny. You—" She pauses, choking back her emotions and the bile creeping up her throat. "You can take the boys to Africa. I'm sure they will have a wonderful time."

Once she hangs up, she slides down the cement wall to the floor. Neither the physical exhaustion from running a multitude of miles nor the thoughts of being away from her children cause it. It's Kentucky and her childhood memories, the ones she banished long ago. They're coming back to her. A dam, impenetrable for decades, built by Penny's brain to protect a traumatized girl, has been weakened. Now she knows she doesn't stand a chance.

July 2009
Atlanta, Georgia

Chapter 6

All by Myself

Traffic in Atlanta is always terrible, but tonight, Penny's in no mood to fight through it. On this ordinary Friday night, with no Braves game jamming up I-20, it still takes her almost forty-five minutes to get home from the airport. The entire way, she keeps reliving the nightmare that unfolded in front of hundreds of travelers next to the American Airlines ticket counter at Jackson-Hatfield.

First was the awkward face-to-face with Teddy's new wife, Jessica, who was decked out in a hot-pink Juicy Couture velour tracksuit, quintessential Jennifer Lopez, right down to the bedazzled monogram on her voluptuous chest and a large diamond cross lying in the pit of her cleavage. Brutus—or rather, Tess Walker—was lurking behind her new best friend, desperately avoiding all eye contact with Penny. But nothing compared to Penny's final moments with the boys. Though Trey put up a good front, his brothers weren't that strong. Drew did his best to hide his emotions, constantly hugging his mother, while Sammy remained oblivious to the fact that his mother wouldn't be traveling with him until Penny stopped walking with the group at the security line. Ten minutes of hysterics and tantrums ensued before Teddy pried the toddler from his mother's arms. Sammy's tears soaked through Penny's linen shirt. Though she'd been mentally preparing herself for weeks, dreading the moment she would say goodbye to the boys, it never occurred to her they'd be filled with the same apprehension and sadness.

The Dutch colonial is now dark and empty. Sounds of laughter, video games, and balls bouncing against the walls are not there to greet her. She feels utterly alone. Penny opens the refrigerator, pulls out a bottle of Duckhorn sauvignon blanc, and pours a generous serving. Not bothering to turn on a light, she sits down on the family room couch. In complete darkness, she relives the events of the last hour over and over again in her mind. As she's about to make her way to the kitchen for a refill, since the first glass of wine slid down her throat a little too quickly, she spots headlights pulling into her driveway. Company, in light of the incident at the airport, isn't something she wants. When the doorbell rings, she scans the room, looking for places to hide. All the lights in the house are off, for darkness best suits her woefulness. Perhaps they'll leave, thinking she's not home.

"Penny, we know you're in there! Open the door."

Peeking through the kitchen window, Penny spots her friends Leslie Newman, Annie Grant, and Dakota.

"I just got a blowout, and it's hot as hell out here. My hair's starting to frizz!" Dakota yells through the door.

Penny shakes her head in defeat. It's no use trying to hide from them now. Besides, Dakota knows where she keeps the spare key, and she has no problem using it whenever she pleases.

"Hey there. I wasn't expecting you." Penny opens the door and welcomes her uninvited guests to her little pity party. "What a pleasant surprise."

"Pleasant surprise, my ass. Were you hiding from us?" Dakota asks.

"No," Penny replies quickly.

"Then why's it so dark in here?"

Penny flips the kitchen light switch. "I wasn't hiding. Just walked in the door from the airport."

"Yeah, right," Dakota says, nodding toward the open bottle of wine on the counter.

"Hey," Leslie greets Penny with a kiss on the cheek. "How are you holding up?"

"I'm fine. Thank you."

"We thought you needed a little company. So we brought some friends," Annie says, holding up two bottles of Sonoma-Cutrer chardonnay. "But only one glass for me. I'm the DD tonight." She breezes past Penny.

"Good to know," Penny says.

"And we thought you could use a little food too," Leslie adds, setting up a buffet on the marble island. "Tonight, you're eating more than cheese and crackers for dinner."

"I don't know why you wouldn't let us go with you. I mean, Teddy, Jessica, and Tess at once? You needed some backup," Annie says, pulling out silverware for dinner. Her friends know their way around her kitchen as if it's their own.

"Because she's stubborn. That's why." Dakota mixes a large glass of gin and tonic.

"She's not stubborn. She's tenacious," Leslie says, winking. "Besides, she's a big girl and knows how to handle herself."

"Thank you, Leslie," Penny says. "I'm a big girl who handled herself so well tonight that I've already downed a glass of wine, a generous pour, at that. In the dark. By myself. I was ready to pour my second glass when I saw you. Then I entertained the idea of hiding in my own house. From my friends. So yes, I really have my life together."

Leslie gasps. "Was it that bad?"

"Yes, it was. But not with Teddy or Jessica. Not even Tess, who never spoke. It was Sammy."

After Penny relays the story of her last moments with her toddler, Annie places her hand on her chest. "That sounds terrible." She's always been Penny's most tenderhearted friend.

"Sammy's a little trouper. He's probably asleep by now," Dakota says, waving off Penny's concerns. "Besides, there's nothing you can do about it. He's Teddy's problem now."

"Come on. Let's eat before it gets cold." Leslie guides them toward the food and away from any more talk about the airport. Covering the island are white boxes full of eggplant rollatini, linguine with clam sauce, and veal piccata. The dinner's designed to lift Penny's spirits—and quite possibly her weight.

After they finish their Italian feast, and the kitchen's back in order, they make their way to the cozy living room with their glasses of wine to chat some more.

"Thank you for being here tonight, even if you barged in on me. Uninvited. Still, I'm happy you're here," Penny says, raising her glass to the group to show her appreciation.

"So, you're leaving tomorrow for Kentucky?" Annie asks.

"Yep. Six a.m. on the dot."

"Let me guess. Your bags are packed, and the car is gassed up and ready to go. I bet you even have your clothes laid out, right?" Leslie smiles.

"Of course her car is packed." Annie chuckles. "God, I wish I were that with it. I can't manage to pack until about thirty minutes before I'm supposed to leave."

"That's why you're always an hour late," Leslie says.

"So, what's the plan for the next two weeks?" Annie giggles because there's always a plan for Penny.

"You could just look at one of the dozens of flowcharts she's made for her time in Kentucky," Dakota says. "That will tell you how she plans on spending every waking moment. She's even mapped out times when she goes to the bathroom."

"Very funny," Penny says. "And for your information, I've only made two."

"Two too many, if you ask me."

Leslie swats at Dakota's hand. "Don't listen to her. I'd like to know what you're going to do up there."

Penny takes a sip of her wine. "Hit the ground running. Boxing, tagging, throwing away trash. If I work around the clock, I should be done with the house in twelve days."

"Are you going to rent a moving truck to bring all that stuff back home with you?" Annie asks.

Penny shakes her head. "I only want a few things from Ruby Ray's, and they can all fit in the back of my car. Just little reminders of her. Keepsakes that were special. Once I've finished sorting through the house, my aunts will come over to take whatever they want. They can have it all, as far as I'm concerned."

When Ruby Ray's last will and testament was read out loud, it caused a nuclear meltdown within the family. No one knew the matriarch had made her last living grandchild the sole beneficiary of the house on Dogwood Lane along with all the contents in it. In doing so, she cut out her two elderly money-grubbing sisters and, most importantly, her own daughter.

"Hold on a sec," Dakota interjects. "You're going to give everything to them? Who, may I remind you, have treated you like shit over all this?"

"Why?" Annie asks.

"Because it means more to them than it does to me. I only want a few things. Besides, they won't miss them to begin with because they hold no monetary value. Just sentimental."

"Why do you think your grandmother singled you out? Giving you everything instead of them?" Leslie asks.

"No clue." Penny shrugs. "Ruby Ray wasn't very close to her daughter. After Molly moved to Paducah, we didn't see much of her. I've only met her a handful of times. She's kept her distance. As for Ruby Ray's sisters, I think my grandmother only tolerated them out of familial obligation. She used to say, 'Sometimes family is like a raisin cookie. Nobody picks 'em. Nobody even likes 'em. But if you're hungry enough, you'll learn how to swallow one in a crunch.'" A grin comes to Penny's lips as she remembers her grandmother's unique insights into life. Plus, she was spot-on about raisin cookies. "Since my aunts were upset about being cut out of the will, I decided I'll rectify it by letting them take whatever they want. I'm also splitting the proceeds from the sale of the house, fifty-fifty."

"You have a kind heart," Leslie says, giving Penny a tender smile.

"A fucking bleeding one, if you ask me." Dakota gives Penny a disapproving glare.

"You can't pack the whole time you're there. You'll be exhausted," Annie says, changing the subject. "Maybe you can spend some time with your family or some of your high school friends."

"My friend Kelly's coming over one day to help me pack. So are Jimmy Neal and his wife, Laura. They've been lifesavers, taking care of the house for me this year. And as Dakota likes to remind me, I'm sure I'll run into several relatives while I'm there as well."

"Anyone else you want to run into?" Dakota asks, a wicked grin spreading across her face.

"No, Dakota. No one else," Penny says, glaring at her tipsy friend in hopes she can squelch her inquiry.

"Are you sure?"

"Yes, I'm sure."

"Wait. Why do I get the feeling there's someone we don't know about?" Annie asks, her eyebrows shooting up.

"It's nothing," Penny says too quickly.

"Oh, I definitely don't believe you now. You're holding out on us," Leslie says, rubbing her hands together with excitement.

"Come on. Spill it," Annie demands.

"He's just some guy I used to know," Penny says, looking down at her wine glass, trying her best to look nonchalant.

"Bullshit!" Dakota roars.

After grabbing a throw pillow from her couch, Penny launches it toward Dakota's head.

"Hey! Watch the glass. You could've spilled my drink!" Dakota shrieks, throwing the pillow back. "And he's not just some guy, and you know it."

"What are you two talking about?" Annie asks.

"Bradley! There, I said it," Penny blurts. "Can we move along now?"

Looking utterly confused, Leslie asks, "Who's Bradley?"

"Bradley Hitchens. That's who," Dakota adds with gusto. "Who happens to be Penny's first love. Her first in many ways."

Leslie and Annie gasp. This is a side of Penny they'd never been privy to.

"Dakota!" Penny throws her overpriced pillow back at her naughty counterpart, this time with more urgency.

"Your first?" Leslie squeals. This boring Friday night of eating lukewarm Italian noodles while sipping costly wine has taken a turn.

"Dakota, you're cut off," Penny tells her. "And he was *not* my first. He's a guy I knew a million years ago. We went to school together. That's all."

"I'm not buying that," Annie says. "All this time, we thought Teddy was your first love. Now, there's this mysterious man. We need details."

"He's not mysterious. He's a dentist, for goodness' sake. We were friends. Really."

"Liar. Should I tell them, or do you want me to?" Dakota giggles while downing the last bit of her gin with very little tonic.

"No," Penny says. Though these women have been her friends for almost a decade, she's been tight-lipped in regard to her life in Kentucky. They know her immediate family, parents, and all three siblings died long ago, but they're oblivious to the ugly details surrounding her childhood. Penny would prefer to keep it that way.

"Come on. Tell us," Annie and Leslie beg.

Taking a long drink of wine to steady her nerves, Penny allows herself to go back to Kentucky and her complicated memories of her first love. "Bradley Hitchens." She sighs, still nervous about the mention of his name. "I don't remember meeting him. Camden's a small town, so you just kind of know everyone. We were in the same grade, even though he was a year older than me. We were in class together a few times in elementary school, but we didn't become friends until my eighth-grade year. Right after Zelda divorced her third husband, Earl the Squirrel—"

"Wait," Annie says. "Why do you call your stepfather Earl the Squirrel?"

"I gave all my stepfathers nicknames. Kind of like a little mnemonic device," Penny explains.

Annie and Leslie are clueless that her mother said "I do" eight times. However, this isn't the time or the place to give a full dissertation on the love life of one Zelda Ray Allen Devasher Mitchell Downing Pinson Stanley White.

"As for Earl, I called him Earl the Squirrel because he looked just like one. He had these beady little eyes that darted back and forth, and he had terrible buckteeth. He was definitely Zelda's least attractive husband," Penny says then takes another sip of wine. "And cherry on top, we went out in the front yard and shot one for supper once a week. That man *loved* fried squirrel."

"Oh god! What on Earth does squirrel taste like?" Leslie asks, horrified, turning green at the notion.

"Well, it doesn't taste like chicken," Penny tells her with the seriousness of a woman who's consumed the culinary treat.

"Enough with the *Deliverance* portion of your childhood," Dakota says. "You're trying to avoid talking about him by sidetracking us with the stupid squirrel story."

"Sorry, but Annie asked."

"Dakota's right. You're stalling," Leslie says.

"Okay. Back to Bradley," Penny says, readying herself once again to think of *him*. After all these years, she still can't say his name without her cheeks turning red. She still crushes on the first boy who took an interest in her. But with Bradley, there's much more. "He was the starting quarterback for the football team. Played varsity basketball in the winter. Ran the four hundred meters in spring. Class president all four years." A smile forms on her lips. "Even though he was the most popular boy in school, he wasn't a jerk or a snob. He treated everyone the same, with respect. But most importantly, he was *kind*. And when I was desperate for some kindness in my life, he gave it to me. He became my safe place. I trusted him." Her eyes start to water.

The room is still. Leslie and Annie, clutching their libations like pearls, are on the edges of their seats.

"Dakota's right, though. He was my first but not in *that* way. He was the first boy who ever gave me flowers, purple irises, which are still my favorite. He was the first boy I slow danced with. 'Heaven' by Bryan Adams. Every time I hear that song, I still think of him. He was the first boy who cupped my face in his hands and gave me my first real kiss. One that no other kiss has ever quite measured up to. And he was the first boy who told me he loved me."

The room is so quiet you could hear a pin drop.

"What happened to him?" Leslie asks.

After swallowing hard, Penny tells them, "He's living in Camden. Raising his two daughters."

"He's married?" Annie asks, disappointment filling her voice.

"No. He's a widower. His wife..." Penny looks hard at Dakota. "His wife died in a car accident a while back."

Dakota tosses back what's left of her drink after hearing Penny's voice harden. It's about as soft as barbed wire.

Annie gasps. "She died? Oh my god, that's terrible."

"Yes," Penny whispers. "It was."

"Do you still talk to him?" Leslie asks. "Are you still in touch?"

"No." She shakes her head. "We haven't spoken in twenty years."

"I think we all should go now," Dakota says, standing up.

"Stop it!" Leslie grabs Dakota's elbow, pulling her back down to the couch. She turns to Penny. "Why did you stop talking to him?"

Penny sighs. "He was also the first boy who broke my heart."

"Oh," Leslie whispers as the group once again becomes silent.

After a few moments, Dakota breaks the awkwardness. "Look, it's getting late. We should clean up and let Penny get to bed. We don't want her falling asleep driving up Mount Eagle tomorrow."

"Let's clean up these glasses," Annie offers.

"No, I've got it." Penny's had enough strolling down memory lane. "You guys go on."

"Are you sure?" Annie asks.

"Positive." She leads them to her foyer.

"Okay, then. I guess we'll see you in two weeks," Leslie says. "Sun, sand, and champagne. Love you." She kisses Penny goodbye. "Don't work yourself to death up there. See you in Rosemary."

Pulling Penny in for a warm embrace, Annie says, "Love you, sweetie. Be safe."

"I will," Penny replies, giving her an extra squeeze back.

Dakota waits for the others to make their exits before saying her own goodbyes. "Call me when you get there. Then call me every day so I know you haven't gone completely nuts up there, ready to slit your wrists," Dakota half jokes.

"I promise, even if I'm pissed at you for bringing up Bradley to everyone."

"Sorry about the *wife* coming up," Dakota says, wincing. "My bad. But I'm not sorry about mentioning him. It was necessary. Maybe I lit a fire under your ass, and you can go up there and look him up finally."

"I guarantee you I won't be looking up Bradley Hitchens. He's the last person I want to see." Penny shakes her head.

"Yeah, right."

"Remember, you promised to water my flowers while I'm gone," Penny says, changing the subject. "They need tending to every day. Take care of my girls."

"That's screwed up, you calling your flowers *your girls*. Yes, I promise. I won't kill them while you're gone."

"Thank you."

"In all seriousness, I know how hard Kentucky is going to be," Dakota says. "Are you sure you won't let me come with you?"

"Positive. I'm not sure Camden can handle you or your mouth for two weeks. Bless your heart."

"I love you, Penny Crenshaw, and I don't even like most people."

"I love you, too, but you'd better go before your DD leaves. You're not sleeping here tonight."

As Penny waves goodbye to her friends, watching their car drive into the darkness, she suddenly feels a strong sense of gratitude. Yes, she's still a scorned woman whose children are traveling thousands of miles away from her at this very moment with their bonus mom, but she's also beyond lucky. She has these incredible, thoughtful, ir-ritating women in her life who won't let her go gently into the night, feeling sorry for herself. She has friends—good friends.

Chapter 7

The Tennessee Waltz

The next morning, Penny pulls out of her driveway at 5:58 a.m., two minutes ahead of her self-imposed deadline, to make her way to Kentucky. A little goodbye to her Dutch colonial and her girls, and she's off. The streets around her Buckhead neighborhood are dark and quiet. Atlanta's sleeping in on this hazy Saturday morning. The air is thick with humidity. After all, it's the deep South, and once again, the city will have another stifling July day.

As she makes her way onto I-75, her thoughts go to her boys and the journey to Africa they're still making. Fifteen hours is a long flight for anyone, let alone a toddler who had a meltdown right before takeoff. Remembering Sammy's cries kept her up most of the night. Sleep is elusive for a mother whose children are halfway across the world. All throughout the night, she prayed Sammy slept through most of it.

Thirty minutes later, the sun begins to rise in the distance over a patch of Georgia pines. When she first moved to the state, she detested them for the needles they dropped in her beloved gardens, not to mention all the kites she lost in their branches with the boys. Yet somehow, she's grown fond of them. Though they're not particularly pretty trees, she's learned to appreciate and even admire their fortitude and strength. No matter how harsh the weather, they still remain optimistic with their greenness. They never turn brown or become beaten down when the circumstances around them change. Their branches never become bare half the year, like their deciduous counterparts, who allow their leaves to escape their branches when the going gets tough, exposing their barren limbs for the world to see. For three hundred sixty-five days a year, the pine remains the same. Maybe Penny can learn a thing or two from her former evergreen nemesis.

Though she loves the life she's built here in the Peach State, deep down, Penny has always known something was missing. Georgia's never filled the void in her.

A large sign welcomes Penny to the Volunteer State as she approaches Chattanooga, causing her mind to drift toward her former husband. Tennessee's the place where she fell in love with the young Theodore Fredrick Crenshaw Jr. back in 1994. He was living in Nashville for one last hoorah of youth, while she was trying her best to keep her head above water, working two jobs.

They met at the Green Hills Grille. He was with friends, enjoying multiple rounds of dirty martinis, while she was busy waiting tables. When she dropped off a plate of the restaurant's famous rattlesnake chicken for the group, his jaw dropped.

"You have the most gorgeous eyes I've ever seen," he said.

Though a cheesy line, it didn't come across as insincere either.

Penny nodded politely and went along with her work, ignoring him. Though she wasn't a knockout by most standards, her eyes always drew compliments.

The next day, he sat in her section and asked her out. She declined. Two nights later, he was back. That went on for a week. On his fifth attempt, Penny reluctantly agreed to a coffee date, not a dinner one because she didn't completely trust Teddy... or the opposite sex, for that matter. She had her reasons.

Everything about him looked good on paper. Smart, dashing, great personality, though a little irresponsible at times, he seemed like the perfect catch. Still, she hesitated.

Soon, she let her guard down, and Teddy drove her to Atlanta to meet his parents only a month into dating. Though Penny had grown up in a small, rural Kentucky town, often living well below the poverty line for the early part of her life, the Crenshaws were welcoming toward her from the start. When Penny explained how her family members were primarily farmers, they didn't make assumptions that her childhood was full of thoroughbreds and mint juleps like some outside Kentucky might assume. Where she grew up, most people didn't have the luxury of a stable full of horses to ride for fun. Hogs, cattle, and chickens filled those barns. When Teddy mentioned the small Christian college she'd attended on scholarship and financial aid, it didn't faze them. They loved how she'd managed higher education on her own. Nor did they bat an eye when they found out she was an English teacher by day at a public high school and a waitress by night just to make the rent. And when it came time for the wedding, they said nothing when she insisted on a small, intimate ceremony in Atlanta without either of her parents in attendance.

To some, Penny was wading outside her depth when she became engaged to Teddy Crenshaw Jr., because in most cases, classes don't mix, especially in marriage. However, it's not unheard of below the Mason-Dixon line for a wealthy man to take a shine to a woman outside his privileged bubble. Today's poor white trash is tomorrow's mother, daughter-in-law, or cochair of the Swan House Ball. It's best not to dig too deep.

The last time Penny spent any time in Tennessee was four years ago, when her husband whisked her away for a romantic weekend to Blackberry Farm. Tucked in the foothills of the Great Smoky Mountains, it's a charming resort known for its world-class cuisine and impeccable service. That's also the last time she remembers the Crenshaws acting like a happy couple.

Each morning on their romantic vacation, before the sun had even peeked through the mountains in the distance, she took long runs around the sprawling property. A thick canopy of trees kept her cool, and rolling hills challenged her endurance. The spectacular East Tennessee sunrises greeting her halfway through her daily minimarathons always took her breath away. As she admired the serene beauty, a sense of peace encompassed her, and she counted the blessings that Mother Nature and Teddy had supplied.

After her runs, she arrived back in time for a quick shower before crawling into bed next to a sleeping Teddy, ready to enjoy their private cabin's handmade mattress with breakfast in bed. Steel-cut oatmeal in a cast-iron ramekin was her preference. Once he stirred, Teddy feasted on griddle cakes covered in warm maple syrup topped with homemade salted butter. They savored the quietness of the room, a bed without children rolling, jumping, or sleeping in it, and sipping their coffees and lattes in peace. A crossword puzzle from the complimentary *New York Times* occupied her, while he feigned interest in the Bloomberg ticker scrolling at breakneck speed across the bottom of the television screen.

On the second day of their adventure, Teddy, who wasn't comfortable in the great outdoors unless on a golf course, tried his hand at fly fishing, much to her amusement. She watched from the bank of the pond, finishing her puzzle and chuckling at his fruitless attempts to cast a line. Not an experienced angler, he would've been clueless if he succeeded anyway. The thought of him holding a slimy fish, let alone finding the fortitude to unhook one, was quite funny to her. Unlike her "cityfied" husband, Penny knew her way around a critter-infested pond, thanks to Pops. Digging around a trout's mouth, releasing it from its painful mistake, wouldn't faze her. A country girl knows bodies of water—creeks, rivers, lakes, tiny streams—can provide a plethora of free food options for the taking. Crappies, brims, catfish, and even crawdaddies can make for a fine meal, if one can catch enough of them while avoiding their painful pincers. All one needs is a bucket of earthworms, maybe an ear of corn in a pinch, a little patience, and a whole lot of luck from the fishing gods. It's too good to pass up. Unlike her husband's gilded childhood, hers was fraught with the uncertainty of where her next meal would be coming from. Hunger overrides any queasiness one might experience from the sight of fish guts or the moral dilemma of consuming something that possesses eyes.

Later, by the same pond where Teddy had "fished," they enjoyed a lazy picnic beneath the golden sun with a basket of food arranged by the attentive staff. They noshed on savory BLT sandwiches on toasted pain de Mie bread dripping with homemade mayonnaise and heirloom tomatoes. A fennel pasta salad mixed with pickled vegetables was the perfect complement. To satisfy her insatiable sweet tooth, they topped off their meal with a couple of fresh-out-of-the-oven chocolate chip cookies perched on the side of small ceramic bowls full of strawberries and fresh cream. Though it was only noon, they threw caution to the wind and indulged in a bottle of Veuve Clicquot champagne. The combination of warm air mixed with a belly full of decadent food and overpriced bubbles caused her eyes to grow heavy. Laying her head upon her azure handwoven throw, she spotted through her thick eyelids Jesus bugs gliding effortlessly across the water before her. Their beautiful dance, skipping across the glassy pond, lulled her into a deep, hypnotic afternoon slumber. Before long, her husband joined in, offering his arm as a pillow.

A soft kiss upon her ear, courtesy of Teddy, brought her back from the land of Nod because more food and pampering awaited them. After a quick wardrobe change, the couple walked the short distance to the main house for an elaborate four-course dinner. They feasted on Wild Alaskan halibut with farm grits cooked in a savory bacon broth and Georgia Little Neck clams. Penny savored every calorie-laden bite.

The third morning of their getaway, they enjoyed a couples massage with lavender oil and bourbon body butter soaking into their skin in the quaint farmhouse spa. Three hours of hot tea and inner peace, their bodies wrapped in white robes while furry slippers kept their toes warm, was the perfect respite. Later that day, Teddy arranged a tour of the kitchen for a private culinary lesson for his wife. While Penny immersed herself in a cauliflower puree with the guidance of the executive chef by her side, Teddy sat back with a glass of cab, enjoying watching her in her element.

They made love their last night at Blackberry Farm. Nine months later, their little souvenir from the trip arrived... Sammy.

Driving up Mount Eagle, Penny's cell phone vibrates, breaking her thoughts. It's a short message from Teddy.

We've arrived. Please don't call or text back. We're exhausted. Call you later.

Though relieved to know they arrived safely in Africa, Penny's irked by the curt text from her ex. However, she needs to shake it off. Her energy and focus must be on the task ahead. Suddenly, sadness pours over her. Packing up her grandmother's house, saying goodbye to Ruby Ray without a Valium-spiked tea, and facing her past with her parents and her siblings is no longer theoretical or something she can discuss with friends over a plate of biscuits or a glass of wine. It's real. In less than three hours, she will be *home*.

Chapter 8

My Old Kentucky Home

The final minutes of Penny's journey is on a quiet, winding back road of rural Kentucky, a stark contrast to Atlanta's congested interstates. She's never gotten used to six lanes filled with semitrucks driving precariously close to her SUV while overpriced sports cars zip in and out, cutting her off. This two-lane road is a nice change of pace, but she forgot how difficult it can be to navigate such a large vehicle along their narrow lanes, which seem to curve in random places for no other reason than to avoid a row of large oak trees here or a field of soybeans there. Yet it's a beautiful drive through the countryside, with swaths of Queen Anne's lace and blue-eyed Marys growing along the landscape. Rustic barns, both working and abandoned, are scattered along the fields. The aromas of hay, livestock, and old leather come flooding back. She spent many hours in her family's tobacco barn as a child, playing hide-and-go-seek with her siblings and cousins.

Though she loves Georgia, its splendor doesn't compare to that of her old Kentucky home. In her biased opinion, Kentucky's the prettiest state in the Union, though it's technically a Commonwealth. The greatest two minutes in sports happen here, the Kentucky Derby. The first Saturday in May, Churchill Downs is always packed with horse lovers from around the world, dressed to the nines. The fairer sex dons over-the-top hats and fascinators, while the men in their midst strut around in their Sunday suits. Kentucky's also the home of the Chevrolet Corvette, with thousands of the luxurious sports cars rolling off the production line in Bowling Green each year. But most importantly, Kentucky's the home to every bourbon under the sun worth drinking. Ninety-five percent of the world's corn-mash whiskey comes from the state. Fast cars and fast horses, moonshine, and Muhammad Ali, Kentucky has given the world many unique gifts.

But as much as she loves the Bluegrass State, it's also the place that still haunts her. All of Penny's immediate family, with the exception of her mother, died here. Jack, Julie, Pops, and now Ruby Ray all rest in a little cemetery next to Penny's childhood church, while Janet's remains reside along a quiet creek bed in the holler next to their old trailer. Janet's final wish was that Penny, her last remaining sibling, scatter her ashes there, the place where the two had played together as children, catching crawdads, corn snakes, and june bugs.

But that's only a snapshot of the painful memories Penny's tried desperately to bury. Kentucky's also home to Charlie Ray, Zelda Too-Many-Last-Names-to-Mention, and Emily Johnston, the unholy trinity in her world—the father, the adulteress, and the holy terror.

Charlie drank like a fish and beat his wife and youngest child throughout her formative years. He was never good with money or employment. So incompetent in fiscal matters, he put the Ray family in an embarrassing bankruptcy, leaving Penny and her siblings penniless—pun intended. Thanks to Charlie, Penny knew the distinctive taste of the government cheese and powdered milk that were distributed around her county for those who lived below the poverty line. Though dead and buried, the man left scars outside as well as in.

Zelda, the adulteress, slept with any man who gave her the slightest compliment, much less bought her a drink. She was no better on the parental front. Without remorse, she left her husband—or rather, husbands—and children alone in the world without the maternal force they needed. Whispers swirled around her reputation, for she'd broken up too many marriages around Camden for it to be swept under the rug. Zelda was Liberty County's very own Elizabeth Taylor, marrying eight times before she passed away. As bad as Charlie was with money, Zelda was worse, regularly accepting food stamps when between husbands. The disapproving glares from those waiting in line at the cash register at the local Houchens grocery store when Zelda accepted their free food was etched in Penny's brain. However, the pangs of hunger and the prospect of no edible food in one's kitchen changes the myth in one's mind regarding the welfare queen sucking off the tit of the government when you're the one doing the sucking. Like Charlie, she, too, is long gone. Though dead and buried in a tiny cemetery outside Panama City, she still haunts Penny.

And Emily, the holy terror, is Penny's very own Nellie Oleson. Lots of little girls have one growing up, a mean girl who chooses to make another's life a living hell by picking on them with mocking and ridicule. Being the daughter of both the town's drunk and fallen woman, Penny was an easy mark, and Emily pounced at every opportunity. Penny lived in a trailer, not even a double-wide, wore hand-me-downs from her sisters, and her puberty was delayed by years. It was all too good to pass up. She was flat chested and flat broke. The insults practically wrote themselves, and they've never left Penny's mind.

When Penny spies the Welcome to Camden, Kentucky, sign, she grips the steering wheel. She's home, and there's no turning back now.

"You can do this," she says to herself. "Be a buttercup. Just be a buttercup."

Minutes later, Penny's driving through the town square, taking in the scenery. Though small, it's still a bustling place. Dozens of people are mingling about this afternoon. Some are heading into Curly Q's beauty shop, while others are dropping by Abbot's Feed & Seed for supplies. Farley's, the local dime store, which has been an anchor for the community since the late forties, is packed to the gills to-day with only one parking spot left in front, while O'Donnell's, the town's much-loved drug store, has a line out the door. Penny suspects it's for the soda bar. They make the best egg cream floats. At least, she hopes they still do. However, those are the only storefronts that look familiar. The rest of the buildings around the square are occupied by businesses she doesn't recognize. A nail salon has replaced Mr. Bew-ley's jewelry store. Next door, there's a medical supply company ad-vertising oxygen tanks for twenty-five percent off where Mary Gay's Fabric Market used to be. A coffee shop has confiscated the space once reserved for Nelson's Shoe Repair, while a florist has taken over Saul's Pizza. A pang of sadness hits her. She loved that place.

Camden has certainly changed over the years. Perhaps if Penny had remained there, the changes wouldn't have seemed so abrupt or startling.

As Penny makes her way down Dogwood Lane, the place Ruby Ray called home for more than forty years, her mind drifts back to when she was a girl. On this smooth piece of pavement, she learned how to roller-skate. She also set up a summer lemonade stand here, selling her grandmother's famous strawberry pies, earning her a few bucks on the side without her parents' knowledge. If they'd caught wind of her little business, they would've gobbled up her earnings to feed their addictions—cigarettes and liquor, an expensive combina-tion.

Pulling into the driveway of 225 Dogwood Lane, Penny admires the beauty of Ruby Ray's home—hers now, with a stroke of her grandmother's pen before she died. She's in awe of the foursquare home painted yellow with green shingles and bordered by a beautiful wraparound porch.

Though she lives in Atlanta, surrounded by seven-figure real es-tate, nothing compares to this place. Six large pink peony—or pee-OH-knee, as they are pronounced in Camden—bushes line the edge of the house's stairs along with dozens of periwinkle and snow-white hydrangea bushes. Two mature maple trees frame the front of the house perfectly. In the summer months, they provide a canopy of shade to protect the house and its occupants from the hot, unforgiving summer sun, and in the fall, their leaves transform into the most spectacular shade of red, putting on an autumn show. To the right of the house stands a tall pink-and-white dogwood that has been grafted into one magnificent tree. It's Penny's favorite climbing tree in the yard, though its rough bark had caused more than a few cuts and scrapes on her knees and elbows. But the star of the front yard is an enormous Southern magnolia to the left of the house. It's the largest in all of Camden and maybe in all of Kentucky. The limbs, having never been pruned, have grown down to the ground, creating a tiny room that's the perfect place to escape. As a child, Penny spent countless hours within their confines, playing house. Ruby Ray helped her decorate her tiny oasis with a small table and chairs, an old set of dishes they found at a yard sale, and a small wooden crate they turned into a couch. They hung sparkling crystals from a broken chandelier they bought at a flea market on the limbs. Pops made a wooden sign with 225 Penny Lane and placed it next to the entry. In Penny's imaginary world, life was peaceful. No child or little beauty queen was ever slapped or kicked around there.

Slowly, she makes her way out of the car, stretching her legs from the long drive. Walking toward the front steps, she spots her grandparents' rocking chairs. Seeing how they are now empty takes her breath away. In those chairs, her grandparents would sit, watching the town pass by for hours on end. Her grandmother snapped peas or shucked corn while her grandfather whittled a piece of cedar wood. Never idle hands for those two.

Not ready to go inside, Penny stalls. She decides to walk around the property to get her bearings. Much to her surprise, her grandmother's perennial beds are thriving. Her cousin Jimmy Neal and his wife, Laura, who've been taking care of the place, have done a splendid job. Ruby Ray's purple asters, black-eyed Susans, delphiniums, sweet Williams, gladiolas, and day lilies are in full bloom. They're magnificent. Her grandmother would be pleased that all her hard work in her flower beds hasn't gone to waste. Her girls are carrying on nicely without her.

Penny moves on to one of Ruby Ray's new dawn rose bushes. Inhaling its fragrance, she closes her eyes. At that moment, she feels a rush of her grandmother's presence surrounding her and is reminded of her cardinal rule of gardening. "Remember, Penny, it doesn't matter how good the soil is or how hardy the stem. Unless a flower catches the eye of the sun every once in a while, it'll never bloom." It was a gentle reminder that Penny, too, needed a little sun cast upon her from time to time.

Continuing around the grounds, Penny admires the large white oak tree with the tire swing Pops installed for her as a child. She chuckles when she spies the mimosa tree her grandfather thought was tacky and wanted to take an axe to, but Ruby Ray insisted its "exotic" blooms reminded her of Hawaii, a place she'd never been. Her grandmother won the argument nonetheless.

Passing the utility barn, she catches the slightest hint of sweetness floating in the air from the climbing jasmine bush. Penny's first bee sting was sustained here, and she always blamed the bush's ambrosial blooms for her pain.

Not only does the property possess an abundance of trees and flowerbeds, but it also has a large flat area, almost a quarter of an acre, where her grandparents planted their "city" garden every summer. They spent hours in silence, lost in their thoughts and tending to their vegetables in unison. Now it's covered with grass, for it became too burdensome for Ruby Ray to continue. When Pops died, her love of gardening did too.

Though the stroll through the two-acre yard was a good idea, Penny's losing valuable time. The self-imposed schedule she made is gnawing away at her, and it's almost one o'clock. Though she's gained an hour, since Atlanta is in the eastern time zone and Camden in the central. But still, the clock is ticking. Time to get to work.

She walks back to the front porch, this time barreling her way up the steps, purposely avoiding a glimpse of the rocking chairs. After unlocking the front door, she's greeted with the familiar smells of her grandmother's home welcoming her back. Though faint, Ruby Ray's White Shoulders perfume still lingers in the air. Instead of bringing a tear to Penny's eye, it brings an earnest smile to her face.

Looking around the space, Penny notices how little the living room has changed. From the marigold afghan her grandmother crocheted back in the Carter years lying along the back of the floral company couch to the sheer curtains covering the metal blinds, which are yellowed from the years of afternoon sunlight pouring in, the space is exactly the same. The forty-year-old green wool carpet has never been replaced, and the mixture of *Southern Living* magazines, *Reader's Digest*, and copies of *National Geographic* scattered about on the cherry coffee table have been staples of the room for as long as she can remember. The end tables framing the love seat in the corner are covered with several yellow number two pencils with bite marks on the sides. Picking one up, Penny chuckles, remembering how her grandmother always had one in her mouth when doing her nightly crossword puzzles here. The room looks as if it's been frozen in time, a relic of the past. She halfway suspects if she keeps looking around, she'll find her grandmother here. What a wonderful gift that would be, to see Ruby Ray one last time.

Suddenly, the grandfather clock in the corner of the room strikes, beginning its hourly chime. The noise startles her, breaking her thoughts. Before it can even finish its singsong greeting, Penny's already annoyed with it. One, it's incredibly loud, and two, the sounds it emits are downright haunting. Now she has her very own Cinderella warning to keep her company for the next two weeks, cautioning her that time is in fact ticking by. Not only that, but it's also perfectly placed just a few feet from her bedroom. Though irritated by her new ticking nemesis, she'll have to brush it aside for the moment. She has a house to pack, and she's on a tight schedule.

Penny opens the door to her SUV and grabs a small suitcase containing the clothing she'll need for Kentucky, like T-shirts, jogging shorts, and tennis shoes, while leaving the suitcase she's packed for Florida, which is filled with swimsuits, sandals, and sundresses, in the backseat. She slips two cardboard flow charts that are color-coordinated and timed down to the minute on how she will spend her time in Camden under her right arm. Trying to be as efficient as possible, she throws a Scout bag containing three bottles of sauvignon blanc she's brought from home over her left shoulder since Liberty County is "dry," and the nearest wine store's thirty miles away. Though she's never liked the idea of drinking alone, packing up this place might require a libation or two in the next few days.

Once she drops off the luggage in her bedroom, she makes her way to the kitchen, hunting for any paper towels, trash bags, or cleaning supplies that may have been left over. Upon entering the room, she's greeted with a Tupperware carrier sitting right in the middle of the kitchen table. The instant she spots it, Penny knows it's from Gracie Belle, Jimmy Neal's mother, welcoming her home with one of her famous lemon-blueberry pound cakes. Though Gracie Belle is only a second cousin by marriage, Penny loves the woman, even more so than most of her blood relations.

Usually, Penny possesses the fortitude to be able to resist unnecessary calories when tempted, but this time, she cannot stop herself. Digging into the buttery concoction, she's met with juicy fresh blueberries bursting with tartness in her mouth. The hint of lemon is a nice twist and the perfect complement to the mounds of sugar her cousin by marriage has put into it. Closing her eyes, she savors every last morsel, even licking her fingers so as to not leave a speck of it behind. As she begins cutting a second piece, she notices a note sitting next to a large bowl of homegrown tomatoes and a basket full of brown eggs from her cousin's coop.

Welcome home, cuz!

Momma wanted to make sure you had something to eat the next couple of weeks, so she stocked the fridge. Said it's about time for you to get a little meat on those tiny bird bones of yours. We need to fatten you up.

Jimmy Neal

PS There's plenty of cardboard boxes, packing tape, and newspapers in the barn. I've arranged for a dumpster to be delivered this afternoon. Trust me. You're going to need it!

Opening her grandmother's ancient Frigidaire, she shakes her head in bewilderment. Yes, her family has indeed stocked the icebox with foods she loves, food that she's not allowed herself the pleasure of consuming since she left Kentucky. Jimmy Neal has carefully arranged twelve bottles, not cans, of Dr. Pepper, her childhood favorite. She's not touched a drop in ten years. Next to the sodas is a huge spiral ham, which Penny is sure has been cured by Gracie Belle herself, with cloves and pineapple baked right in. A yellow box of Velveeta sits next to the ham along with a tub of Hellman's. On the second shelf is a bowl of corn salad made with cream cheese, green peppers, onions, and mounds of mayonnaise. In the door stand two gallons of milk, whole and buttermilk. No wonder heart disease plagues her family.

Before her head can spin out of control from the amount of fat content in such a small space, she cuts a third piece of cake—calories be damned—before leaving the kitchen behind to begin turning on all the window air conditioners. The foursquare is sweltering under the hot July sun—it's at least ninety inside. She hopes by the time she returns from Farley's, it will have cooled down.

Sitting at her grandmother's secretary, Penny jots down a list of all the supplies she needs for the week before heading to the store. It's close enough for her to walk, but she drives instead. All those bags will tucker out her arms.

Upon entering Farley's dime store, Penny's greeted with the sweet aroma of their famous kettle corn, which they've popped every Saturday since the fifties in a Camden tradition. In no scenario will she be able to resist its buttery caramel goodness, so she makes a mental note to pick up a bag when she checks out. Calories be damned—again.

Proceeding up and down the aisles, picking up boxes of trash bags, Pine-Sol, Windex, cleaning rags, and a mammoth canister of Maxwell House coffee, she mentally pats herself on the back. She's going to pack up her grandmother's home properly—with plenty of caffeine coursing through her body.

This is going to be a breeze, she thinks, pushing her buggy full of supplies toward the checkout line and the kettle corn that's been toying with her nose for the last fifteen minutes.

"Penny Ray? Is that you?" the jovial man behind the cash register exclaims, startling her. "It's so good to see you. Lord, you ain't changed a bit, except maybe you got younger!"

Penny doesn't recognize the man standing before her. Unfortunately, his vest with his name tag is turned inside out, so she can't sneak a peek.

"Oh my goodness. It's so good to see you too. How long has it been?" she asks, trying to buy more time to figure out to whom she's speaking.

"Well, I guess the last time I saw you was on our graduation day, and that's been twenty years ago. Where's the time done gone?" the still-nameless gentleman says. But he gives her the valuable clue that they were classmates.

"Good ole class of '89," Penny adds, still struggling to place him.

As the mystery man begins scanning her items, she scans her brain, desperately trying to remember.

"You got a whole lot of cleaning stuff here," he says. "You back in town to pack up your grandmother's house?"

"Why, yes," she says, surprised he knows her intentions by the items in her shopping cart. "Yes, I am. Got in town a little while ago,"

"You ain't gonna have no problem selling that house. Everybody in town wants it."

"Let's hope so."

"I sure am sorry about your loss. I loved your grandmother. Everybody round here did," he says, a soft expression falling upon his face. "You remember when she was our fourth-grade teacher, and she'd sneak me a sausage biscuit from her kitchen every morning? She knew I didn't get nothing to eat at home. Never had another teacher do that for me, and I never forgot it."

Lonnie Davis! Eureka! He sat next to her that year and was frightfully skinny and stayed that way all throughout high school. Nothing bonds classmates like a troubled home life.

"Thank you, Lonnie. She was one of a kind, and she loved all her students, but she had a soft spot for you." Her grandmother had truly cared for the young Lonnie and his well-being, knowing his free lunch at school was his only meal of the day. "How long have you worked here?" Penny asks, genuinely wanting to know the answer, for she's just made her first connection back to the Bluegrass State.

"'Bout eighteen years now. Got promoted to assistant manager a while back, so I don't run the register anymore, unless we're busy or I'm bored. You really get a chance to know your customers when you're checking folks out. What about you? What do you do?"

"Oh, well, I'm a stay-at-home mother. I have three boys. After my first was born, I quit my job. I was an English teacher," she says, trying to mask her embarrassment at giving up her career aspirations. "Before I knew it, I had two more."

"So you went into the family business, then," Lonnie says. "But being a mom, that's the hardest job in the world. God love my wife, but I don't know how she's been able to put up with my crazy son all these years."

Penny giggles. Lonnie's joke has taken the sting out of her lack of professional accolades.

"You know, you could keep Miss Ray's house and move back to Camden with your boys," he says. "We could use a good English teacher round here."

"You're sweet, but my life is in Atlanta now."

"Then don't be a stranger. You hear? Anything else I can get you?"

"Oh! I almost forgot. Can you add a bag of kettle corn?"

"Yes, ma'am. I'd be a little hurt if you didn't buy some. Popped it myself an hour ago," he says, handing her the bag. "That'll be ninety-four seventy-six. Cash or check?"

Farley's is old school and hasn't adapted to a world of credit cards.

"You mean you'd take an out-of-state check from me?"

"You ain't from out of state, Penny Ray. You're still one of us. I'll vouch for you," he says earnestly.

Smiling, she hands Lonnie cash before tossing a handful of kettle corn into her mouth. The second she bites down on her salty-but-sweet treat, a loud cracking noise sounds, and an excruciating pain shooting through her jaw and up into her left eye overwhelms her. Penny moans.

"Oh no! Oh no! Oh no!" Lonnie yells.

A tear slowly rolls down Penny's cheek. "I think I broke my tooth," she whispers, wide-eyed, looking up at a stunned Lonnie.

He covers his face. "I can't believe this is happening again."

"Again? This has happened before?" she asks, flummoxed.

"Popping kettle corn is harder than it looks." Sweat pours from his forehead. "Please don't sue us."

"Sue you?" she repeats. Litigation's the last thing on her mind. The liver taste of blood in her mouth consumes her.

"Yes, sue us. We just settled up with Bertha Evans last month for the same thing. My manager said if I did this again, I'm gonna lose my job!" He shakes his head. "My wife's gonna kill me."

Penny holds her jaw. "I would never sue you, Lonnie." Though right now, she wants to throw the judicial book at him for the pain she's experiencing.

"Thank you, Lord Jesus!" Lonnie clasps his hands together, looking up to the sky in gratitude. "What can I do for you?"

"Please tell me what aisle you keep the ibuprofen on," she says, trying to suppress the irritation filling her voice.

"You wait right here, and I'll grab a bottle. Stay put." Lonnie rushes around the counter.

"What about us?" a customer standing behind Penny asks.

"You just going leave us here? We need to check out too," someone else says.

Lonnie sprints back to the counter and grabs a phone receiver. "Donna Pat, I need another cashier at the front. Stat!" Turning to the crowd, his face ablaze, Lonnie says, "She's on her way. I'll be back in a jiffy."

While Lonnie rushes toward the medicine aisle, Penny closes her eyes, trying to make herself invisible. A childish stunt, hoping the world around her will disappear. However, the people waiting in line behind her begin whispering. Though her eyes are shut, her ears still work. She prays they don't recognize her. In Camden for less than an hour, and already she's a spectacle—in Farley's, of all places.

"You're Charlie Ray's daughter. Ain't ya?" someone asks, causing her pulse to quicken. Turning around, she finds an elderly woman standing behind her, a lit cigarette between her lips.

Penny swallows hard. "Yes, ma'am," she says, her voice trembling. Under her breath, she says a little prayer, hoping her father hasn't wronged this woman in some way.

"You musta been gone a real long time," the woman says, shaking her head. Gray smoke lingers around her ashen locks like a halo.

Curious, Penny asks, "How did you know?" Sometimes you can't tell who is a friend or a foe in these parts. Crazy family feuds are not unheard of. After all, Kentucky's the home of the Hatfields and the McCoys. Those people fought and killed one another for decades over a dispute about a hog.

"'Cause today's the second Saturday of the month. That's why," the old woman says, still taming the smoke around her like a carnie at a county fair.

"What does that mean?" Penny asks.

"Everybody in Camden knows that Lonnie Davis pops the kettle corn on the second Saturday of the month. We're not dumb enough to buy it, let alone put it in our mouths," she says, laughing so hard that her cigarette slips from her lips.

The rest of the crowd begins howling along with the old woman. A Kentucky version of a Greek chorus is now mocking Penny. At this moment, she wishes God would be merciful and create a large sinkhole in the floor of the store to swallow her up. It's not unheard of around Camden. The Mammoth Cave system sits below this town. Twenty-five years ago, the local Dairy Queen's parking lot succumbed to rain, water, and an unforgiving topography, sinking thirty feet into the limestone beneath.

"What's all the commotion up here?" a woman wearing a Farley's vest asks as she saunters toward the crowd.

"Kettle corn. Looks like Lonnie's going to court again."

The clerk takes a long look at Penny and shakes her head without any concern or sympathy before motioning the customers to her counter. "Should've known better. It's the second Saturday of the month."

How can today get any worse? Penny thinks, closing her eyes again.

Then it does.

"This must be your lucky day. Look who I ran into on aisle seven," Lonnie calls out, rushing back to the checkout counter.

Before Penny can turn and see who Lonnie's discovered, she hears a voice. "Hey," the man says. It's smooth and comforting. It's home.

Though her back is to him, Penny knows exactly who Lonnie's found on his mission for pain relief. Goose bumps cover her body, and her stomach twists into a Gordian knot. Slowly turning around, she comes face-to-face with the one person in all of Camden—or rather, the entire world—she had no intention of ever seeing again. Yet here he is, standing before her like a vision. *Or a nightmare.*

"Doc Hitchens, Penny Ray done cracked her tooth on some kettle corn," Lonnie says breathlessly. "She needs help right away. You can fix her, right?"

"It's okay, Lonnie. I'm fine," Penny says, grabbing her bags and looking down, avoiding Bradley's gaze. Not only is she in a great deal of pain, but she's now run into Bradley. This scenario was not part of her plan, which is barreling off a cliff at the moment.

"Don't look like it to me. You've done turned white as a ghost," Lonnie says.

"It's all good. I promise. Just tell me how much I owe you for the ibuprofen," she says, ignoring Bradley's presence.

"It's on me." Lonnie smiles, throwing the bottle into a yellow bag.

Motioning toward the generic bottle of painkillers, Bradley says, "You're going to need more than that." His voice is soft.

"I'll be fine." Her voice is hard.

"I can take a look, if you like," Bradley offers.

"No!" she snaps before finding the decorum to recover. "Thank you, but it's fine. I'm sure it's nothing."

"A cracked tooth isn't nothing." Bradley shakes his head.

"Of course a dentist would say that," she mumbles like a bratty teenager.

Bradley hears the comment and suppresses his smile.

"Awfully convenient, him being here," she whispers in Lonnie's direction.

"Well, I always make time to roam around Farley's on Saturday afternoons, waiting for new patients. It's my busiest day of the week. You know, with the kettle corn and all."

With those words, Penny finally looks up, and her eyes meet his. Though she would never admit it, she's taken aback by the grown-up version of Bradley Hitchens. The salt-and-pepper scruff growing on his square jaw and those perfect cheekbones are a nice addition to her first love's visage. And through his facial hair, Penny still spots *that* dimple on his left cheek. She always loved and was puzzled by it. She found it fascinating that there wasn't another on the right to complement it. It was always her kryptonite. Every girl in Southern Kentucky, Bowling Green, Glasgow, and Tompkinsville longed for a smile from Bradley that was worthy of that single cheek indentation.

While Penny's mind is tangled up with Bradley's looks, poor Lonnie is having a conniption fit of titanic proportions in the middle of the store.

"You're not gonna sue us, are you, Penny?" Lonnie asks.

"I'd sue him, if I were you," Donna Pat pipes up from the other counter.

"Just mind your own beeswax," Lonnie snaps.

"I'm not going to sue you," Penny says.

"Then please let Doc Hitchens take a look," Lonnie replies. "I feel terrible about all this."

Lonnie's supplications finally take their toll on her, breaking her from her trance. Rolling her eyes for show, she agrees to an examination, not for Bradley's sake but for poor Lonnie's. Without touching her, Bradley peers into her mouth. After what feels like an eternity, with her mouth wide open for all of Farley's to see, the good dentist finally speaks.

"There's some blood forming around your back-left molar. I'm afraid it might be an oblique subgingival crack. My office is next door. Why don't we head over, and I'll run some X-rays on you to make sure."

"I'm not going anywhere with you," she says. "Wait, I didn't mean it like that. What I meant to say is I don't want to put you out. I'm fine. I'll go to my dentist when I get back to Atlanta."

"You can't wait that long."

"Why not?"

"Because you'll be in severe pain until it's fixed. You won't be able to eat. Forget about drinking anything that has ice in it. Coffee will be brutal. Trust me. You can't put this off. Miss Paulette is working overtime today, catching up on some bookkeeping, so she can assist me."

"I'm sure you have better things to do this afternoon," Penny says. "Besides, I have a ton of packing in front of me."

"You'd best go on with Doc Hitchens," Lonnie says, inserting himself into the exchange. "He's the only dentist within thirty miles of Camden. Well, except old Jim Hamilton, and he'd never open his place on a Saturday. Plus, I wouldn't want him fixin' my tooth. Would you, Doc?"

"Well, he's a fine dentist, but he teed off an hour ago. I'm fairly confident he won't leave his foursome to open his office today. So, Penny, I guess I'm your man. I mean dentist," he says, chuckling at his own gaffe.

"Are you sure I'm not keeping you from something more important? Family obligations?" Penny asks, thinking of every angle to get out of the dental mess she's found herself in.

"Ace, I mean Ashleigh Cate, is studying abroad this summer in Europe. And Emeree Shae left for Greystone this morning for camp. Then she's off to Hilton Head with my parents for vacation. So my schedule has freed up a bit this summer," he tells her.

Ah yes, the children with the double names and creative spellings. Years ago, when Penny read their birth announcements in the local newspaper, she knew it was their mother's doing. Bradley would never come up with such names. Now she's being petty toward the dead wife of the man who's offering his dental services. The little devil on her shoulder might have won the first round, but the little angel on the other makes her feel bad for her snideness toward the late Mrs. Bradley Hitchens. Reluctantly, Penny nods in agreement, accepting his help.

"I'll take care of these bags," Lonnie says. "Give me your keys, and I'll put them in your car."

"That's sweet of you. It's a white SUV. I think I parked it... Actually, I have no clue where I parked it," she says, flustered from the pain, both physical and emotional. She isn't sure which is worse.

"Don't worry. I'll find it. Look for the Georgia plates, right?" Lonnie smiles.

"Thank you," she says, handing over her keys. She'd forgotten how friendly, accommodating, and trustworthy the people of a small town can be. If this scenario—catastrophe—occurred in Buckhead, she doubts she would receive such care.

"Shall we go, then?" Bradley motions toward the door.

Closing her eyes, Penny nods while once again wishing for a geological event to save her before she can reach his office.

Chapter 9

The Crown

"Look what the cat drug in! Penny Ray, when did you get home?" Miss Paulette exclaims, opening her big arms to demand a hug, which Penny happily obliges.

Paulette Taylor is both an icon around Camden and the town's premier gossip, knowing every one of the town's 4,434 residents and all their little peccadillos. For fifty years, she's worked as a dental hygienist and bookkeeper in this very office. Bradley *inherited* her from Dr. Whalley when he took over the practice ten years ago, but everyone knows who the real boss is around here. Four years of dental school don't stand up to Paulette's half century of care. In her midseventies, she's almost six feet tall and has an enormous beehive that resembles purple cotton candy on top of her head. She adopted the hairstyle back in the sixties and refuses to give up on it. Of course, Penny's related to her through her vast, complicated family tree, which sometimes crosses the same branch or two from time to time.

"I hadn't heard you were back in town. Guess my little spies have lost a step or two." Paulette winks.

"Got here an hour ago," Penny slurs, since her mouth is no longer cooperating.

"I'm afraid Penny's fallen victim to Farley's kettle corn," Bradley says. "I'm fairly confident it's an oblique subgingival crack. We'll need to run some X-rays on her."

Miss Paulette huffs. "Good Lord. They gotta stop selling that stuff or learn how to fix it like Old Man Farley used to. This is the second broken tooth we've had in six weeks from it. I swear we're gonna have to start sending them a bigger Christmas basket for all the customers they keep sending our way!" Her gregarious laugh fills the room.

"Heard it got Bertha Evans too," Penny mumbles.

"Let's prep the room, and can you please call the club and clear my afternoon?" he asks before disappearing.

"Of course, Dr. Hitchens," Miss Paulette says before springing into action, guiding Penny into an exam room. Within minutes, Paulette runs a series of X-rays on Penny's mouth, preps the room, brings out consent-to-treat forms, and places a dental bib around her neck. For a woman her age, Miss Paulette's remarkably efficient.

Now Penny's waiting for Bradley—alone, on her back, in one of his dental chairs. Oh, how her friends will love this little development.

"Good news," Bradley says, walking into the exam room. "Your X-rays show that although you've indeed fractured your tooth, it hasn't affected the pulp."

He holds up an X-ray to the light. Penny squints, pretending she knows how to read it too. She wants to present herself as a woman capable of handling herself.

"Thankfully, you won't require a root canal. I can fix this with a temporary crown. When you get back to Atlanta, you can have a permanent one put on. But still, this is going to take a while."

The words *take a while* catch her attention. Not only will today be a total loss in packing time, but she also fears she'll miss Teddy's phone call about the boys' exploits on the deadly continent of Africa. "Can't you put a filling on it or something? Superglue? Wouldn't that be quicker?"

Chuckling at her absurd suggestion, he says, "A filling will not hold your tooth together. Neither will Superglue. This is the only solution."

Realizing she knows nothing of the dental profession and that her attempts to fix her problem with something sold at a convenience store are futile, Penny can only nod and reluctantly sign the papers. Now, she's at the mercy of Bradley Hitchens for the rest of the afternoon.

"Before we start, would you like a little nitrous oxide? It might help you relax a bit," he says, lowering her chair.

"No, I'm fine. I think I'll pass," she says, wanting to keep her wits about her.

"Are you sure? It might be a little uncomfortable." He lowers his voice. "There's going to be a few shots."

"I've given birth three times. I don't think a couple of needles will bother me," she lies. Penny hates needles, but under these circumstances, pain be damned. A stiff upper lip is her choosing, though she hasn't an English bone in her body or her unfortunate gene pool. The Ray family's made up of fiery Irish and pugnacious Scots. Not even a Scandinavian or German can be found in their mix.

Bradley raises his eyebrows. "Okay, then. No gas for you," he says. "Miss Paulette, we might need some extra numbing gel."

"Sure thing," she says before digging around in a cabinet behind the dental chair.

"Are you ready?" he asks.

Penny takes a deep breath and nods.

"Okay. Here we go."

Bradley gently opens Penny's mouth. His thumb grazes the upper-left corner of her lip. This simple touch causes both of them to freeze and their eyes to lock. While her body stiffens, his falls. The two are at an impossible stalemate.

After what seems like an eternity, he leans in and whispers into her right ear, the good one, "You can't see it at all now, Penny. It looks good. I promise." Then he gives her a reassuring smile. Only he, not Teddy, Dakota, her Kentucky friends, or even Ruby Ray knows how she got that scar on her lip. He's never told another soul, at least as far as she knows.

The scar has been a glaring eyesore for Penny. Over the last twenty years, no matter how hard she and several plastic surgeons have tried, it's never disappeared completely. What's left upon her porcelain skin is a lasting, ugly reminder of a day she wants to forget. Unfortunately, it's not the only one on her face, just the most visible. Thick bangs styled to the left side of her forehead cover the other deep, jagged mark.

As her chin begins to quiver, she mouths, "Thank you." A small tear forms in the corner of her eye. Before it can fall down her cheek, where Miss Paulette can see, Bradley softly brushes it away with his thumb. This moment is between the two of them. It has been for decades.

"Honey, I heard about your divorce, and I'm so sorry," Miss Paulette says, turning around, unwittingly breaking the moment between doctor and patient. "I never did like that husband of yours. I always thought he was a little too big for his britches. And Gracie Belle told me he's already remarried. To some yoga instructor, of all things. He's such a dog. You're better off without him. And look at you. You're the cat's meow, even if you need to gain a pound or two. Or maybe twenty. How 'bout I donate some of mine to the cause." She rubs her thick stomach, laughing at her own joke. "I bet the men of Atlanta are lining up, beating down the door to get a chance to court you. Are you dating, honey?"

Once again, Penny and Bradley's eyes meet. The good dentist seems eager to learn of her dating status. Wanting to end the conversation once and for all, Penny attempts to say, "I'm not ready yet," though it comes out garbled, with all the instruments being placed in her mouth.

Remarkably, both Bradley and Miss Paulette understand. Penny can only assume it's because they've had years of practice in deciphering the words of patients whose mouths have been rendered useless.

"Not ready? Time's a-ticking, young lady. You're in the prime of your life. I swear, you're as bad as Dr. Hitchens here. Lord knows I've tried to fix him up dozens of times with some fine young ladies around town. Even a few in Glasgow, but he won't budge. He's been single for... how many years?" Miss Paulette asks.

"Twelve," he answers stoically.

"Did you hear that? And he still won't date. I even thought about filling out an application to get him on that show. You know, *The Bachelor*? Maybe they can find him somebody." Miss Paulette laughs. "Can you imagine Dr. Hitchens up there on the TV, handing out roses to intoxicated, desperate women?"

"Suction, please," Bradley says.

"You know what I think? Why he won't date?" Miss Paulette continues, ignoring him. "I've long suspected he's been holding out for something better. Or maybe I should say *someone* in particular who moved away a long time ago." She winks at Penny. She knows the two were close at one time. They have a history.

"Would you like that gas now?" Bradley asks again.

This time, Penny nods. She needs something to dull the embarrassment of Miss Paulette's probing questions and innuendos. Bradley places a silly mask on her nose, one she's certain he's used hundreds of times on frightened eight-year-olds. Now it's needed to ease the humiliation of a thirtysomething woman. A few moments later, and after a couple of deep breaths, Penny's arms and legs become warm and tingly then heavy. The tension in her entire body and mind relaxes under its spell. She's floating now and curses herself for not requesting this magical concoction the second she stepped foot

in the door—or better yet, in the state of Kentucky. Her embarrassment, though still there, is no longer paramount in her mind.

As Miss Paulette continues yammering, Penny sneaks little peeks
here and there at Bradley. In her current state, she's mesmerized.
Though most of his face is covered by his surgical mask and glasses,
she finds him to be as intoxicating now as she did as a lovesick
teenager. Age has certainly been his friend. Father Time has not been
as harsh to Bradley Hitchens as she fears he's been to her. His face
has matured, of course. He's in his late thirties, but his wrinkles make
him more attractive, wiser, and more confident, where her crow's-
feet and laugh lines make her feel hollow and tired. The boy with the
baby face, the one she knew and loved, has been replaced by the chis-
eled figure floating above her. The flowing honey-blond hair of his
youth is gone. Now it's peppered with specks of gray. Though short-
er, it's still full and thick. Propecia doesn't seem to be a concern for
him. But his best feature is his eyes. It's not the color, which is hazel
with golden flecks, or the oval shape that draws her in. It's the compassion behind them. Now, they're looking at her once again.

Penny savors the splendor of the man above her. *God, he's gorgeous.* Then she panics. *Did I just say that out loud instead of thinking
it? Damn this gas. Damn this gas.*

Nervously, she begins scanning Bradley and Miss Paulette's ex-
pressions. They seem unaware of her true feelings toward the dentist.
Relieved she hasn't committed a serious faux pas, Penny chides herself. *Get it together. You need to focus. Remember July fourth, 1989?
Who cares how he looks now? Don't look at him. Don't look at him.*

Determined, Penny closes her eyes so she can no longer see him
through her nitrous oxide glasses. To occupy her time in the chair,
she begins making mundane to-do lists, including all the rooms she
must pack and the items she wants to save before her aunts can swipe
any and all valuables they can lay their hands on. But thinking of her
greedy kin only causes her heart to race with anxiety. What she needs

to do is simply clear her mind of all thoughts and worries. *How hard can this be? Just relax,* she reminds herself. *Think of nothing. Especially anything having to do with Bradley Michael Hitchens. Wait, am I using his full name? What's next? Rattling off his birthday, favorite color, and old phone number? Octoberthirteen, blue, and 622-4848. Favorite food? Pepperoni-and-mushroom pizza. Thin crust, extra cheese. First pet? Rudy, a blind cocker spaniel. Worst trait? Biting his fingernails.*

Before she can stop herself, the floodgates of her first love burst wide open, knocking away the icy wall she built around her heart twenty years ago. The man above her, repairing her broken tooth, was at one time the most important person in the world to her. Now he's overtaking her again. This time, instead of fighting back her memories of Bradley, she closes her eyes and allows herself to go back to a moment in time that changed her life for the better. That day, he brought her in from the cold, literally and figuratively. That day, she fell in love with him.

January 1985
Camden, Kentucky

Chapter 10

Cruel Summer

Stop. Rewind. Play.

The lyrics of "Cruel Summer" echoed in Penny's ears as she watched the January rain pelt the windshield of her mother's Chevy Nova, waiting for her to finish her new job and praying no one noticed she was sitting in Bradley Hitchens's driveway. The rain was in steady rhythm with the song, unlike her racing heart. Though Penny begged her mother to let her stay home or spend the afternoon at Ruby Ray's instead, Zelda refused.

"You got that slumber party tonight, and it's right next door. I'm not going to waste the gas money driving you back and forth into town," Zelda said, lighting a cigarette before pulling out of their worn grass driveway.

Stop. Rewind. Play.

The song had become Penny's coping mechanism. Every waking moment, she listened to it, over and over again, on the Sony Walkman that Ruby Ray and Pops had given her for Christmas the month before. She was obsessed with its lyrics, as if the song were written especially for her and the tumultuous summer she had experienced only months before.

Stop. Rewind. Play.

The summer of 1984 had, indeed, been a cruel summer for Penny Ray. Her brother, Jack, finally succumbed to his disease. Cystic fibrosis was always going to have the final say in his life. No matter how valiantly he fought, he was never going to win that war. His disease had not only stolen his childhood, forcing him to grow up too soon and deal with the existential question of life and death as a child, but it had taken away his adulthood as well.

Stop. Rewind. Play.

Janet tried to pick up the slack, helping her little sister cope with their loss. But she was neither warm nor fuzzy. Her focus was on leaving Camden that July for summer classes at Eastern Kentucky University in Richmond. Rather than help a devastated twelve-year-old grapple with the void Jack's death had left, she bolted. Compassion was not in her wheelhouse. Janet's coping mechanism for dealing with the hell her parents had put their family through was detachment from all emotions and people. She was aloof, distant, and downright cold to everyone she encountered.

Stop. Rewind. Play.

Julie, on the other hand, escaped Camden three days after she and Janet graduated high school that May. In the middle of the night, she snuck away to Gatlinburg to elope. John Foster, a gentleman twenty-five years her senior, with whom the family never had the pleasure of a formal introduction until after the deed was done, became her husband. Before the ink was dry on the marriage certificate, he whisked her away to Louisville along with his fifteen-year-old daughter. Julie never looked back or said goodbye. Her coping mechanism for the Ray family dysfunction had been to find a father figure—in her case, an older man with rumored money. Not every little girl was lucky enough to have a father they could love.

Stop. Rewind. Play.

The summer of 1984, Penny lost all three of her siblings in one season. One to death, one to college, and one to marriage, which Penny viewed as a death sentence just the same. Holy matrimony wasn't that much different from dying. Zelda had taught her that lesson.

Stop. Rewind. Play.

For months, Penny had been living a middle school nightmare she couldn't wake from. The rumor mill had gone into overdrive because of her mother. Zelda hadn't just left Earl the Squirrel, her third and most unattractive husband that summer, but she'd done so in spectacular fashion, leaving him for a respected Baptist minister the week after Jack's funeral. The scandal was too egregious for Zelda to walk away scot-free. The good *Christian* ladies at First Camden Baptist Church made sure to fulfill the wrath of God, just in case Zelda's sins had slipped through the cracks and gone unnoticed by the Heavenly Father. It became their mission to teach her a lesson, and they went after her job at the town's library, where she'd worked for two years. Scrambling, Zelda was on the hunt for a new job.

Naturally, the whole school was buzzing with stories about Zelda. They had a Jezebel in their midst. Not only did she have to pay for her sins, but so did her daughter. One life destroyed wasn't enough for the revenge-thirsty townspeople. The next generation needed to do their part as well.

The spring before, at the end of her seventh-grade year, Penny's best friend, Kelly, encouraged her to try out for the school's cheerleading squad. Penny had grown or rather willed herself, into an athlete. Not only was she coordinated, but she also had the ability to spell and clap at the same time, which eluded much of the current squad. Not to mention she was the only girl in school who could manage a roundoff back handspring, a little trick she'd taught herself. She couldn't take trips to the gymnastics studio in Bowling Green to learn such things.

Much to her surprise and Kelly's delight, Penny made the team. However, she wasn't a welcomed addition to the group. Her tumbling prowess alone made her a target of the other girls. They hated

Penny. Every day, they chastised her for being a show-off because she'd mastered a standing back tuck and they had not. She managed a toe touch and both a front and side Herkie. They could not. Her tryout routine was all anyone at school talked about. Theirs were not. But the real nail in Penny's coffin was that she'd taken Tracy Fisher's spot on the squad. Though Tracy couldn't walk and chew gum at the same time, let alone find the beat to a song if it hit her on the head, she was one of *them*, a hapless disciple of the queen bee, Emily Johnston. Nothing was more dangerous in the life of a middle school girl than a cheerleader who possessed undying loyalty from a mindless group of other girls whose only goal in life was not to become the object of the queen bee's disdain. As long as the prepubescent sycophants could avoid Emily's wrath, they followed her scurrilous lead and went along with her contemptible tactics and bullying. Self-preservation was more important to Emily's followers than self-respect.

The girls' bathroom became Penny's personal hell. Some of the most vicious verbal attacks took place within its cold cement confines, away from the watchful eyes of teachers. Tuesday's barrage of insults was just another day in the life of being an outcast.

Stop. Rewind. Play.

"Mrs. Whitlow is, like, a total bitch," Emily moaned, stomping into the restroom. "She's making me invite *everyone* to the cheer sleepover at my house this weekend."

"What? She can't do that," Marcy Simons said. "It's not her call. It's your house. You should be able to invite whoever you want." She spoke with such fake outrage that one would think Mrs. Whitlow had invited Charles Manson over for milk and cookies and bedtime stories.

"She said it's a squad tradition. Every cheerleader has to be included. Whether they're wanted or not. Which *they* are not," Emily said, glaring at Penny.

Penny was in the corner of the bathroom, trying to get dressed at lightning speed so that she could exit with as little damage as possible inflicted upon her self-confidence.

"Even though it's at my house, I can't make any cuts. I mean, she's telling me what to do. She's, like, a total bitch!"

"That's unfair, Emily. You're right. She's, like, a total bitch. Like, totally," Shannon Madison said, trying to support her *friend* by repeating Emily's words like a parrot. She didn't have a mind of her own.

"I told her I shouldn't be expected to let *certain* unchristian people in my house so they can corrupt me and my friends. Some people around here have no morals and don't know right from wrong. Y'all know how much my church family has been hurt. What we went through this summer. The actions of *some* people in this town have ruined our congregation with their lack of respect in my Lord and *my* Savior, Jesus Christ. It hurts my heart," Emily said, dramatically touching the golden cross hanging around her neck. "Like my mother always says, the apple doesn't fall far from the tree."

All the girls nodded, but they didn't dare interrupt their omnipotent leader. Their victim was being set up for more than another innuendo about her mother's reputation.

"But the worst part, which I told Mrs. Whitlow, is that it's one thing to bring a home-wrecker's daughter into my house, because Jesus wants us to love all sinners no matter how terrible they are. But when that same person brings *lice* into my house, into *my* bedroom, and infects the whole squad, I have a right to uninvite them," Emily cried out, pointing at Penny. "We all know how she infected us at our last sleepover with those things. It was awful. My mother is still beside herself, thinking about having to disinfect everything. I mean, she literally has bugs crawling around in her hair. It's so gross."

The other cheerleaders turned their glares toward the source of the great lice epidemic of 1984, Penny Ray.

As she saw the judgment pouring from their eyes, Penny's head tingled, but she didn't flinch or dare make a move to scratch it, fearing it would give Emily more ammunition.

"You see, as captain of this squad, I have to protect my girls—their souls and their hair—from someone as filthy and unchristian as you," Emily said, slowly walking toward her, like an animal toying with its prey right before the kill. "And don't get me started on that mother of yours. The whole school knows the only reason you're even on this squad is because she gave Mr. Petty a blow job after school. Tracy is like a thousand times better than you. And she's a real Christian. So is her mother."

That Penny's mother was a loose woman was no secret, but she'd never serviced the principal in order to get her daughter on the cheer squad. Penny had earned the spot on her own, receiving the most votes, almost twice as many as Emily. The student body chose her by a landslide, and her tormentor hated her even more because of it.

"Some people need to learn where they belong in this world and where they don't, and you don't belong on this cheer squad," Emily said. "Do us all a favor and just quit like you should have done months ago."

"Girls! Hurry up and get dressed. Be in the gym in five minutes," Mrs. Whitlow said, opening the door. "Let's go!"

All the other cheerleaders fell into line, grabbing their backpacks and pom-poms, with the exceptions of Penny and Emily. They remained in a stalemate, staring at each other.

"Quit this team. I mean it," Emily said.

"I'm not a quitter," Penny replied, trying to fake confidence.

"Hmm, we'll see about that. I'm just getting started." She narrowed her eyes. "You have no idea what I've got in store for you this weekend. Trust me. If I were you, I wouldn't step foot in Beacon Hills again. Stay on your side of town. You know, where all the houses have wheels." Emily gave Penny a sadistic smirk before she turned to leave.

Penny drew a deep breath before snapping back, "Careful, Emily. One day, I might just end up living in that precious little neighborhood of yours. You know what they say. Where there's a will, there's a way." A bolt of electricity surged through her body for having the nerve to stand up to her teenaged nemesis.

Emily harumphed. "Like that would ever happen. You living in Beacon Hills? *Unless...*" She brushed her finger across her lips. "You're as good as your mother is at seducing the poor men around Camden. I see how Dusty Ward looks at you in math class. How he follows you around like a lost puppy. You know, I heard he wouldn't leave you alone on Jenny Britt's hayride last fall. I wonder why. Was it because you let him go to second base on that wagon? Or did you let him go *all* the way?"

"That's not true, and you know it," Penny said through clenched teeth.

"Of course it's not true. No boy, including Dusty, has ever touched you. But that's what makes it so much fun." She rubbed her hands together. "Truth is boring. Lies can destroy. Remember, Penny, I always get what I want," Emily purred before walking away.

There was a pep in Emily's step and a bounce in her annoying, blindingly blond ponytail, compliments of heavy use of Sun-In the previous summer. If she weren't so malicious, Penny would have thought Emily the most beautiful girl in all of Camden and maybe in all of Kentucky.

"God has been kind on her face," as Ruby Ray would say. "But he's been hell on her heart."

Once her tormentor left, Penny exhaled heavily. Though she should've been used to the everyday abuse, each incident left her shaken, with adrenaline pulsing through her body. Between Emily, Charlie, and Zelda, she was in a constant state of fight-or-flight. Only thirteen years old, she felt much older. Stress was a thief, chipping away at her youth.

"Penny?" someone whispered from the back stall.

She spun around, looking for the source. "Hello? Who's there?"

"It's me. Suzy." She came out of the stall, pulling her UCA cheer shirt over her thick hips. Puberty was in full battle within Suzy Patterson's body, and Penny envied her for it along with her perfectly permed hair styled with mounds of Aqua Net. It was far and away the best in school, even if it was highly flammable.

Suzy was no friend of hers. She was one of Emily's followers, more than willing to get dirty for her dear leader. Her hands were not clean.

"I had to change in the stall because I'm on my period. Emily likes to make fun of me because my stomach gets really bloated when it's my time of the month. She thinks it's so funny, telling everybody I'm probably pregnant and that's why I'm so fat. Typical Emily. Jealous of something she doesn't have. You know she hasn't gotten *hers* yet," she said with a wicked smile.

Reluctantly, Penny smiled back, knowing she couldn't trust Suzy as far as she could throw her. Plus, she was uncomfortable being in the same menstruation boat with Emily. Mother Nature had decided to skip right past her too.

"Plus, she's super pissed because she and Bradley Hitchens broke up," Suzy said.

Penny's eyes widened. "What? She and Bradley broke up? They've been a thing since—"

"Fifth grade. I know. It's crazy. The perfect couple going down in flames. I heard he passed her a note in social studies that it was over."

Penny bit her lip. "I bet she's really upset."

Suzy crossed her arms. "Don't tell me you feel sorry for her."

"Not exactly."

"As bad as she is to me about my period, it's nothing compared to what she's put you through this year. We all see it. Making fun of your clothes constantly is one thing. I mean, I agree with her. They're kind of tacky, and the jokes about your mom are fair game. I don't have to tell you that she's a train wreck, but lately, Emily is taking it a little too far."

"How?" Penny asked. The other reasons alone should be enough.

"She told us not to catch you during the basket toss last week."

Penny gasped. "You mean that wasn't an accident? I'm still covered in bruises from that fall, and I had to have an X-ray on my wrist."

"Yeah. I know. Sorry about that. At least you didn't break your arm."

"No thanks to you," Penny mumbled.

"The whole lice thing is getting on my nerves. I'm sick and tired of hearing about it. Emily brings it up like a thousand times a day."

"Tell me about it," Penny said before mustering up the strength to defend herself. "I know you probably won't believe me, but I've never had lice."

"Oh, I know," Suzy said.

"You do? How?"

"Because it came from Emily."

"Emily?"

"Yep. She had them first then gave them to the rest of us. I saw them crawling all over her head before you even got to her house," Suzy said.

Penny's jaw dropped with amazement that another cheerleader would be so forthright.

"Didn't you think it was weird that she invited you to the Christmas party in the first place? It wasn't even a mandatory sleepover. Not like this one. It was a setup. I know it. Actually, everyone does. Emily was out for blood when you beat her in tryouts, and she used it to hurt you. Even her mom knew she was the one who had it first because my mom saw her buying lice shampoo at O'Donnell's the day before."

"Why are you telling me this?" Penny asked, still not trusting her fellow cheerleader.

"Don't quit the squad. I know we haven't been very nice to you, and I swear I feel really bad about dropping you like that, but you're a good cheerleader. Like the best one the school's ever had and way better than Emily."

"Thanks for telling me," Penny said softly.

"You're welcome." Suzy smiled before remembering her old self. "Oh, and if you ever tell anyone about the lice, the basket toss, or how Emily can't get her period, I'll make your life miserable. This stays between us. Got it?"

Suzy's words, though somewhat threatening, were still good to hear. Another person in the world or at least at Liberty County Middle School understood she was innocent of Licegate. The only story anyone had been privy to was Emily's version, and it had been gossiped about for months on end.

Stop. Rewind. Play.

Penny's fingers throbbed. The mixture of Kentucky's biting winter rain, reliving yet another round of Emily's bullying, and the impending slumber party had taken a toll on her body. The last time she'd stayed at Emily's house, she was accused of starting a lice outbreak. God only knew what was in store for her tonight—or the plagues she would be blamed for spreading. Scabies, mumps, measles, chicken pox... Emily was probably going through an encyclopedia, looking for diseases. Even "Cruel Summer" couldn't alleviate the pain.

Penny rubbed her shriveled yellow hands together, but instead of helping, it only made them hurt worse. Since Zelda allowed her one minute of heat every half hour while she cleaned, Penny decided to start the car for some much-needed relief.

As she reached for the keys, a tap on the window stopped her. When she looked up, she found Bradley Hitchens smiling down, shivering, his hands shoved into his crisp Levi jeans pockets.

Realizing she could no longer hide, she sighed, rolling down her window.

"Hey," he said. Every girl at Liberty County Middle School dreamed of that word being directed toward them.

"Hey," she replied. A thirteen-year-old girl whose breasts were still in the bud stage was talking to the most popular boy in the entire school. "Hey" was all she could muster.

"What are you doing out here?" Bradley asked. "It's freezing."

"Oh. I'm just waiting for my mom to finish," she said, trying to mask her embarrassment. Zelda was his housekeeper.

"Mrs. Mitchell is doing a great job. I love my mom, but she's not the best around the house. Last week, she turned my basketball shorts pink," he said with a smile.

"Thank you," she replied, noting he called her mother Mrs. Mitchell out of respect rather than Zelda—or worse, maid. "Your parents were so nice to give her a job."

"Why don't you come inside? Hang out with me while your mom finishes?"

"Oh, I don't want to bother you or your parents."

"You wouldn't be bothering me. You'd be doing me a favor by keeping me company. It's too cold and rainy to shoot baskets, and my little sister is really annoying. All she wants to do is play Candyland for the millionth time. Besides, I can't leave a friend out here in the cold."

The word *friend* caused Penny's stomach to flutter. She needed a friend in the worst way, that day of all days. Bradley Hitchens would be a good place to start. "I'm not sure my mom wants me inside while she's working. I'd be in the way," Penny said.

"Mrs. Mitchell just finished the basement, so we can hang out there. She still has the kitchen and the upstairs to do, so she'll be here for a while. Plus, I already asked her permission."

"But what about your mom—"

"I already asked. She couldn't believe you were outside," he explained.

"Only if you're sure."

"Sure I'm sure. Let's go. I'm dying out here," he said, jumping up and down to warm up.

"Thank you," she whispered, rolling up the heavy window, then stepped out of the car.

"Hey, is that the new Walkman?" he asked, motioning to her hand as they walked up the driveway.

"It's not the new one, but it's new to me. I got it for Christmas."

"That's awesome. I wanted one too," he said. "So, what are you listening to?"

"Oh, it's nothing. Something stupid," Penny lied. It had been her musical lifesaver since December. She'd listened to it so much that the tape was wearing thin and could break at any moment.

"Come on, tell me. I'd like to know what you're into. Musically, I mean," he said.

"It's a tape I made of a song I kind of like. It's 'Cruel Summer' by Bananarama. I recorded it off the radio. You know, from the top-forty countdown, so the quality isn't very good. I know it's cheesy, but I like it," Penny said as Bradley opened the door to his house.

"I love that song. It was in a movie I saw this summer called *The Karate Kid.*" He smiled.

As they walked into the Hitchenses' Beacon Hills home, Penny was struck not only by its size, but also its tasteful interior. Ruby Ray's home had nice, pretty furniture and antiques scattered around, but Alexandria Hitchens's taste was exquisite. She didn't have curtains, homemade ones or bought from a Sears catalogue. She had custom draperies that matched the pillows on the plush couches in the formal living room. The kitchen was the size of Penny's trailer. An entire wall of exposed brick surrounded the large oven. It even had a built-in microwave. It was the most beautiful kitchen she'd ever seen, and she thought how wonderful it would be to sit down at the Hitchenses' glass table and have dinner with parents who were both physically and emotionally present asking about her school day while feasting on a homemade meatloaf.

Then Bradley led her downstairs to the large basement and into the family's game room. Penny had never been in one before and was dumbfounded that there were people in the world, much less in Camden, who had so much money and space in their homes that they devoted an entire room to just games. She'd never played one with her own parents, not even checkers. The room was huge and, of course, tastefully decorated, with a large black leather sofa in the middle with two matching recliners on each side facing a projector TV, like the one she'd admired the summer before on *Wheel of Fortune*. In the open space behind the couch sat a pool table covered in red felt with a colorful Tiffany lamp hanging above. Finally, there was a large wooden poker table in the corner of the room next to a pinball machine.

"Have a seat. Want to play some Atari?" he asked, being the consummate host.

"Sure," she said, walking over to the couch to sit.

"Here, let me get that." He moved a copy of *To Kill a Mockingbird*, the book they were studying in English class. "I was trying to read it this morning, but I fell asleep. Have you started it yet?"

"I'm finished," she replied.

"You finished it already? Mrs. Bates just assigned it to us yesterday."

"I finished it two years ago." Penny's voice was small.

"Really? You read it in sixth grade? Why?"

"I love to read, and my mom works—I mean, she used to work at the library. I had access to any book I wanted. I didn't even need a card."

"How many did you read last year?"

Penny paused, mentally counting. "Maybe fifty. Fifty-five?"

"Wow. I can't even get through this one, let alone double digits. I don't know anybody our age who actually likes to read. I only do it because I have no choice. I'm more of a math guy. That's my best subject."

Penny crinkled her nose. "Not me. It's my worst. I hate math."

"And I hate to read. Maybe we can help each other out sometime. Like study together," he said. "Deal?"

"Deal."

"Hey, I meant to tell you the other day in class, you're a great cheerleader."

"Excuse me?"

"I was watching you at our last game, and I can't believe you can do all those flips. You make it look so easy."

"How are you watching me when you're playing in the game? Aren't you supposed to pay attention to the ball instead of the cheerleaders on the sidelines?"

"Well, sometimes I sneak a peek here and there. It's hard *not* to watch you. You're like Mary Lou Retton or something."

"Thank you," Penny said, her cheeks flushed with embarrassment. "But what I've discovered in my one and only year of cheerleading is we're really kind of useless. It's so annoying, chanting the same things over and over again. Do you know how stupid it is to say, 'Be... aggressive. Be, be... aggressive. B-E-A-G-G-R-E-S-S-I-V-E. Be... aggressive'? It's awful. What does that even mean?"

"I think it's important. I like having cheerleaders supporting us." Bradley paused. "Well, maybe not all the cheerleaders. I'm not a big fan of Emily Johnston."

"I thought you guys were pretty tight," Penny said. "Don't you go on family vacations together to Hilton Head every year?" They were all Emily talked about, how she *and* Bradley spent every summer since birth frolicking around in the waves of the Atlantic Ocean. Penny had never been on a vacation, let alone seen an ocean. The way Emily bragged about Hilton Head, South Carolina, made it seem like the most exotic place on earth.

He ran a hand through his hair. "You know we broke up."

"Oh. Wow. I'm sorry to hear that," Penny said, avoiding his gaze.

"Our parents have been friends forever. We live in the same neighborhood. We even go to the same church. I guess that's why she was my girlfriend for so long. It was easy. You know?"

She nodded but had no idea why anyone would ever spend time with Emily Johnston by choice, let alone date her for three years.

"But lately, I've started seeing some things. Like, she really started to change. We used to have a lot of things in common. We'd ride bikes all day or shoot hoops until the sun went down. But now all she cares about is clothes, popularity... and cheerleading."

"She's definitely passionate about that," Penny agreed.

"I don't even know who she is anymore. She's completely different now."

"I get it. It's like she's done a three-sixty?"

Bradley let out a laugh. "You mean a one-eighty?"

Penny winced. "Yeah. Right."

"You weren't kidding about being bad at math."

Her face flushed.

"But that's not why I broke up with her."

"Then why?" She held her breath.

"I started seeing who she really is. How she treats people at school. Especially how she treats you, and it's not cool. I just found out about the whole lice thing. How she was the one who started the rumor that you gave it to all the cheerleaders. I didn't know it came from her."

"The rumor or the lice?" Penny asked.

"Both," he said. "She promised over Christmas break that she wasn't the one who started it. She swore it was Shannon Madison, but I found out this week it was all a lie. I'm sorry she hurt you, Penny. I swear I didn't know. But trust me. I get it now. She didn't just lie. She gave me lice. My sister too."

"If it makes you feel better, they like clean hair."

Bradley laughed. "I guess you read that in some book."

"If you were accused of spreading hair bugs to the popular kids at school, you'd crack one open too and find out what you're up against."

A long silence followed before Penny changed the subject. "It doesn't matter now. Lice, cheerleading, or Emily. I'm just going to get through the season then hang up my pom-poms for good. Coach McDonald saw me running last week and asked me to be on the track team this spring for the high school, then cross-country in the fall. Running's my favorite thing to do, even more than reading."

"That's awesome. Running for the high school is a big deal. And you know the best part about it?"

"What?" she asked.

"No more Emily Johnston. You'll be free of her, at least for a little while, because she can't run across the street without having to stop and catch her breath." Bradley giggled.

For the next two hours, they sat around, playing cards, Atari, and a quick game of Trivial Pursuit. Alexandria, Bradley's affable mother, dropped by a couple of times throughout the afternoon with cookies and hot chocolate, making sure Penny felt at home. How cruel people in Camden could be in regard to Zelda and her daughter was no secret.

The Hitchens home was spotless once Zelda was done. All the laundry was meticulously folded and put away in their respective drawers. Though she hated to admit it, Penny was impressed with her mother's diligence in her new *career*.

"Thank you for having me, Mrs. Hitchens. Your home is really pretty," Penny said.

"All thanks to your mother. She's been a godsend. You're always welcome here," Bradley's mother replied. She leaned in and gave Penny a hug, squeezing extra hard before quietly retreating to the kitchen, leaving the two alone.

"Hey, if you're not doing anything next Saturday, why don't you come back with your mom? We could hang out again," Bradley said, peering down at his feet. "Plus, I want a rematch in Donkey Kong. And Frogger. And Trivial Pursuit, since you beat me in everything we played."

"I'd like that," Penny said. A grin spread across her face.

"Great!" he said. "See you next week?"

"See you next week."

And so began their Saturday ritual—that was, until Zelda found another husband and was no longer desperate enough to clean houses. But those Saturdays became Penny's saving grace and were where her love for Bradley blossomed.

July 2009
Camden, Kentucky

Chapter 11

Time to Pay the Fiddler

"Here are the follow-up instructions," Miss Paulette says, handing Penny the papers as she recovers in the dental chair. "If you have any problems with your temporary crown, call us immediately. Are you feeling all right?"

Penny nods because she is indeed feeling like her old self. Sadly, the nitrous oxide haze has now left her body and her mind.

"We've been pumping you with oxygen for a while now, so you should be good to go. Here are your car keys. Sweet Lonnie brought them by. He's such a good boy, even if he can't pop kettle corn worth a darn." Miss Paulette hands the keys over to Penny. "Honey, it was so good to see you again. Don't be a stranger, you hear? Camden is still your home. Always has been and always will be."

"Thank you," Penny replies, smiling at her proclamation. "Can you tell me how much I owe? I don't have dental insurance, so can I pay now?"

"Dr. Hitchens is in his office. You can settle up with him. It's down the hall." Miss Paulette points with a knowing smile.

As Penny makes her way out of the chair, her legs are heavy and stiff. She glances at her cell phone and shakes her head—the device is all but useless thanks to AT&T's lack of coverage in this part of Kentucky. It's almost four, so she's lost an entire afternoon of packing and a phone call from the boys, all because she lacks the willpower to resist kettle corn.

Making her way down the empty hallway toward Bradley's office, Penny begins to feel an overwhelming sense of guilt for how she treated him at Farley's. That she was a complete bitch is putting it mildly. All Bradley wanted was to help. Perhaps her stroll down memory lane, with the help of dental gas, has softened her a bit. An apology is in order. Now she'll have to eat crow.

Bradley's office door is open. As Penny's about to knock and announce herself, she stops, seeing he's on the phone.

"I understand this is a once-in-a-lifetime opportunity, Ace. However, bungee jumping off a bridge in the middle of the Swiss Alps isn't what I had in mind when you asked to study abroad this summer," Bradley says, pinching the top of his nose in exasperation.

Penny snickers at the absurdity of youth while also envying it at the same time.

"Why don't you think about this a little longer. For your old man's sake. Okay?" he asks, discovering Penny at the door. Nodding and smiling, he listens to one more round of pleas from his daughter a world away while motioning Penny into his office. "I love you too. Let's talk about this some more tomorrow. Get some sleep." A smile crosses his face.

"I'm sorry. I didn't mean to interrupt," Penny says, embarrassed she's been caught inadvertently eavesdropping.

"You're not interrupting. Come on in." Bradley stands up from his desk and welcomes her into his private, wood-paneled confines.

Conjuring up the best forced smile she can, Penny walks in. Immediately, she notices the room is covered in University of Kentucky memorabilia, full of pendants, blue-and-white shakers, and both his undergraduate and dentistry degrees. The Wildcat alum's so dedicated to his alma mater that he proudly displays, on the credenza behind his desk, a picture of his thirteen-year-old self standing next to Rex Chapman. Penny remembers how big a deal it was around school when Bradley met him.

Next to the king of UK basketball are dozens of pictures of his daughters at various stages of their lives, including baby and toddler snapshots galore. Every year of elementary and middle school is documented along with candid photos of various sports. On the wall next to the window are three framed photos side-by-side. The first is a black-and-white clipping from the local newspaper. A precocious girl with an infectious smile, his youngest daughter, Penny presumes, is in full camouflage, holding the rack of a six-point deer she snagged. Every November, *The Camden Times* devotes three pages a week to the deer hunters around Liberty County so that they can show off their yearly kills to the townsfolk. For the boys and girls around Camden, it's a rite of passage to bring down a buck or sometimes a doe then get a shoutout in the paper. Next to the animal carcass is a photo of Bradley and the girls standing on a beach at the edge of the water, their hands intertwined while their arms swing in the air. The golden beams from a late-afternoon sun transform their hair into a rich auburn. The oldest girl is kicking her feet up, splashing salt water toward the camera, while the little one tries to dig her toes into the firm almond sand. It must be Hilton Head, Bradley's favorite beach. The final picture of the three bothers her more than seeing a dead Bambi with blood seeping from its nose. It's of a vibrant teenage girl dressed in a red, white, and blue uniform, striking a pose with pom-poms in the shape of a V over her head.

"A cheerleader?" Penny asks, her right eyebrow arching.

"I know. I know." He winces. "I swore I'd never allow one of my daughters to become one, but she had her heart set on it."

"Well, I see you've raised a psychopath. And the other one likes to kill innocent animals," she says, trying to keep things light.

Nodding in agreement, Bradley chuckles. "Great dad, huh?"

Penny smiles. "In all seriousness, your girls are stunning. Absolutely beautiful." *Just like their mother,* Penny suddenly thinks. Then it hits her. There could be a photograph of her somewhere in this office, such as one of her splashing around in the ocean or building a sandcastle on the beach. Perhaps she got one of those Glamour Shots everyone around Camden was obsessed with back in the early '90s, with lots of makeup and soft lighting. Or worse, maybe he has one of her on their wedding day, when she became Mrs. Bradley Michael Hitchens. That day broke Penny's heart.

Penny scans the room for a photographic reminder, but there are none, giving her a temporary respite.

"Thank you," Bradley says, interrupting Penny's thoughts of his late wife. "They're my world. Even if Ace wants to push my buttons every now and then."

Penny clears her throat, trying to stay on subject. "Sounds like she's having a wonderful time. What an incredible experience." But Penny's mind is still on *her*.

"I'm afraid Ace is more focused on her extracurricular activities in Europe than her studies." He sighs. "The European experience I wanted her to have was more in line with visiting the Louvre and gazing up at the ceiling of the Sistine Chapel. Bungee jumping off a cliff wasn't what I envisioned." He shakes his head. "I can't believe she's even contemplating something so cavalier."

"I thought it was a bridge. Sounds much safer than a cliff," Penny teases, regaining some composure.

"I'm sorry. You're correct. A bridge," he says. "Did Miss Paulette go over the instructions for your follow-up care?"

"Yes, she did. She was quite thorough and professional."

"Good. How are you feeling? No aftereffects from the gas?"

"I feel fine," Penny says. "Except for a massive case of embarrassment."

"Farley's kettle corn has taken down many folk around here. Don't beat yourself up over it." Bradley grins, his dimple peeking through once again.

"Sorry if I was short with you back at Farley's. I was taken aback by the pain then seeing... you."

"No apologies necessary."

"I asked Miss Paulette how much I owe you, and she told me to speak with you. Do you take credit cards, or do you prefer a check?"

"Neither."

"Oh. Well, like I told her, I don't have dental insurance. I never got around to it after the divorce, so this little catastrophe will be out of pocket. There's no reason to bill me and waste the postage. I'll clean it up today."

"Your money's no good here, Penny," he says.

"Excuse me?"

"It's on the house."

"What? No, I couldn't possibly. I have to pay you." It's one thing for Lonnie Davis to throw in a bottle of knock-off Advil on the house, but a thousand-dollar dental procedure is quite another.

"I don't want your money," Bradley says. "I was happy to help you out in your frazzled state."

"I think frazzled is a bit of a stretch," she retorts.

"However, I would like *something* in exchange for my services." A coy smile spreads across his face.

A flush of heat pierces her cheeks. *Is he flirting with me, or am I imagining it?* It's been so long since a man has shown interest in Penny that she can't remember what it feels like.

"I'm a country doctor, you see. Sometimes my patients like to trade things. You know, barter in exchange for my services."

"You've lost me. If you don't want me to pay, then what do you want?"

"Dinner," he says.

"You've got to be kidding me," Penny whispers.

"Dinner. At my place. I'll throw a couple of steaks on the grill and maybe add a bowl of soup for you. We can sit on my back deck and catch up. It's been twenty years since we last spoke, and well, here you are. Back in Camden less than an hour with a dental emergency."

"So that's your price? Dinner?"

"That's my price."

"Bradley, I'm afraid I wouldn't make very good company tonight," she begins, ready to throw out a litany of excuses. "I've been up since five. Four, your time. I drove six hours alone, and my mouth is still numb. I don't think I could even eat if I wanted to. Thank you for your kind invitation—or your blackmail, not sure which—but I can't tonight."

"What about tomorrow?" he quickly counters. "I guarantee your mouth will no longer be numb."

She shakes her head. "I don't think it's a good idea."

"I missed my tee time for you. I made Miss Paulette cancel on my group at the last minute, leaving them without a fourth. Did I mention it was my qualifying round for the club championship? I was heading there before Lonnie found me at Farley's. So you kind of owe it to me for not only being your dental knight in shining armor but also for hurting my golf game and crushing my dreams of a three-peat."

"Now you're throwing in a side of guilt to complement your blackmail?"

"I prefer the term barter. Blackmail is such an ugly word. We're simply negotiating a business arrangement. My services don't come cheap. I'm the second most popular dentist in town. I'm in high demand," he jokes.

"You're not going to take no for an answer, are you?"

"Nope."

"Well, it seems I have no choice in the matter. I can't exactly return my tooth for a refund, since I'm kind of attached to it. So yes, I'll have dinner with you tomorrow night. But it has to be early."

"How about I pick you up at Ruby Ray's? Let's say five. Would that work?"

"Now you're asking me instead of resorting to blackmail?"

"Again, that's an ugly word," he says. "This is a business arrangement. Pure and simple."

"Okay," she says reluctantly. Then she walks out of Bradley's UK-clad office with him behind her and smack dab into Miss Paulette's hefty chest.

Scrambling, Miss Paulette pretends she wasn't listening to their conversation. "C-Call us if you need anything, Penny," she stutters. "With your crown and all." She scurries into the exam room.

"I will," Penny calls, giving the nosy woman the side-eye, while Bradley ignores her antics altogether.

Opening the front door, Bradley says, "Tomorrow, it is. See you at five."

"Fine," Penny says, stepping onto the sidewalk and trying to project an air of annoyance. But deep down, there's a hint of excitement too.

Once she's made it safely to her SUV, she notices Lonnie has placed her bags neatly in the backseat, and an oversize bag of kettle corn sits in the passenger seat with a note attached:

This one's on the house. Sorry about your tooth.

Don't be a stranger.

Lonnie Davis – Farley's assistant manager

Though Lonnie's note and kind gesture of the sweet-yet-deadly treat is nice, Penny makes a vow never to touch the stuff again. Kettle corn caused more than just a broken tooth today. It brought her first love back into her life, and now he's all she can think about, especially the person he used to be. All these years since she left Camden, she's tried to banish him from her mind, the same way she did with Charlie and Zelda. But being home and spending the afternoon with him is causing her to remember the boy she fell in love with, not the teenager who shattered her heart. That's more painful than an oblique subgingival crack in a tooth.

As Penny starts the engine, her first instinct is to drive toward the interstate and back to Atlanta. However, that will only complicate matters. Instead of retreating, she drives the short distance back to Ruby Ray's. Approaching the driveway, she spots a familiar figure rocking in Pops's chair. Now, she's truly home.

"I was just about to send the dogs out for you. Where have you been all afternoon, young lady?" Jimmy Neal, her favorite cousin, asks with his burly arms spread wide, waiting for a hug. "You wouldn't believe me if I told you," she says, walking into his embrace.

"Try me. I've been waiting out here for thirty minutes."

"Why are you sitting on the front porch in this heat?" she asks. "You have a key, remember?"

"I was trying to respect your space, since this is your home, and you're back in town now. So, I ask again. Where have you been all day?"

Opening the front door and heading toward the kitchen, she says, "Flat on my back with Bradley Hitchens. That's where."

"*What?*" he screeches in disbelief, right on her heels. "You've got to be joking."

"No joke. All afternoon, and I'm exhausted." She opens the Frigidaire to look for one of the Dr. Peppers her cousin has supplied her.

"I'm guessing this has something to do with your dental health and not the alternative."

"Ha. Ha."

"Sorry. Go on."

"Apparently, sweet Lonnie Davis from high school hasn't mastered the art of popping Farley's kettle corn, and I broke a tooth on it. And just my luck, Bradley was in the store when it happened. So being the thoughtful dentist he is, the second most popular in town, he offered to fix it for me on the spot."

"You know, it's the second Saturday of the month, Penny."

"Maybe Camden should add that to the welcome sign. Warning hapless visitors of the perils of kettle corn."

"Talk about bad timing. Or good. I'm not sure which." He tries to suppress a devilish grin. "Man, that had to be awkward."

"Go ahead and laugh. I know you want to."

"I'm not laughing *at* you. I'm laughing *with* you."

"Do you hear me laughing? Do you see a smile on my face?"

"No, but you've got to admit how funny this is. Come on. It's been almost twenty years since you last spoke to him, and *today* you run into him with a dental emergency? You've spent an entire afternoon with him, and you don't think it means something?"

"Yes. It means Lonnie Davis shouldn't be popping kettle corn," Penny says then takes a long drink of her calorie-laced Dr. Pepper.

Jimmy Neal whistles. "I can't wait to tell Laura this."

"Keep laughing at your cousin's expense. Don't worry about my pain and humiliation today."

"Looks to me like you need something stronger than a Dr. Pepper right about now."

"You're right. I do. What I want is a glass of wine."

"Well, it's five o'clock somewhere. Right?"

Glancing up at Ruby Ray's kitchen wall clock, Penny sees her opening. "You're right! See? It's already five in Atlanta, so I won't be day drinking, technically, since my body is still on eastern time. Like to join me in a glass?"

Shrugging, Jimmy Neal says, "You know me. I'm up for a nice glass of whatever wine you're drinking." Although a Southern Baptist like the rest of Penny's family, Jimmy Neal doesn't adhere to the no-drinking mandate that's a foundation of the religion. "Jesus turned water into wine, after all" has been his reasoning for a celebratory drink whenever the occasion sees fit to come up.

She opens one of the cupboards and digs out two pink plastic Crystal Oats tumblers, the ones that came in the containers of her grandmother's favorite oatmeal. She fills them to the brim with Duckhorn sauvignon blanc, since there are no wine glasses in the house on Dogwood Lane.

Penny hands her cousin his wine. "I almost feel guilty about drinking in Ruby Ray's house."

"I remember her calling all fermented beverages 'the juice of the devil' a time or two."

"That, she did."

"After the day you're having, cuz, this isn't even optional. It's mandatory. Even Ruby Ray would understand."

"You're right."

"Cheers," they say, clinking their tumblers before retreating to the living room's company couch.

For the next three hours, they catch up on life. Though Penny should be packing, it's been years since she and Jimmy Neal have sat down together for a good chat. While he tells stories about the pitfalls of farming while juggling two daughters and a wife who hates living so far out in the country, she gives him updates on city life in Georgia with three boys. Then talk moves to Ruby Ray's house and Penny's plans to give the proceeds to her aunt Molly and Ruby Ray's cryptic sisters. Like Dakota, Jimmy Neal tells her she's crazy for doing so. They don't warrant a Christmas card from her, let alone a sizable check. Naturally, the blackmail by Dr. Hitchens comes up, with Jimmy Neal teasing her mercilessly for running into her old crush, while Penny tries to deny that it means anything to her.

When the grandfather clock in the corner strikes its hourly reminder, it both startles and infuriates Penny, for she's lost an entire day of packing. "Any suggestions on how I can turn that thing off?"

"A chainsaw?" he offers.

"That would certainly do the trick."

"You look exhausted," Jimmy Neal says.

"I am. It's been a long day, to say the least."

"I'm gonna head out and let you get some sleep. You've got a big day ahead of you." He giggles.

"I'm settling a score. That's all." A hiccup escapes her lips.

"Okay, Penny." He heads for the door, and Penny follows.

"Wait, not a score. That sounds wrong. Like payback. Wait, that's worse. It's not. I'm not paying him back. It's ransom. That's it—ransom. I have no choice in the matter." Clearly, she's intoxicated from two glasses of wine.

"Well, whatever you're doing with Bradley, I'm sure you'll handle it with the utmost grace." He opens the door and steps onto the porch. "However, I was talking about church service tomorrow."

"Church?"

"Willow Creek Baptist. Ten forty-five on the dot."

"Ch-Church? You're asking me to go to church?" she stammers. "Now?"

"Yes, ma'am. To repent for all the wine you drank tonight, you little heathen," he says, nudging her shoulder.

"You helped."

"I had one. You had two. Look, everyone's expecting you tomorrow. In fact, don't kill the messenger, but they've planned a special potluck after the service in your honor." He winces.

"A potluck? For me?" Penny repeats, aghast by the proposition.

"Momma's so happy to have you home again that she organized the whole thing. You have no choice. You gotta go."

"And *now* you tell me? After the day I've had? Plus, you let me down two glasses of wine." She hiccups again.

"I know you hate being the center of attention, but it's all done in the spirit of love and fellowship."

"Of course I'll be there." She sighs. "For Gracie Belle's sake. Not yours."

"Good," he says, giving her a hug of approval for bending to the congregation's will. "See you tomorrow, cuz." Jimmy Neal walks toward his pickup.

"See you tomorrow," she repeats then locks the door behind him and rests her back against the glass window. Since the wine has gone straight to her head, packing at this point is futile. Sleep is the only thing left to do.

When she collapses into the four-poster queen bed, allowing its feather mattress to encompass her, her body gives way. This bed has always provided her with security, a cool embrace where she can melt away from the chaotic world when it torments her. Tonight, she's grateful for its familiarity. Pulling the colorful Lonestar quilt, which her grandmother made for her, around her shoulders, she imagines its corners are her grandmother's loving arms keeping her safe and warm.

As she stares at the ceiling, the exhaustion from the day's events take hold of her body. Her eyelids become heavier with each blink. Instead of fighting it, she closes them. However, her mind isn't cooperating, far from ready to throw in the towel. It's in overdrive from Teddy's curt text and promised call, which never came to fruition, and having her children thousands of miles away on another continent with Jessica "One *N*" Lyn. But that's only one piece of a complicated puzzle of things gnawing at her tonight. Running into Bradley is the real kicker. Twenty years of holding back her heartache is now for naught. Kettle corn and a broken tooth have changed all that. Bradley Hitchens is back in her life. Penny hopes it's for the better. But deep down, she knows it's probably for the worse.

Chapter 12

Amazing Gracie

The grandfather clock outside Penny's bedroom door strikes five a.m. Cursing the bane of her existence, she vows to give the stupid clock to the first person she encounters at Willow Creek Baptist but only if they promise to move it out by dusk. If not, she's going to take a sledgehammer to it, for it has chimed every fifteen minutes throughout the night. Why on Earth her grandparents chose such a nuisance to be in their home is beyond her. Now she's wide awake, though she never really went to sleep. Between her new archnemesis ticking away and Bradley Hitchens swirling around her mind, she was restless throughout the night.

Now that she's awake at this ungodly hour, there's only one thing left to do—lace up her shoes and hit the road. Maybe a good run will settle her. Though it's pitch-black outside, she knows these streets like the back of her hand. She trained throughout high school on this very pavement, pushing herself toward state titles. This piece of concrete was her golden ticket out of Camden—one of the few things in Kentucky that's a welcomed homecoming for her.

Though the sun has yet to arrive, and the humidity's so thick that she can cut it with a knife, she sets out. The second her foot touches Dogwood Lane, she lets out a deep sigh. For the next sixty minutes, she will have peace, even if it's fleeting.

Running ten miles up and down the hilly town seems to do the trick. Penny makes her way back to Ruby Ray's a new woman, ready to tackle the world. A big mug of coffee is needed to start her day.

Rummaging around the kitchen, she finds her grandmother's antiquated percolator. To accompany her thick, tarry beverage, she cuts a tiny sliver of Gracie Bell's lemon blueberry cake, its decadence too tempting to pass up. Then she scrambles one of the free-range eggs from her cousin's hens for a quick breakfast. Having never made the trip to Houchens yesterday for groceries, she has no alternative.

As she finishes her second cup of coffee, the wall telephone rings. She springs up from her seat.

"Hello?"

"Mommy," Sammy says with a scratchy little voice.

"Oh, my sweet baby. I'm so happy to hear your voice. How's Africa?" she asks, grateful Teddy remembered her grandmother's phone number.

"There's no lions here," Sammy whines.

"Well, of course not, silly. You're still in a big city. Lions don't live there. You have to go out into the wild to see them," she says, laughing. Her ex is probably dealing with an angry cub for not spotting one of his pride members the second they arrived. "How was the airplane ride?"

"The plane was big. We had cookies and a TV and a—stop it, Drew. I'm talking to Mommy!" Sammy screams. Penny hears the sounds of him swatting at his brother over the phone.

"Dad said make it quick," Drew says in the background. "We don't have much time. I want to talk too."

"No! I'm talking to Mommy!"

"It's okay," Penny says, trying to broker peace between the brothers from a world away. "We can talk again another time, then you can tell me more about your big trip."

"Hey, Mom," Drew says after successfully pulling the phone away from his brother. Now she hears Sammy wailing in the background.

"Oh, sweetie. It's so good to hear your voice. Is your brother okay?"

"He's fine. Sammy's being a jerk, as usual."

"I'm not a jerk!" Sammy screams. More slapping ensues.

"Dad, get him off me!" Drew yells.

"How was the trip over? Did you like the plane?" she asks, trying to divert her middle son's attention away from her toddler's temper tantrum.

"Yeah, it was cool, but I was glad to get off. It felt like we were on it forever. I'm just tired," he explains.

"I'm sure you are. That's a big trip."

"Are you at Ruby Ray's?"

"Got here yesterday."

"Are you sad being there without her?" Drew asks. He's a kind and empathetic boy. Penny's grateful for his big heart.

"Don't worry about me, sweetie. I'm all good. We'll talk again soon."

"Sure. Here's Trey," he says, handing the phone over to his older brother.

"Hey, Mom," Trey says.

"It's so good to hear your voice. How's Africa?"

"Kind of boring. Dad says things will pick up once we get to the safari."

"I'm sure it will."

"The worst part is Sammy. We should've left him with you. He's been a turd the whole time. He keeps complaining about not seeing lions, even though Dad told him we'll see them soon. It's so annoying."

"Be patient with your little brother. I'm sure he's not adjusted to the time change. I can't imagine Sammy with jet lag."

"He's ruining the trip."

"Just give him a little more time to adjust."

"Whatever."

"I love you, sweetie."

"Love you, too, Mom. Here's Dad."

"Penny," Teddy says. The frostiness in his voice pierces through her soul. *Can you get frostbite over the phone?*

"Thank you so much for the call. I really appreciate it," she says, trying to sound grateful to melt his icy demeanor.

"We tried your cell, but it doesn't work," he tells her in a monotone voice.

"Yes, my cell phone is useless here. The only contact with the outside world I have is this archaic phone. Maybe we can establish a set time for you to call. That way, I'll make sure I'm home, and I won't miss a phone call. Obviously, at a time convenient for you, of course."

"Penny, I think that's a little overkill."

"What about this time?" she continues, ignoring his comment as she musters a small amount of authority in her voice, taking charge of the situation in order to avoid a useless fight. "It's six fifty here now. That would be what? Afternoon for you? Maybe this will be a good time to call. Would that work?"

"Fine. Remember, I'll be the one to make the phone calls." The line goes dead. No "Have a nice day" or even a goodbye.

Swallowing hard to suppress her anger at the brevity of the phone call, Penny hangs up the receiver. Within seconds, the phone rings again. "Teddy?" she asks in hopes her ex has had a change of heart and decided a two-minute phone call with her children isn't sufficient.

"You have a date with Bradley Hitchens?" the person squeals.

"What? Hello?"

"Why didn't you call and tell me? This is *huge*."

Penny closes her eyes. "Good morning, Kelly."

"Good morning? That's all I get?"

Kelly Roark was Penny's first friend and her most devoted one besides Dakota. If need be, Penny could call her up in the middle of the night, asking her to help bury a body. The only question asked in return would be "Who's bringing the shovel?" Such a bona fide friend is hard to come by, and loyalty is the one quality Penny places above all others when it comes to friendships.

"How did I not know this the second it happened?" she asks.

Penny sighs. "Because no one does. It's no big deal," she says, pretending to inspect her fingernails, which is silly, since she's on the phone. Kelly can't see her acting skills.

"No big deal? Really? You haven't spoken to him in twenty years, and *now* you have a date with him?"

"It's not a date. I broke my tooth yesterday at Farley's, and he fixed it. I tried to pay him, but he refused. Then he blackmailed me. I have no choice. Plain and simple. Wait. How do *you* know?"

"Miss Paulette, of course. She told Gina Myers, who was working the cash register at O'Donnell's yesterday, then Gina told Martha Keen over coffee at Darnell's, then Martha told Lois Shipley last night at Mr. Clovis Crunk's visitation at the funeral home, then Lois told *everybody*. Aunt Connie called me this morning with the news."

The classic game of telephone, Camden edition. "Mr. Crunk died? I hate to hear that," she says, hoping to redirect the conversation.

"Yes, he did, God love him. He was as old as dirt, but stop trying to change the subject," Kelly scolds her. "You're going out with Bradley?"

"Again, it's no big deal. I'll have dinner with him, and it will be done. I have no expectations of seeing him again after tonight. He's part of my past. Not my present and certainly not my future."

"So, what are you wearing tonight?" Kelly squeals like she did as a teenage girl at a New Kids on the Block concert.

"Um, clothes," Penny replies.

"I know that. Don't give me attitude."

"Sorry, but I haven't given it any thought. It's not like I'm trying to impress him. I didn't exactly pack an outfit for the occasion. Besides, he saw me yesterday with hardly any makeup on and my frizzy hair tied up in a bun. I wasn't exactly exuding sex appeal. Remember, I'm here to pack up a large, rather cluttered house. Not picking up random dentists."

"Don't get mad at me, but I think this is great," Kelly says.

"You do?"

"Bradley's so nice. Probably the nicest guy in town. Other than that one night when he was an absolute dog. But it was such a long time ago. Just so you know, he asks about you every single time I see him. And last summer, he about jumped out of his skin when I told him you were getting divorced."

"How often could you possibly run into him?"

"Well, Camden's a small town. You know that. I see him at the club. Around the pool or on the driving range. You know, he's the president now," Kelly boasts.

Just hearing the words "the club" causes Penny's heart to flip, for she was never welcome at the Camden Swim and Golf Club growing up, thanks to her Nellie Oleson.

"And sometimes I run into him at football games. Or at the bank, or... when I have a checkup."

"Wait. He's your dentist?" Penny asks, bewildered.

"Yes," Kelly says in a quiet voice.

"For how long?"

"About eight years."

"Eight years? And now you tell me?"

"I didn't want you to get mad at me. Like I'd broken girl code or something. But he's the best dentist in town. Besides, I despise old Dr. Hamilton. Nobody round here wants to go to him. He's as mean as a snake and as blind as a bat. Don't hate me."

"I could never hate you, Kelly. And there's no girl code I'm aware of for going to a competent dental professional who happened to break a girlfriend's heart. I would never put your dental health in jeopardy over any hurt teenage feelings I have toward Bradley."

"Lawsy me. I've prayed about this," Kelly says with a sigh of relief.

They catch up for thirty minutes before saying their goodbyes, cementing their plans for tomorrow to pack up Ruby Ray's with help from Jimmy Neal's wife. But most importantly, Kelly makes Penny pinky swear to call after her evening with Bradley to spill all the night's juicy details.

Once again, as soon as Penny hangs up the phone, another call comes in.

"So, have you lost your fucking mind up there in *Deliverance* country? Should I come up there and rescue you?" Dakota snickers.

"I prefer 'God's country' when referring to my birthplace, and you have *no* idea," Penny says before relaying the events of the last twenty-four hours.

"You're shitting me right now."

"I wish."

"Bradley Hitchens? This is perfect! Exactly what you need. A little illicit summer romance. You're so going to sleep with him. I know it."

"Ew. It's not a romance, illicit or otherwise, and I certainly have no plans of sleeping with him. May I remind you of July fourth, 1989?" Penny shoots back.

"That was twenty years ago. Let it go. Jesus, you can hold on to a grudge."

They continue their conversation, trading barbs and teasing each other. Once Dakota begins offering unwanted sexual advice, Penny quickly ends the call under the pretense that her morning's slipping away. She says her goodbyes to Dakota, promising yet another friend a full report of her evening with Dr. Hitchens.

After she hangs up, she throws on one of Ruby Ray's old gardening shirts, hoping to protect her skin from bees and prickly vines, and heads out the door. Ruby Ray's flowers await, and time's ticking away.

Now her focus is on the bouquets she'll be taking to Willow Creek Baptist church this morning.

The first arrangement is for the church's altar. Her grandmother provided one every Sunday for forty years. Even in the dead of winter, Ruby Ray gathered magnolia leaves and holly branches to adorn the pulpit. She used to say it was her gift to the Lord, and Penny plans to do the same, knowing it would please her grandmother. Plus, it's a fitting thank-you to the congregation for the potluck they'll be serving in her honor. The second arrangement is for Jack, who's buried alongside their grandparents. The third is for Julie. Her husband shipped her body from Louisville before it was even cold, after she succumbed to Von Willebrand disease three years into their ill-advised marriage. Not making enough of an impression on her husband to rest in peace together in a cemetery or even sit on his mantel in a fancy urn was a terrible fate for Julie. The fourth bouquet is the most important. It's for her grandparents' final resting place, which sits on a little plot of land under a large weeping willow tree on a hillside behind the rustic church.

The row of deep-purple gladioli outside the dining room window are the first to capture Penny's attention. Their splendid vibrant-amethyst blooms against the foursquare's yellow walls are striking. A small pang of guilt courses through her body when she draws a sharp gardening knife to cut the stalks. They're almost too perfect to disturb. However, Penny's guilt soon subsides when she spies a bundle of periwinkle hydrangeas a stone's throw away. Willow Creek Baptist church's altar will be decked out in a sea of purple—a little Methodist tip of the hat from the former Baptist.

A spray of magenta sweet williams growing wild along the fence catches her eye next. Paired only with a mason jar, they will make a fine arrangement for Jack's grave. He always loved the simple things in life, anything small and unappreciated, like him. He required no fuss. Julie, however, necessitates more attention than their big brother, for she was used to having the spotlight placed upon her. Since roses are the queen of any garden, it's only fitting her bouquet will be full of them, since Julie was a beauty queen herself. The peach tea roses, which always garnered ribbons for Ruby Ray at the county fair, will make a fitting arrangement for her.

Though Penny's being extra careful while cutting the last bloom, since this particular rose bush bears the most cantankerous thorns she has ever encountered, her shirt sleeve still catches in the twisted vines, and she accidentally drops her basket. When she leans over to pick it up, she sees something that leaves her in awe—a lone fuchsia gerbera daisy growing all by itself. Ruby Ray never took a liking to this particular flower and never planted them in her gardens. Yet somehow, one has found its way here and grown out of spite. As soon as Penny sees it, she plucks it for someone special.

Finally, it's time to select the flowers for Ruby Ray and Pops. The pink New Dawns are the natural choice, since they were her grandmother's favorite flower. Vines from the white star jasmine bush, which is covered in honeybees, will make a beautiful arrangement in the cobalt-blue glass pitcher sitting in the kitchen. Only Penny's love for her grandmother allows her the fortitude to fight off stinging insects for the sake of floral design. Finishing her whimsical masterpiece, she places large muscadine grape leaves around the edges of the pitcher. The arrangement is worthy of a *Martha Stewart Living* cover.

After tending to the tiny scratches on her hands and arms, Penny hops into the claw-foot bathtub in the foursquare's one and only full bath to rinse off. Her grandmother never took a liking to showers, vowing to never have one installed. In a bid to look presentable, Penny spends half an hour attempting to straighten her persnickety mane with the help of a round brush and a scorching hair dryer. After that, she applies a tasteful amount of Bobbi Brown makeup to her glistening face in the un-air-conditioned bathroom. She applies light lip gloss, a small amount of eye shadow, and mascara to enhance her blue eyes. The navy Rebecca Taylor dress and the nude espadrilles she's packed for Florida are the final touch.

Willow Creek Baptist is, as folks around Camden would say, a haul from town, a twenty-minute drive along the hilly back roads of Liberty County. This is no "city" church. It's as country as the day is long, quite different from the more refined, somewhat uptight church Penny attends in Atlanta and has grown accustomed to. Though Methodists and Baptists are technically kissing cousins in the world of evangelicals, they tend to do things differently in regard to worship. The Baptists, at least in Penny's experience at Willow Creek, wear their hearts—or rather, their Christianity—on their sleeves for all the world to see. An opportunity to shout out an Amen during the sermon or testify to the congregation about how Jesus has saved their weary souls from eternal damnation is never missed. A Methodist, on the other hand, would rather pull out their fingernails one by one. They would prefer a waterboarding to making a peep during service. *Giving intimate details of their salvation in front of a packed sanctuary? That's unheard of.*

When Penny finally spies the white steeple with a cross in the distance, after making multiple trips down multiple hollers, she sees there's only one parking spot left in the gravel lot. Word about a food shindig of biblical proportions must be out around the community. But before she faces the good people of Willow Creek, Penny must first pay her respects to the Ray family members buried on top of the hill. With flowers in hand, she makes her way up to their final resting places.

Halfway up, she notices the bright saddles she ordered for her family's granite headstones in May. Four times a year, she makes a call to the Liberty County florist for seasonal artificial flowers. It gives her comfort to know that the family's spots in the cemetery are a little less dreary throughout the year. The silk pink peonies, white roses, and spider lilies are holding up nicely under the harsh summer sun. No fading, she notes.

Approaching the graves, she spots a smaller saddleless headstone a few feet away from the others. Charlie's plot, all by itself, where it belongs. No bouquet for him. Not even a dandelion has been plucked for his sake. Penny keeps moving without so much as a silent prayer.

She spots Jack's headstone and quickens her pace to get to him. The verse etched in stone, *Blessed are the pure in heart, for they shall see God*, greets her. She remembers how Ruby Ray insisted on including the verse from Matthew for her only grandson, even though it cost the family hundreds of extra dollars. But her grandmother was right. It summed up Jack's short life perfectly. As Penny lays the sweet williams beneath his headstone, her chin quivers. She misses her brother. He's the one paternal force in her life besides Pops she's ever known.

After giving her brother's stone a gentle kiss, she moves on to the next one, her sister's. *I have fought the good fight, I have finished the race, I have kept the faith* was the verse selected for Julie. After Ruby Ray made such a fuss over Jack's headstone, she needed to do the same for her granddaughter. Julie's tribute had Ruby Ray and half her quilting group digging around the Bible for hours. Finally, the book of Timothy gave her the inspiration. Of all the Ray children, Julie was the religious one, almost fanatical in her beliefs. As Penny places roses upon the cool stone, her thumb brushes across the smooth surface. She closes her eyes. *Two down, one to go.*

Though Penny has two sisters, she can only visit one at Willow Creek. Janet insisted upon cremation and had her ashes spread along the side of a creek to piss off her Baptist family one last time. In honor of her sister's bold decision to go against family burial protocols, Penny begins plucking the petals from the lone fuchsia gerbera daisy she found earlier. Suddenly, a gust of wind scatters the petals throughout the cemetery like confetti on New Year's Eve. Maybe Janet's spirit is here with the rest of the family.

As much as Penny misses her siblings, the person she longs for most has the freshest grave and the greenest grass on the hill. *She is clothed with strength and dignity* is etched across Ruby Ray's side of the double headstone she shares with Pops. Seeing it causes Penny's heart to skip a beat as she thinks of how much she worried over her selection of the verse from Proverbs for her grandmother's tribute, wanting to get it just right.

Biting the inside of her cheeks in an effort to suppress her emotions, Penny lays the bouquet filled with her grandmother's girls on the lush ground. This is the closest she's been to her touchstone in a year. She feels an overwhelming sense of loneliness, and her eyes fill with tears. Save for her aunt Molly, with whom she has no relationship, Penny is the last remaining Ray. Though she still has kinfolk—cousins and great-aunts and -uncles who'll be greeting her in a matter of minutes—her real family is all gone. Penny's the only one above ground. Now she's the matriarch of this tortured clan, an ancestral memory keeper who's spent most of her life trying to forget her history.

It's too much for Penny. Grief is a beast, and she's powerless under it. As she's about to surrender to it completely, falling down the dark rabbit hole of despair, a red cardinal flies over her shoulder and lands upon one of the weeping willow's kelly-green branches only a few feet away. Though she's startled at first by its proximity, a wave of gratitude floods over her as she remembers the old wives' tale Ruby Ray used to say about the bird when they were gardening together. "When you see a cardinal, Penny, it's a visitor from heaven. A loved one reminding the world that they're watching over you."

Staring at her feathered angel, knowing it's only a coincidence, Penny smiles. Tears of sorrow turn into ones of joy. There's something deeply comforting about nature and good timing. Though she has her doubts about religion, never speaking of them to another soul, she'll take this divine celestial message with her for the day.

"Goodbye, Ruby Ray," she whispers before turning around and making her way back down the hill. Now Penny has the strength to face her spiritual family.

After fetching the flowers for the altar from her car and corralling both her mascara and her emotions, Penny walks toward the packed front porch of the church. Historically, it's customary at Willow Creek for the men and a few women to go outside for a quick smoke break between Sunday school and worship. Two hours without a tobacco hit was deemed cruel, so the elders of the church designated five minutes for the nicotine caucus. She takes in a deep breath of smoke-free air before walking up the steps. Then she hears a familiar voice.

"Penny Ray? You best get on up here, purdy lady, and give me some sugar," Uncle Floyd says through a thick cloud of cigarette smoke escaping through his nose. He's dressed in his heavy polyester Sunday suit. Uncle Floyd's a relic at Willow Creek Baptist, having just celebrated his ninety-first birthday back in the spring, an amazing feat with the two-pack-a-day habit he's been nursing for the last eighty years. As the elder deacon of the church, he never misses an opportunity to be in the house of the Lord, setting a good example for the rest of the flock.

"Good to see you," Penny replies, kissing his wrinkled cheek. "I see you still haven't quit those things yet." She motions to her great-uncle's addiction.

"I'll get around to it one day. Still got some time," he says with a wink.

"Heard you had a little scare last winter," she said, referring to his health.

"Well, let's put it this way. I'd have to feel better in order to die." He roars with laughter and takes a long drag off his unfiltered Camel.

The tobacco-loving crowd laughs with him, and Penny can only shake her head, amused by his proclamation.

"Your ears musta been burning, 'cause I was just talking about you!" Gracie Belle comes rushing out of Willow Creek's sanctuary and onto the smoky front porch, her arms wide, ready to greet her cousin.

Instinctively, Penny puts her right foot in front of her left, readying herself for the onslaught of bear hugs. A loss of balance will not happen today.

"I can't tell you how happy I am to see you." Gracie Belle beams, scooping Penny up for a tight embrace to her bosom.

"It's good to see you too," Penny whispers, desperately struggling for air while also trying to protect the bouquet from being crushed.

"We've missed you like crazy, sweet child," Gracie Belle proclaims, not noticing she's suffocating her second-cousin-by-marriage.

"I've missed you too," Penny says while slipping free of the woman's clutches.

"And you brought flowers. They're the prettiest things I've ever seen," Gracie Belle proclaims, placing her hand on her chest.

"Thank you for organizing the lunch today, Gracie Belle. You *really* shouldn't have gone to all the trouble."

"It's no trouble at all. When Jimmy Neal told me you were coming home, I was fit to be tied." Gracie Belle pats Penny on the back with such force that she fears her breakfast will come spilling onto the concrete porch. "Lord, it's good to have you home!"

"Can you tell she's a little excited to see you?" Laura, Jimmy Neal's wife, says with a wink. Her chocolate-brown eyes dance with excitement. She was Penny's friend long before she became her cousin through marriage.

"You think?" Penny smiles. "Good to see you, Laura," she says, hugging her old counterpart.

"You too." Laura squeezes back.

"Let's get off this porch before I hack up a lung." Gracie Belle swats away the smoke surrounding them. "Laura, can you get Granddaddy into his pew now?" she asks, nodding toward her father-in-law, Floyd.

"Reckon I can find it myself. Been sitting in the same spot ever' Sunday for ninety-one years," Floyd snaps.

"I know you can find it, Granddaddy, but church is getting ready to start, and you don't need another one of them cancer sticks. You know what the doctor said."

"I'll be in directly." Floyd lights up another Camel out of spite.

"I give up. You're as stubborn as a mule. Don't complain to me when you get another bout of pneumonia or worse." Gracie Belle fans herself in fake exasperation. "Come on," she says, dragging both Penny and her bouquet into Willow Creek's simple sanctuary. "She's here."

"Penny Ray!" the congregation cheers in unison with the same fanfare given to the prodigal son returning home. That biblical story has always bothered Penny, for she feels the younger son was a consummate screwup, throwing away his money, while the older one dutifully worked next to his father. Yet somehow the irresponsible son was celebrated for his spendthrift ways. *There's forgiveness, then there's codependency* is Penny's take on the parable.

Heat rises to Penny's face as she begins greeting the adoring crowd with handshakes and hugs. Being the object of everyone's attention isn't something she's comfortable with, but she'll have to brush off her distaste for the limelight for a few minutes because the people of Willow Creek Baptist Church are like family to her. They all love her, which fills Penny with a sense of belonging.

"Oh, child. Look at you," the elderly spinster Miss Ada Pickert says, creeping toward the gathering. "You're too skinny." She pokes at Penny's bony arms with her cane. "Are you eating enough since your divorce? It must be awful to be divorced. Have you repented of your sinful ways?" She's cut right to the chase in less than ten seconds.

"Hello, Miss Pickert. It's so good to see you," Penny replies robotically, trying to mask her displeasure at having her crappy life laid bare by one of the few members of Willow Creek she isn't related to.

"And have you quit the drugs, child?" the old woman asks.

Gracie Belle balks. "Penny was never on drugs. Her Yankee friend roofied her before Ruby Ray's funeral last year. To help with her nerves. That's all. You know you can't trust a New Yorker."

"And is it true you've become an atheist?" Miss Pickert continues to a stunned Penny.

Gracie Belle gasps in horror at the absurd accusation. "She's a Methodist. That's all, and we *still* love her in spite of it."

Squinting, Miss Ada is about to get in her last dig of the day. "Just remember who baptized Jesus. John the Baptist not John the Methodist."

"Miss Ada," Penny says, "would you like a free grandfather clock?" If anyone deserves to be tormented by its chimes all night, it's Ada Pickert.

"That thing would drive me crazy, just like it did Homer. Straight to the loony bin, I tell you," she says, describing Penny's new nemesis to a T.

"I don't think you can blame his Alzheimer's on a clock. Genetics may have had something to do with it." Penny smiles.

"Well, he was fine until that thing came into the house," she retorts. The old bag of bones might be on to something. Penny was ready to pull her hair out after one night of its annoying tolls. Maybe it played a part in Pops's neurological disease after all.

"Having fun yet, cuz?" Jimmy Neal teases as he walks up.

"Loads." Penny rolls her eyes. "Does that woman really think John the Baptist was actually a Baptist?"

"What do you think?" Jimmy Neal snickers.

"Good Lord."

After what seems like an eternity, with everyone at Willow Creek fawning over Penny's arrival—or in Miss Ada's case, nitpicking at her flaws—Gracie Belle starts playing a grand rendition of "When We All Get to Heaven" on the Story and Clark upright, a cue for everyone to take their seats and prepare their hearts for worship. In awe, Penny listens to her cousin play her instrument by ear, stroking every key with flair and showing off her self-taught skills.

"Please turn your hymnals to page 161, 'There Is Power in the Blood.' Let's stand and rejoice in the presence of our Lord," Melvin Ray, Penny's other living great-uncle and Willow Creek's long-standing song leader, says in a baritone voice. Unlike most of his siblings, Melvin has avoided cigarettes his entire life, though he sounds like he's sucked down fifty a day. If circumstances had been different, he could've been on the stage of the Grand Ole Opry. He's a mix of Hank Williams and Johnny Cash rolled into one—without the drugs and alcohol, of course.

Melvin leads them in two more stanzas before Brother Hitt wobbles up the steps to the pulpit for the church announcements. "Good morning!" the round young minister exclaims. "It's a good day to be in the house of the Lord. Can I get an amen?"

"Amen!" the congregation, sans Penny, answers back on cue.

"A bit of housekeeping this morning with a few announcements. Our youth group will be making their spiritual journey to Brownsville this week to spend the next six days at Camp Joy. I think we have nine going this year, and I believe that's the most we've ever had register. Please lift them up in your prayers for a safe trip and that there will be lives saved. Also, please keep the Centers family in your prayers this week as Brother Freddy goes in for much-needed back surgery in Bowling Green."

The congregation nods in agreement that Brother Freddy's name will indeed be crossing their lips before suppertime around their tables and before their weary heads rest upon their pillows.

"All right, then," the preacher continues, "I have one last announcement. Directly following our service today, we'll be having a potluck luncheon in the fellowship hall, honoring the homecoming of Ms. Penny Ray. Penny, will you please stand up so that everybody can get a good look at you?"

Beads of sweat form along the back of Penny's neck. Having to stand up and be singled out at this moment is too much for her nervous system. Though her first instinct is to slide down and hide under her oak pew, which has been polished so thoroughly that it's as slick as a frozen pond, that's not an option for a grown woman. With no way out of this pickle, she does as she's told and is greeted by loud applause.

"Now, I don't know Penny all that good. She was gone long before I took over as your pastor, but I did know her grandmother. And well, she was one of the finest Christian women I've ever had the pleasure of preaching to. And let me tell you what. Sister Ruby Ray kept me on my toes every Sunday. She knew the Bible better than the Apostle Paul himself, and she wasn't afraid to let me know if I got something wrong." He lets out a boisterous laugh, and the crowd says yet another amen in agreement. "Everybody in this church loved her, and we are so pleased to have her granddaughter here with us today, especially since most of y'all are kin to her. Now, Brother Melvin, can we get another song of praise?"

The service hasn't changed since Penny was a child. After the second song of praise, an offering is taken. Penny's thankful she remembered to bring cash. At her new church, she writes a check once a year instead of performing the weekly ritual of throwing a wad of cash into the plate. After the tithes are collected, Brother Hitt begins his sermon, continuing the sacred tradition of Willow Creek's fire-and-brimstone brand. His face turns three different shades of red during his rant about how the country is falling prey to sin and fornication just like Sodom and Gomorrah did. Slapping his right hand onto the wooden pulpit, he reminds everyone what God did to those people.

"Repent!" he cries out. "Or risk an eternity in Hell!"

After the fiery sermon, which lasts forty-five minutes, Brother Hitt asks Uncle Melvin to sing all five stanzas of "Just as I Am" for the altar call.

"The sinners in our midst must be saved," he keeps repeating.

Yet no one budges. So desperate for a soul to save on this day, the robust preacher asks the congregation if they should participate in a good old-fashioned handshake to stir up the Holy Spirit. However, he's only greeted with blank stares and a few paltry amens in the back. It's becoming apparent to all, Brother Hitt included, no one's coming clean today. There's food downstairs, and this flock would rather fill their stomachs than their souls. Finally, the disappointed preacher calls it a day and dismisses the crowd.

Making her way down the narrow steps to the basement, Penny catches a whiff of the familiar aromas floating up the staircase, transporting her to another time. It smells like Ruby Ray's kitchen used to. While it causes her throat to tighten, it also fills her with a sense of joy and belonging. Food has the ability to comfort people in a way nothing else can. Though this meal will be centered around her, she will allow herself to delight in this fellowship for the next hour. A smile spreads across her lips, and she relaxes a bit.

Walking into the cinder block fellowship hall with linoleum flooring, Penny sees long, rectangular tables in the middle of the room. They're overflowing with food, all made from scratch with recipes not from cookbooks but from memory, the way it should be. As Ruby Ray taught Penny from a young age, "When you come to a potluck at Willow Creek Baptist Church, not only do you bring your best, most trusted dish, but you put it in your finest Corningware or crystal platter that's been handed down to you by your great-grand-mother."

To begin the buffet, boundless salad options are available. They're not the green kind, though, other than the fluffy pistachio salad made with a blend of Cool Whip and crushed pineapple. These "salads" contain no lettuce or vegetables and are delightful concoctions of flavored Jell-O, copious amounts of cream cheese, mounds of sugar, and chunks of fruit. Frozen strawberry fluff, mandarin orange salad, and of course, ambrosia dripping with marshmallows and flaky coconut are placed at the beginning of the immense table.

Following the salad selection are the mammoth bowls of beans—green beans, pole beans, and soup beans cooked with ham hock and simmered overnight. Not a nutrient is left in them. They've been boiled into submission. Next to the butter beans is the selection of cornmeal okra. Everyone at Willow Creek has a different take on how to cook the gooey pods, but there's always a common denominator, that it be fried within an inch of its life. Next to the varieties of okra are dozens of Pyrex dishes. Every vegetable under the sun has been turned into a casserole. Carrots, corn, broccoli, squash, and even cabbage have been transformed into little culinary masterpieces by simply putting a little love and a whole lot of butter, cheese, and Ritz crackers into them. Then there are the potatoes, which are in a category by themselves. Bowls full of the starchy root vegetable lie across the table as far as the eye can see, from mashed, boiled, scalloped, twice baked, to the most popular creation of all—the potato salad. Willow Creek has always had two dueling versions. First is Leeta Ray's Southern recipe with the right blend of hot onion, green pepper, yellow mustard, egg, and Miracle Whip topped off with a generous dusting of Hungarian paprika. The other is from the kitchen of Davonna Ray, Leeta's daughter-in-law, who's a former Michigander. One would've thought she'd slapped the baby Jesus sideways when she introduced her German creation made from vinegar, Dijon mustard, and parsley, of all things, to Willow Creek's congregation. However, Davonna's years of persistence, never giving up on her salad, won over more than a few fans in the crowd, Penny included. A potluck wouldn't be the same without it now.

After the galore of potatoes, which contain enough salt to make a cardiologist shudder, comes a vast array of bread choices. No boring store-bought rolls here but ones made from scratch. These women brought out their finest creations, including warm cornbread sticks with chunks of bacon cooked into the batter, Kentucky spoon bread, yeasty Sally Lunn bread, and a heaping plate of angel biscuits with a side of strawberry preserves.

But the star of the show, the main attraction of any Baptist potluck, is at the end of the table: a mountain of fried chicken. The fine women of Willow Creek knew how to prepare it: a salt bath, thick buttermilk batter, and hot cast iron skillets full of Crisco. The crispier and saltier, the better. And they cook not just the breasts, legs, and wings, but also the giblets. Those in the front of the line tear through the gizzards, hearts, and livers before those behind them have a chance to pick up a plate.

Finally, in the corner of the room, is a bountiful display of desserts. The creamy yet spicy hummingbird cake has always been Penny's favorite, though she has a soft spot for the airy angel food as well. The pies are equally enticing. Choosing one is impossible. The chocolate chess is always a favorite of the menfolk, while the coconut cream, with meringues so high they resemble perfect little mountains, is more to the liking of the softer sex. Plates of cookies—chocolate oatmeal and cinnamon butterscotch—are scattered about, pleasing the younger ones. There isn't a raisin cookie in sight. These women knew better.

But one dessert stands out, the one Miss Sadie Reese has perfected over the years—the punchbowl trifle. Miss Reese has constructed her decadent masterpiece in her grandmother's Depression-era glass bowl thousands of times. Golden yellow cake surrounded by layers of syrupy pineapple, maraschino cherries, and homemade vanilla pudding fill the bowl. To finish the masterpiece, she tops it with whipped cream made with a quarter cup of Maker's Mark, her secret ingredient. No one in the teetotaling crowd knows about the bourbon, but they lap it up like hungry dogs, blissfully unaware of their sin. It's so irresistible that Penny has two helpings of the morally corrupt dessert.

"Gracie Belle, you've outdone yourself," Penny says, laying her head upon her cousin's shoulder after the meal, stuffed to the gills.

"This is what family does, Penny. We celebrate with one another. Don't ever forget that," Gracie Belle says, kissing the top of her head.

"Thanks to you, I'll have to run twenty miles tomorrow to burn off all the fat and calories I consumed today." Penny tugs at the waistline of her dress. "I haven't eaten like this in years."

"You're as thin as a politician's promise. I think you can spare a pound or two." Gracie Belle smiles, patting her knee.

"I'd better get going. I've got a lot to do today," Penny says.

"Oh, I know." Gracie Belle winks.

"Know what?"

"About your plans this evening."

"I'm going to wring Jimmy Neal's neck." Penny rolls her eyes.

"Honey, he didn't tell me nothing. Lord knows he's as tight as a tick with information. I heard it last night at the funeral home."

"Of course you did." Penny shakes her head at the efficiency with which the rumor mill of Camden runs. In less than twenty-four hours, the entire town knows about her date with Bradley. "It's no big deal. He was kind enough to fix my tooth, so I agreed to dinner. That's all."

"It doesn't matter what *it* is. You just have a good time tonight. Lord knows, you need it, child," Gracie Belle tells her as their eyes meet.

"It's only dinner," Penny mumbles.

"Why don't I stop by Wednesday to help you pack," Gracie Belle says, changing the subject. "I can be there all day."

Relieved that Bradley's no longer the topic of their conversation, Penny says, "Thank you," and hugs Gracie Belle around the neck.

"You're welcome." The warmth in her voice is better than a long summer day by the creek. This woman loves her.

Though she wants to savor this moment in the loving, understanding arms enveloping her, Penny finally pulls away. "By the way, would you want a slightly used grandfather clock that keeps you up all night?" Penny asks. "It can be yours on Wednesday."

"Is it driving you crazy?" Gracie Belle laughs.

"It kept me up most of the night."

"It's a beautiful clock. I think you should keep it. It'll make a nice heirloom one day."

"Maybe, if it makes it through the night. If I find a sledgehammer today, it's toast."

"You never know, sweet girl." Gracie Belle smiles. "It might just grow on you."

Chapter 13

Penny's Got a Gun

T minus two hours and twenty-three minutes until Bradley's dinner demand is met. If Penny hurries, she can get in at least two good hours of packing before his dreaded arrival. Today, she vows to keep her head down and actually pack. A broken tooth will not stop her now.

Before going into the house, she enters the barn to grab a stack of the boxes Jimmy Neal has provided. After a quick wardrobe change into her favorite Kentucky T-shirt, which has lasted longer than her marriage, she's off. The plan is to pack one room at a time by separating everything into three categories—items she wants to keep, items she knows Aunt Molly and Ruby Ray's barracuda sisters will fight to the death over, and finally, straight-up trash.

Clearing out her grandparents' bedroom is the first thing on her agenda. It's a relic and hasn't changed one iota since her grandparents bought the house more than forty years ago. The aged wallpaper, which has started to peel in the corners, has never been replaced. An antique bedroom suite, given to the couple as a wedding present by Ruby Ray's mother, hasn't moved an inch since the sixties. Even the pictures hanging on the walls are exactly the same.

Within minutes of entering the bedroom, Penny comes to the startling realization that her grandmother was, before her death, teetering precariously close to hoarding territory. As she thinks of how much packing, organizing, and mounds of trash she faces, her head begins to pound. The dumpster out back, she fears, will be full after one room.

Though she works at breakneck speed, it takes her an hour to clean out just the small closet. Penny the Planner didn't foresee this scenario, and she's irritated by her lack of efficiency as well as Ruby Ray's penchant for clutter. *One closet down, eight more to go. And three more bedrooms. And a formal dining room. And a living room. And a den. And a kitchen. And a basement.*

"At this rate, I'll be here till Thanksgiving," she grumbles, looking around the room in defeat.

Looking at the cherry bed, she contemplates collapsing onto it, pulling up the covers, and calling it a day. Maybe she could find a moving company to do the heavy lifting. Camden doesn't have one, but Bowling Green or Nashville has dozens of them. Let the professionals work their magic on Ruby Ray's. However, that feeling lasts about five seconds, until the gnawing guilt of responsibility hits her. She could never let a stranger go through her grandmother's beloved items. That wouldn't be right.

Instead of taking the easy way out, she decides to pull up her boot straps and knock out another packing obstacle, more determined than ever to get the job done. With a box in one hand and a trash bag in the other, she walks over to Pops's bedside table. Without thinking, she opens the top drawer. Looking down, she's greeted with only three items—a Bible, a pile of embroidered cotton handkerchiefs, and Pops's Colt Frontier Scout revolver. The second she lays eyes on the gun, Penny's knees buckle, causing her to collapse to the wooden floor. Her ears burn, and her hands become cold and clammy. She's transported back to the day that rocked her to her core, when she realized what she was capable of if pushed past the breaking point.

That was the day Penny got her scars, the ones she's been desperately trying to hide from the world for decades.

April 15, 1989
Camden, Kentucky

Chapter 14

Scarface

"Three seconds. That's all. Three seconds, and you'll own the state record," Coach McDonald said with a stopwatch in his left hand, patting an exhausted Penny on the back with his right. "This is a once-in-a-lifetime opportunity."

"I'll try harder next time. I promise," Penny said with what little breath she still had in her lungs, praying she wouldn't expel the contents of her school lunch onto his feet.

"You're a senior now, Penny. There're only a few weeks and a couple of meets left to break it before graduation. There's nothing I want more than to see you own the thirty-two hundred all to yourself. School records and regional titles are nice, but to have a state record and title, that's something else entirely."

"I want it, too, Coach." Penny leaned over and put her hands on her knees, trying to get air back into her lungs. She truly wanted nothing more—other than being with Bradley Hitchens—than to become the best runner in the state. Throughout her preteen and teenage years, she'd willed her body into a perfect running machine through grit, determination, and hard work. But that only took her so far. Something else drove her as well, a much darker and sinister reason. "I mean you saw that little one with the belly poking out. Lord knows she ain't no beauty queen." Those cruel words from long ago had stuck to Penny's fragile psyche like gum to a shoe. They were on a continuous loop in her brain. Not only had running made her into a state contender, it had also transformed her body. Her belly no longer poked out, and her body-fat count was in the single digits.

"Keep working. Dig deeper. You can do it. I'm sure of it. Now, hit the showers," the coach commanded.

"Yes, sir," Penny said, making her way upright. Three seconds sounded simple enough, but in terms of running, it might as well be three thousand seconds. One could only do so much digging.

Walking toward the locker room, Penny began to feel the teenage weight of the world fall upon her tiny shoulders. Between the state record looming over her, the prospect of college on the horizon, and the pressure she put on herself to ace her final exams and finish fourth in her class, one spot ahead of Bradley, the pressure was starting to take its toll on her. But that was only a small piece of the complicated puzzle of her worries. Naturally, her parents' antics haunted her as well. First, divorce number five was hovering over her mother's head. *Another one bites the dust.* And Charlie was unemployed again and drinking heavily. His boorish behavior around town was causing a magnitude of problems for the Ray family. But not all of her stress was home related. Penny still had to navigate the pitfalls of high school, mainly avoiding Emily Johnston at all costs. Though Penny had prayed for some kind of divine intervention to cause her nemesis to have a change of heart, her prayers had been left unanswered. Age and time had not tempered Emily's vicious tongue, only made it sharper and more cunning. The girl was ruthless. The week before, she complained to Penny's bosses at Sonic Drive-In and everyone within earshot that she found a hair in her food, naturally pointing the finger at the beleaguered carhop who was juggling both school and a thirty-hour work week. Luckily for Penny, Mr. Beasley didn't buy what Emily was trying to sell, but she still got her meal for free, and Penny's hair once again became a point of ridicule within Emily's hive of demented bees. But the real stressor consuming Penny's mind over the past few weeks was finding a suitable dress she could afford for prom. The event was fast approaching, and she didn't have the luxury of blowing her hard-earned money on such frivolous things as a sequined gown.

"You're getting so close," Bradley said, running up behind her. "Coach said three seconds."

"I know, but it feels like an eternity. I'm not sure how much harder I can push before my lungs explode."

"You've got this. I know it."

"Thanks for the encouragement. Hey, how was your time today?" She genuinely wanted to know. Bradley's highs were her highs, and his lows, though he'd never experienced those, would be hers as well.

"Fifty-two flat. Not bad. But not great. I might place at district. Maybe a solid showing at regionals, but that's where my track career will end. I'm not State material like some people around here." He nudged her.

Likewise, Penny's highs were his highs, and her lows would be his as well.

"I don't feel like State material right now," she mumbled, defeat in her voice.

"You'll get there. I have no doubt," Bradley said. "Hey, want to head over to Saul's and grab a pizza before your shift tonight? We can get a little studying in too."

The word pizza made Penny's stomach queasy, and she felt an instant wave of nausea. "I'm not working. I have the night off," she explained while trying to regain control of her stomach.

"Great! I could really use some help on my final paper for Mrs. Holland's class."

"Let me get this straight," Penny said, cocking her head. "You're going to use my writing skills and love of Sylvia Plath to help you ace your paper so that you can leapfrog me and take my spot at fourth? Did you even read *The Bell Jar*?"

"Of course I did," he protested. "But I hated it and didn't understand a word of it. Besides, if I don't help you with Kirkland's trig final, you'll be toast. Goodbye fourth. Say hello to fifth, Penny Ray. You need me as much as I need you." A mischievous grin took over his face.

"Yes, I do." Penny chuckled. They both knew she needed him more for his math prowess than he needed her for her writing abilities. "But I can't right now. I'm going to the bank, then I'm off for another training run to find those elusive three seconds I need for glory. Maybe we can meet up after I run."

"The bank? Why are you going there?"

"Well, if you must know, I'm going to take some money out of my savings account to buy a dress." She paused. "For prom."

"Prom? What's that? Haven't heard of it," he deadpanned. "Do you have a date, Miss Ray?"

"No, Mr. Hitchens, I do not have a date. That implies I have a romantic connection with someone. As we both know, I have no time for such things. I'm going to prom with a friend, remember?"

"An exceptional friend, I hear. Who happens to be your mathematical saving grace, since you can't manage to count above five without help from your little fingers," he said, smiling, that dimple peeking through.

"Meet you at Saul's at seven, my saving grace?"

"Meet you at seven," he repeated, running past her and into the locker room with newfound energy.

Though the two designated their relationship as platonic for the world to see, they were fooling no one besides themselves. The lines of friendship had been crossed on several occasions, sharing kisses and other forbidden teenage sexual curiosities. However, they'd never crossed *the* line.

After she showered and redressed in her acid jeans and a baggy sweatshirt, Penny made her way to Camden National Bank in Pops's borrowed 1975 blue Ford pickup truck. The night before, she'd negotiated a deal for a prom dress from her fellow carhop at Sonic. The periwinkle-blue sequined gown would cost her one hundred twenty-five dollars, a steal in her mind, since it was the most beautiful dress she'd ever seen.

"Good afternoon. How can I help you?" the bank teller asked with a warm smile.

"Hello, Mrs. Proctor. I'm here to withdraw money from my savings account. Here's my passbook with the account number on it," Penny said matter-of-factly, handing over her documents.

"Thank you. You're very prepared. Makes my job easier." Mrs. Proctor winked before scanning through the small book Penny kept with all the deposits she'd made over the years.

Babysitting jobs, two years' worth of Sonic shifts, and even her old lemonade stand money had all been saved. Because of her diligence, Penny's little nest egg had grown to $2,409.06 with interest.

"Do you have your ID on you?" the teller asked.

"Here," Penny said, handing over her driver's license.

"Oh, I see you're only seventeen. That makes you a minor. You'll need the parent whose name is on the account to come with you to withdraw this money."

"I didn't know either one of my parents' names was even on the account," Penny said as her pulse quickened. Ruby Ray had helped her set up the account when she was a small child, so she'd assumed only her name was used.

"Let me check and see who's listed," the teller replied before typing on the computer. After what seemed like an eternity, Mrs. Proctor looked up, her face ashen. "Honey, how much do you think you have in this account?"

"Two thousand four hundred nine dollars and six cents," Penny said, pointing at her diligent bookkeeping. "It's right there."

The kind bank teller turned another color right before Penny's eyes. "It says here there's only nine dollars left. Your cosigner withdrew twenty-four hundred of it a couple of days ago." Mrs. Proctor swallowed hard before delivering the last part of the sad news. "It was Charlie Ray."

"*What?*" Penny yelled in disbelief. "How can that be? It's my account. I had no idea he had access to it. I'm the only person who's ever put money in it. It's my name on the account, not his." Tears of anger filled her eyes.

"Well, by law, he has the right to withdraw the funds, since his name is on the account," the teller whispered.

"I didn't put his name on it. He's the last person in the world I'd trust with money. There has to be a mistake. It's my money. I swear," Penny said, breaking down.

"Why don't you come back tomorrow with your father so we can straighten all this out. Maybe your grandmother could come along too," Mrs. Proctor said nervously, checking the clock over Penny's shoulder. "It's closing time."

"You're worried about your closing time when all my money's been stolen?"

"Honey, my hands are tied. Your daddy had access to the account, so it's not technically stolen," she mumbled.

"Of course it was stolen! I worked for it, not him!"

"I'm sorry, but there's nothing you can do about it today."

"We'll see about that," Penny said, grabbing her savings book from the teller's hands.

She headed straight to Ruby Ray's. In a few minutes, her grandmother would know of her son's duplicity as well.

Pulling Pops's truck into the driveway, Penny saw it. Sitting next to the barn was a fire-engine-red Dodge Ram. There was no question where her savings had gone. A wave of pure anger crashed upon her as she barreled up the steps, reeling from her father's brazenness.

"Ruby Ray!" she yelled, running into the house in a state of sheer panic. "Ruby Ray, where are you?"

"Quit your hemming and hollering. She ain't here," Charlie said, stumbling out of her grandparents' bedroom. He was drunk, and although she knew better than to poke the bear in that state, her unbridled emotions took over.

"Where's Ruby Ray?" she asked, staring at her father with disgust.

"Like I sssaid, she ain't here. Went over to FFFountain RRRun for some kind of revival," he slurred.

"I see you got yourself a new truck," Penny said, venom dripping from her lips. Her brow furrowed in anger.

"Why, yes. Yes, I did. She's a real beauty, ain't she? Been saving a *real* long time for her," he said after taking a long swig from his Evan Williams bottle, winking. "Figured this was the perfect time and all."

"Where'd you get the money for it? We both know you haven't had a job in months." Charlie had given up farming years ago. His last foray into gainful employment ended when a fellow postal employee smelled alcohol on his breath after he crashed his mail truck—yet another Ray scandal to fill the gossip for the busybodies around town.

"Well, like I said, I've been saving up for it. Years, in fact. Takes a lot of hard work to come up with that kind of dough." He sneered.

"You're a liar, Charlie Ray!" Penny shouted. The raw anger in her voice came from deep within, pent up for years. "You didn't buy that truck with your money. You stole it from *my* savings account!"

"Little girl, you'd better watch your tone with me! I didn't steal no money. It was mine."

"That's not true, and you know it! I worked for it, and I want it back right now, or I'm going to call the police."

He laughed. "Yeah, you go right ahead and call 'em up," he said, losing his balance. "While you're at it, tell my buddy Ricky I said hi."

"I mean it. Give it back, or I'll call 'em!"

"We both know they ain't gonna do shit to me. My name was on the account." The large blue vein running down the middle of his forehead began thickening. The telltale sign his temper was getting the best of him usually caused Penny to back off. But she ignored it.

"Your name wasn't supposed to be on my account. I didn't know!"

"Hell, it was news to me too. I just found out myself the other day when I stumbled across your little book in Momma's safe. Figured I'd better go on and spend my hard-earned cash before it was too late. You know, before my daughter can waste it on a prom dress. Or worse, college," he said, winking.

"You're not getting away with this, Charlie. I'm calling the police!" Penny screamed, rushing past him toward the phone next to the bed. It was time Charlie Wayne Ray finally got what he deserved.

However, before she managed a second step into the room, Penny was stopped dead in her tracks, blindsided by her father's right fist to her jaw. The sucker punch was so powerful that it knocked her off her feet, sending her crashing into the corner of the bed and splitting her lip. At first, she had no idea what had happened, too stunned from the intense pain. A loud ringing sound came from her left ear. Soon, warm blood poured from her mouth, which brought her back to reality.

"I'll do whatever I goddamned please! You hear me, little girl?" Charlie roared as he began kicking her in the stomach with his steel-toed farm boots while she lay helpless on the ground.

Air was forced from her lungs. No matter how hard she tried to fill them—gasping, fighting, clawing—she couldn't manage the simple task.

"I'm your father, and I can do whatever I want. You hear me?" He snarled, again kicking Penny as she attempted to regain her footing, knocking her back down. "That money is mine!" His eyes were jet black, like a shark when it attacks.

In an attempt to make herself as small a target as possible, Penny curled into a tiny ball, hoping to save herself from his heavy boots and ferociousness. But it only fueled his onslaught. Grabbing a head full of her thick hair with his left hand, he lifted her off the ground and slapped her blood-covered face with his right. With each strike, her body cried out in agony. The heat from each impact felt like thousands of searing needles puncturing her skin all at once. He finally slowed down when his own hand began to bleed. But he wasn't finished yet. His harshest blow was still to come.

"Next time you come after me, little girl, you'd better bring more than an idle threat," he said before smashing her forehead into the hardwood floor, making it split open.

"You want some more? Or have you learned your lesson yet?" He panted, wiping his brow, which was pouring with sweat. "I can't hear you," he taunted as Penny lay bleeding.

When she failed to respond, he went in for more, infuriated by her silence. However, instead of sustaining another brutal round, she was ready. When Charlie raised his clenched fist, though every inch of Penny's body was screaming in agony, she managed to roll onto her back. With all her might, she struck her father in his less-than-stellar family jewels with such force that he instantly fell to the ground, howling in pain. Penny's strong quad muscles, developed from thousands of miles running, had taken him by surprise.

A kicked dog will holler.

Seeing her father was temporarily stunned and immobile, Penny set her sights on Pops's bedside table. Using her right elbow, she dragged her body across the floor, leaving a trail of blood in her wake. One thing could save her. With her last bit of strength, she grabbed the drawer. It smashed down upon her bloody nose, causing another deep gash, while its contents scattered about the room. After the shock wore off, she spotted it. No more than two feet in front of her was Pops's revolver. Everyone within the Ray family knew their patriarch kept it loaded with three bullets in case of emergencies. Wide-eyed, with adrenaline coursing through her body, she grabbed it as if it was her last lifeline on Earth and pointed it at her father, who was attempting to stand up on the other side of the room.

"Now, what are you gonna do with that?" he asked, stumbling to his feet. The color hadn't returned to his face.

"Exactly what you taught me to do with it," Penny replied as she pointed the gun toward him. Calmness flooded over her. Her index finger, resting on the trigger, was relaxed. For a moment, she'd almost forgotten about the unspeakable pain pulsating throughout her ribcage and the blood running down her face, all because she had something she'd never possessed before—control. Five pounds of it securely gripped in her right hand.

"You don't even know how to shoot that thing."

"Wanna bet?" She cocked back the hammer, loading a bullet into the chamber. "*You* taught me how to shoot this gun," she said with confidence. "And if you remember, I was a pretty good shot."

"You can't hit the broadside of a barn. Besides, you won't shoot me. We both know you ain't got it in you. You're fooling yourself."

"I could shoot a squirrel out of a tree fifty yards away by the time I was ten years old, and you don't think I can hit you at point-blank range? Who's fooling who now, Charlie?"

"You ain't gonna shoot me, and you know it," he hissed, lunging toward her and trying to grab the revolver.

Without hesitation, Penny pulled the trigger. A bullet whizzed by Charlie's right ear, narrowly missing him and lodging in the bedroom wall next to the family picture they'd taken when she was a toddler. The loud cracking sound caused him to fall to the ground.

"You move again, and I'll end you. We both know I got two more bullets in the chamber. That was a warning shot. I missed on purpose," she said, a steely resolve in her voice. "I won't miss again."

"You're gonna kill your own father in cold blood?" Suddenly, he sobered up.

"I wouldn't be killing my father. I've never had one of those."

"Penny, please." Charlie's voice quivered.

"I'm done." She edged closer. "I'm done with your drinking, your lying, your stealing, and most importantly, I'm done with the beatings," she said, her voice cracking. "I've been your punching bag since I was four years old, and it's over! If you ever lay another hand on me, if you so much as spit in my direction, there won't be a warning shot next time. Do you hear me? You will never touch me again. This ain't no idle threat, Charlie."

He closed his eyes and nodded.

"And you'll get me back all the money you stole. If you don't, I'll tell Ruby Ray about my savings account. Got it?"

He nodded again.

"Now, go. Get out of here."

After stumbling to his feet, Charlie slowly backed out of the room. As soon as he reached the hall, he sprinted toward his new pickup.

When he was gone, Penny's knees gave way, and she collapsed from exhaustion. The adrenaline that had allowed her the fortitude and strength to defend herself left her body, leaving her in excruciating pain. Her ribs were certainly fractured. She labored for air, and an uncontrollable shaking from the pain of broken bones took over. Blood continued to pour from her mouth and nose as well as the gash above her eye, so she grabbed the first soft thing within reach. A cluster of Pops's handkerchiefs helped absorb the profuse amount of blood she was losing. All she had left to do was to lie on the cold floor, paralyzed by the thought that her father would return, ready to finish what he started. But worse than Charlie's wrath, she feared herself even more. She'd lost her moral compass by coming within inches of murdering her father. That was worse than any physical blow he'd landed.

When she sat up, figuring out how to explain it all away—the bullet hole, her injuries, the blood everywhere—the room started spinning. Darkness closed in on her, and despite her best efforts, she complied with her body's wishes and passed out.

"Penny! Penny! My God, what happened to you?" Bradley asked in a panic, stroking her cheek.

"B-Bradley?" Penny stuttered, confused by her surroundings.

"Don't move. I'm calling for help."

"No," she said, clutching his arm. Just the simple movement made her wince from pain. "I'm fine. Give me a minute."

"You're not fine. I need to get you to the hospital."

"What?" Penny asked, straining to hear him.

"I said I need to get you to the hospital."

"What are you doing here? How did you find me?"

"I waited at Saul's and got worried because you were late. I've been driving around, trying to find you. Then I came here. I knocked, but you didn't answer. So I looked in the window and saw you lying here."

"What time is it?"

"It's almost eight."

"What?"

"Eight. It's almost eight," he repeated. "What happened? Do you remember?"

A long silence ensued before Penny nodded, her chin quivering.

"Tell me," he commanded. "Why are you covered in blood?"

"Charlie." Her voice cracked from embarrassment.

"Your father did this to you? Where is he? I'll rip his head off!"

"No, Bradley. Please don't!" she wailed.

"What kind of man does this?" he yelled. "I'm calling the police!"

"No! You can't," Penny cried out as she managed the strength to sit up, only to collapse into his arms.

"Shh," he said, catching her, cradling her mangled body. "I've got you. I'm here now. He won't hurt you again. I promise. I'm going to grab the phone and call the police. Okay?"

"You can't call the police," she moaned.

"Don't worry. They'll be here in a few minutes."

"You can't call them."

"Why not?"

"If you do, they'll arrest me," she said in a small voice.

"What on earth could they arrest you for?"

"For... attempted murder," she said, weeping into his arms.

After a few minutes of uncontrollable crying, she calmed down enough to explain what had transpired with her father.

"Penny, he was beating you. You had to defend yourself. Don't you realize that man could have killed you? The police will understand," Bradley said.

"No. They won't. Ricky Lambert is the chief of police now, and he's Charlie's best friend. He's been covering up for him for years. Trust me. If I press charges, he could ruin my life."

"This is an open-and-shut case. You had no choice."

"No," she said, peering up at him. "Even if the police believe me, then what happens? The whole town will know what I'm capable of. And Emily, can you imagine what she'll say? She'll tell the whole school how I'm the girl she's been warning about all these years. My father beats me up, so I pull a gun on him? I mean, who does that, Bradley? Who points a gun at their own father and shoots?" She started crying again, not from the pain but from the shame. "And what if Belmont finds out? They're a Christian college. They won't want someone like me at their school. I'll lose my scholarship and my one chance to escape this hellhole." She sobbed. Tears mixed with blood streamed down her face.

"Calm down," Bradley said, pulling her in for a careful embrace. "Charlie has to pay for what he did to you. Everyone will understand."

"No. They won't. People will never look at me the same. They'll think I'm just as crazy as he is. No one can ever know what happened here. I need your help. Please."

"That's what I'm trying to do here. To help you."

"We can say I had some kind of accident running. You found me up on Beech Hill Way. I slipped on some gravel or something, and I fell into a ditch. Maybe landed on a rock. That could explain the blood," she said, her eyes darting back and forth as she tried to think of a way to cover her tracks.

"Penny..."

"No one would have to know. It was an accident. That's all. But the gun. I need help with the gun," she continued.

"This is crazy."

"Pops always keeps three bullets in his revolver, so if he checks, he'll know something's wrong. I need you to take out the used casing and go upstairs for another one. He keeps them in a closet. We need to replace the bullet I used on Charlie."

"Slow down."

Penny's eyes moved over Bradley's shoulder. "But the bullet hole. If we move that picture over a little to the left, it will cover it up. Ruby Ray never changes those pictures, so she'll never know the difference. But this room. We need to straighten it up. Clean up the blood."

"You're in shock. None of this is making sense."

So focused on the cover-up plan, Penny ignored his comment. "My jeans. They have blood all over them and probably gun residue. We'll have to throw them away. Besides, if I was out for a run, I would've been in shorts or sweatpants. Not jeans. I keep them in the bottom drawer of my bedroom. Can you grab me a pair?"

"Penny," he began, lowering his voice, trying once again to calm her. "Your father has to pay for what he did."

"It doesn't matter. All I need is for you to help me. Help me keep my secret. My scholarship. I have to get out of Camden, Bradley. Or I'll die," she said, breaking down completely.

"Okay. I'll help you," he said quietly. "I don't agree with this, but I'll do what you want."

"What?" she asked. Her hearing was becoming a concern.

"I said I will help you," he repeated, almost shouting.

"Thank you." She squeezed his arm, relieved that her dark secret would never see the light of day.

Springing into action, Bradley followed Penny's convoluted instructions on how to cover up the scene of the crime. After placing Pops's Colt revolver back in the drawer, loaded with three bullets instead of two, he moved to the wall. After finding a hammer in the basement, he rehung the family portrait to cover the bullet hole. He used a roll of paper towels to clean up the blood, which was puddled on Ruby Ray's shiny hardwood floors. Then he stuffed the evidence into a trash bag. After the room was back in order, he grabbed a pair of sweatpants for her to change into. When he finished dressing her, he picked up her up, cradling her in his arms, and carried her out to his car. In complete silence, other than her labored breaths, they made their way to the Liberty County ER.

"Just the person I wanted to talk to," Dr. Woodward said, motioning for Bradley to come into Penny's room. "Were you able to get ahold of Penny's kin while you waited?"

Clearing his throat, Bradley said, "I called her grandparents. They're on their way." Bradley looked at Penny. "My parents are coming too."

"That's good," Dr. Woodward said. "Family is important in a time like this."

Bradley nodded.

"Did you get something to eat as well?" she asked. "Our cafeteria isn't all that bad."

"I wasn't exactly hungry."

"I suppose not, after all your heroics tonight. Penny was just telling me how you searched for her when she didn't show up for your study date. She's lucky to have a friend like you."

Bradley nodded again.

"She also told me how she slipped on some gravel and fell into a ditch, landing on a rather large rock. Is that right?" Dr. Woodward asked, turning toward her.

"Yes, ma'am," Penny lied.

"Is that right, Bradley?"

"Yes, ma'am," he repeated.

"Here's the thing, though." Dr. Woodward narrowed her eyes. "Penny has several broken ribs. Four, in fact. On both her left *and* right sides. Just how many times did you land on that rock, Penny?"

"I-I don't know. M-Maybe I rolled on it a couple of times." Penny's pulse quickened. She hadn't thought that part of her story through.

"Must have been one hell of a rock to inflict this much damage. And your face. You have multiple lacerations on your forehead and one on your left lip, which I'm afraid is going to leave a pretty nasty scar. Not to mention the large hematoma forming around your jaw, and your torso is covered in bruises. Yet there're no cuts or scrapes on your legs. Or arms. Nothing on your hands, knees, or elbows. No dirt or mud from the ditch. How do you explain this?"

"I don't know. It all happened so fast," Penny said, her voice cracking.

"And did I mention you've ruptured your eardrum?" The doctor continued her interrogation. "Are you telling me a rock did that?"

"Yes, ma'am."

"I see." Dr. Woodward pursed her lips, staring a hole through Penny. "And, Bradley, how did you know where to look in the first place? Why that particular ditch? I mean, there're hundreds of ditches she could've fallen into. How did you even spot her? Especially at dusk?"

"I guess I was lucky."

"Lucky?" the doctor repeated incredulously. "Come on. We all know you're both lying. Penny's injuries are more in line with being beaten up rather than falling into a ditch. Look, I've known you both all your lives. You're good kids. I know that, but it's time to come clean. Tell me what really happened tonight." Genuine concern filled her voice.

The room was still, and Penny held her breath out of fear of discovery. The truth was about to come out. She was an attempted murderess being exposed under the glare of the cold fluorescent lights.

"We already did," Bradley said, breaking the silence. "It's simple. Penny was out on a training run. She's been pushing hard for State next month. Did you know she's got a real shot at a title in the thirty-two hundred?"

Dr. Woodward crossed her arms. "Go on."

"Somehow, Penny lost her footing on some gravel and slipped and fell into a ditch. That's all. Nothing more," he explained. A sudden rush of confidence and sincerity filled his voice. "I wouldn't lie about something like this."

"Is that the story you're sticking with, Bradley?" Dr. Woodward asked, one eyebrow raised.

"Yes, ma'am." He nodded.

"Are you sure?" Dr. Woodward asked slowly.

"It is."

"Well..." The doctor shook her head. "I guess Penny just slipped, then." Though she obviously didn't believe a word of it. "I hate to tell you this, Penny, but I'm afraid you won't be able to practice for a while. Competitive running and broken ribs don't mix. It'll take about six weeks to heal. By summertime, you'll be back to training."

An unspeakable disappointment shot through Penny's body after hearing the doctor's prognosis. Charlie had stolen yet another thing from her—State.

"Dr. Woodward." A young nurse poked her head through the curtain. "Miss Ray's grandparents are in the waiting room. They're real anxious to see her."

"Tell them I'm on my way to speak with them," she replied before taking Penny by the hand. "I'm admitting you to the hospital. Don't be scared, but you'll be here for a few days."

"Okay," Penny said, choking back tears. She'd never stayed in a hospital overnight, at least not in the traditional sense. Penny had spent countless nights on multiple green couches and unforgiving chairs in waiting rooms all around the Bluegrass State's finest health institutions in support of her sickly siblings, always the one standing vigil in their support. She'd never been the actual patient and was taken aback by the prospect.

"A plastic surgeon from Bowling Green is on his way to stitch you up," Dr. Woodward continued, breaking Penny's terrifying thoughts. "I'd do it myself if it weren't on your face, but this requires a specialist. Trust me. In a few years, you'll appreciate his work much more than mine. I've also called in a specialist to evaluate your eardrum. I'm afraid you might lose your hearing in that ear."

"Thank you," Penny said and swallowed hard. A scar was one thing to deal with, but to permanently lose a sense was quite another.

"And if you ever feel in danger of *tripping* again," the doctor continued, "here's my number." She placed a card at the foot of her hospital bed. "I'll make sure you're protected from loose gravel."

Those words caused Penny to lock eyes with Dr. Woodward for the first time. No longer was she the bland medical professional going through the motions of piecing a patient back together. The woman understood. Judging by the compassion pouring from her almond eyes and her spot-on questioning earlier, Penny concluded that perhaps her doctor knew a thing or two about the plight of a battered daughter from the hand of an alcoholic father.

Once the doctor left the room, Bradley rushed to Penny's side, and they held each other in a long embrace.

"Thank you," she whispered. "For protecting me."

"Always. I'll always protect you," he whispered back in her right ear. "I'm sorry about State."

She shook her head. "It doesn't matter. As long as I keep my scholarship, that's all I care about. I'm sorry about prom," she said, her voice quivering. The dance meant something to her.

"What do you mean?" he asked, releasing himself from their embrace to look her in the eye.

"I can't go to prom like this," she said, motioning to her bloody, swollen face. "You heard what Dr. Woodward said. I'm going to have some pretty big scars. Like some teenage Frankenstein's monster. Besides, Charlie stole the money for my dress. Who knows if I'll ever see a dime of it."

"Penny Ray, you're still the most beautiful girl in the world. Scars or no scars," he said, caressing her cheek. "Who cares what dress you wear to prom? As long as we're together, that's all that matters. Don't let him take this away from you too." He leaned in slowly and gave her a kiss on the lips. It was so soft and gentle that she was certain he feared he could shatter her broken body into a million pieces simply by touching her. And he was right. At that moment, she was as fragile as a robin's egg. But it wasn't just from what her father's cruel hand had done to her—it was what Bradley had seen. She feared he would never look at her the same again.

That night, after Penny implored her grandparents, most of the Ray and Hitchens families, Kelly, and even Coach McDonald to return home, Bradley snuck back into the hospital and into her room and her bed. Stroking her hair, he held her while she slept heavily because of a powerful potion of narcotics Dr. Woodward had prescribed. But what kept her in the hypnotic state, why Penny allowed herself to succumb to the drugs in the first place, was knowing her best friend was near.

July 2009
Camden, Kentucky

Chapter 15

Picture

P enny scrambles around Ruby Ray's house, trying to get ready for her dinner with Bradley. She's wasted the last hour sitting on the floor of her grandparents' bedroom, clutching her knees to her chest, rocking back and forth, and reliving that horrible day with Charlie. Though the memory is still raw and painful twenty years later, she's found a deep comfort in how wonderful, understanding, and protective Bradley was that day, the way he cared for her after he found her unconscious on her grandparents' floor. And most importantly, he's never spoken a word of it to anyone, keeping her secret until the end.

Having less than fifteen minutes to change clothes, freshen her makeup, and tame her frizzy locks, she does her best to look presentable. Thanks to the stifling Kentucky humidity, her hair now resembles a rabid Chia Pet. It's grown to twice its original size. Her smooth coif from this morning is long gone. She curses herself for not taking Dakota's advice and trying a Keratin treatment back in Atlanta to tame her tresses. A messy ponytail is the only option left, since she doesn't have the time or the energy to fight anymore. Because she wasn't expecting dinner dates with old flames while in Camden, she once again digs into the suitcase she's packed for Florida. A royal-blue knit sundress, her go-to for summer trips, since it never wrinkles, and she can dress it up or down, is the perfect choice. Along with her espadrilles from this morning, it's a fitting outfit for the occasion.

As Penny's new nemesis strikes five, the doorbell rings. Bradley's arrived, ready for his dinner demand. Taking in a long, deep breath to shake off her nerves, Penny makes her move to the door. Once she lays eyes upon him, however, that breath is stolen from her. Standing in the doorway with a crooked grin, he reminds her of the playful boy she was so hopelessly in love with all those years ago.

"Wow," Bradley says, admiring her. "You look stunning tonight, Penny. I've always loved you in blue."

A rush of heat strikes her face as she blushes like an awestruck schoolgirl. This time, there's no doubt he's flirting with her. "You're right on time," she says, redirecting attention from her burning cheeks.

"Of course. I'm a doctor. It's important to be punctual. Speaking of which, how's the tooth?"

"Ever the professional," she replies. "It's fine. No pain whatsoever."

"Good to hear."

"I see you have something behind your back." She points.

"Yes, I do," he says, pulling out a bunch of Ruby Ray's periwinkle hydrangeas. "I know they're not purple irises. Apparently, those went out of season a month ago. But I thought these were close enough. Besides, your grandmother's yard has always been my favorite florist in town. I've never been able to resist the urge to pick a flower or two."

"I remember." Penny giggles. "And so did she. I believe my grandmother caught you stealing from her a time or two. As I recall, she was as mad as a wet hen about your thievery."

"She gave me quite the tongue-lashing. But her granddaughter was always the recipient of my bounty, so that softened her a bit."

"Thank you for the beautiful flowers. You stole. From me. So thoughtful," she says, accepting them.

"You're welcome."

"Come on in. Let me put these in some water before we go."

Bradley follows her inside. "Wow. This house hasn't changed a bit in twenty years."

"More like forty," Penny says on her way to the kitchen.

"You've got a lot of packing to do." He looks around the cluttered living room. "How long are you in town?"

"Until the twenty-fourth. I should have the house cleared out by then. After that, I'm off to the Panhandle for a girls' trip." She walks back into the living room with the bouquet.

"I see you're on a tight schedule. Shocking." He chuckles.

"That, I am."

"Where are your boys? Don't you have three?"

"Yes, I do. Trey, Drew, and Sammy. They're with their father... and their new stepmother. On an African safari for the next twenty-one days. But who's counting."

He whistles. "Wow. Africa. That's a pretty big trip."

"That, it is. I've never been away from them more than a few days, so this is very new for me. Not being in constant mommy mode."

"Do you two get along? You and your ex?"

"Well, let's put it this way. My twelve-year-old is closer in age to his new stepmother than I am."

"Got it," he says, raising his eyebrows.

"Enough about Teddy. Are we ready to go? I have a ransom demand to fulfill, and as we both know, I'm on a tight schedule."

"Let's go." He laughs, opening the front door.

"Where's your car?" Penny asks, puzzled there's no vehicle in sight.

"I thought we could walk to my house."

"Beacon Hills is two miles from here," she replies. He moved back to his old neighborhood when he returned to Camden after dental school.

"Weren't you a distance runner back in the day? You can walk that in your sleep," he says, leading her down the street.

"We're really doing this? Walking?" she asks, not amused by his plan.

"Yep. We're walking."

"Okay," she says, glaring at her espadrilles, which are not ideal footwear for the occasion.

Making their way along the tree-lined sidewalk of Dogwood Lane, they pass five houses: 223, 221, 219, and 217. Though Penny is nervous, excitement brews inside her. Doing her best to contain both emotions, she keeps her eyes straight ahead, avoiding Bradley altogether and pretending she's calm, cool, and collected. In reality, she's a duck on a pond. To the outside world, she's gliding across the water, but underneath the surface, she's flailing around, trying her best to stay afloat.

Suddenly, Bradley stops in front of 215 Dogwood Lane and proclaims, "We're here."

A beautiful slate-blue Craftsman bungalow stands before her. "This is the Robertsons' place."

"Not anymore. It's the Hitchens abode now."

"Since when?"

He beams. "Bought it last October after Mr. Robertson moved to Lafayette to be with his son. It's the perfect location. My office is just up the street, in case I have dental emergencies. Did you know kettle corn is deadly around here?"

Ignoring his joke, Penny says, "So you're only five doors down from me."

"I guess that makes us neighbors. At least until you sell Ruby Ray's."

"You know, I've always loved this house. But I've never been inside," she says, admiring its beauty.

He guides her up the porch steps and opens the wooden door. "Well, that's about to change."

Walking in, Penny scans the space. She's immediately impressed by his decorative touches in the open living room and dining area. Though he's a single man, his taste is impeccable. He obviously learned a thing or two from his mother. "This is incredible."

"Thank you. I still have some work left, but I've enjoyed the process. Stripped all the hardwoods myself, painted everywhere, and I replaced all the fixtures. Even gutted the kitchen and the bathrooms. I'm pretty happy with it."

"You did it yourself? How did you find the time?"

"Well, my girls are older now. They don't need their old man as much as they used to." He chuckles. "Ace—I mean, Ashleigh Cate is in college up in Lexington. Just finished her first year, and Emeree Shae's in the middle of a dreaded teenage-drama-filled high school saga. It's like a soap opera. My baby's never home. So I've spent a lot of lonesome nights knee-deep in Sheetrock and polyurethane."

"It looks like you've put all those lonesome nights to good use."

"If you think my carpentry skills are something, wait until you try one of my steaks. I'm much better with a grill than I am with a hammer."

"A top chef too. You're full of surprises, aren't you?"

"Come on. Your dinner awaits," Bradley says, guiding her down the hall and into the kitchen. "Can I get you something to drink? Maybe a glass of wine before we head out to the deck and fire up the grill?"

"Thank you. I'd like that."

Bradley pulls a bottle of Duckhorn from his stainless-steel refrigerator. "You like sauvignon blanc, right?"

Penny shakes her head. "That's my favorite wine," she says, stunned by the coincidence. "How did you know?"

"I have a confession to make. I stole it." He laughs while removing the cork before pouring her a glass.

"You stole it?" Penny asks, pretending to be aghast by the notion.

"Well, I didn't steal it exactly. Your cousin did. I texted Jimmy Neal yesterday, explaining you were coming over for dinner. Since I didn't take you for a beer lover, I wanted to have something you'd like. So long story short, your cousin swiped a bottle of yours last night. No liquor stores in Bowling Green carry it. Trust me—I called around. Apparently, Penny Ray has expensive taste in wine."

"First my flowers and now my wine. Did you steal our steaks too?"

"Wouldn't you like to know." He pulls out a Coors Light and twists the top off before throwing it into the trash can in the corner. His irresistible dimple on his left cheek peeks through. "Come on. Let's go outside and get this ransom dinner started."

For the next hour, they spend the twilight of the afternoon enjoying their adult beverages on Bradley's wooden deck. While Penny sits in a chaise lounge at his insistence, watching thick clouds move in from the west, Bradley works the grill, searing their filets to the perfect temperature while taking sips of his beer. His eyes rarely leave hers.

Sitting down at a small table with twinkling white lights strung overhead—his daughters' decorative touch, he explains—they toast their meal. Feasting on the delectable dinner of medium-rare peppered filets and grilled corn on the cob, they catch up. Penny lovingly speaks of her adventures in raising three rambunctious boys. Broken bones, trips to batting cages, and SpongeBob fill her days. Bradley regales her with his exploits in braiding, mastering both French and fishtails, before explaining his daughters' former love for Dora, who was much more than an explorer in his mind. Later, she confesses her unexpected love of Atlanta, traffic and all. Somehow, she's even found a way to support UGA football. Chiding her for her foolish devotion to the Bulldogs, Bradley reminds Penny that the Cats are always superior in all sports.

Surprisingly, it's been a relaxing evening for Penny. The embarrassment she experienced at Farley's less than twenty-four hours ago has dissipated. However, the waistline of her dress is tightening. Kentucky's doing a number on her willpower. Under normal circumstances, she would vow to rectify her caloric lapse with another brutal run tomorrow morning. However, all she can do is bask in the glory of her food coma, enjoying the ride.

Bradley pours Penny another glass of wine. "So do you miss it? Being a teacher?"

Penny swirls the yellow liquid in her goblet. This has been a sore subject for her for years. "Part of me does. Don't get me wrong—nothing's more fulfilling than staying home with my boys, but deep down, I miss the classroom. It's magical when you see the look on a student's face when they fall in love with a certain book or when they make a connection with a writer's work you know is about to knock their socks off."

"You always did have your head stuck in a book throughout high school."

She smiles. "Yes, I did."

"Then why don't you go back?" He takes a long pull of his beer.

"Back to teaching?"

"Yes."

Penny sets down her glass. "Two words. Divorce decree."

Bradley raises his eyebrows.

"I can't go back to full-time employment until Sammy starts school, and that's not for another two years."

"Why does your ex-husband get to have that power over you?"

Penny sighs. "Because it's what he genuinely craves, and it's easier to go along rather than fight it. Besides, I can't be too upset. The money I received from the divorce allows me to live comfortably enough that I don't need a job. At least Teddy saw to that."

"Sounds like a swell guy," Bradley says.

"Enough about my ex. Let's talk about this dinner, which was delicious." She leans back, satisfied from another filling meal.

"See? An evening with me wasn't so bad after all. Was it?"

"It's been lovely," she says shyly, her face heating once again. "We're even now. Your blackmail has been paid in full."

"I prefer the term barter. Remember?"

A smile takes over Penny's face. "Barter, it is. If that lets you sleep at night."

"Oh, I sleep like a rock," Bradley counters. "No problem there."

"I bet."

"Would you like a cup of coffee with dessert?"

"Dessert?" Penny tries to regain her wits. "I don't think I can eat another bite."

"It's a peach cobbler."

"You made a cobbler?" she asks, incredulous at the thought.

"I think you know me better than that." He grins. "I can grill, but I'm no baker. Miss Paulette donated it. She even brought over a gallon of Breyers to top it off."

"Vanilla bean or extra creamy?"

"Better," he says. "Butter pecan."

"Of course it is." Penny can only shake her head. Butter pecan is her favorite flavor. Bradley's remembered her sugary kryptonite, and he's using it against her. "Well, I could never resist a cobbler from a long-lost family member. I'll have a small helping. But first I'm cleaning up these dishes."

"Not on your life."

"I insist. I can't leave you with this mess."

"You're my guest."

"Please."

"Okay. I'll make an exception for you. But first, dessert. These dishes can wait a few more minutes. Don't go anywhere," he says before heading into the kitchen.

Now alone, Penny stands up to stretch her legs. A small stroll around the wooden deck will give her stomach a little relief from the heavy meal and help make a little room for the buttery treat coming her way. Walking along the edge of the deck, she looks out into the backyard. Bradley has quite the green thumb. Six large terracotta planters fill the space. They're overflowing with red geraniums, white impatiens, vinca vines, asparagus ferns, and creeping Jenny. They're a wonderful combination of annuals. Then she spies another row of white lights twinkling in the corner of the yard. Next to a row of magnolias, they're dangling from the branches of two lavender crape myrtle trees, creating a little outdoor living room. A hearty Japanese maple next to an iron settee complements the area, while four teak chairs surround a stone fire pit. The place is perfect for a family to enjoy.

For a moment, she allows herself to imagine Bradley and his girls enjoying a fall evening here. Wrapped in plaid flannel blankets with burgundy leaves falling from the maple's branches surrounding them, they roast hot dogs and marshmallows on wooden sticks, laughing and sharing stories. Maybe they cut their jack-o'-lanterns there each October, next to a roaring fire, hints of hickory burning in the night air and clinging to their sweaters and knit hats like a sweet perfume. Maybe his girls scatter handfuls of the seeds along the fence row in hopes a new pumpkin might grow next year. Her boys always tried the same thing every Halloween at their old house. So taken with her imaginary vision of Bradley's family, she doesn't hear his return to the deck.

"A penny for your thoughts," he says softly.

Startled by his words, Penny quickly turns around, embarrassed at being caught daydreaming about him. In her rush to recover from her momentary lapse, her left espadrille catches the ridge in the deck, causing her ankle to twist and her balance to fail. Stumbling, she falls into Bradley's arms and into two heaping bowls of Miss Paulette's sublime dessert.

"Oh my god. I didn't hear you." Penny gasps, noticing their bodies are now stuck together from all the sugar his dental assistant has dumped into her concoction. Twenty years have passed since their last embrace, and that's more startling than being covered in gooey filling and buttery crust. However, Penny doesn't pull away from him. Nor does Bradley try to release her. They stand there, frozen.

"Are you always this accident prone, Penny Ray, or just with me?"

Once again, Penny's cheeks betray her.

As she stares up into his hazel eyes, her heart melts faster than the ice cream covering her favorite sundress. "I guess it's something about Kentucky," she whispers.

"I'm beginning to regret my decision to warm up that cobbler."

"Why?"

"Because there's a hot peach in a place no fruit should ever be," he says, his left dimple peeking through. Finally, the moment breaks, and they begin laughing at their predicament.

"I'm definitely having a problem with food this week," she says, breaking away from his arms.

"First kettle corn, now cobbler," Bradley says, grabbing a napkin from the table and offering it to her while neglecting his own clothing. "I can't wait to see what's next."

"I bet." She smiles while trying to rid herself of the dessert covering her body. "I'm a mess. I don't think a piece of cloth is going to rectify my situation. May I use your powder room instead?"

"Why don't you use the girls' bathroom upstairs? It's much nicer, and because they're gone, I'm certain it's clean. For once."

Relieved, she says, "Thank you," while carefully scooping up the bottom of her dress in an attempt to contain the mess. She wouldn't dare leave a trail of little peach pieces around his home like a Southern Hansel and Gretel.

"It's the second door on the right," he tells her.

Now that a graceful exit is impossible, she scurries off the deck toward the wooden L-shaped staircase, hoping to salvage her dress—and maybe a little dignity in the process.

Once upstairs, Penny begins searching for the right door. So flustered, she's forgotten Bradley's simple directions. Opening the first door she comes to, she discovers a bedroom instead. Judging by the wooden ES sign hanging on the wall, she assumes it's his youngest daughter's room. Obviously, Emeree Shae is a big UK fan, just like her dad. It's dripping with blue-and-white checkerboard. A poster of Walter McCarty dunking over a hapless guy from Vanderbilt hangs above a wicker bed along with seven banners commemorating the school's national championships in basketball. Closing the door, Penny smiles, realizing Bradley has raised a true fan who respects the old regime of players.

Then she spots another door. This time, she's greeted by a violet bedroom that must be Ace's. Completely different from her little sister's shrine to Kentucky, it's tastefully decorated, from the Laura Ashley down comforter and matching floral curtains to the carefully creased pillows in the window seat. Over the white iron bed is a shrine to her sorority, Delta Delta Delta, along with her pledge class composite. The walls are covered in bulletin boards full of dried-up corsages from high school dances, concert tickets, and cheerleading ribbons, while her desk and dressers are full of framed pictures of friends.

As Penny's about to leave, continuing her quest to find the girls' bathroom, a picture on Ashleigh Cate's bedside table catches her eye. Though she knows it's wrong to invade the girl's sanctuary, Penny can't help herself. For some reason, she's drawn to the eight-by-ten photograph like a moth to a flame. A closer look is needed. Approaching, she sees it's of a baby dressed in an exquisite white smocked dress. Her tiny head rests upon a woman's chest. The woman is wearing a matching long white gown. The two look identical, down to their inescapable blond locks. The photo is an exquisite display of affection between the two, showing the unbreakable bond of mother and daughter. Leaning in, Penny stares at the woman Bradley chose and who gave birth to his two beautiful daughters. The one he vowed before God he would love, honor, and cherish— Emily Johnston.

Nausea rushes over Penny, and warm tears fall down her cheeks. It's been twenty years since she last laid eyes upon Emily. Back then, all Penny could see was the cruel and merciless teenager. Now, all she sees is the loving and devoted mother. *The wife.*

So focused on her face, Penny doesn't hear Bradley come up the steps.

"There you are," he says, walking into the room. "I was afraid you got lost. You've been gone ten minutes."

Surprised at being caught in Ace's bedroom uninvited and embarrassed by how long she's been upstairs, Penny knocks the photograph off the table, and it tumbles to the ground. Quickly, she bends down to pick it up, trying to cover for her mistake.

Noticing what she's seen, Bradley rushes to her side. "Penny, I'm so sorry."

Penny stares down at the photo of her childhood tormentor as she holds it in her shaking hand. "I shouldn't be in here," she whispers.

"I completely forgot about that. Ace loves it."

"It's a beautiful picture," she says, still gazing at it, before clearing her throat. "I'm so sorry for your loss, Bradley. It must have been hard on you when she died."

His jaw tightens. "The girls miss their mother."

"I'm sure they do. It's hard growing up without one." Her voice quivers, for she has first-hand knowledge on that front.

"Penny." Bradley reaches toward her face to wipe away her tears, which he's caused. "I need to explain something to you."

Recoiling from his touch and especially his explanation, she stands up and places the photograph back on the table. "We'd better get to those dishes," she tells him, desperate to get as far away from Ace's room or any more talk of Emily as possible. Before Bradley can say another word, Penny's halfway down the steps, making her way to the kitchen. The last thing in the world she wants to do is relive that night.

In keeping with her word, Penny stays long enough to do the dishes, though every fiber in her body screams to run back to Ruby Ray's, bury herself under her Lonestar quilt, and call it a night. For twenty minutes, they work in awkward silence, still covered in cobbler, side by side at his farm sink. Penny washes while Bradley dries. The easy, flirtatious repartee from earlier is long gone. In its place is an uncomfortable iciness.

"That's the last one," she says, handing him a ceramic serving bowl for his finishing touch.

A long silence follows before thunder begins rumbling in the distance, breaking the moment. In unison, they look toward the kitchen window to see what's heading their way. Now their attention is focused on the brewing storm outside while they avoid the one brewing within.

Sensing an opportunity to escape, Penny says, "I'd better get going before it starts to storm. I overheard some people saying at church today that we're in for some bad weather tonight."

"Let me grab an umbrella. I'll walk you back."

"No. You stay here. It's just a little drizzle. It's so close that I'll be back at Ruby Ray's in no time."

"It's getting dark, it's starting to rain, and I hear thunder. I won't take no for an answer."

Though it will take her only a couple of minutes to walk home, Penny agrees to his gentlemanly request. If she argues the point now, she'll be wasting her time and breath.

A rush of cool air with hints of petrichor greet them as he opens the front door. Bradley opens his mammoth golf umbrella, and they make their way down the street in complete silence. Instead of the excitement of earlier, the journey back to 225 Dogwood Lane is a dreary affair. Twenty years of resentment, hurt, and misunderstanding have ruined the evening.

"Thank you for walking me back," Penny says, fumbling with her keys before unlocking the front door. "You've always had a penchant for protecting me."

A deep sadness fills his eyes. "Not always."

Those words are too painful to address now, so she ignores them. Desperate to change the subject, she says, "Look, I'm glad I got to see you again, Bradley. Even if I had to break a tooth in the process. Really. It's been too long."

Sorrow clouds his face. "Yes, it has."

Another long and awkward pause ensues as they stare at each other in silence.

"Well, I guess this is goodbye, then," she says, smiling. Without thinking, she reaches up to give him a small send-off hug. The instant she touches him, she regrets her decision. As she places her arms around his neck, his soft scruff brushes her cheek, sending a tingle down her spine and a flutter into her stomach. Now his succulent lips are resting next to her ear, and she can feel his warm breath upon her neck, causing her skin to prickle and her eyes to widen. She's trapped in his arms once again, this time by her own doing.

As she's about to pull away, Bradley whispers, "I never meant to hurt you, Penny. It was the biggest mistake of my life."

Those simple words of regret crush her. She's always hoped he felt that way about that night twenty years ago, but hearing it from his lips causes her to melt into his arms. Closing her eyes, she says, "I know, Bradley. I know."

Letting out a long sigh, he lowers his head deep into Penny's shoulder, pulling her body closer to his. Though her mind tells her to push him away, her body refuses. Instead, she relaxes into his arms, resting her head against his. The familiar scent of musk and amber from Bradley's hair floats in the air. Penny inhales a long, deep breath of the intoxicating aroma. He smells the same as he did in high school, the way he did during their first kiss. *Would his tongue taste the same too?* Soon, before Penny knows what's happening, her fingers are running through his hair while his lips brush across her collarbone. The delicate touch causes the tingle from her spine to travel much deeper into her body. A warm flush of excitement rushes between her legs, causing her to gasp.

As another roll of thunder claps in the distance, and the rain begins pouring, Bradley's lips find their way to her neck. At first, his kisses are soft like a butterfly's wings, almost tickling her. But soon, they grow more urgent, his mouth more passionate. As he makes his way to her right ear, his breath grows warmer, while his tongue deliciously teases her. When he reaches her flushed cheeks, which are burning from excitement, Penny knows he's coming for her lips next. As she's about to open her mouth and take him in, the photograph from earlier floods her mind. Though she tries, she can't banish the image of Emily. The pain from that night all those years ago consumes her. Grabbing him by the nape of his neck, she pulls his left ear to her lips.

"I can't do this again," she whispers, her chin trembling. "I can't let you back in."

In a low voice, he says, "I know."

With tears flooding her eyes, she says, "Goodbye, Bradley."

Chapter 16

Stormy Weather

Penny once again scrambles around Ruby Ray's living room, this time trying to settle herself after her evening with Bradley. Ashamed, aroused, and longing for more, she left him on her grandmother's front porch in a thunderstorm an hour ago. God only knows what he's thinking. A simple dinner went off the rails over one photograph. But it wasn't just a picture—it was a haunting reminder of Emily Johnston, the person who'd changed both their lives.

To squelch her thoughts of Bradley, freeing both her mind and body from lusting after him, she decides to spend the rest of the evening packing. Instead of going back into her grandparents' emotional booby trap of a bedroom, this time, she'll focus on her own, the one her grandparents had given her after she'd been left homeless by Zelda. She might run across a few embarrassing yearbooks or a couple of reminders of her unfortunate eighties fashion choices. Maybe she will discover some old Belmont sweatshirts or perhaps a few ribbons from her running days but nothing that would send her into a tailspin like Pops's revolver did earlier. This room will be easy to sort through.

After removing her sticky clothing covered in ice cream and changing back into her packing clothes, she finishes the room in less than two hours. All the contents have been boxed, tagged, or thrown away. Only her suitcases and the cherry bedroom suite remain. So focused on her work, Penny didn't even notice the first round of thunderstorms that pounded the foursquare with torrential rain or the dozens of lightning strikes. That in itself was a godsend. She's hated thunderstorms since childhood because of their unpredictability.

Before she can move on to another room, she has one final job left. Fearing Ruby Ray has stuffed even more clutter underneath her bed and behind the lace bed skirt, she crawls on her stomach to check. Much to her surprise, Penny's greeted with one single shoe-box. However, it's out of arm's reach.

Penny tries to squeeze into the tiny space to reach the box and hits her head against the bedframe.

"Shit."

Once her vision returns, she recognizes what she's latched on to. Once upon a time, it belonged to her. Gazing down at the azure-and-silver box, which is decorated with stickers and hearts, Penny is left speechless. The last time she saw it, twenty years ago, was when she threw it and all its contents into the garbage in a fit of unbridled hurt and rage. She never thought she'd see it again, but here it is, resting in her hands. Though she knows she should throw it away a second time, she can't resist taking one last peek.

Lifting the lid, Penny finds a teenage shrine dedicated to Bradley. Slowly, she removes the items in the box one by one, each object bringing back a unique time-stamped memory from their love story: pressed flowers he gave her, silly notes he wrote, and ticket stubs from all the movies they watched together. She kept it all. Digging further, she comes upon dozens of photographs of them, from their track team picture for the yearbook to a Polaroid of him playing basketball in his driveway, which she took while her mother cleaned his house.

However, one photograph in particular catches her attention, one of a young Penny and Bradley standing underneath a white archway covered with ivy and red roses. A Class of 1989 banner hangs in the background. She picks up the prom night photo to take a closer look. The periwinkle dress, which she'd worked so hard to buy, is still as exquisite as she remembers. But even a dress that beautiful couldn't hide her face covered in yellow bruises and pink scars.

Shuddering at her younger self, she begins to toss the photograph back into the box, closing it forever, but something stops her. The corner of a baby-blue book peeks from under a stack of newspaper clippings of Bradley's athletic endeavors. Instantly, Penny knows it's the journal she kept throughout high school. Writing down your secret thoughts as a hormonal teenager is a recipe for disaster, a treasure trove for nosy mothers snooping around for details on their daughter's exploits. Fortunately for Penny, Zelda didn't care what she did, and she's certain Ruby Ray would never pry into her diary. After opening the book, she begins turning the pages, forgetting how much she naively divulged.

March 10, 1986

She's done it again. Zelda has wrecked another one of her marriages, and she's getting divorced. Again. For the fourth time. Shouldn't the government step in and take away her ability to get married? How many times can they stand by and let her wreak havoc on another idiotic man? She's out of control. Babbling Bruce lasted all of five months. They got married in October. Now she's dropped him for a truck driver. I can't say I blame her, though. Bruce never shut up, because he loved the sound of his own voice.

Of course, Emily's eating it up. Today in the cafeteria, she started singing the chorus to "Maneater." I wanted to die. After the vile song, which she shared with the entire freshman class, she went on and on about how my mother has broken up another marriage. Zelda's the town's biggest slut, after all. A statue should be erected in her honor. Then Emily repeated her favorite line. The one I've heard hundreds of times. "The apple doesn't fall far from the tree." Obviously, I sleep

around too. Like my mother. Why won't she leave me alone? What did
I ever do to her other than give her imaginary lice?

But I swear this to God or whatever is in the great beyond, I will
never *become Zelda. I will save myself, my virginity, for my husband.*
And I will never get divorced. Ever. I'll prove Emily wrong.

September 16, 1986

I've officially moved in with Ruby Ray and Pops. Zelda has moved
to Hopkinsville with Terry the Trucker. She's gone for now. Two hours
away. I guess I won't see her very much anymore, and I hate to admit it,
but I'm relieved. At least Emily has lost one of her best insult generators.
Farewell, Zelda!

November 13, 1986

Bradley got his driver's license today! He passed with flying colors. I
still have another year to go before I get mine. A fact he keeps reminding
me of. But that's not the best part because newsflash, he wants to take
me out this weekend for dinner and a movie! This will be my first date...
ever.

November 15, 1986

Wow! Tonight was the greatest night of my life. My first date!

Bradley took me to Bowling Green, and we had dinner at Raffer-
ty's. I've never been there before. Ruby Ray says it's too overpriced for
its own good, and nobody with a lick of sense needs to spend more than
eight dollars on a meal. After I scanned the menu, I decided to order
the house salad with water, since it was the cheapest thing I could find,
because Bradley insisted on paying. But it was delicious. Croutons, lit-

tle tomatoes, real bacon, and Thousand Island dressing. It's now my favorite meal.

After dinner, we went to the mall to catch Stand by Me. *I've been talking about the novella nonstop since last summer. How much I loved it. I guess he wanted to see what all the fuss was about.*

During the part in the movie where Chris tells Gordie how he hates his family because they embarrass him, Bradley reached over and touched my hand. He knows I have the same complicated feelings about my parents. After that, he didn't let go for the rest of the movie.

Driving home, we listened to Elton John the whole way. I think "Tiny Dancer" might be my new favorite song. Since Ruby Ray gave me an eleven o'clock curfew, and because we still had an hour left to kill, we drove over to the Camden Swim and Golf Club. We jumped into his dad's golf cart and started driving around the course. It was so exciting.

When I started shivering from the cold, or maybe it was from my nerves, Bradley stopped and offered me his letterman's jacket. After he wrapped it around my shoulders, and I thanked him, he leaned in and kissed me. I mean, he really kissed me. We kissed forever. I could've stayed there all night.

August 15, 1988

Today sucked. Sorry for the offensive and juvenile language, but I can find no better words to describe my day. I officially became a senior in high school. A new start, a new school year, a new beginning. But it doesn't feel new to me. I'm still the recipient of every cruel and callous joke Emily Johnston can throw at me. This girl will not let up. I mean, it's been five years already! I pray she tires of me, but I have a feeling she never will.

Today's barrage of insults was twofold, courtesy of both my parents. Zelda's latest affair with our town's mayor has been exposed. That's right—when my mother's fifth marriage didn't work out, she moved back to Camden, looking for fresh meat. Thank God she's kept her distance, but her exploits still haunt me. Now, she's moving to Panama City to start a new life with the disgraced politician, leaving behind his wife and four kids. Emily loved bringing that up. Remember the apple?

Then she moved on to Charlie's arrest last week. He went to jail for public intoxication at the soda counter in O'Donnell's, and he was drunker than Cooter Brown. Not drunk as a skunk, as if those creatures were known for their addictive tendencies. Not even drunk to high heaven, as if God wanted to be brought into estimating someone's sobriety. No, Charlie was on the Cooter Brown level. He was so hammered that he couldn't remember his name. Of course, Ruby Ray bailed him out. I would've left him there to rot, if it was up to me.

But Bradley, like always, came to my defense, telling Emily to back off. He even got her to apologize to me. He still thinks there's hope for her. But as we turned to walk away, Emily flipped me the bird.

Bradley's been a lifesaver this summer, and we've been getting closer. We spend all our free time together, running, studying, and making out like rabbits. But I'm starting to think he's getting impatient with me. Not that he ever complains, but I think he wants more than just long kisses and a couple of trips to third base every now and then. He wants to sleep with me. I can see it every time we stop from crossing that line. The pain and frustration in his eyes. But I can't do it. I can't sleep with him. I can't become Zelda. I hope he waits for me.

April 19, 1989
   I got out of the hospital this morning.
   Four days and thirty-nine stitches later, I'm home.
   Charlie Ray did this.
   He stole my money then beat me.
   I grabbed Pops's gun, and I pulled the trigger.
   There's a bullet hole in the wall to prove it.

I almost killed my father.
I wanted to kill my father.
I made Bradley lie for me.
I'm a terrible person.
Can life get any worse?

May 7, 1989

Last night was my senior prom. I had my doubts about going in the first place. My face hasn't healed, and no amount of makeup can hide what Charlie did to me, but Bradley and Ruby Ray insisted I go and enjoy myself.

Luckily, I was still able to buy my dress. Charlie returned half my money last week. I doubt I'll ever see the rest.

After we got to the gymnasium, I was surprised I was having so much fun. We took pictures. Danced a little. It was a good night until you-know-who showed up with her mindless groupies. After Bradley left to grab some punch, Emily started in. She told everyone I was wearing a "used" prom dress from a knocked-up Sonic carhop. A hand-me-down, of all things. "How embarrassing," she kept repeating. Then she moved on to my face. She even gave me a little nickname, Scarface. Her friends loved that. In no time, it'd spread around the gym like wildfire.

As if my night couldn't get any worse, then came the announcement of prom king and queen. You'll never guess whose names they called out. Bradley Hitchens and Emily Johnston. I watched as they were crowned on stage by our principal. As if that weren't bad enough, next came their dance. The whole school was forced to watch.

On her way to the center of the gym, Emily stopped and winked at me before giving me a smile on that smug face of hers. I wanted to die rather than watch her dance with Bradley, but that's where my night changed. Instead of following Emily, he grabbed my hand and led me into the circle. My legs were shaking. I didn't know what to do.

There were the three of us, standing in front of the whole school. Then he wrapped his hands around my waist, and we started dancing, leaving Emily all alone, completely embarrassed. I think it was the first time in her life she was truly speechless. She ran off crying.

I decided right then and there I will finally give myself to Bradley Hitchens. When I told him, he whispered into my ear and told me he loved me. It was the best moment of my life.

May 8, 1989

Shannon Madison admitted to Mr. Woods this morning she helped Emily rig the vote for prom king and queen. Emily will be in his office first thing Monday for her punishment. Can life get any better?

July 4, 1989

I'm an idiot! I broke up with Bradley an hour ago. Tonight was going to be the night I was giving my virginity to him. I thought I was ready. I really did. But I backed out at the last second.

Bradley's been planning this night all summer. He even picked the spot, on a blanket at the Camden golf course, under the stars. The same place as our first kiss. It was perfect, and now I've ruined it.

We were so close, but all I could think about was Zelda and how I don't want to be like her. I panicked. I told him to stop. Our relationship had gotten too intense for me. I needed some space. He begged me to reconsider. Not about sleeping with him but about taking a break. He kept telling me he didn't want to lose me, but I refused. I told him to leave me alone. He never said another word to me after that. Nothing when we got dressed. Not even on the ride home. Silence.

I can't believe I've lost him. What's wrong with me? What am I going to do?

July 11, 1989

 It's been a week, and I haven't spoken to Bradley once. He won't re-turn my calls. I miss him.

July 20, 1989

 I had an epiphany last night. Big word, I know, but in eleven days, I'll be a college undergrad. It dawned on me I've been so hell-bent on, so consumed by, preserving my virginity so that I can prove to the world, prove to Emily, that I'm nothing like Zelda that I totally forgot why I wanted to give it to Bradley in the first place. Because I love him. It's that simple.

 I never asked him what he wanted. I never asked if he would wait for me. He went along with my wishes. But what about his wishes? What about his needs? It's like I used my virginity as a shield, protecting me from becoming my mother's daughter by getting the same reputation as her, so I ended up using it as a weapon. Dangling it in front of him. I've been so selfish.

 It was my idea to have sex in the first place. I told him I wanted to sleep with him at prom. Not the other way around. He never pushed me. He waited. He's waited for years.

 Bradley has loved, protected, and lied for me. He's seen me at my worst, and he's never left my side. I love him.

 I will no longer be consumed with my reputation, Zelda, those damned apples, or Emily Johnston.

 I pray I can make it right before I leave for Nashville.

July 24, 1989

I've become so desperate that I've resorted to writing letters to Bradley, since he won't return my calls. I've apologized, again and again, for my behavior that night. Still, no reply. It's like he's dropped off the face of the planet. Other than camping outside his house and stalking him, I don't know what to do.

July 27, 1989

    I've officially retired as a carhop. My days at Sonic are over. I can hang up my roller skates for good. Tonight, the owners threw me a going-away party before I waited on my last customer of the evening, Shannon Madison. How fitting that one of Emily's minions would be the bookend to my career. When I saw her sitting in her new Camaro, I prepared myself for yet another one of her assaults. She's learned from the best, after all. But instead of accosting me, she apologized. I think she used the words "That was so high school. It was a lifetime ago," even though it's only been six weeks since graduation. I guess people can change.

    No word on the Bradley front. I've become so desperate to make things right between us that I've recruited Jimmy Neal to speak on my behalf. They're about to be roommates at UK in a few weeks. Maybe he can get through to him. I've invited Bradley over to Ruby Ray's Sunday night for one final apology. Or at the very least, we can say a proper goodbye before he goes to Lexington and I head off for Nashville. Maybe he'll accept my offer.

July 31, 1989

    Bradley was a no-show last night. I guess he's moved on. I can't blame him. I broke it off with him. Not the other way around.

I'm leaving in a few minutes for Belmont. This will be my last entry for a while. Sorry I can't take you with me, but I've never met my room-mates before. I can't trust you with anyone. You've been a friend to me. I know you're only paper, but you've provided a safe place. A place to share my feelings. I'll miss you.

October 8, 1989
 Goodbye, Bradley Hitchens.

After Penny reads her words from twenty years ago, she closes the journal and clutches it close to her chest. Memories from that day come flooding back to her as if it were yesterday. On one of the worst days ever, an unexpected visitor showed up, giving her news that changed her life forever.

October 8, 1989
Camden, Kentucky

Chapter 17

Don't Shoot the Messenger

"Jimmy Neal? What on earth are you doing here?" Penny exclaimed, jumping out of Pops's old Ford truck. After sprinting up the steps of Ruby Ray's porch, she gave her beloved cousin a long hug. It had been two months since she'd last seen him, when she'd set off to Nashville and he for Lexington, going their separate ways on their paths to higher education.

"Hey, cuz," he said, giving her an extra squeeze. "I was in the neighborhood, so I thought I'd stop by."

"In the neighborhood? Yeah, right. You're only off by a few hundred miles. Seriously, why are you in Camden?"

"Came home to see you."

"Me? How did you know I was back in town?"

"Ruby Ray told Momma that you were coming home to celebrate her birthday. Yours too," he explained uncomfortably. "Happy birthday, by the way."

"Thanks." She laughed.

"How's the season going?" he asked, though it seemed he had other things on his mind.

"Well…" She sighed. "I've discovered I'm a mediocre college runner at best. I'm there to help the team with points. That's about it. My coach is great, and I love my teammates. That helps with my athletic limitations."

"So you're happy in Nashville?" he asked while fiddling with a stray maple leaf. He seemed off.

"I am. It's different from Camden. It's so big. I'm still getting used to the traffic, and I get lost at least three times a week. But I miss home. I miss my friends. I miss you," she said. *I miss Bradley.*

"I've missed you too," he said, giving her another quick embrace.

"What about you? How's UK?"

"I like it, but it's harder than I expected. I'll manage," he said.

"Well, I'm glad to see you, but you still haven't told me why you're here. I don't think you drove two hours just to wish me a happy birthday. You know you could've called or sent a card. That would've been easier."

"This isn't about your birthday," he confessed before closing his eyes. "Bradley sent me."

Hearing his name caused her heart to skip a beat. Since leaving Camden back in July, she'd thought of him nonstop. Though Jimmy Neal was his roommate, Penny vowed never to put him in the middle of their "relationship" again after Bradley ignored her invitation to say goodbye.

"Why did he send you? If he has something to say to me, maybe he should do it himself," she replied with sudden bitterness. Deep down, she was outraged Bradley had sent someone to do his bidding. Not to mention he'd gone radio silent for three months, never answering the dozens of letters she'd written him. He didn't even have the courtesy to call her back after the innumerable messages she'd left with his mother and sister.

"Let's sit down," Jimmy Neal said, leading her by the hand.

Her pulse quickened. *No conversation ends well when someone asks you to sit.*

"I don't even know where to start." He shook his head and gave a nervous laugh she'd never heard before.

"You're scaring me. Spit it out, Jimmy Neal."

"Do you remember last summer?" he asked, composing himself.

"Of course I remember. It just happened," she said, frustrated.

Jimmy Neal steadied himself before closing his eyes. "Do you remember the night of the Fourth of July?"

Instantly, Penny's heart sank. The Fourth of July had been on a continuous loop in her mind for months. Why her cousin, of all people, was bringing it up caused her pulse to go into overdrive.

Heat ran up her neck. "Yes," she said, her nostrils flaring. "Why are you asking about it?"

"Because a few days ago, Bradley told me what happened between the two of you that night. He told me everything."

She cocked her head. "What did he tell you?"

"He told me how you were going to take your relationship...to the next level." He obviously chose his words with the utmost care to avoid embarrassing her further.

"I can't believe this. Why did he tell you those things?" She shook her head.

"Let me finish," he said, placing his hand upon hers. "There was a big party that night at the Spillway. After Bradley dropped you off, he met up with some of us. The second we saw him, we knew something was wrong. He wasn't acting like himself. Wouldn't talk to anybody. Didn't want to joke around. All he wanted to do was drink."

Penny stiffened. "Bradley was drinking?"

"Only a beer, maybe two. He didn't really have the chance to get wasted, because a few minutes after he got there, a bunch of sheriff deputies showed up."

"The police were called?"

"Yeah. Lights, sirens, yelling for us to freeze. The whole nine yards. I guess it wasn't the smartest place to have a party. On state property during a holiday."

"Then what happened?" Penny asked.

"Well, we all panicked, since our asses were about to be thrown in jail for underage drinking. We ran to our cars to leave, but some of them were blocked by the police. We were trapped. Bradley's was one of them, so he jumped into the first one he could."

"I don't understand why you're telling me all this."

"Because it was Emily's car he got into. She was the one who drove him home that night."

Penny froze, unable to respond.

"There's no way to sugarcoat this, so I'm just going to say it." He covered his face with his hands. "They ended up *together* that night."

All the blood in Penny's body went cold. At that moment, she realized what her cousin was trying to explain. Bradley, the person she loved with her whole heart, had slept with Emily Johnston.

"No," she whispered.

Jimmy Neal moved closer. "That's the reason he didn't return any of your calls. Why he wouldn't see you before you left for college. Because he was so ashamed about what he did. He hates himself."

"I don't believe this."

"I know. I didn't believe it when he told me either."

"No. I mean I don't believe it happened. Bradley would never do that. Not with her." Penny's eyes pleaded with Jimmy Neal's.

"Penny. It happened."

"If Emily slept with him, trust me—she would've bragged about it all around town. Made certain that I knew. Of all the things in the world she can hurt me with, this is it. No way she could've kept this a secret."

"Maybe she's too embarrassed to talk about it."

Penny snorted. "Embarrassed? Emily Johnston? I doubt it."

"I don't think it worked out the way she planned."

"What does that even mean?" she shot back. "Why didn't she shout it from the rooftops?"

"Maybe because she knew his heart wasn't in it. You're the one he loves. She knows that. Hell, the whole town knows it. I guess that's not something she wants to go bragging about. How she was second to you again. Especially in that situation."

Nausea rolls through Penny's body. "Why didn't he tell me himself? Why send you? Or better yet, why even tell me in the first place?" she said, her voice breaking.

"On Thursday, Bradley's parents came up to see him," Jimmy Neal began. "Mr. and Mrs. Johnston came along too." The muscle in his jaw twitched.

"So? Everybody knows the Hitchenses and the Johnstons have been friends forever. They're neighbors."

"They brought Emily along too." Jimmy Neal's voice lowered to a whisper.

The word "Emily" cut like a dagger through her heart. It had new meaning to it.

Jimmy Neal placed his hand on her shoulder before continuing, "You need to know Bradley's first thoughts were of you. Only you."

"Why is this relevant? I don't care about—" She tried not to break down in a flood of tears. "*This!*" she screamed. "I guess Bradley and Emily are a couple now. Again. Everyone knows she's been after him for years."

As soon as those words passed her lips, her body went limp. She understood why Bradley had sent her favorite cousin hundreds of miles to see her.

"Oh dear God," Penny said under her breath. "She's pregnant."

"Yes," Jimmy Neal replied, confirming the worst-case scenario, one Penny hadn't prepared for. "There's more. Yesterday, they got married in Lexington."

Bile crept up Penny's throat. She covered her mouth with her trembling hand, hoping she wouldn't vomit all over her cousin.

"You know how it works around Camden. Bradley's a stand-up guy. He did the honorable thing by marrying her and giving that baby his name. Everybody knows he doesn't love Emily. Hell, he doesn't even like her. But Betty and Roger were pretty adamant. They forced him into this. They even brought his parents to make sure he did the right thing."

"So they're really married," she replied, still paralyzed from the news.

"They are. Emily's going to finish the semester at U of L before she moves to Lexington—" He cleared his throat. "To have the baby. The Hitchenses have agreed to take care of everything financially. I guess having rich parents pays off." No Ray had ever been so lucky.

A long silence followed before he pulled an envelope from the back pocket of his Lee jeans. "Bradley wrote you a letter."

"Are you serious?" Penny snorted at the absurdity of the situation. He'd sent her kin to do his dirty work and written a Dear John—or Dear Jane—letter. "You keep it. I don't care what it says."

Jimmy Neal folded it neatly and put it back in his pocket. "Just so you know, I wanted to kick his ass for betraying you. But Bradley's a good guy. One night doesn't change that. He's sorry about all this. It was a mistake. A big one, I know, but everybody makes them. I mean, he's a guy, Penny. Trust me—we don't always think things through first. Especially when it comes to *that*. He loves you. He wants to be with you."

Penny shook her head. "He's a married man now."

"In name only. It was one stupid night."

"That resulted in a child," she added, choking back emotions. When Penny stood, her legs felt like jelly. Somehow, she managed her way up the steps and headed toward the front door. Before walking inside, she stopped. "Is there anything else you want to share with me today?"

"No. Is there anything you want me to tell Bradley for you?"

"Yes." She paused and swallowed. "I never thought anyone in this world could hurt me as much as Charlie Ray has. Tell Bradley I was wrong."

Once Jimmy Neal left, Penny threw away her memory box. But before Penny cast the items into the garbage can next to Ruby Ray's barn, she made one last entry in her journal. Her story— their story—needed an ending.

Goodbye, Bradley Hitchens, she wrote.

There was nothing left to say.

July 2009
Camden, Kentucky

Chapter 18

I Can See Clearly Now

"Twelve twenty-three," Penny whispers into the darkness after looking at her useless iPhone.

Once again, sleep is elusive. Between the thunderstorm raging outside her bedroom window and knowing that in seven minutes, the damn clock will remind her she's still awake, she's a bundle of nervous energy. Tonight's stroll down memory lane, courtesy of her teenage-love box dedicated to Bradley, isn't helping matters either. She can't stop thinking about him. Now she's torn between the two Bradleys of her past. On one hand, he was the boy who protected, lied for, and loved her through all the chaos of her life, but on the other, he was the boy who shattered her heart into a million pieces by sleeping with Emily Johnston. Thinking of how he hopped into her tormentor's bed—or rather, the backseat of her car—after Penny denied him sex that Fourth of July night causes Penny's blood pressure to spike. Her body is drenched in sweat.

Frustrated, she jumps out of bed and heads toward the kitchen for a glass of water to cool down. Standing at the sink, filling her glass to the brim, she watches the storm grow more intense by the second. The trees in the yard whip back and forth from the violent winds. Ruby Ray's rose bushes scratch the old, rusted window screens like the fingers of witches who are trying to lure a child into a boiling cauldron. Loud claps of thunder fill the sky, causing the yellow foursquare to shake, startling Penny. Mother Nature's angry tonight, but she isn't the only one. Penny's hand trembles as she raises the glass to her lips, spilling water onto the floor.

Then the truth of why she's so angry tonight hits her like a bolt of lightning crashing through the green shingles above. She's been too afraid to admit it. It's not that she still wants Bradley. She's never stopped wanting him, even after he married Emily and, more importantly, after she married Teddy. What's eating her alive tonight is not Bradley's betrayal twenty years ago. He might have crushed her as a naive teenager, but what she did to him as a grown woman was worse, and she's been too stubborn to even think about it, let alone admit it.

On a snowy night six months after Penny married Teddy, Charlie was rushed to St. Thomas Hospital in Nashville after he was found slumped over on a sidewalk in Gallatin. After running tests, they concluded he was brain dead. Only machines were keeping him alive. Trying to spare Ruby Ray the impossible choice of removing her son from life support, Penny stepped in, offering to sign the papers herself. But before she could go through with it, she hesitated.

Conflicted, she confessed her sins to a priest as they sat in the back pew of the hospital chapel. With uncertainty and regret, in vivid detail, she explained how she almost killed her father all those years ago and how she still wished him harm every day of his life.

"How can I be his executioner now, for all intents and purposes, after what's happened between us?" she asked. "Is this mercy, not allowing him to linger for months in a vegetative state? Or is it revenge for all he's done? All he's denied me?"

"Forgiveness," he said, squeezing Penny's frigid hand, "is a virtue of the brave."

A priest quoting a Hindu politician made perfect sense. At that moment, Penny decided to be merciful and just to a man who was neither, allowing him to go peacefully into the great beyond.

However, unlike the Hollywood depiction of life-support removal as a peaceful event, the end is rarely serene. For a man who was deemed to be dead by all medical standards, Charlie held on for five agonizing hours after the last tube was removed. Just as Penny began doubting her decision, she noticed the sure signs of a body giving way. As she listened, his labored breaths turned raspy, and the death rattle settled in, his tortured life finally slipping away in front of her. She pitied him.

Then she did something she would never be able to rationalize, let alone tell anyone. She pulled the hard plastic hospital chair from the corner of the room and placed it next to his bed. After a long, steady breath, she picked up his leathered hand, which was stained yellow from years of cigarettes, and held it. It was the first time they'd touched in years. Not since the violent altercation resulting in her pulling a gun on him had there been physical contact between them.

Though her throat ached, she sang the old hymn "Softly and Tenderly."

As Penny pushed out the last words of the song, Charlie drew his final breath.

Two days later, in the freezing Kentucky wind and rain, he was laid to rest in the Willow Creek Baptist Church Cemetery. The service was swift—no eulogy, only a scripture reading from the book of Lamentations and one stanza of "Amazing Grace," and not even a prayer. For such a simple event and for a man no one loved or even liked, a large crowd gathered. Familiar faces, most of whom Penny hadn't seen in years, were packed together around the grave.

But one face in particular caught her attention instantly and took her breath away. Standing at the back, next to the black Gardner & Son hearse, was Bradley Hitchens. When their eyes met, Penny was filled with an overwhelming sense of relief, knowing he was near. He mouthed, "I'm sorry," and she nodded back, staring at her best friend. The look between them conveyed so much—compassion, comfort, friendship, and most importantly, love.

Collapsing into a fit of sobs in front of the crowd and her new husband, Penny was suddenly inconsolable. The breakdown had nothing to do with Charlie. It was because of Bradley. Once again, he was there for her, like always. He couldn't allow her to go through the experience of burying a man like her father without him, even if they no longer spoke.

Two years later, when Emily died, Penny didn't even send a condolence card, let alone make the trek up to Kentucky to pay her respects. No matter how vile Emily had been to her, Bradley deserved better. A single father of two small children whose wife had been killed in a terrible car accident, he must have been devastated. Selfishly, Penny denied him her comfort and forgiveness in his time of need. Even Charlie got a sliver of compassion as he slipped away that cold January night, and he'd been a monster to her. After all these years, Penny's heart breaks whenever she thinks of Bradley, not because of the night of the Fourth of July, 1989, but because of the afternoon of March 16, 1997, the day of Emily's funeral.

She's been a damned fool, so needlessly bitter that she's tossed away the last twenty years of her life by refusing to forgive the one person who deserves it the most—the keeper of her deep secrets and the protector of her soul.

After throwing her glass into the sink, she rushes out her grandmother's front door barefoot, not bothering to lock it. Running down Dogwood Lane, she ignores the howling storm and pays no attention to the stinging rain. Right now, all she thinks of is Bradley.

She sprints up the bungalow's steps then knocks on the wooden door as if her life depends on it. "Bradley?" she yells. "Bradley, I need to talk to you!"

Minutes pass but no answer.

"Please open the door," she says as the wind picks up, pelting her with branches, leaves, and even more rain. Though the porch is covered, it provides Penny no respite from the storm's fury. If she had a lick of sense, she would run for safety instead of standing out in the open, drenched to the bone, but she persists. When a tree limb comes crashing down across the street paired with a blinding bolt of lightning and a deafening clap of thunder—a sign that the eye of the storm is indeed upon her—she keeps knocking. Though she knows she should seek cover immediately, she ignores her instincts and stands firm. She must rectify her mistake tonight. "Please, Bradley."

Finally, the front porch light turns on, and Bradley opens the door. "Penny?" Bradley asks, confused and wiping the sleep from his eyes. "What on earth are you doing here?"

"What I should've done years ago," she says, tears pouring down her face.

Another flash of lightning illuminates the sky. "Come inside," Bradley says. "It's not safe out here."

"No." She shakes her head. "Not until I make this right."

"I don't understand."

"Emily." Her voice trembles. "When she died, I should've been there for you. But I wasn't. I was wrong."

Now wide awake, Bradley says, "I never expected it. Not after what she—" He swallows hard. "What *I* did to you. I betrayed you."

"That doesn't matter anymore," she says, her chin quivering. "It was one night, Bradley. One stupid night. I get it now. You were a kid. You made a mistake, and I've wasted decades of my life trying to punish you for it."

"I deserved it and then some."

"No. You didn't. You were my friend. My best friend, and I cut you out of my life over it, forgetting all the wonderful things you did for me. If it wasn't for you, I'm not sure I would have survived Camden."

"That wasn't me, Penny. You did that all on your own. You're the fighter."

She rushes into his arms. "I'm so sorry I didn't give you a second chance. Please forgive me." This time, she will not regret or leave this embrace. Not tonight.

"Don't you dare apologize to me," he says, clutching her.

"I love you, Bradley. I always have," she whispers into his ear. "I've never stopped."

After those words pass through Penny's lips, Bradley scoops her into his arms. "I love you too," he says, carrying her into his bungalow.

Chapter 19

Here Comes the Sun

"Good morning," Bradley says, kissing Penny's cheek. Before she can open her eyes, the burnt-sugar aroma floating in the air triggers an instant rush of gratitude. For the first time in her life, Penny feels she's finally home.

When she opens her heavy eyelids, he comes into focus. He's wearing an untied plaid robe and the same worn sweatpants he had on last night when she leaped into his arms, soaked with rain. His bare chest, peeking through, which she laid her head upon and which lulled her into a deep slumber only hours ago, catches her eye. Now it's her favorite place on Earth, and she longs to lie across it again.

"Good morning to you too," she says.

"I thought you might need this." He hands her a mug of coffee.

"You have no idea," she says, sitting up from the sofa while covering her unmentionables with the blanket that kept them warm throughout the night. Her wet clothes, which he tossed aside after removing them from her body, remain in the corner of the room.

"There's breakfast in the kitchen. I thought you might be hungry."

"I'm famished," she says, thinking of the reason for her newfound appetite.

"It's all ready," he says, playing with one of her many curls that have appeared this morning, thanks to last night's rain.

"What time is it?" she asks.

"It's a little after seven. Why?"

"I'm supposed to meet Kelly and Laura at eight to pack."

"Don't worry. You have plenty of time. Come on. Let's eat." He offers his hand.

"Okay," she replies, not moving.

"What are you waiting for?"

"For you to turn around," she says.

A crooked grin spreads across his face. "Why?"

"Because as we both know, I'm missing some key wardrobe items under here," she says shyly. The morning sun is pouring into the room now. Certain things, especially the body of a woman who's thrice given birth, look different in the light of day than they do in the dead of night.

"Oh, I know," he teases. "Clothing is optional for breakfast today."

"Could I have something to put—"

Before she finishes her sentence, he pulls off his plaid flannel robe and gives it to her.

She accepts his cozy gift with a grateful smile. "Thank you."

"Come on," he says. "Let's eat."

As they make their way into the sunny kitchen, Penny notices a single red rose in the center of the wooden table. "Please tell me you didn't run over to Ruby Ray's this morning to steal that."

"No," he whispers into her ear before taking the opportunity to give it a little nibble. "That one's mine."

Bradley pulls out a wooden chair for her, and Penny smiles at her host for not only his hospitality but his impeccable manners as well. Pulling the chair closer to the table, she's impressed with Bradley's culinary skills. Laid before her is a large plate of fluffy scrambled eggs cooked in cream with black pepper on top accompanied by a thick piece of buttery toast. A bowl of fresh blackberries sits next to a glass of orange juice.

"This is incredible," Penny says and digs into the scrumptious meal.

"I'm glad you approve." He leans back in his chair and watches her devour the breakfast. "So, what's your plan today?"

"Well, as you know, Kelly and Laura are coming over to pack. Then I'm meeting with Pat McGuire, the real estate agent Jimmy Neal recommended, this afternoon. So I guess I'll be in the weeds today." She takes another large bite. "Plus, I'm a little behind schedule. Thanks to you."

"What about tonight?"

"Packing," she tells him, devouring the toast.

"Why don't I stop by? I'll help you. My last appointment is at four today."

"You don't need to do that. Trust me. Ruby Ray's could be on an episode of *Hoarders*. I'm sure you have something better to do."

Grinning, he says, "Oh, I can think of *something* I want to do. However, it kind of involves you."

"I bet." She giggles.

"Look, I have no parental responsibilities for the next few weeks with the girls away, which is kind of new for me, so I've got plenty of time on my hands. And I know exactly what I want to do with them."

"You're so thoughtful," she replies sarcastically.

"Seriously, I want to help."

"That's very sweet of you, but there's a ton of work to do over there. More than even I bargained for."

"A little hard work doesn't scare me."

Penny gasps. "Oh no." She puts her hands over her face, covering her dismay. "I just remembered. How am I going to get home? I can't walk back to Ruby Ray's like this. What if someone sees me?" Her clothes are still drenched from last night's storm, and she's wearing only Bradley's robe.

"Perhaps you should've thought of that before running practically naked in the middle of a thunderstorm, banging on random people's doors."

"Can we be serious for a second here?" she says, for this is no laughing matter. There's a pressing wardrobe problem at hand.

"Don't worry." He caresses her cheek. "I won't let you do the walk of shame down the streets of Camden. I'll drive you home."

"Wearing this?" She motions to his robe. "Or worse, in my T-shirt, which I'm sure is still soaked from last night."

"A wet T-shirt?" He grins. "This morning is getting better and better."

"Stop it." She playfully swats at his arm. "This isn't funny. What am I going to do?"

Laughing, he says, "Okay. Okay. You can borrow one of my shirts. See? Problem solved."

"Thank you," she says, relieved.

"You're welcome. Now, finish your breakfast, then I'll sneak you back over to Ruby Ray's and past all the nosy busybodies of Camden. They'll never know you were here."

After cleaning her plate with the ferociousness of a long-haul trucker on a cross-country journey, which surprises not only Penny but Bradley as well, she throws on one of his UK shirts along with her running shorts, which have dried out a bit. Unlike her shirt, at least they're wearable for a few minutes.

"See? Not another soul in sight," he says, pulling into Ruby Ray's driveway. "Your secret is safe with me."

"Thank you for bringing me home. Again." Penny opens her door. This is the second time in twelve hours he's delivered her safely back to Ruby Ray's.

"My pleasure," Bradley whispers before pulling her in for a long kiss.

Happily, Penny obliges. Though she has a million things to do, and locking lips with her high-school sweetheart in broad daylight isn't the best idea, she brushes those concerns aside because she cannot resist him after last night. She's throwing caution to the wind, enjoying both this moment and his tongue, which is gently tickling hers.

"Why is Aunt Penny kissing Dr. Hitchens?" comes a tiny voice, startling them.

They break away from their heated embrace, only to discover little Emma Roark looking quite perplexed by the whole affair.

"Emma! Come here!" Kelly exclaims, running after her. Once she sees what her daughter has just witnessed, she bursts into a fit of laughter.

Penny panics. "Emma? What are you doing here?"

"We're helping you pack. Remember?" the wide-eyed seven-year-old says, crossing her arms.

"Yes, honey. I remember. But I thought you and your mommy were coming over at *eight*." Penny stares a hole through her friend.

"My car had a flat this morning, and Timmy didn't have time to fix it, so he dropped us off before he headed to work," Kelly explains while trying to suppress her amusement. "I *tried* calling you."

"Why were you kissing Dr. Hitchens?" Emma stomps, demanding her original question be answered.

"I-I wasn't kissing him," Penny stammers, avoiding the child's glare. "I was *thanking* him."

"Why?" Emma asks.

"Well..." Penny pauses, thinking of something to shut down her interrogation. "I went out for a run this morning, and I got lost. Dr. Hitchens found me. He was nice enough to drive me home. Isn't that right?" Penny turns to Bradley for help.

"Um, yes," he replies. "That's right."

"But if you were running, where are your shoes?" the precocious child asks.

In unison, everyone looks down at Penny's bare feet.

"Come on, Emma. Let's go inside and let Aunt Penny finish *thanking* Dr. Hitchens," Kelly says, winking at Penny while taking her daughter's hand and leading her away.

"That went splendidly," Penny deadpans after the two leave.

"Running? Why did you say that?" Bradley asks, laughing.

"I panicked." She shakes her head. "I'd better get inside and face the music. Kelly's going to have a field day with this one."

"I'm sure she will." He raises his eyebrows.

"Maybe Emma can go to work with you today."

"No way. I already have my hands full tending to cavity-laced children. Don't think I need another nosy kid hanging around."

Smiling, Penny says, "Okay, then. See you at five?"

"I don't know if I can wait that long."

"We're packing tonight," she says half-heartedly. "Remember?"

"We'll see about that."

Watching Bradley drive away, Penny thinks about how much has changed in only a matter of hours. The weight she's been carrying around for decades has been lifted from her. How wonderfully unburdened she feels right now. This morning, the sun is shining a little brighter, and the honeysuckle growing along Ruby Ray's barn smells sweeter. Even the birds are singing with more gusto. Gratitude for having Bradley back in her life fills her soul. He's where he should have been all along.

A couple of minutes pass, and Penny knows it's time to face the music. Walking toward Ruby Ray's back door, she prepares herself for the onslaught of questions from both Kelly and her pint-sized Sherlock Holmes coming her way.

"What was that?" Kelly exclaims, grabbing Penny's arm the second she enters the house and pushing her into the one and only bathroom.

"It's not how it looks," she replies in a guilty voice.

"Not how it looks? You come rolling up to your grandmother's house at the crack of dawn, wearing nothing but an oversized T-shirt and what I pray are a pair of shorts under there." She swats at Penny's exposed legs. "And you seem to be missing your shoes *and* bra. You want me to believe it's not how it looks? Should I tell you how it looks?"

"You're right. I know *how* it looks."

"You slept with Bradley last night?" Kelly begins clapping with glee.

"No, I didn't."

"Really? Your hair tells another story, Missy," Kelly says, tugging at one of Penny's curls.

"We didn't have sex. I just spent the night on his couch."

"So this is all innocent? You want me to believe you had a little slumber party with my dentist?" she taunts.

"Mommy?" comes Emma's tiny voice from outside the door.

Kelly holds up a finger to Penny's face. "Don't move. We're not done yet." She cracks the door. "Yes, honey?" she asks.

"Why did Aunt Penny have a slumber party last night with your dentist?"

"Now, Emma, you know it's not polite to eavesdrop on adult conversations," her mother scolds her while trying to shut the door.

"But if she had a party, why didn't she invite you? Doesn't it hurt your feelings?" the indignant child asks.

Penny pokes her head through the opening. "Sweetie. Aunt Penny did *not* have a slumber party. And of course, if I did, I would've invited your mommy."

"Emma, go to the kitchen and get something to eat," her mother commands.

"But I'm not hungry," Emma says, crossing her arms in protest and stomping her little foot. This child is indeed hungry—hungry for gossip.

"What the hell happened to you?" Laura asks, walking in Ruby Ray's side door, holding a cardboard carrier of watered-down Minit Mart coffees. Unknowingly, she's stumbled upon the Camden Inquisition.

"Mommy, she said a bad word," Emma says in a tattletale voice.

"Yes, she did. I'll wash her mouth out with soap later. Now, go to the kitchen, and stay there," Kelly tells her while pulling Laura into the bathroom.

"Am I missing something here?" Laura asks.

"Only that your husband's cousin had sex with Bradley Hitchens last night," Kelly says.

Laura almost drops the coffees. "What?"

"For the last time, we didn't have sex," Penny protests.

"Has she looked in a mirror?" Laura asks, turning Penny around so that she can see what they do.

Once she catches a glimpse of her reflection, Penny's startled, not by her disheveled appearance or her frazzled poodle hair, compliments of last night's rain, but by the radiant glow upon her face. She's positively effervescent. Forgiveness and letting go of twenty years of resentment have done a number on her appearance. They're better than any Botox Dakota suggested she try.

"*Now* will you tell us what happened?" Kelly pleads.

"Okay, okay," Penny says before relaying the events of the previous evening—the flowers, the dinner, the flirting, the picture of Emily, her porch, the journal, the thunderstorm, his porch, the kiss, the couch.

"So you slept with him. Right?" Kelly asks, digging for more details.

"No. For the last time, we didn't have sex."

"Why not?" Laura asks.

"Because we weren't exactly... prepared."

"What on earth does that mean?" Kelly snaps.

"Do I have to spell it out for you? I'm a divorced woman who hasn't been concerned with certain things in a long time." She pauses again, hoping they'll catch on to her train of thought. However, judging by the blank stares on their faces, she'll need to elaborate. "Bradley wasn't expecting me to show up at his door in the middle of the night, so he wasn't exactly dressed for the part. So to speak."

"Ohhh," her friends say slowly in unison.

"Well, I guess if anyone knows the dangers of unprotected sex, it's Bradley Hitchens," Laura says.

"Laura!" Kelly shoots her a glare of displeasure.

Laura winces. "Oh, sorry."

Penny smiles at her faux pas.

"You know, he could've gone out. To a store?" Kelly says gently. "To make a purchase?"

"At one o'clock in the morning? In Camden, Kentucky?" Penny asks, arching an eyebrow.

"She's got a point," Laura says, turning to Kelly. "The whole town would know by now."

"But why do you look that way? You look..." Kelly searches for the right words. "So relaxed. So happy. So satisfied."

"Because I'm all of those things," Penny gushes. "I let it go. My bitterness, my anger, my hurt. I forgave Bradley last night, which I should've done years ago. Plus, I did something completely impulsive for the first time in my life. I was free. Running down the street in the pouring rain just to get to him. I've never wanted anyone or anything more in my life. It was the most passionate night of my life."

"I guess kissing can be hot," Kelly concedes. "It can be satisfying. Even gratifying, I suppose."

"Well," Penny says with a wicked giggle. "I didn't say we *only* kissed."

"What?" They gasp as Penny rushes out of the bathroom, only to discover Little Miss Nosy Rosie standing before her.

"What does passionate mean?" the tiny version of Miss Paulette asks.

"I'll let your mommy explain that one," Penny says, skipping past the tiny tot into the kitchen, ready to begin her day. This morning, Miss Ray has a new bounce in her step.

Chapter 20

Some Like It Hot

"Right on time. As usual," Penny says, opening the door to welcome her newest worker bee this evening. For a woman who's been knee-deep in Bubble Wrap and cobwebs all day, she feels rather refreshed and full of energy.

"Always. I'm a professional, after all," Bradley says.

"Are you ready to get started?" she asks before noticing the impish grin skewing his thin, asymmetrical lips to the left side of his face. Packing up Ruby Ray's is the last thing on his mind. "You're insufferable." Though packing is the last thing on her mind as well.

"I'm not sure what you're talking about, Penny. I'm strictly here to work," he teases.

"Yeah, right."

For the next three hours, they work in the stifling heat that fills every nook and cranny of the foursquare. Unfortunately, Penny's agenda tonight has them focusing on packing up the upstairs den, the room with the oldest and least efficient air conditioning unit. While she boxes and tags, Bradley carries loads of trash to the dumpster. The time Penny spent primping before his arrival was in vain. What little makeup she applied has now melted down her face. But Bradley doesn't seem to notice. Penny's caught him several times sneaking glimpses of other parts of her body.

As the grandfather clock strikes nine, it suddenly occurs to Penny—they haven't stopped to eat. Though Bradley insists he's here to help, she's mortified she's forgotten to provide a meal, something in exchange for his services. Slipping away to whip up a culinary feast, Penny realizes upon entering the kitchen that she's poorly equipped. With all the twists and turns since her arrival in Camden, the trip to Houchens for groceries hasn't even crossed her mind. That is, until now, as she stares into Ruby Ray's Frigidaire filled only with the provisions her cousins provided at the beginning of the week. Gracie Belle's country ham is her only option at this point. Using the salty meat as the main attraction, she slices up two of the homegrown tomatoes sitting on the table and sprinkles them with pepper. Generous dollops of mayonnaise spread across both sides of six slices of Colonial Bread finish off the three sandwiches she's rushed to make—one for her, two for Bradley. The corn salad, full of cream cheese and calories, which she's avoided at all costs, will complement this hodgepodge of a meal perfectly. She even cuts a slice of Gracie Belle's blueberry pound cake, though it's a thin one, since she's eaten most of it over the last few days, and places it on the side of the plate.

Within seconds of sitting down at the chrome and Formica dinette, Bradley inhales both sandwiches and devours the blueberry cake slice in one bite.

"That hit the spot," he says before finishing off his Dr. Pepper.

It amuses Penny that he would drink one, since most dentists scold their patients about the evils of sugary drinks.

"I was starving."

"I'm so sorry I didn't feed you earlier tonight or plan for a better meal. I was so focused on the house and my meeting with Mr. McGuire today that it completely slipped my mind," Penny explains. Embarrassment fills her voice for not showing off her culinary skills. "I'll do better next time."

"So there's a next time? Are you planning to work me to death the entire time you're home?" he responds while wiping the sweat from his brow. Ruby Ray's kitchen is just as hot as upstairs.

"I-I didn't mean it like that," she stammers. Again, her cheeks heat.

Before they can get any warmer, he pulls her in for a long, reassuring kiss. When their lips meet, it's the first time they've touched since his arrival. Though there's been a strong undercurrent of sexual tension throughout the evening, they pushed through. If they'd picked up where they left off this morning, they wouldn't have lasted ten seconds before tearing off their clothes and ravaging each other's bodies.

"Well, you've got me for the next eleven days. And nights. Like it or not. I'm at your beck and call, even if the heat is brutal in this kitchen."

"I know. It's awful," she says, fanning herself with a paper napkin before dabbing the back of her neck with it. "My grandparents never liked the idea of something as frivolous as central air conditioning. Or as they called it, bought air. They thought it was a waste of money, so they installed these window units, which are older than me. Mr. McGuire said I should rip them out and install a central air unit. If not, he'll have to cut the asking price by ten grand."

"Ouch."

"Tell me about it. But he seems very excited about the prospect of selling. In fact, he's already had three inquiries about the house since word got out I was home."

"That's good news, I suppose," he says, sadness filling his voice. "Are you sure you want to sell?"

"I'm sure. This place shouldn't go empty any longer, and I can't keep asking Jimmy Neal to take care of it. I want a family to enjoy this place. To love it like my grandparents did."

"But this place is the last thing anchoring you to Kentucky. I know what it *means* to you. Are you sure you want to cut it loose?"

"Positive," she tells him, though the little birdie in the back of her mind is singing a different tune. "Especially right now, since it's as hot as Hades in here." She hopes the joke will break the heavy moment.

"I think I've lost ten pounds since I arrived," he says.

"I guess I've gotten soft in my older years, because I forgot how hot this house gets in the summer."

"Hey, I have an idea," Bradley says, pushing away from the table.

"That sounds ominous." Penny gives him the side-eye.

"Do you trust me?" he asks, extending his hand.

The sound of his voice and the words he uses make her dizzy. "I think so," she tells him before interrupting herself. "Wait. No, I don't think so. I know so." She reaches for his hand.

Right now, she trusts him completely, something she's never done before.

Chapter 21

Full Moon of Kentucky

"The Camden Swim and Golf Club?" Penny asks, her voice dripping with sarcasm. "Of all the places in the world we could've gone, you brought me here?"

"It's not what you think," Bradley tells her. "Come on. You'll see."

As he guides her through the darkness, his hands are warm around hers, his thumbs caressing her palms for reassurance. At this moment, she'll follow him to Timbuktu, if he asks. He stops at a chain-link fence that secures the club's swimming pool.

"You want to cool down? Here's your chance," he says, making his way up the fence.

"Bradley! This is breaking and entering. It's illegal," she whispers. Scratch that. She won't follow him down the slippery slope to a life of crime.

"We're not robbing a bank. We're just taking a dip in the pool. Where's your sense of adventure?"

"This is insane. What if we get caught?"

"I'm president of the club. We won't get caught."

"If you're the president of the club, where's your key?"

While he scales the fence like a professional, she watches, still frozen with fear. So many times in her thirty-seven years, she's missed out on opportunities because she never gathered the nerve to take the first step.

"Come on. Live a little. It's just the two of us. It's late, and it's hot. The sky's not falling tonight, Chicken Little," he teases.

235

"It's a big-ass sky, and the night is young," Penny shoots back.

"I know it's not in your nature," he says, leaping to the ground. "But not everything has to be planned. Be impulsive for once in your life."

The words "be impulsive" catch her attention. The last time she gave impulsivity a chance, less than twenty-four hours ago, she was rewarded handsomely with a night she'll never forget.

To hell with it. Before she can talk herself out of breaking into the Camden Swim and Golf Club, debating all of the ramifications an action such as this can incur, she's halfway up the fence, surprising both herself and Bradley with her climbing abilities.

"That's the spirit," he says as she jumps into his arms.

"Well." Penny sighs. "Here goes nothing." She strips down to her birthday suit.

"Wow," Bradley mouths, seeming stunned by Penny's impetuousness. Without dipping her toes in to check the temperature, she dives headfirst into the unknown. Not to mention she's upped the ante by disrobing completely.

A few seconds later, she resurfaces. "So, what are you waiting for?"

At this moment, Penny doesn't know who she is. She's a poised seductress who's now toying with her prey. But she likes it. The velvety water cascading over her nude body, tickling her sex, has empowered her. Right now, she feels alive in a way she's never felt before.

"Miss Ray, you never cease to amaze me," Bradley says before undressing then joining in their lawlessness with his own beautiful entrance into the pool. For a moment, he vanishes. Though the waning moon provides some light, the water's dark beneath her, almost impenetrable, causing her heart to flutter. Before she can allow her mind to think of all the worst-case scenarios, his hands glide over her legs as he swims up from below.

"That wasn't nice," she whispers into his ear, wrapping her legs around his waist. "Teasing me like that."

"I want to do more than tease you, Penny," he replies in a low voice before turning his attention to her neck and the spot just shy of her right ear. He discovered the place last night on his couch, enticing her with his tongue and warm breath in such a way that Penny almost climaxed on the spot. His ability to make her cry out in pleasure without going for the cheap thrill of fondling her breasts is exhilarating. There's more to a woman's body, more to her erogenous zones, than that.

The world around them stops as their bodies become one beneath a blanket of stars, in the cool water. The rhythmic sounds of katydids in the distance provide the music, and lightning bugs float above the pool, furnishing the ambiance. Flashes of yellow and green twinkle across the dark night. It's just the two of them, lost in the moment—until there are three.

"Evening, folks" comes a stern voice behind a blinding flashlight. In a panic, Penny slips beneath the surface of the water, hoping to hide from the glaring light and from the person who's discovered their little tryst. Left with no other strategy, she decides to hold her breath and hope for the best. Although years of running have provided her with exceptional lung capacity, even she can't stay there all night. However, she thinks she'll at least give it a try, until the searing heat from her chest and the pounding of her heart are too much to bear.

Resurfacing, frantically gasping for air, she hears the man let out a gregarious laugh.

"Now, that was impressive. How long would you say she held her breath, Doc?" The voice is familiar.

"About thirty seconds," Bradley replies, still treading water in the middle of the deep end of the pool.

"Aw, hell. I'd say she was down there at least a minute," the man says, amused by her stunt.

Though still light-headed from her oxygen-depriving stunt, Penny has the acumen to cover her breasts with one arm while using the other to stay afloat. Being the consummate gentleman, Bradley places her behind him and guides her to the edge of the pool.

"Think you can turn that thing off now, Dustin?" Bradley asks.

"It's Officer Ward to you, Doc." Dustin rears back in laughter.

"Dusty? Dusty Ward? Is that you?" Penny asks, clearing the water from her eyes. The last time she saw her classmate was on their graduation day. He left town for basic training the morning after he received his diploma, and she hasn't seen him since.

"Penny Ray. You're the last person in the world I ever thought I'd catch skinny-dipping at the country club." He chuckles. "Have y'all been drinking?"

It's a valid question, under the circumstances. Bradley Hitchens, a pillar of the community—a medical professional, no less—and Penny Ray, who's long since left Camden's city limits, are not the typical public-nudity suspects.

"Sadly, not a drop," Penny says. She realizes that being intoxicated and jumping into a pool sans clothing would be a more understandable explanation than being stone-cold sober.

"Dustin, can you put the light down?" Bradley asks again.

"Sure thing, Doc." This time, his friend obliges and turns his attention toward Penny. "I heard you were back in town. I'll be honest with you. I hoped I'd bump into you again, but this is a *real* treat."

"I'm sure it is," Bradley mumbles.

"It's good to see you, Dusty. I mean Officer Ward. I didn't know you moved back to Camden. I thought you were stationed somewhere in Japan."

"Well, I was there for a while. And Germany. And Kuwait. Been all over the world, but nothing compares to Kentucky. When I retired from the military a few years ago, I came home and joined the police force," Dusty says, patriotic pride brimming in his voice.

"What's going on out there?" comes an agitated elderly voice from the distance.

"It's all right, Miss Eunice. There's nothing to worry about. You can go back inside," Dusty tells the woman, who's standing on her porch.

"Did you catch 'em?" she asks with gusto.

"Nothing to see here. Please remain on your porch, ma'am."

"'Nothing to see here'? I saw them with my own eyes. Driving up here, turning off their lights, trying to go unnoticed. Then they climbed up that fence and jumped into the pool. I know they're in there. Who is it?"

"Just a couple of crazy teenagers. I've got this now, Miss Eunice. You can go back inside. They won't be bothering you again tonight."

"I'm sick to death of these kids thinking they can come up here and use this pool whenever they please. This is a private club, you know. My father was one of the founding members, and he wouldn't have put up with this kind of tomfoolery in his day. It's a disgrace. I'm calling Dr. Hitchens first thing tomorrow morning. We need more lights up here, and we should prosecute those little heathens to the fullest extent of the law." Miss Eunice points. "You hear me? The president of our club will be calling your parents tomorrow!"

"I'm sure Dr. Hitchens is *abreast* of the situation, ma'am," Dusty says, clearly suppressing the urge to giggle. Upon his arrival, he may have caught a glimpse of one of Penny's. "Good night, Miss Eunice."

The old woman dramatically slams her door.

"I guess I'll be getting an earful from her tomorrow," Bradley says.

"You know, I agree with her. It's best to throw the book at trespassers," Dusty replies.

"Are we free to go, or are you going to haul us down to the station?"

"You're free to go, Doc. Get your clothes back on, and skedaddle on out of here before Miss Eunice comes down and makes a citizen's arrest."

"Thank you, Officer Ward," Penny says, relieved she won't be facing a mugshot for her ill-timed dabble into juvenile delinquency twenty years too late.

"It's Dusty to you, Penny Ray. Don't worry. Your secret's safe with me."

"I doubt that," Bradley mutters.

"You'd better leave this one alone, though." Dusty points to Bradley. "He's a bad influence on you."

Penny giggles at his proclamation.

"Good night, Dustin," Bradley says curtly.

"Good night, Doc. See you Saturday for our round. By the way, I think I'll need four or five mulligans when we play. You know, in exchange for my silence for what I saw here tonight," Dusty says with a wink. "I'd best get on over to Miss Eunice's to smooth things out. Good to see you, Penny. Don't be a stranger."

Once Dusty leaves, Penny kicks water in Bradley's face. "Did you hear that? You're a bad influence on me," she says, swimming toward the ladder. For a woman who's been caught buck naked, as they say in these parts, by the Camden Police in the same pool where Emily Johnston humiliated her back in ninth grade after she got her first period, she's surprisingly jovial—buoyant and carefree. Before she can exit the pool, Bradley reaches for her waist, spinning her around to face him.

"What? Plotting something else we can do to get the police called on us tonight? Wait—I have a great idea. Why don't we toilet paper a couple of yards while we're at it? I've always wanted to exact my revenge on Shannon Madison for the hit she did on Ruby Ray's my sophomore year. Let's go on a misdemeanor crime spree," she jokes, putting her arms around his neck. "Or better yet, we could make a run for Crook's. Pick up a six-pack. Maybe shotgun a beer or two on the square." It's a reference to an establishment across the Tennessee line that sold beer and wine coolers to the entire teenage population of Camden back in the eighties. No fake ID or facial hair was needed. One just had to stand upright.

After a long pause, Bradley says, "I love you, Penny." He stares into her eyes with the seriousness of a man who's no longer toying with hypotheticals or flirtatious banter. "I'd like the chance to finally show you how much."

His words are intoxicating, leaving her warm and weak in his arms. It's time, she realizes. Twenty years is long enough. There's nothing on Earth she wants to do more than to finally make love to him.

"Then take me home, Dr. Hitchens," she says, pulling him in for one last kiss before finally cementing their relationship once and for all.

Chapter 22

About Last Night

"What are you doing?" Bradley asks in a husky voice.

Penny bolts upright. "Oh. I was trying to be quiet. To let you sleep," she whispers.

"Where are you sneaking off to? And why are you whispering? We're the only ones here," he says. A sleepy grin crosses his face as he leans up on his elbow.

"Right," she says. "I didn't mean to wake you. I was heading back to Ruby Ray's to change. I need to go for a run."

"Now? It's pitch-black outside. Don't leave me." He pulls her into his arms and gives her a long kiss. His lips, soft and warm, caress Penny's with the same tenderness he showed last night after taking her *home*, his home, to finally make love to her. He was not only an attentive lover but an understanding one as well, sensing she was nervous. She had only shared her bed with one man before, and taking a new lover at her age, no matter how much she's wanted and longed for him, was still daunting. All the years of running and kale salads couldn't reverse the damage three pregnancies inflicted upon her body.

"You know I don't want to leave, but the boys are calling me this morning. I have to be back in time not to miss them. Besides, I need a good sweat."

"So you're a love-'em-and-leave-'em kind of girl, I see."

"Bradley." She sighs. The last thing she wants to do is leave his bed, the place where they finally consummated their long-overdue love for each other. If she had her druthers, she would crawl back in for more, but her thirty-year habitude is screaming. Even now, she's incapable of silencing it.

"I know you need it," he says, caressing her cheek with his finger.

Bradley never judged or mocked her motives or desires when it came to her routines. He had a unique understanding of how important they were to her. What truly motivated Penny Ray was an unquenchable need for control over something in her life. The spiraling family chaos in her formative years created a void. For Penny, she found she could fill that space by controlling one thing as a young girl—her body. And she did so by running. It wasn't a sport or a hobby to her. It became her defense mechanism. Though they never spoke of it, they both understood it was there and would probably never leave Penny's psyche.

"Give me a minute," he says. "I'll join you."

"For ten miles?" she asks, amused.

"Ten?" His voice cracks.

Bradley Hitchens is the epitome of strength and vigor, which he displayed to Penny only hours ago—twice, in fact. But ten miles isn't something one dabbles with. That's serious mileage.

"I didn't think so."

"Wait," he says, rising from his bed in protest. "You know, I can run too. Remember, I placed fourth at Sub-State."

"In the four hundred," she says. "That's a sprint race."

"Ouch," he moans, putting on a T-shirt. "Well, I'm going, like it or not. Besides, I don't like you running around town in the dark."

"It's Camden. It's completely safe. Plus, I ran Sunday morning and survived," she protests. Penny would never entertain the idea of running before sunrise in a city as big as Atlanta, even in a place like Buckhead with a strong police presence. But Camden's different. It's a small town. This is a tight-knit community of people completely intertwined with one another. Here, they know not only their neighbors' names, first, middle, and last, but birthdays and anniversaries as well. Penny's never given her safety a second thought on these streets. Lord knows they were safer than that of her own home.

"I'm not some damsel in distress who needs protection."

"This isn't some macho thing. I can assure you. You can take care of yourself. I know that."

"So why all the fuss?"

"Maybe I can't stand the thought of being away from you for one second," he says, slipping on his running shoes.

"Wow. That's some line."

"Not if it's the truth." His left dimple, which has always been her kryptonite, peeks through.

"Okay," she says. "Try to keep up."

Mile one: the warm-up

Darkness surrounds them as they begin jogging down Dogwood Lane before turning right onto Walnut Drive. Penny's muscles come back to life while her lungs tingle with heat as they quicken their pace. The sun, still resting below the horizon, will not greet them for another half hour. The only light to guide their way on this early morning, besides the antiquated street lamps lining the streets, is the waning moon lazily hovering low in the black sky. It's ready to call it a night so that it can surrender its luminescence to the sun. It's the same moon that only hours ago provided an ideal setting for their little foray into skinny-dipping at the country club. Later, its blue beams peeked through the windows of Bradley's bedroom, allowing enough light that Penny could look into the eyes of the man she loves as he gently slipped himself into her body.

Mile Two: pick up the pace and clear the mind.

The air, sodden with humidity, is still and eerily quiet. The white-throated sparrows and northern cardinals who usually usher in the dawn have not yet ventured out of their nests to sing their glorious morning songs, boasting of their strength and vitality. The noisy cicadas and chirping tree crickets tuckered out long ago. No dogs bark in the distance. No cars move about. The only sounds are their feet striking the concrete in unison along with their rhythmic inhalations and exhalations. They're in sync, just as they were only a few hours ago in his bed, moving as one, slowly at first, savoring those first moments of raw intimacy, then faster when their bodies craved more. The memory, still fresh and exciting, causes her stomach to flutter.

Mile Three: the heart is pumping.

The third mile of Penny's runs are always her favorite. By this point, her arms and legs, stiff from the previous night's slumber, relax a bit. This is when she starts pushing herself. *Go faster. Get stronger. Forget the pain.*

It's unusual for Penny to run with a partner. She finds it tedious to carry on polite conversations with chatty companions. This is the time she allows herself to clear her mind and restore balance to her life. Preferring the solitude of being a lone wolf, she only wants the company of her trusty iPod. Having to keep up with anyone else's pace irritates her. Those who attempt the daunting task of tagging along with her are either too fast, hitting a wall and cutting her runs short, or too slow, making it feel as if she's doing nothing more than geriatric power-walking at the mall. There's never a "just right" speed for the insatiable running Goldilocks. However, this morning, Bradley's meeting her step for step, exceeding her expectations, just as he did last night.

Taking a peek at her "new" partner, she can't help but admire what a physical specimen he is. His rippling biceps, dripping with perspiration, cause her heart to flutter as she remembers how those very arms carried her into his bedroom. She held on to them, digging in with her nails when he thrust himself into her. Penny stumbles, tripping over her feet, thinking about that moment. Bradley notices.

Mile Four: the heart is pumping... for other reasons now.

This morning's run is not going as planned. Penny's mind isn't clear. In fact, it's racing. Bradley and the love they made are consuming her, causing her body to react in unexpected ways. Every time she attempts to sneak a peek in his direction, she remembers how he felt inside her. This is a new development for her, being completely, unabashedly aroused by something as simple as a memory. It's an unexpected, yet magnificent turn of events.

By now, Bradley begins noticing her repeated glances in his direction. It's also obvious her gait's off. She's stumbled more than once and isn't her running self. He gives her a simple smile. Once again, his left dimple peeks through. When she sees his expression, it reminds her of how he looked last night, wearing an expression of pure joy and satisfaction. She stumbles again. The throbbing between her legs is becoming unbearable. Finally, she's had enough.

Mile Five: the realization

"What are we doing?" she asks, coming to a stop at the intersection of Holland Avenue and Beech Hill Way.

"I've been asking myself that very question for five miles," he replies, putting his hands on his knees to try to catch his breath. Apparently, he's been faking his tempo, or rather Penny's, in a bid to keep up.

"I don't want to do this right now," she says, shaking her head and staring at a row of sycamore trees in the distance. They're glowing like fire, compliments of the burnt-orange sunbeams peeking through.

"Thank God," he whispers, panting.

"This is insane." She wants to kick herself for her stupidity. "We should be lying in your bed instead of running around Camden at the crack of dawn."

"I wish you'd had this epiphany forty-five minutes ago." He chuckles.

"Ten mornings. That's all we have left. *Ten.* And this is what I choose to do? Go for a run at this ungodly hour. Dragging you along with me. Practically killing you in the process."

"I think the practically-killing-me part is a bit of an overstatement. I kept up," he says, defending his athletic prowess while attempting to stand upright.

"Let's go back." She shakes her head at the realization of her foolishness of wasting one of their mornings together. Thinking back to yesterday's breakfast, she curses herself. It was the most glorious morning of her life, one that could've been replicated had she taken a moment to simply relax. Time's now more precious than gold, and it's ticking away, slipping through her fingers. "Ruby Ray's is less than a mile from here, if we cut up Beech Hill." She points toward the monstrous incline to the right. "We'll even walk home, if you like." She senses the steepest hill in Camden, though only half a mile in length, might as well be Mount Everest for Bradley at this point.

"Sounds like a plan," he says before pulling her in for a kiss. The sweat dripping from their bodies seems to cause him no concern. His tongue, warm and salty, tickles hers. "So, what are we going to do once we get back?" The good dentist appears to be having his own delicious thoughts of last night as well.

"I can finally show off my culinary skills and make you an omelet. Ham, of course, since it's all I've got. Or we could enjoy a bitter cup of coffee compliments of Ruby Ray's percolator. Or... we can make love for the rest of the morning and forget about breakfast."

"To hell with walking. I'll race you." He slaps her bottom before tackling Beech Hill with gusto.

Mile Six: It's the climb.

The last mile of their journey is the fastest they've completed thus far, even with the sadistic hill in their way. Once they hit the steps of the front porch, they're in each other's arms. As she fumbles with her keys, trying to unlock the front door, Bradley's hand makes its way up her shirt, laying claim to her right breast. Stumbling into the living room, readying themselves for a morning of bliss, they begin removing each other's sweaty clothes.

"Well, I guess we know what you've been up to since you got home" comes a surly voice from the corner of the living room.

Startled, Penny pulls away from Bradley's arms while pushing her T-shirt back down.

"Is that who I think it is?" Bradley whispers into Penny's ear.

"Yep. The two horsemen of the apocalypse," she replies in disgust.

From her biblical training, Penny knows there are four, but the nickname fits her great-aunts to a T. Pearl Sutton Garrison is the Red Rider, always preparing for war. Her tongue is as sweet as vinegar, and a kind word hasn't passed her lips since the 1940s. Ruby Ray's baby sister is known around Camden for her wicked temper, which has often landed her in trouble with the law. The walls inside the Liberty County Jail have been her second home after picking fights at the local pool hall when an illegal bet or game went sideways. Opal Sutton Talbot, on the other hand, is the Pale Rider, representing death. She was born nine months to the day after Ruby Ray, and her skin has always had an unnatural, unpleasant greenish tint to it, just like her soul. One foot has been firmly stuck in the grave since her birth.

How these two miserable souls were related to—and worse, outlived—her grandmother is beyond Penny's comprehension. Not to mention Penny never forgave them after they tried to swindle Pops out of a prime piece of farmland back in the eighties. Those are big deals around here, land and taking advantage of family. Ruby Ray may have let bygones be bygones with her sisters, but Penny certainly hasn't forgotten. After their duplicity, her familial allegiances leaned toward the Rays of Willow Creek rather than the Suttons of Sulphur Springs. It's a fitting place for them, after all.

"What on earth are you two doing here? And how did you get in? The door was locked," Penny says, both dumbstruck and incensed at the intrusion into her personal space.

"This is *my* sister's house," Pearl says, standing up. "I can come here anytime I like."

"*Was* your sister's house," Penny corrects her under her breath, trying to mask her anger. "But you didn't answer my question. How did you get in here?"

"I know where Ruby Ray hides the spare key," Pearl replies, holding it up like some prized catfish she snagged from the Barren River.

Raisin cookies, for some reason, come flooding to Penny's mind at the moment. Comparing these opportunistic women to them, like her grandmother did, is an insult to baked goods everywhere. Penny decides on the spot these two miserable souls are walnuts instead, hard and ugly on the outside, full of bitterness on the inside.

"You two shouldn't be here unannounced," Penny tells them.

"I'm sorry," the shrunken Opal says after taking a hit from her ever-present portable oxygen tank. "Did we interrupt something?" A wicked grin spreads across her haggard face.

"We've heard the rumors swirling around town," Aunt Pearl chimes in. "'Bout how you've been messin' around with ole Doc Hitchens here since you got home. But I would've thought you'd have more respect for your grandmother's memory, my sister's memory, than to do it under her roof."

Deep breaths, Penny reminds herself. *Murder's still a capital crime in the state of Kentucky. The Commonwealth can still fire up "Ole Sparky" whenever needed.* "I was expecting you *next Thursday*." Penny pauses for effect. "When I invited you."

"We thought we'd best get over here before the house was empty. We've heard how you've done thrown away all our sister's treasures. Dumping them into the trash without a care in the world. Her memories. Why on earth she left you this place is beyond me. Lord knows you don't need the money," she says, again struggling for air. She almost sounds like a country version of Darth Vader.

By now, Bradley's heard enough and can no longer remain silent. "Ladies, I really don't think—"

"This ain't none of your business, Doc," Opal tells him.

"Stay out of it. This is a family matter. We've got a bone to pick with this one," Pearl says, motioning toward Penny. "She's been cherry-picking the antiques. Hogging it all. Shipping truckloads back to Atlanta. Or worse, giving away all the valuables to strangers. Ada Pickert done told us you offered up the grandfather clock to her at church. She ain't even family. This is our inheritance."

Good ole Ada Pickert, the Methodist-hating pot stirrer. "I can assure you I've only thrown out trash. Copious amounts, if you need to know. Apparently, your sister was quite the pack rat. As for your claims that I'm somehow 'cherry-picking' the valuables, you have nothing to worry about. Like I told you last week, I'm giving both you and Aunt Molly the opportunity to take all the furniture and keepsakes in the house you want. They're yours."

"Then it's settled. We're gonna stay right here and watch you pack and start taking what rightfully belongs to us," Pearl says.

"You can come back next week. After I've had a chance to organize the house. Right now, I'm asking you to leave."

"You rushing us outta here?" Opal asks.

"No. But I have a lot of work to do, and I'm also expecting a call from my boys this morning. I'd like some privacy." Penny sighs, closing her eyes, exhausted by their antics. She wants to give them a piece of her mind rather than a piece of her inheritance.

"Oh, they done called already," Pearl tells her. "Had a nice chat with your husband this morning after you left. Or rather got home then left again."

"Excuse me?" Penny asks, confused. Not only does Pearl seem to know her comings and goings, suggesting she's keeping tabs on her, but more importantly, she's taken the phone call from her boys in Africa. "You answered my phone?"

"It's Ruby Ray's phone, young lady. It was ringing off the hook. What was she supposed to do?" Opal asks.

"What did you tell him?"

"Well, he asked for you, and I explained you were out," Pearl says. "Considering the hour, he seemed confused. So he asked if I knew where you could be. I told him I had a sneaking suspicion you might be out with good ole Doc Hitchens. Told him how you've been gallivanting around town with him since the second you got back." A wicked grin takes over her wrinkled face. "Also, I might have mentioned, in passing, how you got caught skinny-dipping last night at the country club. As I understand it, the police had to get involved. That seemed to prick up his ears. As it should, since you're still married to him in the eyes of God."

Under normal circumstances, Nadine Penelope Ray Crenshaw would've backed down, allowing these vile blood relations to run roughshod over her. In her thirty-seven years, she's mastered the role of peacemaker, even when doing so often bit her in the proverbial ass. No good deed goes unpunished. But something inside her snaps. No, it explodes.

"First of all, *Aunt* Pearl, Teddy is no longer my husband. He's my *ex*-husband. It's none of his business what I do or who I see. He's in Africa. With his *new* wife, celebrating his *new* marriage," Penny says. Anger causes her pulse to race, making her cheeks heat. "He has no say in my personal life any longer. As for you two, you have no right to come into my house. Yes, Opal, it's *mine*," she says, preventing her aunt from speaking. "What I do here in Kentucky doesn't concern you. I'm a grown woman, and I don't answer to either of you. Please leave."

The forcefulness in Penny's voice fails to sway the gemstone aunts. They stand their ground like defiant three-year-olds, refusing to relent to her wishes. After what seems like an eternity of silence, all parties partaking in a stare off, Penny speaks.

"If you refuse to leave, I'll call the police. As you've so kindly pointed out, I'm quite familiar with them after last night."

"Ladies, I think it's best you go." Bradley motions toward the door.

Realizing Penny isn't budging, they decide to cut their losses for the day. "This ain't over." Pearl huffs, walking toward the door.

"It never is." Penny shakes her head.

After the self-righteous pair vacate the premises, Penny's eyes begin to sting. She's been trying to conceal her emotions from Opal and Pearl's onslaught. "I don't know why Ruby Ray left me this house," she whispers. "It's only caused grief and pain for everyone concerned."

Bradley gathers her into his arms. "She did it because she loved you," he replies, stroking her hair.

"Ten days. I've got to get through the next ten days, and I'll be finished with all this," she tells him. "My aunts. This house. Kentucky. Once and for all." She tucks her head deep into his chest.

"I get it. But I hope you don't wash your hands of everything and everyone here. There are a lot of people who love you." He pauses before continuing. "Jimmy Neal, Gracie Belle, your friends. Me."

In her anger at her aunt's accusations and insinuations, Penny realizes it's caused her to inadvertently throw the baby—aka her relationship with Bradley—out with the bathwater.

"I'm sorry. I didn't mean it. Yes, I'm finished with Opal, Pearl, and this house, but I'm not finished with you." She breaks away from his chest. "Not by a long shot."

"I'm glad to hear that," he says, relief filling his voice. "We only have a few days left together. Let's make the most of them."

"You're right, Bradley. Let's not waste a second of it."

Chapter 23

The X Factor

"That's the last load," Bradley says, looking around Ruby Ray's now-barren living room.

"I can't believe we're almost finished. We got through it so fast," Penny whispers with a hint of sadness as she scans the room. Only the furniture, including the damned grandfather clock, which Bradley now hates as much as Penny, remains. The pictures on the walls, the magazines scattered about, and the trinkets and personal effects that make a home warm and inviting are all gone. The house is cold.

"Well, you've worked me like a mule for the past week. That's why we finished so quickly," Bradley says, coming up behind her and slipping his arms around her waist.

"For everything you've done, I'll never be able to repay you."

"I can think of something," he says, kissing her neck.

The past ten days have been a whirlwind for Penny. She's spent them organizing quilts and afghans, sorting through old mail and magazines, and giving away clothes and shoes to the local Goodwill, all while showing the house to potential buyers. But her nights always belonged to Bradley. As soon as his last patient walked out of his office, he was right on their heels, heading toward Ruby Ray's. Even Miss Paulette was in on the action, picking up the slack and even rescheduling appointments. She seemed to be thrilled at the prospect that Dr. Hitchens had finally discovered a love life. Unbeknownst to her and most of Camden, Bradley had dated since his wife's passing. He wasn't a monk, after all. But he was discreet.

"That's about everything," he says, surveying the room.

"Not everything."

"What's left?"

She forces a smile upon her dewy face. "Tomorrow. We'll talk about it then." Something's on her mind, but Bradley doesn't press her.

"Okay. Tomorrow, then. Ready to head out?" He opens the door, and they begin making their customary short walk back to his bungalow—their place.

Exhausted, she collapses onto his couch. He pours a heaping glass of sauvignon blanc for her then grabs a beer for himself. The crisp wine is needed after a long day of packing, but more importantly, it settles her nerves. Tomorrow fills her with dread. Not only will she be running interference with her aunts, watching them fight like two cats strung over a clothesline, clawing each other's eyes out over Ruby Ray's dining room set or Pops's knife collection, but she'll also be facing one last packing obstacle, the one she's been avoiding.

While Bradley fiddles with the stereo in the corner, Penny curls up on his leather couch. The place holds many fond memories for them. This is her favorite part of their nightly routine. The sex is incredible, and she always looks forward to it, but this is the time when she feels most connected to him, sitting down, talking, listening—being heard.

The woody sounds of an electric guitar begin floating in the air, filling the room. It's haunting, almost pleading. The light brush of a snare drum keeping the beat catches her attention.

"I love this song." She smiles after recognizing Ray LaMontagne's distinct sound. He's a staple on The Coffee House, her go-to station on her car radio.

"Me too," he says, joining her on the couch and taking a long drink from his bottle.

Penny closes her eyes, resting her head against the back of the couch. This is the first time today she's stopped, and it feels so good. With the words to "Let It Be Me" humming in her ears and the wine coursing through her body, she sinks deeper into the cushions. The tension in her neck, in her entire body, slowly melts away.

As Ray belts out the chorus, Bradley leans in and asks, "May I have this dance?"

Her eyes flutter open. "What?"

"You heard me."

"You want to dance? Now?"

"Yes, I do."

"It's almost ten o'clock at night. On a Tuesday. Why would you want to do that now?"

"Because you look so beautiful at this moment that I can't help myself."

"Beautiful? My hair's a mess, and I've been packing all day. You can do better than that." She takes a draw off her wine.

"You've never looked better."

She suppresses a smile. "Your compliments aren't enough to get me off this couch."

"Okay." He traces her collarbone with his finger. "Maybe I want to dance with you because it's been twenty years since we had a chance to."

"That's a long time."

"You remember our first song? Back when we were kids?"

"'Heaven,'" she whispers.

He stands up, taking her glass and setting it on the coffee table. "Dance with me, Penny."

"Give me one good reason."

"Because I want the chance to hold the woman I love in my arms while I still can."

Those words pierce her heart. She isn't the only one who knows their summer affair will be coming to an end. The glass carriage of their newfound relationship will be replaced by the big fat pumpkin of reality in a matter of hours, and there's nothing she can do to stop time from ticking away. As silly as dancing barefoot in the dark, dressed in a dirty T-shirt, is, she accepts his offer.

She wraps her arms around his neck while he places his hands on her hips. Their bodies begin moving to the music. She's sorely out of practice. Her dance card has been empty for years, another thing in her life she's missed out on. This simple pleasure has all but been forgotten by her, but tonight, she'll dance, savoring every minute, every second of being in his arms. This is a memory that will live on forever.

Finally, when they can no longer contain their desires, they make love on the chestnut sofa to the acoustic guitar of "Winter Birds."

As she lays her head on his chest, Penny's eyes become heavy. Safety mixed with satisfaction is better than any sleeping pill she could ever try. As she's about to slip into a deep slumber, his voice brings her back from the land of Nod.

"Where do we go from here?" he whispers.

"What do you mean?"

"You're leaving Friday. What happens to *us*?"

The word *us* spins around in her head. Whether she's ready to admit it or not, she's in a relationship with her childhood sweetheart, who's now her adult lover. It's a valid question.

This is the conversation she's been avoiding. Any discussion of the future has been sidestepped all week. They both have children and carry the responsibilities that come with parenthood. Blissfully skipping into a metaphorical sunset with that kind of heavy baggage isn't so simple. The real world has real expectations. Sometimes there are no happy endings. Bradley's girls anchor him to Kentucky, and outside his self-deprecating humor, he's the most popular dentist in town. He's built a thriving practice since his return to Camden, while her life is set firmly in Atlanta with her boys. But geography is only one obstacle they face.

"I'm sure we'll keep in touch. We can call. Or text. Maybe you can come to Atlanta for a visit sometime," she says.

"That was convincing."

"I'm not sure what you want me to say."

Bradley's chest rises and falls. "I can't lose you again. We've lost too much time already. All because of me."

"Don't. Like I told you when I showed up at your doorstep, all's forgiven when it comes to Emily."

"But will it ever be forgotten?"

Those words leave her speechless. He's right. Forgiveness doesn't necessarily mean you can forget.

"I'm afraid there will always be something between us unless you finally know the truth about that night, even if it's not pretty," Bradley says.

"To be honest with you, I've always wondered."

"I'm sure you have."

Penny takes a deep breath and lets it out slowly. "Okay, I'm ready to listen."

"Are you sure?"

She nods.

"After we left the party at the spillway, when the police showed up, I told Emily I didn't want to go home. I couldn't risk the chance of running into my parents. Not with beer on my breath. So Emily and I drove around. We started talking. Talking about you and me."

"About what we almost did that night?" Penny asks softly.

"Yes," he says. "That came up."

"Go on."

"Later that night, we found ourselves at another party. This time at Suzy Patterson's. You remember her?"

Penny glances down at her wrist, which she almost broke after Suzy dropped her during a middle school cheerleading stunt. "How could I forget."

"There were about twenty people there. A few who came from the spillway party. Shannon Madison was there, of course. They were all playing truth or dare." He pauses. "With tequila shots."

"Oh."

"I'll spare you the details, but Emily and I joined in. After a couple of rounds, we sure as hell didn't need to drive home, so Suzy told us we could spend the night, since her parents were out of town for the Fourth."

"Okay," Penny says, bracing herself for the rest of the story.

"Then it was Shannon's turn again. That's when she dared Emily to either tell a truth or kiss me."

Penny cleared her throat. "I'm pretty sure I know what she chose."

"Emily chose the truth," Bradley says.

A chill runs down Penny's spine. The Emily Johnston she knew wouldn't know the truth if it sat on her. "What did Shannon ask?"

"If Emily had been keeping a secret from me. One that she'd been protecting me from for years, knowing it would break my heart if it was ever discovered."

Penny's pulse quickens. "What secret?"

Bradley takes in a deep breath. "That since eighth grade, the only reason you liked me and kept stringing me along for so long was so you could finally get away from your family. Out of your mother's house and into one in Beacon Hills."

Penny's fingers tingle. "What?"

"Shannon said you were so desperate to live there that you would stop at nothing to make it happen. You even bragged about it to Emily, saying something like, 'Where there's a will, there's a way.' Then Suzy confirmed it. She said she heard you use the same words one day in the bathroom but didn't know what it meant."

Hot bile creeps up Penny's throat. They had twisted her innocent words into something sinister. "Bradley, I did say those words, but—but it's not like that. I was trying to stand up to Emily. You never crossed my mind. I wasn't your friend for money or a house in Beacon Hills. Far from it."

Bradley pulls Penny's body closer to his. "I know, but at the time, I wasn't thinking straight. After they dropped their little bomb on me, I stormed out of Suzy's house, but Emily followed. Once she caught up, she told me she was sorry I'd found out. She'd always tried protecting me. In that moment, she reminded me of the girl I used to know, the one I cared for. The one who was my friend. After that, any good judgment on my part flew out the window. I let my guard down. I was angry and confused. Mix in a couple of shots of tequila and some raging hormones. Well... Like my father always told me, one mistake can change the course of your life. God, was he spot-on about that."

A deafening silence fills the room before Bradley breaks it. "There's no excuse for what I did that night. I hated being a cheater."

"I had already broken up with you by the time you slept with Emily. So technically, you didn't cheat on me."

"You're letting me off on a technicality?"

"It's not my place to judge, Bradley. It was a mistake. I have to let it go. Once and for all."

"So we can finally move on? No more Emily?" Bradley asks.

Penny bites her lip. "I have one last question. Something I've always wondered about."

"What is it?"

"After you got married, did you ever love her?" she asks timidly.

"No," he says in a low voice. A long pause follows. "And I'll regret it until my dying day."

The room's deathly quiet, and Penny's mind begins spinning with endless possibilities on why he would regret not loving Emily.

"The first year of our marriage..." He swallows hard. "I never touched her. I didn't even kiss her on our wedding day. I was so angry about everything. That night. Her parents. My parents. The wedding. The baby." He pauses. "You. All I could think about was you."

Those words take Penny back to that painful summer, the fall when he married Emily, and the spring when he became a father to a little girl.

"I didn't hate her, though. I was indifferent toward her. Which was worse," he says with regret in his voice. "I barely spent any time in our apartment. Instead, I lived at the library to avoid her. Never bothered to eat any of the dinners she made for us. Never even said a thank-you for trying. Skipped all the childbirth classes she signed us up for, leaving her to go it alone. I was a terrible husband, and I never missed the chance to show her. I was cruel with my silence, and I let her go through a pregnancy that I was responsible for without a kind word. Or even a smile. I was a monster."

This is an unexpected turn of events in the storyline Penny created in her mind regarding his marriage. Based on her vast knowledge of Emily's cruelty, she rightfully assumed Emily was the monster in the marriage, not the other way around.

"But..." The next question is the most important one. No matter how hard she tried, she never understood. "Why did you...?" She can't wrap her mind, let alone her lips, around what she needs to say.

"Have another child with her?"

Penny nods.

"After Ashleigh Cate was born, my world changed." His chest swells with pride. "When I held her for the first time, I can't explain it, but Ace became my world, and I'd do anything to keep her happy and safe. Even if it meant staying with her mother for a little while. But before I could even process what it really meant to be a father or to become a decent husband, Emily sank into a deep depression. For months, she never left the bed. Wouldn't shower or eat. Never looked at or touched the baby. I didn't know what was wrong with her. I was still a kid myself. I ignored the signs she was in trouble until the day she walked out the front door in nothing but a nightgown onto Versailles Road in rush-hour traffic. It wasn't just the baby blues—it was a full-blown post-partum episode. And it was my fault. I left her alone all those months while she was pregnant, in a new town with no friends. All I did was blame her for my life being destroyed, never once thinking her life had changed too. It took six months in a hospital before she got better, and when she came home, she was... a really good mom.

"I promised if she got better, I'd try to be a real husband. We found a church group and a pastor we liked who encouraged me to honor my vows. We tried to live together as a couple, but my heart was never in it. She knew it. My heart was still with you, and she knew that too."

Hearing how he'd never forgotten her, even after he was married, causes Penny's throat to tighten.

"A few years later, Ace became obsessed with having a little sister. It was all she talked about, and Emily was desperate for another child. She was an incredible mother, believe it or not, but I didn't want to bring another baby into the marriage. I was going through the motions. Then one day, I heard the news you were getting married, and well, it crushed me that you'd moved on. I realized I'd lost you forever, so I relented. Ace got the sister she wanted, and I fell in love all over again with another beautiful girl. It should've been a happy time, but no matter how hard I tried, I still couldn't make myself love Emily. I wasn't interested in being married, and she knew it."

His voice softens. "But then I noticed she no longer cared. Because Emily wasn't interested in being with me anymore either."

Penny's heart quickens.

"A few months later, I found out she was having an affair with a guy from our small group at church. Nice guy. Really. A law student at UK. Actually, I liked him a lot," he explains with no malice in his voice.

"I'm so sorry," Penny whispers, knowing how much unfaithfulness hurts.

"Don't be. Emily deserved a little happiness after what I put her through. As cruel as she was as a teenager, motherhood softened her. I was fine with her leaving me for Tony. Deep down, I was relieved. She found someone she loved, and he loved her back. She deserved that. But before we filed the separation papers, she had the accident. Since it would only hurt the girls and Emily's parents if the affair came out, Tony and I agreed to keep it between us. He went back to his wife, and I moved to Camden to start my practice. I'll never forgive myself for Emily. She never got the chance to be with the love of her life."

His candor and openness leaves Penny speechless. A new light has been shed upon her tormentor. Emily Johnston Hitchens had her own complicated, difficult life as well. She was human, too, with real feelings and real emotions, and she suffered unimaginable pain. No longer was she the one-dimensional antagonist in Penny's story. Emily had her own burdens to bear.

"What?" Penny asks. So deep in her thoughts, processing the new version of Emily, she didn't hear his question.

"Does this change how you feel about me?" Bradley repeats.

Without hesitation, she leaves the safe confines of his chest and arms. Leaning over him before gently brushing her finger across his cheek, she says, "Of course not. You're a good man, Bradley. Being in a loveless marriage doesn't change that." For once, she's reassuring him, not the other way around. "To be honest with you, I've had my own doubts about my marriage for years. I'm afraid I didn't love Teddy, at least not the way a wife should love her husband. I hoped I had. I even thought I did. But this week with you has solidified those doubts. My love for him was more platonic than romantic."

With a look of relief, Bradley pulls her back into his arms. Tonight, they've finally put Emily to rest. She's now behind them. "So, I ask again. Where do we go from here?"

"I don't know," Penny says, sighing deeply. "I just don't know." Tucking her head into his shoulder, she prays the answer will come to her soon.

Chapter 24

A Nightmare on Dogwood Lane

"Tired of my eggs already?" Bradley asks.

"No," she says. "They're wonderful."

"You've been making crop circles with them for twenty minutes. You haven't touched your food, and your coffee's cold. I know something's wrong. Is this about last night?"

"W-What? No. It has nothing to do with that. Actually, I'm glad we finally talked about it. I promise this has nothing to do with Emily. Or Teddy."

"Then what's on your mind? I know something's bothering you. Is this about your aunts? Dealing with them today?"

"It's not about them. Besides, I have Gracie Belle coming over to run interference."

"Then what is it?"

A long, awkward silence ensues before she begins. "Could you help me do one last thing before you go to work today?"

"Of course."

"Let's go," she says, pushing away from the table.

After the short walk down Dogwood Lane, they arrive at Ruby Ray's, where she leads him down the long hallway and into her grandmother's bedroom.

"What's left to do in here?" Bradley asks, looking around the room. Only the antique cherry bedroom suite remains. No quilts, books, or personal effects, only the furniture, which will be gobbled up in a few hours by Penny's edacious aunts.

Without saying a word, she lets her gaze lead his toward Pops's bedside table. Then it seems to dawn on him why she's brought him into this room, of all rooms, asking for his help.

"I see," he says in a low voice. "What do you want me to do with it?"

"I don't care. Just get rid of it, please."

Without saying a word, Bradley walks over to the bedside table. After grabbing the revolver, he discreetly places it behind his back, under the waistband of his pants. Penny Ray will never lay eyes upon it again.

"Is that all?" he asks gently.

"The picture," she says, pointing at the family portrait, which he moved a mere two inches to the left all those years ago. "There's still a bullet lodged behind it. I can't leave it for the new owners to find."

"Okay. I'll stop by Farley's today for putty and sandpaper. It's a quick fix, but I'm afraid we won't be able to match the wallpaper."

She shakes her head. "It doesn't matter. Mr. McGuire told me whoever buys this house will have to strip it down. It's peeling in the corners already."

"I'll take care of it after work," he tells her before pausing. "I wish you'd asked me to clear out this room for you. I can't imagine it was easy."

"I didn't. Gracie Belle packed it up last week. I started cleaning it out myself last Sunday before our ransom dinner. I wasn't thinking. When I opened that drawer, when I saw it, I was stunned. After all these years, it still took my breath away. I haven't stepped foot in here since. Kept the door closed. When I asked Gracie Belle to box up the room but to leave the bedside tables and the picture alone, she did. No questions asked."

"Gracie Belle is a kind woman."

"Yes, she is."

"Are you sure I can't help you today?"

"You already have," she says, leaning into his chest.

He wraps his arms around her. She's going to miss this place. Not Camden. Not Kentucky. Not even this beautiful foursquare. It's Bradley's embrace she'll long for. Inhaling a long, deep breath, she closes her eyes, wanting to capture his aroma so that she can take it back with her to Georgia.

"Penny" comes an acerbic voice from the living room, breaking the moment. "Where are you?"

"Who's that?" he asks.

"Who do you think?" Penny replies, exasperated. "One of the horsemen of the apocalypse."

"I thought your aunts weren't coming over until eight."

"Penny?" Pearl cries out again, stomping down the hallway while slamming doors in her wake.

"Do you think something as simple as time would deter her? Actually, I'm surprised she wasn't on the front porch at the crack of dawn."

Pearl walks into the bedroom, discovering them. "Well, of course *you're* here," she hisses at Bradley like a feral cat.

"Aunt Pearl. So good to see you," Penny says, plastering a fake smile upon her face.

"It's time to get this show on the road. You've been puttin' us off all week." Pearl huffs, snapping her fingers in a bid to get things moving. "Opal and my grandsons are outside with the trailer. We want what rightfully belongs to us."

Whether it's Pearl's demand of heirlooms that don't belong to her or the discourtesy of her snapping fingers, Penny becomes incensed. Her aunt's rudeness gives her the tiniest backbone to finally stand up to the incorrigible woman. "I'm sure you're quite prepared and eager to begin, but we can't start without Aunt Molly. Remember your niece? Your sister's daughter?" Penny's voice drips with mockery.

"I know what she wants," Pearl says. "She won't mind if we go on without her."

Clearly, the woman's lying. Though Molly and Pearl became uneasy allies in the fight against Penny in Ruby Ray's Last Will and Testament battle, it's a shaky alliance at best. The gloves will come off the second one of them makes a move toward the deep freezer or the mahogany Chippendale secretary.

"We're going to wait for her just to be safe," Penny insists. "Shouldn't Aunt Molly have a say in what she wants?"

"That ain't fair! I knew Ruby Ray first," Pearl says. The pact is crumbling before Penny's eyes, much to her amusement. Her great-aunt's terrible excuse regarding inheritance rights is childish.

"Nothing happens until Aunt Molly arrives. That's final."

"What are we supposed to do for the next hour?" Pearl complains, crossing her arms over her thick stomach. "Wait outside in the truck?"

"Aunt Pearl, you're family. I would never leave you in a truck to melt away on a hot July morning." Penny smiles. "You're more than welcome to wait out on the front porch instead. In the shade, of course."

In a huff, Pearl exits the room to tattle to the others about her great-niece's unbending rules. There'll be no head start for them.

Bradley leans down and whispers in Penny's ear, "I like this side of you."

"It was kind of gratifying. Putting her in her place," she says, shocked by her newfound authority.

"Remember to stand your ground. I'll check in on you a little later," he says with a wink before heading out to the office. "Go get 'em, tiger."

Penny follows Bradley onto the porch, where Pearl, Opal, and a gaggle of Garrison boys, her third cousins on the Sutton side of her family, now wait. While smoking their Marlboro Reds, they shoot daggers with their eyes toward Penny.

"Good morning." Penny nods, acknowledging her guests and their glares.

"Morning," Opal replies with a stiff upper lip, taking a hit off her oxygen tank. Apparently, she's received word from her sister about the equal playing field Penny's just leveled.

"We'll get started as soon as Aunt Molly arrives. Please make yourselves comfortable," Penny says to the crowd, motioning toward the rocking chairs. "Oh, and if you don't mind, please don't smoke on the property today. As you know, it's a hazard for Aunt Opal and her oxygen tank to be near lit cigarettes. We wouldn't want anything to happen to her. Now, would we?" She smiles again, though her aunt's safety is the last thing on her mind. The noxious fumes floating about are what bother her.

An hour later, as the pesky grandfather clock strikes eight, Aunt Molly arrives from Paducah. With her, she's brought an oversized U-Haul truck and her second husband, John, an effeminate, lanky man, whom Penny's only met twice before. Three bulky men follow the couple up the steps. They need the help—John doesn't look like he could handle the pain of a hangnail, much less lift a heavy couch or cherry hutch. Molly's entourage and preparation skills are impressive, overshadowing Pearl and Opal's futile attempts. The gemstone aunts' flatbed trailer is puny in comparison to Molly's mammoth rental. Not to mention the scrawny Garrison boys, all six of them put together, couldn't match the strength of just one of Molly's muscular movers.

The contrast between Molly and Ruby Ray's sisters doesn't end there. Where the gemstone aunts are uncouth and crude, the acting-before-thinking type, Molly Ray Montgomery is polished and refined, calculating and cold. Where Opal and Pearl are old and haggard from years of hard living and from the treatment of even harder men, Molly's ageless and beautiful from years of easy living and being indulged by the opposite sex. Though not particularly rich, Aunt Molly's always lived very comfortably, thanks to the loveless marriage pacts she's made with her two husbands and the sprinkling of lovers on the side. However, there's never enough money to satisfy her, because she's always thirsted for more. Today, she's prepared for battle.

As strained as Penny's relationship has been with her aunt, especially after Ruby Ray's Last Will and Testament, Penny still greets Molly with a short hug. It's reciprocated with a frosty kiss on Penny's right cheek.

"Good to see you, Penny," Molly says. Both she and Penny know she doesn't mean a word of it.

"Good to see you too," Penny replies with a little more emotion than her aunt's sentiments.

For a woman in her early sixties, Molly looks a decade younger. She's a striking woman who possesses perfect cheekbones and a painfully flattering silver bob. Her effortless beauty causes Penny to both envy and admire her. Not to mention Molly's makeup is always on point—not too heavy, not too light. How she managed that face and hair after a two-hour drive down the William Natcher Parkway this morning is beyond Penny.

"The boys? Are they here?" Molly asks, pretending to search for her great-nephews. It's obvious she doesn't care for little ones, having forgone motherhood, but she keeps up appearances. Having Penny's boys around would make it much harder to play the role of victim today. Children soften uncomfortable situations. Molly needs this day to be as unpleasant as possible for her niece so that she'll come out the victor.

"No. They're with Teddy on a family vacation."

"Oh. I see. Sorry to miss them." She sighs with no sorrow in her voice.

"Can we get started now?" Pearl asks, tapping her foot. Even she sees this is a charade, and it's wearing thin.

"Yes, Aunt Pearl," Penny replies.

"Time's a-wasting," Opal says breathlessly.

"Is there some sort of plan here today?" Molly waves her hand gracefully in the faces of her allies.

Penny suppresses the urge to smile, seeing Molly dismissing her aunts' presence. The Axis of Aunts is already crumbling less than a minute in.

"Yes, I have a plan," Penny says after spying Gracie Belle walking up the sidewalk. Her one-woman reinforcement has arrived right on time.

"Well, what are you waiting for?" Pearl asks. The woman is like an eager child on Easter Sunday, preparing to make a charge at a field of eggs.

"Good morning, ladies," Gracie Belle says, walking into the lion's den. Or in this case, a wraparound porch full of rocking chairs and swings.

Pearl points. "What's she doing here? That woman ain't family."

"Actually, Gracie Belle *is* family. She's part of the *Ray* family, not the *Suttons*," Penny says slowly, making it clear she wants no part in this branch of her family tree. "But that's not important right now. I've asked her here today so she can *help* you. I know how emotional it will be for you, going through Ruby Ray's belongings, her keepsakes, knowing how much you all loved her."

"I don't need no help," Pearl interjects. "I'm fine."

"Of course you are, Aunt Pearl. You were always the strong one," Penny says smugly. "But just the same, she'll be right by your side during this emotional day." Gracie Belle's presence has nothing to do with emotional support. Penny hopes having an extra set of eyes on the two cantankerous women will keep them and their salty tongues in line.

"Can we begin?" Molly asks once again. There's a walnut dining room suite she covets. Once Penny releases the hounds, she'll be making a beeline for it.

"Well, I guess it's up to you," Penny says, looking at Molly. "Since you're Ruby Ray's only surviving child, I think it's only fitting that you pick first. Take it all, as far as I'm concerned. If there's anything left..." She turns toward Pearl and Opal. "You can have the rest."

"*What?*" all three aunts exclaim. Molly's tone is one of disbelief, while the gemstone aunts' are of outrage and horror.

"You can't do that!" Pearl yelps while Opal collapses onto a rocking chair, thousands of dollars slipping through her wretched fingers. Desperate for more air, Opal begins sucking more oxygen from her tank while her sister ignores her altogether.

"Yes, I can, Aunt Pearl. And I just did. As the sole beneficiary of the estate, I can decide how we proceed. I think Aunt Molly deserves first right of refusal. Don't worry. I'm sure she'll leave you a few keepsakes. Some sentimental reminders of Ruby Ray. Because isn't that why you're all here? To have a little piece of her? A memory?"

"I won't stand for this!" Pearl howls.

"I don't suppose there's much you can do about it now," Gracie Belle says without empathy or sympathy. "Let's sit down and have some iced tea while Molly figures out what she wants. I think a little privacy is fittin' in a time like this."

Taking Pearl by the arm, Gracie Belle guides her to a rocking chair.

"Penny, I-I..." Molly struggles for the right words. "Don't know what to say."

"There's nothing to say. You were Ruby Ray's daughter. All this should've been yours from the start. Not mine. Certainly not those two." Penny motions toward her aunts, where her great-aunts are bellyaching to Pearl's grandsons, who are in a state of shock.

"Don't you want... anything?"

"Well, I did take a few things," Penny mumbles. Even now, though Penny's a grown woman, her aunt still intimidates her.

"Let me guess—Ruby Ray's glass basket vase?" Molly asks.

"Yes, and a couple of her Willow Creek cookbooks and cast-iron skillets." Her aunt will never miss those items, since they are of no monetary value. "And two quilts. The Lonestar on my bed and the cornflower-blue cross-stitch. It was always my favorite," she adds, worried it might set off her aunt. Even though Molly has been given free rein to take whatever she wants in the house, the quilts could fetch top dollar at festivals around Kentucky, especially since they were stitched by Ruby Ray.

Molly clears her throat. "That's fair."

Penny almost laughs. Of course it's more than fair. She's giving her aunt all the belongings in the house. But even now, with the generosity being shown to her, Molly Montgomery has no problem looking this gift horse in the mouth.

"You'd better get started, then," Penny says. "I'm not sure how long Gracie Belle can corral Pearl and Opal over there."

"I won't take it all. I'll leave a few items for them," Molly says, trying to suppress her smugness. "Maybe Ruby Ray's hideous guest bedroom suite. I've always hated it. That should calm them down a bit."

"I doubt it. Nothing's going to soothe those two today."

"John!" Molly barks at her mealy-mouthed husband, who's been watching the absurd dynamics of his wife's family. "Retrieve the movers. We have work to do."

As efficient as Penny has been, preparing the house for this day, packing, organizing, boxing, and labeling, Molly and her movers are on a different level. They're a well-oiled machine, methodical in their movements. Within six hours, they're finished. Stuffed into the Montgomerys' silver Mercedes SUV are dozens of quilts, afghans, lace tablecloths, and most of the china and silverware. The U-Haul's packed full of lamps, two couches, multiple chairs, the entire dining room set, Ruby Ray's bedroom suite, the mahogany secretary, three coffee tables, and the deep freezer from the barn, ready to make their way west to Paducah, completely out of reach of Pearl and Opal's clutches. If Aunt Molly planned to leave a bone for the two, she certainly made it a tiny one.

During Molly's frenzy of acquiring all the goods in each room, the gemstone aunts and their gangly grandsons swept in from behind, taking what was left. So desperate for any tiny breadcrumbs left, they snatched up everything in sight, grabbing the percolator, a box of chipped coffee mugs, all the Crystal Oat plastic cups, and every edition for the last ten years of both *Southern Living* and *National Geographic*. Even Penny's half-empty canister of Maxwell House coffee was swiped for no other reason than it still remained. Nothing's left, not even a teaspoon. It's as if a swarm of locusts descended on 225 Dogwood Lane on that hot July day, almost biblical and comical at the same time. Penny suspects Pearl and Opal will be hosting a rather large yard sale in the weeks to come, selling everything their grubby little hands snatched today, but Penny lets it go.

When the day finally comes to a merciful close, with Opal and Pearl cramming the last of the old canning jars onto their tobacco trailer and Molly's movers shutting the U-Haul's mammoth doors, Penny knows the end is near. Only two items remain in the vacant yellow foursquare with green shingles and shutters to match—the family portrait in Ruby Ray's bedroom covering the bullet hole and the damned grandfather clock sitting in the living room, not because the clock wasn't coveted by all three aunts. They had a small fight right after lunch over it. No, it's because Penny couldn't part with her ticking tormentor, for some inescapable reason.

As she waves—perhaps a little too enthusiastically—goodbye to her family, Penny realizes it's the last time she'll ever lay eyes on her aunts. They're exiting her life forever, since their common thread is gone. Perhaps they'll finally send her that elusive Christmas card she's been waiting for year after year. Maybe upon receiving the ample checks from the proceeds of the house, they'll call and thank her. But Penny doubts it. It isn't in any of their natures to send holiday correspondence, much less a thank-you note, since that requires gratitude.

When her aunts barely acknowledge Penny's send-off with their own weak flicks of their wrists, she knows they'll never be satisfied, even with the unexpected windfall of thousands of dollars coming their way in a few weeks.

Chapter 25

How to Lose a Guy in One Day

"**M**s. Crenshaw!" Pat McGuire, Camden's premier Realtor, cries out, waving his hands furiously over his head as he trots up Dogwood Lane. "I've got great news."

"Mr. McGuire. Good to see you," Penny replies, standing up from the front steps of Ruby Ray's wraparound porch.

"Good Lord, child, why are you sittin' out here in this heat? It's hotter than a goat's butt in a pepper patch," he admonishes her while dabbing his thick brow with his monogrammed handkerchief.

"I came out here to say goodbye to my aunts a little while ago. Guess I lost track of time." She has no good explanation for sitting on a scorching concrete porch in the unforgiving afternoon sun. Maybe the empty house is too depressing to face. "What news are you talking about?"

"All three buyers have agreed to our terms!" He's floating on cloud nine and the prospect of the six percent commission he'll be pocketing, since he's representing both sides. "It's up to you who gets this charming abode," he says with enthusiasm. Or it could be a shot of celebratory Maker's Mark from the bottle he keeps under his desk at his office that has lifted his spirits a bit.

"Really?" Her enthusiasm doesn't match the diminutive Realtor's.

"Yes, honey. All three have agreed to pay the asking price of one hundred forty-five thousand as long as it passes the inspection.

Which it's gonna. And the best part, no contingencies with any of 'em," he says with a little hiccup escaping his lips.

"What do I do?"

"Pick one, sweetheart. It's unheard of to have so many buyers for a house in Camden, especially in this terrible market."

"Oh," she says, sitting back down on the steps. "How do I do it?"

Following her lead, he sits down alongside her, pulling a plethora of papers from his old leather briefcase, which has the same monogram on it as his handkerchief.

"What we have here is a mini bidding war. Buyer One asks you to expedite the closing in two weeks. After seeing that godawful tobacco trailer weaving down the street by my office a while ago, I'm sure your crazy aunts done picked this place clean like a wake of vultures. I think it's safe to assume there ain't nothing left in there, so that won't be a problem." He giggles, throwing a side of Kentucky shade onto Pearl and Opal.

Penny smiles at his spot-on observation of her kinfolk.

"Now, Buyer Two wants the closing in forty-five days and wants you to leave all the draperies and light fixtures in place. They're also asking for you to remove all those hideous air conditioners from the windows then repair any damage to the wood and paint after said removal. A little too persnickety for my liking, and the wife is saucy, if you know what I mean." He crinkles his nose. The man loves to dish out a little real estate gossip. "And Buyer Three wants the closing in thirty days. They said nothing about air conditioners or draperies, thank the good Lord."

"And none of them are planning to tear it down?" Penny asks, motioning to her beloved house.

"Honey, this is Camden. Nobody round here is gonna spend almost a hundred fifty thousand dollars to tear down a house. Whoever buys it will have some remodeling to do on the inside. Especially since there's only one bathroom. But no, the house will remain intact," he says, wiping the sweat off his heavy brow. "This place has great curbside appeal. Nobody would dare touch the outside."

"It's all happening so fast."

"Of course it's happening fast. We priced this thing to move. Hell's bells, come to think of it, I probably priced it too low. Never should've cut ten thousand off the price to make up for the lack of central air," he mumbles. "Oh, and one more thing—all three ask that you leave the floor safe in the master closet. I hope you didn't let those cuckoo birds hitch it onto their dilapidated wagon, heading for whatever Podunk holler those two crawled out from." He giggles.

"The safe?"

"Yes, the safe! Are you telling me you plumb forgot about it?" he asks, outraged by the notion. "It's a five-hundred-pound monstrosity just sitting there. How did you miss it, child?"

"I didn't go in that room much," she said, embarrassed she missed such a big item. Shockingly, so did all three aunts.

His face lights up. "You'd better shake a tail feather and open that thing up. Lord knows what's in there. Life insurance policies, stock and bond certificates. Hell, I bet you'll find the deed to the house in there. A treasure trove could be waiting for you."

"No," she says, shaking her head in confusion. "I have the deed and all her paperwork. Ruby Ray's lawyer gave me all those papers after her funeral last year."

"Best check it. Just in case. I hope you know the combination to that thing, because the buyer, whoever it is, will need it."

"I know it."

"Good," he says, relief filling his voice. Penny suspects it's because a locksmith might cut into his commission. "Now, back to business. Who's it gonna be? Buyer One, Two, or Three?"

His excitement is the same as that of Penny's children on Christmas Eve. The man loves to close a deal.

"Since you know them all, maybe you should pick. I only want someone who'll love this place as much as my grandparents did. Someone who will take care of Ruby Ray's girls," she says, nostalgia filling her voice.

"What in tarnation does that mean? What girls are you talkin' about?"

"Never mind." She sighs. "Who do you think I should pick?" She stands up. This is all too final for her liking.

"My gut says you should go with Buyer One," he says, matter-of-factly. "Personally, I like them best. They're good, God-fearing people." With this buyer's requested expedited closing time, Mr. McGuire will be getting his commission sooner rather than later. It's a win-win for him.

"Fine."

"Praise Jesus," he says, throwing his head up toward the sky. "I'll draw up the paperwork this afternoon."

"Thank you." Penny can almost see the old man mentally spending his commission.

"Doc Hitchens," Mr. McGuire says as Bradley walks up the sidewalk. "You should congratulate Penny here. She just sold her house."

A flash of disappointment crosses Bradley's face, which both Penny and Mr. McGuire notice.

"Congratulations," he says.

"Good Lord. You two could depress a bride on her wedding day." Mr. McGuire huffs. "Penny, I'll stop by first thing in the morning with all the closing papers. Then I'll be wiring a very *large* sum of money into your bank account. Maybe that'll turn that frown upside down."

Once the huffy Realtor vacates the premises, no doubt on a mission for more Maker's Mark, Bradley says, "Looks like you survived your aunts today."

"Looks like you went to Farley's." She motions to the yellow bag in his right hand.

"I did." He gives her a gentle smile of reassurance. "Putty, sandpaper, and..." He reaches into the plastic sack. "A Hershey's bar." Bradley holds up Penny's favorite candy.

The chocolate breaks the heavy moment. "Aw, you shouldn't have." She giggles.

"I didn't. This is for me. Since you always forget to feed me when I work, I brought my own provisions," he says, his left dimple appearing. "I was afraid of starvation."

"Ha-ha," she says while he tosses her the sweet treat. "It'd better have almonds."

"Of course. I have a good memory."

"Yes, you do," she says, looking down at the candy. "Well..." She sighs. "I guess it's time we patch up that hole. It's long overdue." She tries to mask how hard it will be to see the bullet again. It came within inches of ending her father's life all those years ago. Even chocolate can't make that better.

"I'll take care of it. Shouldn't take but a couple of minutes. After I finish with the wall, let's go back to my place for a nice dinner. I sent Miss Paulette over to Houchens this afternoon to grab a couple of filets for us."

"Did you pay for them this time?" A chuckle escapes her lips as she remembers their first dinner together.

"Wouldn't you like to know," he says with a wink.

"Dinner sounds wonderful. Thank you." She gives him a little kiss. "Come on. Let's get this over with."

Taking his hand, she leads him inside. It's time to face the last reminder she has of Charlie. Dutifully, Bradley goes into the bedroom while leaving Penny safely outside in the hallway.

After a few moments, he calls to her. "Um, Penny, can you come in here, please?"

"What's wrong?" she asks, poking her head through the door.

He has a confused expression on his face. "It's... Well, it's gone."

"What's gone?" she asks, rushing into the room.

Pointing, Bradley says, "The bullet. The hole. It's gone."

"What?" Penny whispers. Only a small white circle of Sheetrock remains. "Where did it go?" She lightly rubs her shaking finger over the spot where the bullet should be.

"Maybe Charlie fixed it."

The thought of her father doing anything helpful is absurd. "I doubt it." Penny shakes her head.

"Well. Someone did."

As they stand in silence, glaring at the hole where Pops's Colt revolver bullet should be, the wall phone in the hallway begins ringing. So lost in her thoughts, Penny doesn't flinch. Her mind is racing as she thinks of all the possibilities of where the bullet could have disappeared to. Apparently, it vanished into thin air.

"Penny," Bradley says, trying to bring her back into reality. "There's a Ruth Higgins on the phone for you. Said it's urgent."

"Who?" Penny squints.

"Ruth Higgins," he repeats slowly. "She says she's your attorney?"

"Oh. Right," she whispers before swallowing hard. "She's my *divorce* attorney." Dread fills her voice. They never call with good news.

"Hello? Penny?" comes a crisp voice through the line.

"Yes."

"God, you're a hard woman to get ahold of. I've been leaving dozens of messages for you on your cell phone all day."

"I'm in Kentucky. The cell service here is nonexistent."

"That's what Dakota Reisner told me. I called her when I couldn't get you. She gave me this number."

"Ruth, why *are* you calling me?" Penny asks, struggling to get the words out, since a lump as big as a grapefruit is taking up space in her throat.

"Did you get arrested last week?"

Penny gasps. "What?"

"Did you get arrested for..." Papers shuffle in the background. "For public nudity and breaking and entering at the Camden Swim and Golf Club?"

Penny freezes. Ruth Higgins, attorney at law, in Atlanta, Georgia, somehow knows about that night.

"Penny?" she barks, trying to get her attention after she's fallen silent. "Did you get arrested last week?"

"No. I wasn't arrested."

"Well, your former husband and his attorneys are alleging you did. It's all right here in black and white," Ruth explains. "And who is this dentist with you? Bradley Hitchens?"

"He's a friend," Penny says, her voice cracking with fear. Ruth knows not only his name but his profession as well. "How did you find out about this?"

"It's all laid out in a complaint they messengered over to me this morning."

"What complaint?"

"Teddy's prepared to file a motion with the court, questioning your fitness as a parent. He's threatening to seek primary physical custody of the boys," Ruth tells her in her own forced empathetic way. A compassionate divorce attorney is an oxymoron, like watching a bull navigate through a china shop. It's unnatural, and nothing will go unscathed. Their job is to get down and dirty to fight ruthlessly for their clients, not to dwell on the emotional well-being of those they represent. That's the therapist's job.

"Are you kidding?" Penny's shoulders fall.

"This is no joke, I'm afraid," Ruth says with a softer tone after hearing her distress. "Let's start from the beginning. Why would your ex-husband claim you were arrested last week? Were you at this club?"

The lump in Penny's throat is now the size of a bowling ball. It's growing exponentially by the second. "Yes, I *was* at the Camden Swim and Golf Club last week."

"Hmm," Ruth says. "So you *were* arrested then?" Judgment oozes from her voice.

"No, Ruth, I wasn't arrested. But it's true the police were called by a nosy neighbor who saw us swimming in the pool. And no, I was not wearing a bathing suit at the time, but the officer on the scene let us go without incident. That's all. Just a warning. Not even a stern one."

"That's a relief, I suppose. I'll need the name of the officer who responded to the call so I can fight that accusation. However, you still haven't answered the second part of my question. Who's Bradley Hitchens?"

Penny has been trying to answer that question for twenty years and still doesn't know.

"Like I said before, he's a friend."

"According to Teddy's complaint, he's a hell of a lot more than that. I hate to tell you this, but you've been followed by a private detective for the last week. They've been tracking all of your and this Dr. Hitchens fellow's comings and goings."

Nausea rolls through Penny's body at the thought of her summer romance with Bradley, their most intimate moments, having been chronicled by some hack watching from the front seat of some sleazy car parked on the street. Maybe Teddy's detective hid in the row of juniper bushes outside Bradley's living room window, watching their every move and peering through the end of a camera lens as they danced together last night. Of all the cruelty her former spouse has subjected her to in the last year, this is by far the worst. He's violated her privacy.

"What does this mean?" Penny closes her eyes, preparing herself for the worst-case scenario. Old fears take hold. Old habits die hard and don't go away after one blissful week.

"Other than your ex-husband is a vengeful asshole?" Ruth says bluntly. "It means we'll most likely have to fight this in court."

"I can't believe this."

"This is a bullshit filing, without a doubt, especially since you weren't arrested, thank God. But the court will still have to hear the case if he proceeds. Any time one parent makes an allegation like this, warranted or not, it must be explored."

"What happens next?"

"First, I'll send a letter denying their ludicrous claims of your arrest. Next, my paralegal will prepare an immediate motion of dismissal. Since there were no charges brought against you, there's no merit to the question of your fitness as a mother. Then I'll remind the good attorneys at McGinn, Litchfield, and Crocket that filing a petition of this magnitude, leveling an accusation such as this without proof, could be viewed as harassment on the part of their client, and I'll let them know I'm preparing my own countermotion for malicious litigation if they don't drop the case immediately," she says, her pit bull nature shining through.

"Will it work?" Penny asks with a tiny bit of hopefulness.

"Probably not." Ruth sighs. "Look, I'm going out of town for a conference in Seattle Monday, but I'll be back in the office the following week. My assistant will reach out to you, and we'll set up an appointment to meet in person. While I'm gone, feel free to call if something comes up."

"Anything else?" Penny's voice quivers.

"Yeah. Keep your damned clothes on, and stay out of swimming pools," she warns her before landing her final piece of lawyerly advice. "And cool it with the dentist for a little while."

"Really?"

"Until things settle down. Even though Teddy's accusations have no merit, you should still mind your p's and q's right now. Don't give him any more fodder to use against you," Ruth says. "I hate that I'm even suggesting this. You're a single woman, and under normal circumstances, you can date and go out with whomever you please. But these aren't normal circumstances. Like I told you, it takes one judge, one favor called in to the right person, to muddy up this case. I know this isn't fair in any way, shape, or form, but I have a case to win, and you have three children's lives that are being toyed with for no other reason than one parent wanting to stick it to the other. Do us both a favor, and just keep your distance from your *friend* for a little while. Do you understand?"

"Yes," Penny whispers. Now she's being forced to say goodbye again to Bradley Hitchens, not on her terms but rather on Teddy's.

"Good. It's settled. We'll talk soon." Ruth hangs up.

Penny stands there motionless for minutes, still clutching the receiver. Her fingers are numb and white as the dial tone rings in her ear. Another edict from her ex-husband has been laid before her.

Bradley walks in. "Is everything okay?" He's been waiting patiently in the kitchen during the call.

"No."

"What was that about?"

"Teddy," she says then clears her throat while hanging up the phone. "He's threatening legal action against me."

"For what?"

"He's doubting my fitness as a mother."

He scoffs. "That's a joke. Right?"

"No. Far from it."

"On what grounds?"

"Apparently, our little stunt and subsequent arrests at Camden Country Club seem to have caught his attention," she says. "Breaking and entering, not to mention public nudity. Has a nice legal ring to it."

"What? You weren't arrested!"

"Not just me. *We*. We were arrested. Teddy's dragging you into this as well."

"Me?"

"Yes, you. And the cherry on top—he's had a private detective following us around all week. Documenting our comings and goings. Watching our every move. I'm sure there're photographs."

"Who the hell does he think he is?" Bradley asks, shaking his head in anger. "You're not his wife anymore. He has no say in your life."

"It doesn't matter. He's threatening to take away my children." Her voice finally breaks.

Bradley pulls her to his chest. "That will never happen."

She pushes him away. "You don't know that. If Teddy wants something, he gets it. Trust me."

"He'll never take away your children. He's doing this to scare you."

"Well, it's working," she says. "God, I should've seen this coming. He's been so strange all week when the boys called. I knew something was off with him."

"He's a bully, Penny. No court will ever take him seriously," he says, trying to pull her in for a second embrace.

Once again, she recoils at his touch. "Stop saying that! You have no idea who or what I'm up against here."

He puts his hands up. "You're right. I can't imagine how hard this is for you. Come on. Let's go back to my place and talk this through," he says, reaching for her.

Again, she pulls away. "No," she says sternly.

"No? No to what?"

"I'm not going with you."

"I don't understand. Why not?"

"I have a lot to think about. I want to be alone."

"You don't need to be alone right now," he says.

Of course she doesn't need to be alone, but Ruth Higgins has given her three monumental reasons for self-imposed isolation—Trey, Drew, and Sammy. "I think it's best you go," she says.

"Best I go? I'm not leaving you like this," he says, reaching for her again.

"Stop touching me!" she yells, slipping away from his hands. "You should go. Now."

"I don't understand why you're pushing me away. All I want to do is help."

"If you want to help, then leave."

"Why are you acting like this?"

"Because my attorney thinks we should keep our distance from each other while I fight this out in court."

"That's ludicrous advice. You're not married anymore. He can't decide what you do or who you see. It's not his place. You've done nothing wrong here."

"*Other than being completely irresponsible and going skinny-dipping at a private club?*" she yells.

"We didn't hurt anyone. It was harmless fun."

"Well, my ex is taking me to court because of it. Not so harmless now, is it, Bradley?"

"Penny, I'm sorry about that."

"It doesn't matter now." She shakes her head. "It's over."

"What's over? Us? All because your ex-husband is some jealous, spiteful jerk who threatens to drag you into court on trumped-up charges because you found a little happiness with someone else? You know that's what all this is about. He can't stand the thought of you being happy, so he's trying to take it from you. Don't let him win."

"What do you want me to do?"

"Don't bow down to him. Face him head-on."

"Easy for you to say. You don't have a dog in this fight," she hisses like a cornered snake. She hates herself for how she's acting toward him, but she has no choice.

"You don't think I'm invested here? I love you, Penny, and I'll stand by you through all this."

"From Kentucky?" she retorts, crossing her arms.

"What does that mean?"

"You're in Camden, and I'm in Atlanta. How on earth could this ever work? I mean, who are we kidding here? This was never going to develop into a long-term relationship. This was a fling. A summer affair. It was just sex."

"Don't say that. We both know it was more. A lot more. What we've shared over the last week wasn't some seedy friends-with-benefits fling. You know that."

"You asked me last night where we go from here, and you know what? There's nothing past *here*. Past Kentucky. We never had a future together. It was over before it even started, and the sooner we realize it, the better."

"Who says we don't have a future?"

"Just what are you proposing here? A long-distance relationship?" Penny asks. "You really think that can work?"

"It might. There are other possibilities."

"Other possibilities? Like what, Bradley? Are you asking me to move back to Camden? Pack up my children so you and I can play house together? I'm sure Teddy will be totally agreeable to that, considering he's already threatening to sue me for custody for an arrest he's conjured up. I'm sure he'd be thrilled to have his children live six hours away."

"Stop it, Penny," he says, lowering his voice.

"Or better yet, maybe you could move to Atlanta. You can give up the successful dental practice you've been building for ten years while proceeding to drag your teenage daughters away from the only home they've ever known. Away from their friends, from their grandparents, to live with me, a woman they've never met. I'm sure that will work out beautifully."

"Why are you doing this?"

"Because I have no choice!" she yells, her hands shaking. Her maternal instinct has kicked in, taking over her rational thinking. Her role as a mother is being threatened.

"I'd never put you or your boys in jeopardy," he tells her. "I want to help."

"If you want to help, *please* go. I'm begging you," she says.

He reaches for her one last time. "Penny, please."

"Get out!" she screams, twisting away from his touch yet again. "For the love of God, Bradley, just leave."

"Don't do this," he pleads, shaking his head.

"I can't... I can't lose my boys," she says, weeping as soon as the words leave her.

Bradley closes his eyes. Once again, their fate is sealed. Penny Ray is banishing him from her life, just like she did when they were teenagers. Then, it was for the sake of his unborn child. Now, it's for the good of her three. Being a parent requires sacrifices, sometimes brutal ones.

Before opening the door, obeying her command to leave, Bradley turns to her. "You're a fighter, Penny Ray. Remember that. It was the first thing I fell in love with." A bittersweet smile forms on his lips. "Don't let someone like Teddy Crenshaw be the one who finally breaks you and steals your fire. He's not worth it." Bradley walks out the door and pulls it shut behind him.

Standing alone in Ruby Ray's now-barren house, Penny begins looking around through her glassy eyes. Never in her life has she been more heartbroken and lost. Though she loved Bradley with all her heart as a young girl and a teenager, the adult bond they've formed in the last two weeks is on a different level. He isn't just her lover, the man who has intimate knowledge of her body, making it cry out in ways she's never known, but he has given her a glimpse into what a healthy relationship could be like—one of trust, laughter, and compassion. Now it's gone.

As she's about to collapse from emotional exhaustion, the telephone rings again. Fearing it's Ruth calling to deliver another round of catastrophic news, she answers. "Hello?"

"Penny? Is everything okay?"

"Dakota?"

"Yes, it's Dakota. I'm with Leslie. You're on speaker."

"Hey, sweetie," Leslie chimes in.

"Hey," Penny replies.

"What's going on? Ruth Higgins called, wanting to know how to get ahold of you. She wouldn't tell me anything. Typical fucking lawyer."

"Teddy," Penny whispers.

"What the fuck did he do now?"

Through tears and hiccups, Penny explains the whole ordeal with her ex-husband, including casting away the man she loves.

"That's the shittiest legal advice I've ever heard," Dakota says. "Teddy can't drag you to court because you're finally getting laid. You're single, for Christ's sake. You can screw the entire Falcons offensive line if you want, and he can't say a thing."

"Oh, Penny. I'm so sorry you're going through this," Leslie says with a little more empathy.

"I can't believe she told you to break it off with Bradley," Dakota fumes.

"I had no choice."

"There's always a choice," Dakota says. "Teddy's a jealous asshole. He can't stand that you've finally moved on from the divorce. Moved on from him, with Bradley Hitchens, of all people. You know that's what this is about. He's trying to punish you."

"It doesn't matter," Penny says, wiping her nose with her T-shirt since there's no tissue left in the house, thanks to her aunts. "It was never going to work out with Bradley. It was going to end. Eventually. Teddy just expedited it."

"That's bullshit, and you know it," Dakota says. "You've never sounded so happy, so alive, as you have these last two weeks, and we both know why. Don't let him take that from you."

"But Ruth—"

"Forget Ruth. She's covering her own ass because she doesn't want to lose her case, or more importantly, she doesn't want to look bad in front of McGinn, Litchfield, and Cock Sucker."

"Crocket," Penny corrects her.

"I have to agree with Dakota," Leslie says in a more conciliatory tone. "I think your attorney's advice is a little drastic. You've done nothing wrong, and it's no one's business, especially Teddy's, who you date."

"God, I should never have jumped into that pool," Penny says, chiding herself for the irresponsible decision, which has snowballed into the nightmare she's living in.

"Stop it," Dakota says. "It was the best decision of your life, and you know it. Finally, you let go for a little while. You stopped being such a tight-ass—I'm sorry, but you are—and you actually lived a little. You've spent the last two weeks—which may I remind you you've been dreading like the plague for more than a year—blissfully happy. Don't let Bradley go. Not without a fight."

"It's too late. There's no going back now."

"Isn't that what you thought twenty years ago? No door is shut forever."

"Call him, Penny," Leslie adds.

"I appreciate your advice, but I think I need to go."

"You sound tired. Why don't you lie down and get some rest," Leslie tells her, not knowing her advice is useless, for not even a folding chair or a pillow remain at Ruby Ray's.

"Leslie's right. Get some rest, because you have a long drive ahead of you tomorrow. We'll talk about this then."

"Florida." Penny winces. She forgot about their girls' trip. Living it up in the Sunshine State is the last thing on her mind.

"Yes, Florida." Dakota huffs.

"I'm not sure I'm up for it now, with everything that's going on. Besides, I'm afraid I won't be the best company. I think I should go back to Atlanta instead."

"Screw that! You're coming tomorrow, whether you like it or not."

"Sitting alone at home, worrying about this custody mess, isn't going to help," Leslie says. "Besides, you said Ruth's out of town next week, so it's not like you can do anything about it now. In light of everything today, you could use a little break. Come to Rosemary with us tomorrow. It'll be good for you."

"You know how much I appreciate your invitation, but I think I'll pass."

"I swear to God, if you're not at Leslie's house by sunset tomorrow, I'll get in my car, drive back to Atlanta, and drag your skinny ass down to 30A myself. Kicking and screaming the whole way, if I have to. Don't try me. You know I'll do it," Dakota says. "Your stupid ex-husband isn't going to fuck this up too."

Bluffing and making idle threats isn't Dakota's style. "Fine. I'll come," Penny says, defeated.

"Finally, she takes my advice," Dakota says.

Advice isn't the word Penny would use in this scenario. Threat of bodily harm is more in line.

"We'll be there around four. A glass of sparkling rosé will be waiting for you," Leslie adds.

"Thank you," Penny says, though her heart isn't in it.

"See you tomorrow. We love you," they say in unison before ending the call.

Now Penny's alone in Buyer One's empty house. Only the cherry grandfather clock, still ticking away, chiming every quarter hour, will be keeping her company tonight. Though she knows it will drive her crazy, it's oddly comforting to have it near. The final hours she has left in Kentucky, T minus fourteen and counting, won't be spent in the arms of the man she loves but rather on the cold, hard floor of her grandmother's living room, wrapped in Ruby Ray's cornflower-blue cross-stitch quilt. The reason she's alone tonight isn't Teddy Crenshaw. It's because Penny Ray is too afraid to fight back.

Chapter 26

Fort Knox

"Good Lord almighty, what happened to you?" Pat McGuire asks, standing in the front door with his mouth agape, staring at Penny's disheveled appearance.

"Nothing," Penny says, annoyed that her real estate broker seems to be judging her and the bags under her eyes.

"You look like you didn't sleep a wink last night." He shakes his head.

"Do you have the papers?" she asks curtly. She's in no mood for small talk this morning, especially after a restless night trying to sleep on the floor. Of course, she could've called Jimmy Neal or Kelly, asking for a place to stay. Gracie Belle would die if she knew where she'd slept. But they would ask too many questions, chastising her for being a fool to end it with Bradley. She couldn't bear listening to their well-meaning advice.

"I have them all here, ready to sign." He pats his monogrammed briefcase while ignoring her short tone. "Commissions make the world go around, sweetheart, and today, I'd wrestle in the mud with a pig if I had to."

"Do you have a pen?" she asks, since all her belongings, purse included, are already packed in her Land Cruiser in the driveway.

"You're a grumpy bumpy this morning," he jokes.

However, Mr. McGuire's treading on thin ice. He's unaware Aunt Pearl seized the last remnants of the Maxwell House coffee canister from the kitchen yesterday. Camden doesn't have a Starbucks for a quick caffeine hit or even a McDonald's in a clutch, so Penny's trying to be human without her beloved beverage.

"Here you go," he says, quickly handing over his blue rollerball pen as he follows her into the kitchen.

Since there's no table left in the house to provide a hard surface to sign the documents, she uses the Formica counter next to the sink for the closing. Spreading out a plethora of papers before her, Mr. McGuire begins instructing Penny on where to sign. "Gonna need your John Hancock on a few pages."

Penny complies and begins scribbling her name and the date wherever he points. After a couple of minutes, the task is complete.

"Voilà! You've officially sold 225 Dogwood Lane. Congratulations," Mr. McGuire says, brimming with pride over another successful transaction.

"Thank you for selling it so quickly."

"This ain't my first rodeo, sweetheart." He giggles.

"I'm sure it's not."

"Oh, by the way, what are you gonna do with that ticking time bomb out there?" He points toward the living room and the grandfather clock.

She winces. "I'm having it shipped to Atlanta. Is it okay if Jimmy Neal comes by tomorrow to pick it up?"

"Couldn't part with it, I see. You must be a glutton for punishment," he says with a wink. "I'll come by and let him in myself."

"I guess you'll need these," she says, handing over the keys.

"Yes, I do. All that's left now is the combination to the safe."

"The safe." She closes her eyes, embarrassed she's once again overlooked it.

"Don't tell me you forgot about it again. What is it with you and that thang?"

"I completely forgot."

"I swear you're gonna make me lose my religion."

"I had some things on my mind yesterday," she explains while trying to hide her embarrassment.

"What's the combination?" he asks, preparing to write it down on his palm.

"Ten, three, nineteen, seventy-one."

"What is that? Some kind of date?"

"My birthday," she tells him.

"Oh, I see." He clears his throat. "Well, you better get your tiny heinie in there and clear that thing out. I'd love to stay, but I've gotta skedaddle right on out of here. Got myself a showing over in Lucas in an hour. Just close the door behind you when you leave. I'll come by later to lock up."

"Thanks again," she says. The corners of her eyes burn.

"Are you okay, hon?" Mr. McGuire asks.

"I guess I'm a little emotional. All this is coming to an end so fast. It's harder to say goodbye to Ruby Ray's and Kentucky than I thought it would be. To be honest with you, I'm a little lost right now."

"Penny, just because you don't have a house here no more don't mean you don't have a home."

His words and insight take her breath away. He has just the wisdom she's in desperate need of at the moment.

"Besides, nobody ever really *leaves* Kentucky nohow. Hell, it's in our blood, whether we like it or not."

Penny smiles. "That's nice to hear."

"It was a pleasure doing business with you, Penny. If you're ever in need of a Realtor in Camden again, call me. And don't forget to recommend me to your family. Lord knows there's enough of 'em," he says before departing.

It's done. The foursquare is no longer in the Ray family. After forty-three years, it's in Buyer One's hands to love and make memories here. A little part of her envies them because they'll be the ones gathering in the kitchen on Thanksgiving morning like she used to as a girl. She loved sneaking bites of Ruby Ray's peppery cornbread dressing while fighting with her siblings over licking the mixing spoon dripping with thick homemade whipped cream needed for the pumpkin pies baking in the oven. The new owners will be the ones spending their Easter weekends here, making hot cross buns and dyeing Easter eggs. As a little girl, Penny spent hours in the dining room with her grandmother, preparing for the Willow Creek annual egg hunt. Newspapers lined the table, which was full of boiled eggs, food coloring, and teacups scattered about. The smells of vinegar come rushing back to her.

Dwelling on those memories will get Penny no closer to Florida, so she clears her mind and focuses all her energy on the one task that's left in Kentucky: the elusive safe, which Pops bought at a bank liquidation auction for no other reason than it was for sale. Since she's facing hours in her car, making her way to the Panhandle, there's no use in putting it off any longer. Using the combination, she spins the wheel left and right, left and right before jerking up the lever.

As she opens the door, not knowing what she'll find, she's greeted with a single white envelope, no documents or stashes of cash, no diamonds, rubies, or pearls—which is preposterous in the first place because her grandmother never owned any jewelry other than her gold wedding band and a few costume brooches—and not even a pair of earrings, as her grandmother never pierced her ears.

Curious, Penny picks up the lonely artifact, feeling a little like Geraldo Rivera after opening Al Capone's safe. But when she looks closer, she realizes she's discovered something more precious than gold—a letter with her name on it, in Ruby Ray's distinctive handwriting, for her grandmother lived in a time when penmanship was celebrated, and she took great pride in hers.

Without hesitation, Penny opens it.

April 16, 2008

My Dearest Penny,

Tonight, I've been doing a little soul searching. I'm taking an inventory of my life. If Oprah can do it, so can I.

For the past few months, I've been feeling poorly. A little under the weather. Every morning when I wake up, I'm so tired that I have to go back to bed. In February, my doctor ran some tests, and he diagnosed me with acute lymphocytic leukemia. The prognosis is never good, but for an eighty-six-year-old woman, it's a death sentence. He said without treatment I've got about a month. Spending my final days in a hospital, hooked up to needles filling me full of poison just so I can have a few more weeks on this earth, is the last thing I want. I've lived long enough. Longer than I should've. It's unnatural to outlive a child or worse, three grandchildren. I politely told him I'm ready to meet my maker and see my Homer again. On my own terms, which includes keeping this to myself. I want to die in peace without people fussing over me, especially you.

Tonight, I've been grappling with the age-old questions of life and death. Did I lead a good life? Did I do right by the people I love? And for the most part, I've felt like I have. But I'm afraid when it comes to you, I failed. Badly. All because I never protected you from your daddy.

I was a weak woman when it came to my son. I knew what kind of man he was. A mean, violent drunk. Yet I still loved him. He was my child, my firstborn, and I could never turn my back on him. I'm afraid I loved him to death because of my inability to hold him accountable for anything. I knew he'd been hitting your momma long before that Fourth of July night, but I did nothing. I said nothing. After he hit you right in front of me, I should've cut him out of my life right then and there, but I didn't. I continued to give him money, a place to live when he quit job after job, with no consequences for his actions. The experts call it codependency nowadays, but back then, I didn't know better. But I should've.

Penny, I know your daddy never stopped hitting you. Even though I never saw it again with my own eyes and you never made a peep about it, I suspected it for years until my worst fears were confirmed last spring. I'd grown tired of waking up every day to the same old wallpaper in my bedroom, so I hired a handyman to come over and strip it down for me. When he started pulling the pictures off the walls, he found a bullet lodged behind our family portrait. After he dug it out, I realized it came from your granddaddy's revolver. I didn't understand how it got there, but I had a gut feeling it had something to do with you. I told him to patch up the hole and go home. I was keeping the wallpaper after all.

What I did next was shameful. I went to your room and pulled out the old journal you kept all throughout high school. I found it in the garbage after you threw it away in anger years ago. Couldn't bear the thought of you casting your memories aside like that, so I dug it out for safekeeping, hoping one day you might like to see it again. Please know I never opened it before that day. Never touched a page. It would've been a violation of your privacy, but I needed answers. I thought your journal might give me some insight.

I can't begin to tell you how sorry I am for what happened to you, Penny. When I read what your daddy did to you, what you had to do to protect yourself from him, my heart sank. All those broken bones you suffered, the scars you still carry on your face to this day, are as much my fault as Charlie's. If I'd stood up to him when he hit you the first time—or your mother, for that matter—you would never have been put in that horrible position in the first place. I let you down. Me. I was a coward then, and I'm a coward now because I'm writing you a letter, begging for forgiveness in death, instead of asking for it face-to-face in life.

Though there's nothing I could ever do to make up for my transgressions, I changed my will, leaving you this house. I know it's silly, thinking a slab of wood and some Sheetrock could make up for the years of pain and suffering you've endured, but it's my way of trying to rectify my mistakes. I don't care what you do with the place, because it's yours now. Don't let Molly or my sisters push you around over it. It's been months since I laid eyes on my own daughter, and Opal and Pearl have been divvying up my belongings between themselves for years, just waiting for me to kick the bucket.

Penny, you had a hard time growing up. Fear, I'm afraid, has been your driving force because you never felt safe. That's my fault. Because I failed to protect you. Don't live in fear anymore. It'll suck the life right out of you. All your life, you've had to fight something or someone in order to survive. It's my hope, one day, you'll get the chance to actually fight for *something instead.*

I love you, and take care of my babies.
Love,
Ruby Ray

After Penny finishes the letter, her eyes well up, and her vision blurs. But these tears are not just coming from a place of sorrow after learning her grandmother spent her final days knowing the end was near and chose to hide it so that she could die alone. They're also full of relief. Now, Penny has closure as to why Ruby Ray singled her out, leaving this yellow foursquare in her care. She'd spent a year racking her brain. Though it wasn't necessary, because Penny loved Ruby Ray unconditionally and could never hold her responsible for Charlie's transgressions, she understands the rationale behind the odd decision. In a strange way, it's almost comforting, knowing that her grandmother discovered the dark secret she's spent decades trying to bury deep within. At least another person besides Bradley knew what happened to her and the abuse she suffered. And like Bradley, her grandmother's love didn't waver because of it. That in itself is a gift. Penny always worried it had somehow made her less than.

Still in awe that she has this tiny part of Ruby Ray in her hands, she looks down at the letter. A tear falls onto the paper, landing upon one particular line.

Fear, I'm afraid, has been your driving force because you never felt safe. That's my fault.

Ruby Ray's right about the first part. Fear has certainly been Penny's driving force. But it was no fault of her grandmother's. This falls squarely on Penny's shoulders. She allowed this beast to rule over her, letting it silently suffocate her while it dictated every choice she has made. If Penny doesn't make a stand now, it *will* suck the life right out of her, just as Ruby Ray warned. This cycle must end, not just for her sake but for her children's as well.

Standing in Buyer One's vacant house, Penny makes a silent promise to herself. When she returns home to Atlanta, she'll finally open up about her past and talk about it honestly. She may not be ready to discuss it in detail with her friends yet, but a therapist might be a good place to start. Penny's only attempt at self-help has been running. After all these years and thousands of miles, it hasn't accomplished much besides torn ligaments and lost toenails. She's still in the same place with the same problems, spinning around and around. She's no different from a hamster on a wheel. The faster she goes, the quicker she gets nowhere.

But gaining self-awareness and baring her tattered soul to a professional is only one piece of the complicated puzzle. Penny can't just sit by, idling her time away. She needs to begin this long journey toward freedom today. And she knows exactly where her first baby step needs to be directed, and it's only five doors away. If she's going to live her life unbridled, there's no time like the present.

When Penny has finished crying, she kisses the envelope and places it in her pocket. "Time for me to go fight for something, Ruby Ray."

Then she rushes out of 225 Dogwood Lane for the last time.

Chapter 27

Crazy for You

"Bradley! Please open up!" Penny pounds on the front door to the bungalow for the second time in less than ten days. Unlike the last time, she's in broad daylight. The sun is shining brightly, and there's not a cloud in the sky. If she weren't so consumed with her quest to find him, she could almost stop and enjoy the songs the birds are chirping. It's a sharp contrast to the night she rushed here—the one full of thunder and doom. But somehow, against nature and odds, the outlook is much more ominous. "It's me. I need to talk to you."

A few seconds pass, though it seems much longer, and she begins beating on the door again.

"Are you in there? All I'm asking for is five minutes," she says. "I need to apologize." Urgency fills her voice, every word accompanied by another round of banging, causing her palms to sting. "Please open the door."

Seconds fade into minutes, yet the house remains eerily still. Beads of sweat roll down Penny's neck and back, but she keeps knocking at the door.

"I was an idiot yesterday. I shouldn't have listened to Ruth. And those things I said to you were absolutely wrong. Open up. Please, Bradley." Penny rests her forehead against the door. "I love you. I always have, and I always will."

"Well, the whole town knows *that* already" comes an elderly voice from behind her.

Penny spins around. "Miss Ada? Where in the world did you come from?"

Ada Pickert's eyes bulge. "Good Lord in the heavens, what's wrong with you? You're all drenched in sweat, and your face is redder than a beefsteak tomato. Are you having a hot flash?"

Penny gasps. "No, ma'am."

"Then you're back on the drugs again, I see," she says in a knowing tone.

Penny bristles at the allegation. "I'm not on drugs!" This is the second time in two weeks that Ada Pickert has accused her of this very thing. The last time was in the sanctuary of Willow Creek Baptist Church.

"So you're naturally this way?" Miss Ada flicks her hand. "Acting a fool in public?"

Penny takes a deep breath. "I realize I might look out of sorts at the moment, but I really need to speak with Dr. Hitchens," she says. "I was knocking on his door. That's all."

The old woman shakes her head. "You could've woken the dead with all that banging."

"Miss Ada, what *are* you even doing here?" Thirty seconds of a conversation with this woman is as pleasant as passing a kidney stone the size of the Rock of Gibraltar.

"I was on my way to Ruby Ray's to pick up that grandfather clock you promised me. When I saw you beating down that door like some crazy woman, I stopped. I'm a concerned citizen. That's all."

Penny's nostrils flare. "I'm not crazy."

"Words spoken by every serial killer," Miss Ada deadpans.

"Just so you know, I've decided to keep that grandfather clock after all," Penny says.

Miss Ada's wrinkled face contorts. "What? You offered it to me two weeks ago. In the house of the Lord, of all places. I made a special trip to town. Drove ten miles for it."

"You still drive?" Penny's aghast that the state of Kentucky allows Miss Ada to operate a motor vehicle while wearing her thick coke-bottle glasses.

"You listen to me, young lady. I came for that clock, and I'm not leaving without it."

"I said no. I'm keeping it."

"I borrowed a trailer for the occasion, so I'm taking it."

"You can't have it." Penny's voice grows louder.

"It's mine."

"*No. No. No!*" Penny screams at the top of her lungs. "I'm done with being told what to do and just rolling over and taking it! I'm done with being pushed around by the likes of you. I'm done with being polite, trying to make everyone else around me happy just to keep the peace. I'm sick to death of being the good Southern woman who minds her p's and q's, biting my tongue until it's raw, while getting my heart stomped on in the process. I'm done. D-O-N-E!"

Penny turns her attention toward the occupant of a dark sedan that's been parked across the street since her arrival at Bradley's doorstep. Then she dramatically shoots a middle finger in their direction. "And I'm done with you too! I hope my ex-husband has paid you plenty of money, because I'm about to rock your world. I can't wait for you to tell him what I'm about to do next!"

Miss Ada shakes her head. "I *knew* it was the menopause."

"I'm not in menopause!" Penny's arms flail about.

"You just shot poor Lamar Crane the bird."

"Who?"

"The eighty-year-old man who delivers the *Camden Times* to the good folks around town every Thursday, rain or shine."

"Oh no."

"And on Sunday mornings, he's in the pulpit, saving souls at Amos Methodist. He's the senior pastor."

Penny covers her face. She just gave a man of the cloth an offensive gesture. "I'm so sorry. I thought he was someone else."

"Now will you tell me what's going on with you, child? Lamar may be a Methodist, but even he doesn't deserve that."

"It's just—I've lost him. I've lost him for a second time." Penny breaks down in tears and sobs.

Easing Penny to the steps, Miss Ada asks, "Lost who, honey? Who did you lose?" Her tone isn't hospitable, but her touch tells a different story.

"Bradley." Tears roll down Penny's cheeks. "I've lost Bradley. Again."

Miss Ada reaches into her purse, pulls out a well-loved handkerchief, and offers it to Penny. "From what I hear, you were having quite the summer romance with Doc Hitchens. Didn't you two get caught skinny-dipping in the country club pool? At least, that's the story that's been going around town. Not that I get all hot and bothered by rumors and the sorts. Not my monkey, not my circus."

"There's no summer romance now. Far from it." She blows her nose.

"What happened? Tell me, child," Miss Ada says sweetly—or as sweetly as Ada Pickert can manage.

Penny opens the floodgates of truth, telling her all that transpired, from Ruth's directive to how she threw Bradley out of Ruby Ray's house yesterday to the letter she found moments ago in the safe. It's oddly natural and freeing for Penny to speak with such candor. Surprisingly, the elderly woman listens without judgement.

"Do you have a bobby pin on you?" Miss Ada asks.

Penny's brow furrows. "Excuse me?"

"Or a credit card? I suppose that would do." She stands and hobbles over to inspect the door.

"What on earth are you talking about?" Penny follows her.

"I've been known to pick a lock a time or two. Back in my day, it came in handy. I can probably have us inside in a couple of minutes."

Penny lets out a nervous laugh. "Who are you?"

A warm expression crosses Miss Ada's face. "A woman much like you. I know that feeling. How the power of love can cause you to lose all control of your sensibilities. And in your case, a little dignity."

Penny's unable to respond.

"What? You don't think I've ever been in love? I may not look like it now, but a long time ago, I was quite the catch around these parts. A real drink of water." Miss Ada gives Penny an impish grin. "When I reached a certain age, several young bucks came sniffing around me, but I paid no attention to any of 'em because my heart belonged to Hexel Jarvis. He was a lovely man. And let me tell you something—Hex was just as taken with me as I was with him."

"What happened?" Penny asks.

"Well, this might come as a surprise to you, but I used to have a salty side."

Used to? Penny suppresses the urge to say it out loud.

"My daddy said I was full of piss and vinegar. Can you believe a father talking about his own daughter that way? He was right, of course, but it never bothered Hex. He loved my stubbornness. My sassy side. Or so I thought, until the night of our engagement party. We had an argument. I may have pushed Hex's buttons a bit, but I thought it would pass. The next morning, when he showed up at my house, demanding that I apologize, it infuriated me. I was right in my mind, so I dug in my heels and refused. Once that happened, Hex called off the wedding on the spot."

"He called off the wedding? Over one fight?"

"Sure did. I remember it like it was yesterday. Sunday, December seventh, 1941."

Penny remembers that date from history class. "I'm so sorry."

Miss Ada stares into the distance. "A week later, Hex left for the army, and I never saw him again."

"Oh, Miss Ada. Did he die in World War II?" Penny grabs her chest, her heart breaking for the old woman.

"No!" Her head snaps around. "He didn't die in that war or any other. He failed his physical then up and married my ungrateful sister and moved to Indianapolis. Then they started popping out children like Pez."

Penny gasps. "Oh. That's... That's a terrible thing to happen."

"Don't you see what I'm telling you here?" she asks.

"That you probably didn't have a great relationship with your sister after that?" Penny says.

"No, child! Remember what Ruby Ray said in her letter? How it's time to start fighting? But not for Bradley—or any man, for that matter. You have to start fighting for yourself. You." She places her hand, which has paper-thin skin and is full of thick blue veins, over Penny's heart. "When you start doing that, then everything else will fall into place."

Their eyes meet.

"You're a wise woman, Miss Ada. And a kind one as well."

"Now, don't go tellin' the whole town that. I've got a reputation, you know." She gives Penny a sly wink.

"Thank you for your sage advice, but I'm not going to break into Bradley's house. I'm desperate but not pathetic."

"How about taking a peek inside? Just to see if he's in there."

"First you encourage me to pick a lock, and now you want me to become a Peeping Tom?"

"I'll cover you from behind." Miss Ada begins swaying back and forth against her cane, craning her neck in the search for onlookers.

Bending down, Penny looks through the window to the living room, which holds such fond memories for her, but it's dark and quiet. The brown leather couch she slept on while wrapped in Bradley's warm arms and where she's made love to him numerous times is empty. The pillows she laid her head on and the blanket she slept under that stormy night last week are neatly arranged. There's no mug of piping-hot coffee sitting on the reclaimed wood table where Bradley usually enjoys his caffeinated brew. No morning newspapers are scattered about. No lights come from the kitchen or the hallway leading to the master bedroom.

Penny stands up. "No one's home."

"Go look in the garage."

"His garage? Why?"

Miss Ada huffs. "If his car's still there, you know he's avoiding you. If that's the case, we should pack it up and call it a day. I've got some strong homemade wine back at my house. We could open up a bottle and spend the day basking in the warm glow of fermented grapes."

"You drink wine?"

Miss Ada slams her cane against the wood planks of the porch. "You'd better believe I do. How else do you think I survived living in a town full of gossips? Thank the good Lord I ain't one of 'em."

Penny shakes her head in astonishment at Miss Ada's lack of self-awareness. But she's an ally now, and Penny would fight to the death for her.

"If his car is gone, we still got a fightin' chance," Miss Ada says. "Don't ya see?"

Penny's eyes widen.

"Go." She points with her cane.

Penny rushes to the back of the property toward the detached garage. A little window sits on the side. She stands on her tiptoes, but she's too short. Searching for another option, she spies a cement block next to the fire pit. Penny places it under the window and looks inside.

"Well?" Miss Ada asks as she rounds the corner.

Penny shakes her head. "Empty."

"It's seven thirty in the morning on a Thursday. There's only one logical place that man could be, and it's only three blocks away."

"His office!" Penny leaps from her concrete perch and rushes past Miss Ada.

"Go get 'em, child." Miss Ada's voice is full of excitement.

"Miss Paulette!" Penny says, bursting into the office lobby. Her lungs are on fire, and her face is drenched in sweat.

Miss Paulette gasps. "Penny Ray? What in tarnation are you doing here?" A pile of medical charts lie beneath her.

"I'm so sorry I startled you." Penny begins frantically picking up the mess she's caused while gulping in air. Distance running and sprinting are two different beasts.

"You just about gave me a heart attack." Miss Paulette fans her face with her hand. "And look at your feet. What did you do to them?"

Looking down, Penny notices her bloody toes. Running in flip-flops instead of athletic shoes was a mistake. Oddly enough, with the amount of skin missing from them, there's no pain. "I must have scraped them on the sidewalk when I ran here. It's nothing."

"You ran here? In those shoes and in this heat? Have you lost your mind?"

Wide-eyed, Penny says, "Maybe."

Miss Paulette reaches for Penny's arm then gently leads her to a chair. "You need to sit down and cool off a bit. Let me get you some water."

"I'm not thirsty."

Miss Paulette fills a paper cup. "Running around like a chicken with your head cut off in the middle of July is plumb foolishness. Are you trying to give yourself heatstroke?"

"No, ma'am."

Handing Penny the cup, Miss Paulette says, "Drink up, then tell me what's gotten you in such a tizzy this morning."

Penny downs the water in one gulp. "Bradley. Is he here?"

"Dr. Hitchens?" Miss Paulette's expression changes from concern to *concern*. "Why, no, honey. I'm afraid not."

"It's *really* important that I talk to him. The sooner, the better. If it wouldn't be too much trouble, do you mind if I stay here and wait? I promise I won't get in your way."

Miss Paulette takes in a deep breath before slowly letting it out. "You could, but I'm afraid you'd be waiting a real long time."

"What do you mean? Doesn't he usually see his first patient at eight?"

"He called me late last night and asked me to clear his schedule."

"You mean he's not coming to work today?"

"Not today or for the six after that," Miss Paulette tells her. "I'm only here this morning to get caught up on some billing and charts."

"Where's Doc Hitchens?" Miss Ada yells breathlessly.

"Ada Pickert?" Miss Paulette asks in wonderment. "Where did you come from?" She peers behind Ada through the open door. "And did you just park your car in the middle of the street?"

"I didn't have time to find a spot. Besides, that trailer is a bear to navigate. But never mind all that. We've got pressing matters here. Where's Doc Hitchens?"

Penny turns toward Miss Ada. "He's not here."

"Like I was telling Penny before you abandoned your car in the middle of the town square, he cleared his schedule. I've never known him to cancel one appointment, let alone a week of them. He even asked Dr. Hamilton to fill in for him in case of emergencies."

"That alone should tell you something is terribly wrong, if he'd leave his patients' dental care in the hands of that old coot," Miss Ada says. "Thank the good Lord that Lonnie Davis doesn't pop the kettle corn this weekend, or the town of Camden might never survive."

Miss Paulette's eyes narrow. "If you don't mind my asking, Penny, did something happen between you and Dr. Hitchens?"

"You could say that. We had an argument that was all my fault."

"And your stupid ex-husband's too," Miss Ada adds.

"It went off the rails so quickly," Penny says.

"I bet it wasn't all that bad. Dr. Hitchens has been sweet on you for too long to walk away over a little tiff," Miss Paulette says.

"I think it was more than a tiff," Miss Ada mumbles.

"I've just made the second-biggest mistake of my life. Unfortunately, Bradley's been involved in both."

"Maybe you should apologize," Miss Paulette says. "That's as good a place to start as any."

"I would if I could, but I can't seem to find him. Before I came here, I went to his house."

Miss Ada shakes her head. "You should've seen her. She was beating on that door like a crazy woman."

Penny turns to Miss Ada. "I thought we worked through that. I'm not crazy."

"Of course you're not." Miss Ada pats Penny's arm. "But you did shoot the bird in poor Lamar Crane's direction."

Miss Paulette's eyes widen. "You mean Reverend Crane? My minister?"

"One and the same," Miss Ada confirms.

"It-It was just a big misunderstanding. I swear I didn't know he was a minister. I thought he was the private investigator my ex-husband hired to spy on Bradley and me all week."

Miss Paulette clutches her chest. "There's a private investigator following you around too?"

"There's a lot of moving pieces here, Paulette. We ain't got time to explain everything right now," Miss Ada snaps.

"Well, have you tried calling him?" Miss Paulette asks.

Penny shakes her head. "I left my phone back in my car at Ruby Ray's."

Miss Paulette picks up the office phone. "Let's try his mobile. Shall we?" Miss Paulette punches in the number with the ease of a woman who could dial it in her sleep and hands the receiver to Penny.

"This is Bradley Hitchens." Penny's heart skips a beat at just the sound of his voice. "I'm unavailable at the moment. Please leave your name, message, and number after the beep, and I'll get back to you. If this is a dental emergency, please contact Dr. Jim Hamilton." The tone sounds.

Penny hands the receiver back to Miss Paulette. "I got his voice mail."

"We'll try him again," Miss Paulette says. "He's probably on the other line."

Again, the call goes to voice mail. Penny shakes her head.

"One more time." This time, Miss Paulette's more urgent with her fingers as she dials the number.

Again, they get voice mail.

"He's not answering."

"Oh, I bet he's just misplaced his mobile this morning. Dr. Hitchens has been known to do that a time or two," she says.

Their eyes meet. Miss Paulette is trying to spare her feelings by telling her a little white lie. Bradley's phone is attached to his hip at all times. Last week alone, he made two trips back to the office after hours, one at midnight when a child fell out of bed, cracking three permanent teeth, and the other when an elderly patient suffered an abscess. That case interrupted a particularly passionate session of lovemaking on Bradley's kitchen table.

"Aren't you leaving town this morning?" Miss Paulette says. "You're going on a trip with some of your friends to the Panhandle, right?"

"I went to Florida once," Miss Ada interrupts. "Boca with a man named Stuart. For some reason, everybody called him Bob. It was terribly hot down there, and the mosquitos were the size of my fist." She holds one up. "Or maybe it was Cuba."

Miss Paulette and Penny stare at Miss Ada, their mouths agape. The woman certainly has had an interesting life, one that under normal circumstances would fascinate Penny, but right now, she has more pressing matters.

"My trip will have to wait. I need to speak to Bradley. I think I'll stay in Camden for a few more days," she says, her voice brimming with determination.

Miss Paulette places her hand on Penny's shoulder. "If you stay here, I'm afraid you'll just be piddling around in an empty house, wasting your time. Dr. Hitchens could be out of town, for all we know. Go soak up some sunshine with your friends."

"I agree," Miss Ada chimes in. "Besides, the sun will do you good. You're looking awfully pasty, if you ask me." She pinches Penny's skin.

Penny turns to Miss Ada. "Did I ask for your opinion?"

"Go on your trip, and you can call Dr. Hitchens on your way," Miss Paulette says.

"I guess you're right."

"Of course I am," the older women say in unison.

"But I'm not giving up. I promise," Penny says.

"That's my girl." Miss Ada winks.

"I can't thank both of you enough for what you've done for me today," Penny says before taking them into her arms for a long embrace. "Truly."

Miss Ada pulls back. "I don't know what Paulette Taylor did. She just made a phone call. I was the one willing to break the law for you. Remember?"

"And that's something I'll never forget," Penny says. "Miss Ada, can I ask one last question?"

"Sure."

"How in the world were you going to move that clock all by yourself? Did you really think it through?"

"I'm a lot stronger than I look," she says, holding up her wispy arm to show off her muscles. "Remember, I'm full of piss and vinegar. Never forget that."

"Yes, ma'am." Penny smiles. "That, you are."

"Now it's time you get a little bit of it for yourself too."

Chapter 28

Feels like Home

An hour later, as Penny is merging onto I-65, like magic, her cell phone starts lighting up like the Rockefeller Center Christmas tree. After two weeks of no service, bars begin popping up across the top of the screen, followed by a flood of texts, voice mails, and missed-call notifications.

"Finally!" Penny cries out, changing lanes and looking for an exit where she can pull over. With the amount of adrenaline pulsing through her body, she knows it's not a smart idea to drive and talk to Bradley at the same time.

Once her car is in park, she dials his number.

"Come on. Come on," she says, tapping her fingers on the steering wheel.

"This is Bradley Hitchens. I'm unavailable at the moment. Please leave your name, message, and number after the beep, and I'll get back to you. If this is a dental emergency, please contact Dr. Jim Hamilton." Again, the tone sounds.

This time, instead of hanging up, she takes a deep breath and says, "Bradley, it's me. Penny. I-I don't even know what to say about yesterday except I'm sorry. I should never have treated you like that. Never spoken to you so cruelly. I was scared. I was upset. I was wrong. Please call me back when you get the chance. I'll be in my car for a while."

She hopes once Bradley hears that message, he'll call and tell her his whereabouts. It doesn't matter where he is. She will make a beeline toward him to apologize in person, girls' trip be damned—or Dakota's threats of bodily harm.

An hour goes by, and she still hears nothing from Bradley. After passing Nashville, Penny begins getting anxious. If a detour north is needed, say to Lexington, a place where he has a number of friends he might visit, she doesn't want to continue going any farther south, so she picks up her phone and calls him.

Once again, she reaches his voice mail.

"It's me. Sorry to keep calling. I don't want to bother you, but I really need to apologize for yesterday. I'm so sorry, Bradley. Truly, I am. These past few days... It was so much more than just sex. It was—" Penny's voice cracks. "Everything."

As she's closing in on the Tennessee-Alabama border, her phone rings. Without checking the screen, she answers.

"Hello?"

"You'd better be through Birmingham by now."

"Dakota." Disappointment pours from Penny's voice.

"Wow, it's great to talk to you too. Where are you?"

"Just past Pulaski."

"Where the hell is that?"

"It's in Tennessee."

"Why are you still in Tennessee?" Dakota asks crisply.

Penny bites her lip. "I got a late start this morning. I left Camden later than I planned."

"Why?"

"I went out this morning." She pauses. "Searching for Bradley."

"Bradley? I thought you cut him loose yesterday."

"Yes, I did, but I realized I should never have listened to Ruth in the first place. I can't let Teddy dictate my life forever. No matter what he's threatening."

"It's about fucking time. I'm glad you're thinking clearer now. So, have you talked to him yet?"

"No."

"Why not?"

"Because I can't seem to find him. I went to his house this morning then to his office. His assistant suspects he left town for a few days."

"Did you try calling?"

"Five times. But I've only left two messages."

"Why don't you lay off the phone calls for a while? At least until you get through Alabama. If he wants to talk to you, he'll call back."

"I was an idiot," Penny says.

"Yes, you were. Remember, I told you so yesterday."

Penny lets out a sigh. "I know you did."

"Shoot me a text when you're an hour out from Rosemary so that we'll be ready with that glass of sparkling rosé Leslie promised you."

"At this point, I think I might need the whole bottle instead."

"We can make that happen." Dakota laughs. "And one more thing. If you get the urge to call Bradley again, or worse, call his mother, trying to figure out where he is—don't. That would be crossing into Glen Close territory, and you don't want to come across as the creepy-stalker type."

"I would never call his mother," Penny lies. She's been debating that very scenario for the last thirty miles, checking to see if Bradley has headed toward Hilton Head to spend the week with his parents and Emeree Shae.

"Sure, Penny," Dakota says before hanging up.

Five and a half hours later, Penny crosses into the panhandle of Florida. So grateful to see the sign welcoming her to the Sunshine State, she almost sheds tears of joy. She was beginning to think she would never get out of Alabama, which she now believes is the longest state in the union. She heeds Dakota's advice and resists the urge to call

Bradley for a sixth time, since it was one step away from boiling a bunny on a stovetop, in her friend's opinion.

At the Tom Thumb in DeFuniak Springs, Penny makes a quick stop, her second of the trip, after realizing both she and her car are driving on fumes. She hasn't made time for a proper lunch. Munching on a bag of boiled peanuts while filling up her tank, she sends Dakota a text.

Almost there. Just crossed into Florida. Should be in Rosemary in an hour. Followed your advice. Left Bradley alone, and he, in turn, has reciprocated the gesture. Crickets.

Dakota replies almost immediately. *Good girl. Get your ass here in time for sunset. Don't bother with your bags. Just head out to the beach. Same spot as always.*

The picturesque beach town of Rosemary is finally in Penny's sights, signaling that her long day is mercifully coming to an end. Thick olive tree canopies lining East Water Street greet her. This little seaside town is indeed charming, from its cobblestone sidewalks meandering through the quaint main street bustling with outdoor restaurants and stores to the wooden boardwalks transporting visitors to the sugary-white sand that this stretch of coastline is famous for.

Looking around, Penny realizes she's blessed. Experiencing something as magnificent as the turquoise waters that the Gulf of Mexico provides is a gift. Her younger self would've given her eyeteeth just to see an ocean, let alone have the opportunity to dip her toes into a body of water that wasn't a freezing creek or a stagnant pond. Now, because of the generosity of Leslie, she'll take in glorious sunrises while sipping cappuccinos in the mornings then toasting to the sunsets with glasses of Veuve Clicquot in the evenings. A home with full, unobstructed views of the gulf is a precious jewel. One must remember to count their blessings. Penny chides herself for her melancholy attitude earlier, refusing to be like her aunt Molly. She won't look this gift horse in the mouth. No matter how bad the last twenty-four hours have been, she'll appreciate what God and Leslie Newman have provided, regardless of how miserable the state of her personal life.

After making a left onto Rosemary Avenue, she parks her SUV next to a row of saw palmettos in the first spot she finds, right around the corner from Leslie's. Being the amenable friend she is, she heeds Dakota's instructions to bypass the unpacking process and go straight to the beach. Instead of collapsing onto one of the white plush sofas in the great room and calling it a day, she makes her way to walkover B, toward the place her Atlanta friends have enjoyed for years. Here is where they discovered a love for Elin Hilderbrand books, the perfect summer beach reads, while indulging in home-made pimento cheese sandwiches and warm crab dip. This is one of Penny's favorite places on Earth, and it has nothing to do with the million-dollar views. The bonds of friendship were solidified on this sand.

As soon as she opens the gate to the dune walkover, granting her beach access, she's greeted with a warm rush of salty air welcoming her back like an old friend. Penny's heart skips a beat as she catches her first glimpse of the Gulf of Mexico during the peak of the golden hour, that magical time of day that beachgoers wait for, sweating through hours of sun and heat to have those precious ten minutes of perfection or the opportunity for the quintessential family portrait. It's magnificent.

Slipping off her sandals, she takes a moment to dig her feet into the cool, velvety sand, then she sets out to find her friends. Choosing to walk along the water's edge to feel the warm water rushing over her ankles, she begins thinking of her friends. Perhaps she'll find them lounging in their SeaOats beach chairs in an intimate circle, sharing stories while enjoying pre-dinner appetizers. A melted brie drizzled with honey is always a crowd pleaser on a lazy afternoon like this. She can picture Annie on her phone, trying to make reservations at Café Thirty-A for a late dinner. Annie's always ready for a night out. Dakota will be making other plans, of course, poring over a stack of paper menus from local restaurants. A night in is always her preference. She'll do her best to entice the group by ordering Rubens from Wild Olives. Maybe a pesto chicken pizza from Fat Daddy's will do the trick. Naturally, Leslie, being the perfect hostess, will be busy refilling empty glasses. Her custom-made Caspari napkins, matching her home's décor to a T, are given to all. A tiny smile escapes Penny's lips as she thinks of her dear friends and the roles they play.

As she approaches their spot, just shy of the Eastern Green, she notices no chairs are set up today. No circle has been formed. No afternoon cocktails are being consumed. At first, she assumes it's her vision. The sun's especially bright this afternoon, and her sunglasses are still in her car on North Briland. Placing her hand over her eyes, she can only make out the outline of a lone figure. So focused on who she's approaching, Penny trips over a small child who's building a monstrous sandcastle in the hard sand a few yards from the water. When the tower he's just completed buckles under the weight of her left foot, he spirals into a mix of rage and anguish. As Penny stops to apologize to the boy's understanding mother for ruining his architectural masterpiece, she looks again at the lone figure. The person standing in the place where her friends should be is a man, a rather tall one.

"Oh my god," she whispers, moving toward him.

Her pace quickens the closer she gets, until she's in a full-blown sprint, trying her best to keep her balance in Rosemary's thick white sand. With each step she takes, her heart beats faster.

"Bradley?" she asks, struggling to catch her breath. "Is it really you?"

"Hello, Penny." His voice is warm like always, but his expression gives nothing away, and she doesn't know if he's happy to see her or ready to give her a piece of his mind.

"I—I don't know what to say."

Bradley doesn't respond. He just looks at her with the same blank expression.

"About yesterday. The way I acted at Ruby Ray's? I have no words." Shame fills her voice. "I was wrong on every level. You were only trying to help. Like always. I'm so sorry."

Once again, Bradley remains silent. Only the waves crashing into the shoreline and the sounds of seagulls fill the air.

"I went to your house first thing this morning to apologize. I pounded on your door for a good fifteen minutes. If that wasn't bad enough, I flipped off some poor preacher, then I ran to your office in a pair of flimsy flip-flops, looking for you, and in the process, I took a layer of skin off my toes. I'm sure Camden will be abuzz with all my antics."

Bradley raises his eyebrows but says nothing.

"To be honest with you, I was on the verge of losing it today," Penny says in a quiet voice.

Bradley finally speaks. "I know."

"Excuse me?"

"Miss Paulette told me. She filled me in on my drive down. Said you and Miss Ada Pickert were quite determined to find me, and somehow, in the process, you two have become unlikely friends."

"Wait a minute. Why *are* you in Rosemary?"

"I came to see you."

"Me? How could you possibly know I'd be in this very spot? At this very moment?"

"Dakota," he says, grinning.

"Dakota?" she repeats, dumbfounded.

"She called me last night. Actually, it was more like a conference call. Or a surprise attack. I'm not sure which. Leslie and Annie were on the call too."

"I don't believe this," she says, shaking her head.

"Somehow, she tracked down my cell number and told me to get my ass—her language not mine—down to Florida ASAP to fight for you. If not, she was prepared to drive to Kentucky and bring me here. Using force if necessary."

"That doesn't sound like her," Penny responds playfully. She can almost hear her friend's conversation with Bradley in her head.

"She also had a few choice words in regard to your ex-husband and your attorney as well. Your friend really likes the F word, doesn't she?"

Penny nods. "Yes, she does."

"So I heeded her advice—or rather, command—to get down here. Left Camden at the crack of dawn."

Looking around, Penny asks, "Where are the girls?"

"In Atlanta."

"What?"

"They took some kind of vote last night and decided to forgo the girls' trip this week. They want you to enjoy yourself and forget about Teddy. At least for a little while. They gave us Leslie's house instead."

"I can't believe it. That's so generous."

"Yes, it is. You have some very good friends, Penny Ray. They did, however, make me promise you'll fulfill some kind of list Dakota's set out for you. Something to do with mimosas and a place called George's, and you have to go dancing at Red Bar. But Dakota said you can skip the part with a stranger now. Says you've already fulfilled that quota."

Penny's face heats. She knows exactly what Dakota was alluding to.

"So I'm here. Here for you," he says, taking her hand in his. Their fingers lace together. "If you want me to go, I'll understand. I'm not going to hurt you or your boys. Please know that."

The thought of him shutting down his practice for a week and driving hours on end to see her is overwhelming. "I'm so sorry about yesterday."

"Don't be. You have nothing to apologize for."

"Yes. Yes, I do. I should never have spoken to you like that. It was wrong on every level. You were only trying to help. Like always."

"You were scared. I get that," he says, gazing down into her eyes.

"I threw you out of my house. Be honest. You had to be angry with me."

"Don't get me wrong. When I left Ruby Ray's yesterday, I was furious, but it wasn't directed at you."

Penny tilts her head and narrows her eyes.

"Okay, maybe I was mad at you for about five minutes, but I knew, deep down, it was the fear talking."

Penny draws in a deep breath of briny air. "A wise woman told me that it's time I stop living in fear. I'm not saying I won't have triggers from time to time, but I'm not going to run away anymore. Especially from you. I promise."

"I'm glad to hear that."

"Bradley, when I told you what we shared was a summer fling, just sex, I was lying. It was so much more than that to me. I still don't know what *this* is, but I'm willing to try to find out if you still are. So this time I ask you: where do we go from here?"

Seeming to gather his thoughts, he takes a moment to gaze upon the majestic auburn glow of the waves crashing upon the shoreline. "Two weeks ago, we were given a gift. A second chance, compliments of Lonnie Davis, kettle corn, and divine timing. Now, we have a third chance from the generosity of your spirited friends."

"I think the word is *pushy*," she replies. *Spirited* is too diplomatic for her friends.

"That's another way of putting it," he concedes with a chuckle before continuing. "Penny, I can't remember a time in my life when I didn't love you. From the day I found you sitting alone in your mother's car to the day you trusted me enough to carry you into that hospital. My heart has always belonged to you. Always."

He brushes a curl away from Penny's face before grazing his thumb across her lips and her scar, which she's been so protective of her entire life. Instead of recoiling, this time, she allows Bradley's healing caress to continue. With each stroke, his touch feels like he's finally erasing it, not just the one on the outside but the one she carries inside as well.

"I don't know what's going to happen," he continues, "or where we go from here. But the one thing I do know is we have seven days in this special place. Let's not waste a second of it."

This isn't some grand proposal from the second most popular dentist in Camden in which he's sweeping her off her feet, forgetting not only his responsibilities but hers as well to live happily ever after in Atlanta or Kentucky. This is something more. Something better. Bradley's offering Penny a chance to finally live in the moment, letting go of her insatiable need for planning and mapping out every minute of her life, filling it with endless to-do lists and regimented schedules. This is a once-in-a-lifetime opportunity to cast aside Penny the Planner, at least for a few days, in a breathtaking setting where she can enjoy the present instead of constantly worrying about the past or the future. *How can anyone be happy in life if they're always dreading and preparing for the end of something before the beginning can even happen?* In doing so, one misses out on the most important, the most beautiful part of life—what happens in the middle. It's well past time Penelope Ray Crenshaw discovers it for herself.

"Well, Dr. Hitchens." Penny sighs and wraps her arms around his waist. She stares up at him, the golden light encompassing them both. "Maybe the third time can finally be our charm."

October 24, 2009
Atlanta, Georgia

Epilogue

The Silence of the Lambs

Tonight's the night, the one Penny's intimate circle of friends mark on their calendars years in advance—the Newmans' annual Fall Festival. Leslie's little soiree isn't a run-of-the-mill autumn get-together—it's *the* event among Atlanta's young socialites. Held on the third Saturday night in October, to avoid conflicting with the Georgia-Florida game the following weekend, it's the place to be seen among the who's who of the trendy set of Buckhead.

Every year, the Newmans open their sprawling home in Tuxedo Park to their friends and friends' friends. The guests are a mixture of people from all over the city, from Leslie's ALTA tennis team to her husband's business and political contacts. Large clear tents are erected in the back of the estate. Rustic walnut farm tables dripping with café au lait dahlias, peach roses, antique green hydrangeas, persimmons, and tiny white pumpkins fill the space. Upon arrival, guests are greeted with a signature cocktail that Leslie collaborates on with some of the city's trendiest mixologists, creating a concoction that will have her friends buzzed and buzzing about it for months to come.

After an extended cocktail hour, with the waitstaff doling out scrumptious hors d'oeuvres, they invite their guests to sit for a three-course dinner. Once the gingerbread shortcakes with spicy pumpkin gelato are gobbled up, the couple introduce the entertainment for the evening. Last year, they secured Journey to perform for their intimate backyard bash. But as much fun as dancing the night away to the best bands from the seventies and eighties can be, the real event, the main attraction, is the annual costume contest.

The Newmans love to dress up whenever the occasion arises. To encourage their more refined or rather uptight friends to join the fun, they put out extra incentives to jostle the creative juices. The winner of best costume will not only receive the title of champion along with bragging rights and accolades for the next year, but their name will be engraved onto a sterling-silver bowl for posterity, and a substantial check will be donated to the winner's charity of choice. It's rumored to be in the ballpark of five digits and start with a two.

The title's a coveted crown. Everyone wants to be victorious, and it has nothing to do with the philanthropic hearts of Atlanta wanting to make the world a better place. This is war, plain and simple. Some couples spend thousands of dollars on custom-made costumes for a shot to become the victor.

Last year, Penny skipped the party. Teddy's affair and his upcoming nuptials to his Pilates instructor were the talk of the town. The thought of spending an evening with a crowd full of people who'd gossiped behind her back nonstop, or worse, pitied her, was too overwhelming. Instead, Penny spent the evening in bed with Dakota, who bailed on the party in solidarity, watching all eight hours of *The Thorn Birds* to occupy her mind. As bad as Penny's life was at that moment, they surmised, at least she was no Meggie Cleary. But this year, it's time for her to come out of her scorned-woman shell and take back her place in her former society circle—on her terms.

Penny arrives very late, something she would never do otherwise. A grand entrance is needed because she's about to make a statement. She waltzes by Leslie, who spits a mouthful of her caramel apple martini into one of her guests' hair when she sees Penny's ensemble. The next to notice Penny is Teddy, who drops his old-fashioned cocktail in shock, causing the glass to shatter into a million pieces. Soon, the crowd begins to notice what their hostess and Penny's ex have just witnessed, letting out gasps. But once the shock wears off, they give a thunderous roar of cheers and applause.

"Fucking genius," Dakota says in awe.

"That's my girl," Penny's new nanny, Miss Ada, says, beaming at her. Penny has become both her employer and her adopted grand-daughter.

The former Mrs. Theodore Fredrick Crenshaw and North Atlanta High School's newest tenth grade English teacher strolls into the party of the year as none other than Holly Golightly from "Breakfast at Tiffany's." She carries a long cigarette holder in her right hand, while a fake diamond tiara sits upon her coiffed hair. Penny is a perfect vision of Audrey Hepburn circa 1961, right down to the white evening gloves and the little black dress. And the cherry on top—she wears an enormous garish rhinestone tennis bracelet around her tiny wrist, a subtle reference to the humiliation she experienced when she stumbled upon her husband's affair in the posh store.

But there's more to Penny's plan than just the costume. Tonight, she didn't come alone. Right by her side is Dr. Bradley Michael Hitchens, wearing a simple suit and a million-dollar smile. Not only does Ms. Crenshaw walk away with the title of best costume and all the accolades that go with it, but she introduces Bradley to her world on her terms, without fear of retribution from her former husband or his silly custody suit. Tonight, she dances the night away with the visiting Bradley and sparkles like a brand-new diamond under an effervescent Tiffany's light. Atlanta will talk about this night for years.

Three weeks later, Ruth informs Penny that Teddy has decided to drop his custody suit for the Crenshaw boys. His priorities have suddenly shifted. His attention is needed for a new battle on the horizon—an impending divorce from Jessica "One *N*" Lyn.

Acknowledgments

First and foremost, I want to thank Lynn McNamee at Red Adept Publishing. You took a chance on a new writer with absolutely no experience. I am beyond grateful for the opportunity you have given me by providing a home for *Where the Grass Grows Blue*. Lynn, I will never forget what you've done for me.

Rashida Williams, my content editor. Thank you! Thank you! Thank you! (I know how much you love my exclamation points.) Your belief in this story and your enthusiastic love for Penny and Bradley pushed me through those long nights of content edits when I wanted to throw in the towel because I didn't believe in myself. Your advice was instrumental in getting this book where it needed to be. Thank you! (I had to throw one more in.)

Susie Driver, my line editor. There aren't enough words to express my sincere gratitude. I'm in awe of not only your ability with words but also your keen eye. After I spent four years writing this book, you poked holes in my manuscript. You made this story better. You made me work harder.

Many thanks to the incredible staff at Red Adept Publishing, especially Erica Lucke Dean, who was instrumental in designing my amazing cover, which I love! You understood Penny's story and her journey. RAP—y'all have my deepest appreciation. Not only did you answer my questions, but you guided a newbie through the crazy publishing world.

To Blackstone Audio and Liza Fleissig, I'm beyond grateful for the opportunity you've given me. *Where the Grass Grows Blue* has a "voice" because you believed in this story. Thank you.

Stacy Jagger, the person who encouraged me to write in the first place, this only happened because you told me to throw away that yellow book. I hated that yellow book. I cannot thank you enough. I will be forever grateful. Look what we did!

A big thank-you to the Women's Fiction Writers Association. Finding this group has been instrumental in my journey toward publication. I'm especially grateful to Jennifer Klepper, who invited me to join and answered so many questions early on in my querying journey.

My writing friends, Donna N. Carbone, Elizabeth Parman, Cindy Dorminy, and the Tour Guides at Bookish Road Trip—you all have been lifesavers through this process. You've offered sage advice, encouraged me when I wanted to give up, and always lent a sympathetic ear. I couldn't have done this—enduring the highs and lows of getting a book into print—without you. Thank you. Simply the best.

My family—my sister, nieces, nephews, and in-laws—in Tennessee and Georgia, thank you for your support. Asking about my writing process and letting me drone on about how hard publishing is has meant the world to me. I know it was boring. But you listened. My love to you all, and thank you for your patience. Angela, Craig, Cindy, Howard, Rebecca, Chris, Kadyn, Shea, Connor, Addie, and Jack, thank you. And yes, I used some of your names in this book. Only out of love.

LaRecea Gibbs, my late mother, the first writer in our family. My inspiration. As a girl, I watched in awe as you taught English by day and at night and, during the summers, worked multiple jobs while enrolled in multiple classes to hone your craft. No one was more determined. I wouldn't be here without the spirit you instilled in me. Smart. Hard worker. Driven. Mom, this is for you.

Ovaleta Gibbs, my grandmother, the woman who taught me everything. No words are needed. No person has ever held my heart or respect like you. You are the greatest woman I've ever known.

To my friends both in Kentucky and Tennessee—you know who you are—thank you for listening to me talk about this book for the last four years, even though I didn't let you read a word of it until it was ready for publication. Your friendships have kept me going, long before I wrote my first sentence. You all are truly special, and the fact that you have stuck with me through thick and thin is a gift.

The Magnolias. Enough said. No words are needed. That's probably for the best.

Bob Dylan. This story only happened because you and my Methodist minister in Brentwood, Tennessee, came together one Sunday. How weird is that? Completely random, I know. True story.

To the people of the great Commonwealth of Kentucky, you will always hold a special place in my heart. There are no more loyal or kind folks in the world. I'll cherish the gifts you have given me. Forever.

My children, Calister, Alex, Jackson, Will, and Ansley, thank you for giving me space to write the last four years when I needed it and for being proud of what I was trying to do (even if you all thought I was writing a cookbook). Being your mother for the last twenty-five years has been the greatest job I've ever had. Thank you for letting me spread my wings a bit by venturing outside my comfort zone.

Finally, my husband, Patrick. My biggest fan and greatest source of inspiration. None of this would have been possible without your love, encouragement, and ability to leave me alone for hours on end to work late into the night. In my case, past nine o'clock. You have been an instrumental part of my life. Without you, I would never have had the confidence to not only write a book but also publish it. Patrick, you are my world, and you have my whole heart. Always.

About the Author

Hope Gibbs grew up in rural Scottsville, Kentucky. As the daughter of an English teacher, she was raised to value the importance of good storytelling from an early age. Today, she's an avid reader of women's fiction. Drawn to multi-generational family sagas, relationship issues, and the complexities of being a woman, she translates those themes into her own writing.

Hope lives in Tennessee with her husband, her five children, and her persnickety shih tzu, Harley. When she's not on the sidelines, cheering on her family in their various sports, she's on the tennis court, pursuing her own athletic dreams. In her downtime, she loves poring over old church cookbooks, such as the ones from her hometown, singing karaoke, curling up on her favorite chair with a book, and playing board games, especially Trivial Pursuit, if she can find someone up to the task.

Read more at https://www.authorhopegibbs.com.

About the Publisher

Dear Reader,

We hope you enjoyed this book. Please consider leaving a review on your favorite book site.

Visit https://RedAdeptPublishing.com to see our entire catalogue.

Check out our app for short stories, articles, and interviews. You'll also be notified of future releases and special sales.

Made in the USA
Monee, IL
25 April 2023

32358558R00204